LOST SUMMER

Stuart Harrison grew up in England and always wanted to be a novelist. He finally decided to have a go after forty or so other careers failed to work out. He now writes full time and currently lives in Auckland, New Zealand. His website address is www.stuartharrison.com.

STUART HARRISON

Lost Summer

HarperCollins*Publishers*

This novel is entirely a work of fiction. The names,
characters and incidents portrayed in it are the work of the
author's imagination. Any resemblance to actual persons,
living or dead, events or localities is entirely coincidental.

HarperCollins*Publishers*
77–85 Fulham Palace Road,
Hammersmith, London w6 8jb

www.**fire**and**water**.com

This paperback edition 2003
1 3 5 7 9 8 6 4 2

First published in Great Britain by
HarperCollins*Publishers* 2002

ISBN 0 00 713936 5

Set in New Baskerville

Printed and bound in Great Britain by
Clays Ltd, St Ives plc

For Bill and Joan, with thanks

ACKNOWLEDGEMENTS

Thanks to: Emma Stewart, for advice and help; my agent, Stephanie Cabot; and at HarperCollins, Susan Opie, Nick Sayers and all the marketing team, without whom I would not be writing this now.

Part One

CHAPTER ONE

A red light on the side of the phone began to blink on and off, which meant that there was a call. Adam had switched the ringer tone onto mute because sometimes when it rang it startled the hell out of him. Now as he watched the light he made no move to pick up the receiver. It was late; past ten and he knew who it was. He wondered how long she would let it ring before she gave up. He could picture her standing in their living room at home or pacing back and forth from the kitchen. Her mouth would be clamped shut, her lips an unyielding line. The colour of her eyes would be vivid blue; they were a darker shade when she was angry. These days she was angry a lot.

He counted the flashes: seventeen, eighteen. Then the light went out. He waited to see if she would call back but the light remained off. Later, when he got home, or in the morning if she was asleep by then, she would ask where he'd been. He'd say he was working and she'd say she'd phoned, the suspicion in her voice cracking like a whip. He'd tell her he hadn't noticed and then it would start; the familiar argument which would escalate and veer off in different directions but would ultimately come back to the same well-worn theme. He was never home. One day he'd come through the door and she would be gone and then maybe he would be sorry. Accusations flung like rocks. Work! It was always his fucking work! Well, what about her? What about them?

The office he rented was small. A long narrow room above a photography shop in Fulham. He didn't need a lot of space. In fact as a freelancer he could have worked at home easily enough,

3

which he had before he and Louise had married. In those days he could keep whatever hours he wanted. Now he had this place. He even kept a camp bed there for the nights when he was so exhausted he would begin to nod off as he worked.

The notes and pictures for the story he was working on were scattered messily along the long wooden bench that served as his desk. Transcripts of interviews with police, family, neighbours, friends, in fact almost anybody who had come into contact with Elizabeth Mount since she had vanished. Some of the photographs her parents had given him were pinned on the wall. He liked to see the faces of the people he was looking for whenever he glanced up. That way they remained real. They were people not merely names. The more he learned about them the better he felt he knew them. Often he knew more about them than their own families because he learned things from their friends that children rarely tell their parents. Usually about boys (if they were girls, and usually they were) or plans they had to go somewhere or do something their parents wouldn't approve of.

Elizabeth was sixteen. Her friends called her Liz. Her birthday had been in April, three weeks after she'd vanished. It was late May now. The initial inquiry and attendant publicity had tapered off. The official view from the police was that she had run away. She had joined the thousands of others like her who fled their families and home towns each year for the cities, where they melted into the anonymous underbelly of society. Sometimes their families never heard from them again. They changed their names, became involved with drugs, prostitution, criminal activities. All the usual litany of the underclass.

It wasn't as if Adam hadn't heard the story before. He had files crammed full of notes about kids like Liz, mostly girls, though there were a fair percentage of boys too. Runaways. People sent him letters all the time. They used to phone as well until he made his number unlisted. He had a reputation now. Not only did he write about kids that went missing, sometimes he found them. Not always, but enough times that he had made this particular patch of expertise his speciality; he'd achieved a degree of minor fame. A couple of times he'd been interviewed on TV, and lots of times on radio. The families of the missing turned to him out of desperation, when nobody else would help. They asked him to find their children, and sometimes he did. The trouble is they were usually dead.

Was Liz dead? He didn't know. She had vanished one morning on the way to school and hadn't been seen or heard of since. But it turned out she'd taken a change of clothes with her that day. A witness reported seeing her on a train to London but she wasn't wearing her school uniform. An anonymous caller had claimed she was living on the streets near Paddington. The police had her down as a runaway, but her family were adamant that she wasn't the type. But then that was often the case. The family sometimes didn't know what type their children were. Or didn't care. Or were lying to cover up abuse. But then those people weren't the ones who normally contacted Adam.

So far he'd spent five weeks looking for Liz, talking to everybody she had come into contact with. He knew that on the day she vanished she had got on a train to London. One of her friends had finally admitted to him in confidence that Liz had talked about doing it, though she maintained that Liz had meant to come back the same day. Adam didn't know about the anonymous caller. Maybe that was somebody covering their tracks, trying to mislead the police.

He stared at her picture. A smiling girl with brown hair and a few adolescent pimples. Plucked eyebrows, a bit of make-up, trying to look older and more sophisticated than she was, as girls of her age do. She had a boyfriend who swore he hadn't seen her that day. In fact they'd argued a few days earlier. Motive to kill her? Adam didn't think so, and anyway the boy had an alibi for that day. Adam had traced every hour of Liz's movements for the week prior to her getting on that train. Nothing unusual, nothing at all out of the ordinary. No strangers that she'd spoken to, no behaviour that was abnormal either at home or among friends. But one Thursday morning she had boarded the nine o'clock train to Euston and after that nobody had seen or heard of her again. Apart from the anonymous caller. She had simply vanished.

It was past midnight when Adam arrived home. He moved about the flat quietly and when he looked in on Louise she was asleep.

He watched her for a while from the doorway. He felt guilty about what was happening to them. They had been married less than eighteen months. Not very long. Her blonde hair was fanned out on the pillow, visible in the dim light that leaked from the hallway. He remembered the first time he'd seen her in a bar with some friends. She had her back to him and it was her hair he'd first noticed, long and pale yellow so that it looked almost silver. It had jolted a memory and for a brief moment he'd held his breath thinking it was her.

Of course it hadn't been. When Louise turned around she'd met his gaze with her cool blue eyes. There was a resemblance in her face, though only slight. She'd felt him watching her, she'd claimed later. He had pursued her. Plotting his campaign. Seven months later they'd tied the knot at the register office and spent a week in the Caribbean.

He closed the door quietly and went to the living room where he poured a Scotch and lay down on the couch. He'd spent a lot of nights there lately. Sometimes he had dreams and they were peopled by the faces of lost children. They swam in and out of focus. Now and then he dreamed about one in particular. She had dark hair, almost black, that floated about her head in tendrils. Her features were slightly blurred though he knew who she was. She always appeared with her arm outstretched, a mute gesture of appeal, though in her eyes he glimpsed an accusation. Usually when he had that dream he woke up sweating with the bedclothes tangled in a knot.

Beyond the window the rooftops of Islington were lit with the pale, smoky sunlight of early spring. As Adam turned away he noticed the way Paul Morris was watching him. He suddenly felt like a butterfly pinned beneath the scrutiny of an objective collector.

'Sorry, where were we?' Adam asked.

Actually, he quite liked Morris. He didn't look much like a psychologist in his jeans and open-neck shirt, or at least Adam's conception of what a psychologist was supposed to look like. His consulting rooms on the third floor of a terraced Georgian house

6

had a pleasantly casual feel. The walls were pale and the windows flooded the rooms with light and air.

'Last time you were here, we talked about your work,' Morris said. 'Do you think what you do has had an effect on your marriage?'

'Obviously Louise thinks so.'

'Yes, but what do you think?'

Adam started towards his chair and then changed his mind. He preferred to roam around the room during their sessions, looking at books and the prints on the walls, the view beyond the window. At least that way he felt less as if he was being analysed. Morris couldn't be much older than himself. A year or two maybe, which made him what, thirty-three or -four? When he'd agreed to relationship counselling he'd expected somebody older.

Adam paused by the bookcase as he considered how to answer Morris's question. 'Louise would like me to get a regular job with a magazine or something. She'd like me to leave for work at eight-thirty in the morning and be home by seven and have the weekends off.'

'Has she actually said that?'

'Not in so many words perhaps. But she doesn't need to. Louise thinks I put my work before my marriage.'

'And you think the way she feels is unjustified?'

'Yes. No. Not exactly.' Adam moved away from the bookcase and went back to the window. 'Look, the thing is I don't deny that I work long hours, or that I'm away a lot. What I do isn't like being an accountant. The hours aren't regular and they wouldn't be even if I wasn't freelance. The point is I was doing this before I even met Louise. She knew what she was getting into.'

'You know, Louise said that's what you would say.'

'Well she was right,' Adam said sharply.

'I'm not taking sides here,' Morris said. 'I'm just trying to give each of you the other's point of view. Sometimes it's easier coming from an intermediary.'

'Okay. I'm sorry. It's just that Louise and I have been over this a hundred times before.'

'You said that she wants you to give up what you do. Get a regular job. But that isn't what she told me. Actually, she said she always knew how important your work is to you. She says she never had a problem with that before you were married.'

'But now she does.'

'Only because, and these are her words, since you were married you actually spend *more* time working than you did before. A lot more. In fact, Louise used the term obsession. She thinks your work has become an obsession.'

'She doesn't understand,' Adam said. 'She never has. The people I work with have almost lost hope. These are parents whose children are missing. They're desperate but nobody will listen to them. They know something is wrong. The police tell them their kids are runaways but they know it isn't true. They feel it inside. Here!' He thumped his chest for emphasis. 'Sometimes I'm the only chance they feel they have to get at the truth.'

'And you believe that Louise doesn't appreciate any of this?'

'I don't think she understands that when I'm working on a story, I can't just drop it because I have to be home for dinner.'

Morris was reflective for a moment. 'The other day Louise said something else that I found interesting.'

Adam stared out of the window. 'What was that?'

'That she felt after you were married it was almost as if you had changed deliberately. As if you spent more time working in order to shut her out.'

'That isn't true. Look, I'm the way I am because . . .' Adam faltered.

'Because of what?'

'I don't know.'

'You were going to say something then.'

'I was going to say what I do is a part of me. There's nothing I can do about it.'

'That's interesting,' Morris said. 'Can you explain what you mean?'

Christ, he had walked right into that, Adam thought. He moved away from the window and eventually took the chair opposite Morris. He had a choice here. He could back off or he could try to answer Morris's question. He'd never talked about any of it before, not to anyone. But a part of him recognized that he'd been leading up to this for some time. He knew he had to try

8

and explain. Perhaps to himself as much as anyone, and Morris was the first person he'd ever come close to opening up to. He supposed it was because there was an element of the impersonal about a professional relationship. Or maybe it was because then Morris could try to explain it all to Louise. Something he couldn't do himself. Or wouldn't. The result was the same.

'I just meant that isn't our behaviour, the way we are, supposed to be determined by the things that happen when we're young?'

'Much of our personalities is shaped by our early influences, certainly. That and our genes.'

'Nurture over nature?'

'Broadly, though most people perceive that to mean that it's our parents who have the greatest influence over us.'

'You don't agree?' Adam asked, suddenly interested.

Morris shrugged. 'Not directly. As children once we start school our peers become the dominant influencing factor. The attitudes and behaviour of our friends and how we relate to them shape us. More so than our parents.'

Well, he wouldn't argue with that, Adam thought. There was a short silence.

'You were going to say something before. Was it to do with your work? Why you chose your particular field?'

'Yes. I suppose it was,' Adam admitted.

Morris laced his fingers and assumed a practised expression that mixed mild interest and nonjudgemental detachment.

Adam remembered the day they had moved; the changing landscape outside the car window. The sky was overcast, a solid grey mass hanging heavy and leadenly ominous just above the level of the rooftops. Beyond the valley loomed the stark hills that marked the northern edge of the Pennines shrouded in cloud. It seemed about a million miles away from Hampstead.

His mother had smiled encouragingly from the front seat. 'You're going to love it here, Adam. All this beautiful countryside and fresh air.'

He'd wondered which one of them she was trying to convince. He noticed she and Kyle exchange glances.

Castleton turned out to be more of a large village than a town.

9

The main road crossed a stone bridge over the River Gelt before winding past the square, around which were clustered a few shops, a church and a small branch of Barclays bank. The estate was a few miles further on and was approached through wrought-iron gates guarding a road flanked by twin columns of sweet chestnuts. At the end stood a massive sandstone manor. The estate manager's house was out of sight, itself a substantial Edwardian building with a walled garden.

'How old were you?' Morris asked.

'Thirteen. Kyle was my stepfather. My dad died when I was six. Kyle had worked for some international corporation managing Third World projects until he met my mother, and then he decided to settle down and announced he had this job managing an estate in Cumbria.'

'I take it you weren't thrilled with the move.'

'You could say that. I had to leave everything I knew. Friends, school.'

'How did you feel about that?'

Adam smiled wryly. 'I didn't think you people really said that.' Morris smiled, but didn't respond. 'Lonely,' Adam said eventually.

A week after they'd moved Adam rode his bike into Castleton along lanes bordered by hedges and stone walls, past fields full of docile cows. When he reached the town it was mid-morning and people were beginning to emerge from the church.

At the newsagent he picked up *The Sunday Times* for Kyle and the *Observer* for his mother. The girl behind the counter had pale blonde hair and was about his age.

'You must be from the estate,' she said. 'What's your name?'

'Adam,' he answered, surprised. 'How did you know I live on the estate?'

'My friend's dad works there. She said there was a new lad who talks posh.'

He wasn't sure if he ought to be insulted. His cheeks burned. As he left, the old-fashioned bell above the door rang with a silvery note and glancing back he saw the girl watching him with an amused look.

'Bye, Adam.'

He mumbled something in reply.

He came across the boys half a mile from the town. There were three of them sitting on a stone wall, their bikes lying down in the grass. As he drew nearer one of them walked out onto the road. He was tall and solidly built with thick brown hair. He stood with his hands on his hips and waited for Adam to come to a stop.

'Where are you going?' he demanded.

'I live on the estate.'

'You have to pay to go on this road if you're not from 'round here. Fifty pence.'

Adam remembered the thudding of his heart and how his mouth had become suddenly dry. Kyle had once told him that if you could it was better to talk your way out of trouble than to fight. 'Actually, I suppose I am from around here now,' he'd reasoned.

'Actually, I am from around here old chap.'

One of the other boys parodied his accent. He was thin with pinched features and black hair that lay flat on his head. His jeans were filthy and had tears in both knees and the sole of one shoe flapped loose. He reminded Adam of the kids from the tower estate he used to pass on the way home from school who used to yell names and throw stones or even empty bottles.

The boy in the road seemed amused. 'What school do you go to?'

'It's called Kings,' Adam said. 'But I haven't started yet.'

'Fucking grammar boy,' the thin one sneered.

They had given him an ultimatum; pay or fight, otherwise he had to take the long way around.

'What did you do?' Morris asked.

Adam was surprised at how vivid his recall was. He could almost feel the sun on his back making him sweat, the smell of cut hay from the fields mingling with hot tarmac and he experienced again the stinging humiliation of being the victim of bullying. He was alone, an outsider.

He had known he would have to fight or never hear the end of it.

They had said he could choose which one of them he took on. Fucking generous of them. The one who'd stopped him was easily the biggest and exuded a kind of lazy confidence. The thin one was the smallest but obviously a nasty little bastard, as Kyle would say. Which left the one on the wall, who so far hadn't spoken. He was trying to look tough but he was as nervous as Adam was.

They waited for him to decide and when he eventually pointed at the big one he was almost as surprised as they were.

Morris was intrigued. 'Why did you do that?'

The truth was Adam wasn't sure. He'd often wondered if it had been a sudden attack of bravery, the tactical response of those with balls of brass; take out the biggest guy and everybody else falls into line. Or had it been something less heroic. Instinct perhaps?

He shrugged in reply. 'It was all over pretty quickly.'

He'd thrown a few wild punches and remembered at least one connecting with its target, and the expression of pained surprise the other boy wore before he retaliated by swinging his fist in a blur of speed. The blow caught Adam on the cheek with the force of a house brick and knocked him to the ground, but somehow, probably accidentally, he'd managed to grab the other boy's legs. Next thing they were rolling on the tarmac scrabbling and flailing at one another amid shouts of encouragement from the other two.

'Finish him, Dave!'

'Hit him!'

There was blood in Adam's mouth and his lip felt thick and swollen. Tears of humiliation pricked his eyes. His arms were pinned. Get it over with he'd thought. Fucking country bumpkins. He'd remembered his mother always telling him how great it would be living in the country. How London was full of crime and vandals. All those glue sniffers and thugs on the tower estates. But he'd never been beaten up there. He'd never had three kids try to rob him. At least there he'd had his friends.

And then unexpectedly he was being pulled to his feet and the other boy was half smiling as he wiped blood from his nose and examined it with faint surprise.

'Shit! You alright?'

'I think so,' Adam said.

They faced each other awkwardly and then the boy fetched Adam's bike. 'Sorry. It was just a bit of a laugh really.'

Some fucking laugh. The other two boys hung back, the thin one scowling with sullen disappointment.

Adam fell silent, lost in reflection. All these years later and the memory of that day remained as fresh as if it had happened just a day or two ago. He remembered feeling a curious pride for having stood his ground. The boy he'd fought looked at him differently, with a kind of respect. Even then, at that very moment Adam realized that some bond had inexplicably formed between himself and the boy whom he later knew as David. He wasn't the only one to feel it. The thin one who turned out to be called Nick sensed it too. His eyed had glowed with resentment.

'What happened?' Morris asked.

Adam shrugged. 'They let me go. I didn't see them again until term started. It turned out I was going to the same school as the one I had the fight with.'

Morris waited expectantly as if there was more. But Adam didn't feel like going on. He looked at the clock and noted with relief that his time was up.

CHAPTER TWO

The house was set back from the road and all but hidden behind a hedge. All that was visible was the thatched roof, but earlier Adam had wandered past the gate, pausing at the end of the driveway to get a better look. It was the kind of quaint two-storey Sussex village cottage in demand by well-heeled city commuters. Cloud Cottage was the name on the wooden barred gate. A black Labrador trotted over and dutifully though half-heartedly barked before wagging its tail hopefully. It watched with disappointed eyes when he went back to his car.

The first houses on the edge of the village were around the bend several hundred yards away. The railway station was in the next town, where Liz had caught the train to Euston. Mr and Mrs Thomas lived in Cloud Cottage with their three children. Liz had been their baby-sitter until a year earlier, a piece of information Adam had only stumbled across when he'd asked Liz's father, Paul Mount, to go to the station with him a couple of mornings in a row on the very long shot that he would see something or somebody that would open up a new avenue in what had become a fruitless search.

On the second morning Paul had nodded to a middle-aged man in a suit. 'Alan Thomas. He works in the City I think. Liz used to baby-sit for them.'

What was it about Thomas that had triggered some kind of internal alarm? He was just another business commuter like hundreds of others. Nothing to mark him out from anybody else, but discreet questioning had revealed that Liz had stopped baby-sitting for the Thomases a year ago. Why?

'I don't know really,' Paul Mount had said. 'I think it was a bit far and they were often out late.'

Adam had moved into the village pub, which was called the Crown, and for several days had been quietly digging and watching. He knew Alan Thomas caught the seven-thirty-two most days, but sometimes he went in late or not at all. His wife was on the plain side but well groomed. She didn't have any close friends in the village, which wasn't unusual for incomers like the Thomases. They tended to socialize with other people like themselves from the country club up the road. Their children attended private schools.

Adam had learned that the police hadn't interviewed the Thomases. There was no reason to. In the morning he went back to the station and watched the other people who boarded the seven-thirty-two. There was a young woman whom Thomas seemed to know. Adam followed her to her office in the City and after work introduced himself. He said he was a journalist and wondered if she had time for a drink.

'Adam Turner?' Her brow furrowed and then her eyes lit up with recognition. 'I've read something of yours.'

Minor fame had its uses. In a wine bar near the station she answered his questions. He didn't expect her to remember the day Liz had vanished, but in fact she did. Such strokes of fortune happened occasionally and he accepted them as his share of luck. Dig deep enough and often enough and sooner or later something has to fall into place, and he was nothing if not diligent. He hadn't been home for a week.

'Actually, it was my birthday,' she said, as she sipped a Côte de Rhone. 'So I went in late that day. I caught the nine o'clock. Wasn't that the one this girl was supposed to be on?'

'Yes. Did you see her?'

She shook her head. 'If I did I don't remember. I sat next to Alan.'

'Alan Thomas?'

'Do you know him?'

'Not really. He was on the same train?'

'Yes. I remember he said he was running late because his wife was away and he couldn't cope without her or something. He made a joke of it. Anyway he promised to buy me a drink after work, but he never turned up. Actually, I was glad.'

'Why?'

She hesitated. 'It's just that his wife was away, and you know, I wondered if he was making a pass. He didn't actually say anything suggestive or anything. I'm probably being completely unfair.'

'But something made you uncomfortable?'

'A little I suppose.'

'Intuition.'

She shrugged. 'Perhaps.'

But Alan Thomas had sat with her all the way to London, she was positive of that. Had she seen him again after they left the train? She hadn't. Who was to say he hadn't bumped into Liz on the platform?

The next day he went back to London and when he arrived home Louise told him that Morris had phoned. 'You didn't cancel your appointment,' she said. Her arms were folded, a wine glass in one hand.

'I forgot. I'll call him tomorrow.'

'Will you make another time to see him?'

'I don't know. I think I'm on to something with the Liz Mount story. I might have to put Morris off for a little while.'

'Christ!'

She slammed her glass down on the counter.

'Look, it's just temporarily,' he said.

'Right. Your bloody work comes first. Again!'

'Come on, Louise,' he said, and reached for her arm as she swept past.

'Don't touch me!' she yelled, yanking free. 'Just leave me alone!'

'It's not a case of my work coming first, dammit. This girl . . .'

'I don't want to hear about her! I don't want to hear about any of it. There's always some girl, some parent, somebody. Anybody except me! Where do I come in, Adam? Tell me that. Where do I come into your list of bloody priorities?'

'That isn't fair,' he started to say, but she shook her head and turned away. He watched her go, heard the slam of the bedroom door.

❧

Out of guilt Adam called Morris and made an appointment for two days' time. When he arrived at the door he suddenly wondered if there was really any point going inside. That morning he and Louise had argued again. Nothing unusual about that, but it had quickly become a bitter fight. Things had been said by both of them that wouldn't easily be forgotten. The kind of barbed remarks that are designed to inflict maximum damage. He didn't think she deserved that. He didn't either for that matter. By the time he'd left the house they'd both been ashamed to look one another in the eye, and anger had been replaced with the dull knowledge that perhaps this was hopeless.

Deep down, however, Adam knew that Louise's anger stemmed from her frustration with him and he felt badly about that. In the end he kept his appointment and presently found himself at the window while Morris sat behind him, his fingers steepled beneath his chin.

'During our last session you were telling me about Castleton. You mentioned that you felt lonely when you moved there.'

Adam turned around. He'd been thinking about Liz Mount, wondering what his next move ought to be. 'It got better after I started school.'

'The boy you had the fight with went to the same school didn't you say?'

'Yes. His name was David Johnson. Nick and Graham, the other two who were there that day, went to the local comprehensive. David and I got to know each other. We ended up being friends.'

'So, you felt accepted after that?'

'Not exactly. Sometimes.'

When he looked back now, Adam didn't think he'd ever felt accepted. Maybe if it had just been David, or even David and Graham it would have been okay. But Nick had never liked him. He tried to explain.

'Graham was fairly easy-going. A follower I suppose. But when I came along Nick resented me. It didn't help that David and I both

17

went to the grammar school. David's dad owned the local sawmill which had the contract for the wood on the estate, so he and Kyle had a lot to do with each other as well.'

'Nick was jealous?'

'Probably.'

'And what was the effect of that?'

'I think David felt caught in the middle sometimes.'

He recalled a time when they had arranged to go rabbiting. It was early and the town was quiet. They had arranged to meet at the church. Graham and David arrived a few minutes after Adam, but quarter of an hour later there was still no sign of Nick.

'Why don't we ring him?' Adam suggested. There was a phone box on the other side of the square.

'They haven't got a phone,' Graham said.

'Let's go to his house then. He might have slept in or something.'

'It's best if we wait,' David said. 'He'll come when he can.' He started idly scuffing his feet along the path between the gravestones while Graham began examining the palms of his hands.

'I got these bloody blisters yesterday,' he said, picking at the skin.

It was as if invisible shutters had closed. The subject wasn't open for discussion but Adam felt excluded by his lack of understanding. He swallowed his frustration.

During that first year he'd lived in Castleton, Adam had never seen where Nick lived. He knew vaguely where it was; somewhere down past the council houses at the bottom end, close to the eastern edge of the wood, but he'd never been there. A faint air of mystery surrounded Nick's family. Adam knew there was a younger sister who caught the school bus in the mornings and was as scruffy as Nick and just as sullen, and he'd seen their mother around town wearing a shapeless worn coat, her pale blotchy legs bare even in winter. But Adam had never seen Nick's father, James Allen. Nick never mentioned him, and neither did David or Graham.

What little Adam had known he'd overheard in snatches of conversation between Kyle and his mother. Whenever there was poaching on the estate, or there had been an outbreak of theft, Kyle blamed Nick's dad. He heard stories about Allen getting drunk in the local pubs and starting fights with men from the estate. Once he'd seen Nick's mother in town with a black eye. Over time Adam had formed a mental image of the whole family living in Dickensian squalor, terrorized by an evil-tempered thug.

Eventually Nick had turned up that morning but he hadn't offered any explanation for being late.

They rode their bikes out of town across the bridge and took the road that climbed steeply towards the fells. By eight the sun was already warm on their backs and the effort of the climb had made them sweat. At one point he and David had paused to rest. The others were still out of sight around a bend in the road behind them. On one side the road was bounded by a wall, and on the other by a thick hedge. A blackbird flashed by, chattering in alarm.

When the others finally appeared they were pedalling slowly. Nick's bike was a big heavy machine that seemed to be made of cannibalized parts. He was wearing boots that looked too big for him, though the laces were undone. The leather was cracked, and the sole of one had come loose at the toe. It was flapping up and down, making a slapping sound as Nick struggled up the hill. The chain creaked with every turn of the pedals. Creak slap, creak slap.

When they finally caught up Nick dropped his bike on the ground and went to sit on the wall. He dumped the sack that was tied over his shoulder on the grass and it moved as the ferret inside poked and snuffled looking for a way out. Nick lit a cigarette butt he found in his pocket, though he was still panting. He coughed and spat then muttered something under his breath as he lifted his T-shirt to wipe the sweat from his face, revealing for an instant his pale skinny body. There was a vivid purple black bruise the size of a melon across his ribs.

'Bloody hell. What happened to you?' Adam said without thinking.

He knew straight away he should have kept his mouth shut. The others were looking away as if they hadn't seen or heard anything. Nick looked up in surprise, and some ill-defined expression briefly flashed in his face before it was quickly replaced with an angry glare. Abruptly he dropped to the other side of the wall and walked fifty yards up the hill where he sat down.

'A few minutes later David and I started off again,' Adam recounted. 'Nothing was said but I knew I'd crossed a line. David gave me the cold shoulder all the way up the hill. I kept thinking about the look I'd seen on Nick's face. It was shame. I'd embarrassed him.'

'And you felt bad about it?' Morris asked.

'A bit I suppose. But I'd be lying if I said I was that worried. Nick made it clear he didn't like me and the feeling was mutual. Somehow he always managed to turn things around. Like I said, it was mostly because of him that I never really fitted in.'

That day Adam and David had waited for the others at a place known as the Giant's Chair. It was a rock formation that roughly resembled a huge seat. Local legend had it that a race of giants had once roamed the fells and this was all that was left of their existence. It was easy to climb to the top by the gently sloping grassy rise on one side, but once in the seat itself the drop was a sheer one. It was like standing on the edge of a cliff. From there the road was visible, winding back down to the valley. The town was out of sight but parts of Castleton Wood could still be seen. A pine forest lay to the north, and fringed inside its southern edge was Cold Tarn, a natural deep lake that even on a day like this, when the sun was beating down from a cloudless sky, appeared black. Sometimes they fished for pike and perch there, and in season wildfowlers stood in the reeds that fringed the shore to shoot ducks. Behind them, Cold Fell rose 600 metres above sea level at the northern extent of the Pennines.

Back the way they'd come two tiny figures were visible more than a mile away, moving slowly up the steepest part of the hill.

Adam had pulled a book from his pack and started reading while David sat with his feet dangling over the edge of the rocks, chewing on a stem of grass.

'What's that you're reading?' David asked after a while.

Adam silently held it up so that he could see the cover but he didn't say anything.

'*The Crystal Cave?* What's it about?'

'I'll let you read it when I've finished.' He was being sarcastic because David didn't read anything unless it was about sport.

For a while David tossed small pieces of rock out into the open, seeing how far he could throw them. Eventually he stopped and said, 'What's up with you?'

Adam put his book down. 'So, now you're talking to me again, is that it?'

'What do you mean?'

'Come on. You haven't said a bloody word since we left the others.'

David found another stone, and threw it hard out into the air where it dropped from sight.

'I just said it without thinking,' Adam said. 'For Christ's sake I didn't mean to embarrass him or anything.'

But if David had heard him, he didn't give any sign of it. He picked up another stone and threw it out into the air.

'How do you think he got that bruise anyway?' Adam said, though David kept his back turned and didn't reply. He sensed that David's refusal to talk about it stemmed from loyalty to Nick, but the reasons behind it were something Adam was excluded from. At first he'd tried to make friends with Nick, but every gesture he'd made was openly rejected. Once Kyle had offered to give all four of them a lift to Carlisle so they could go to a film they all wanted to see but Nick had refused to go at the last minute even though Kyle had said he'd pay for all of them. It had developed into an argument and in the end Adam had had enough.

'You'd go if David's dad was paying though wouldn't you?'

Nick had glared at him and clenched his fists. 'Fuck you, grammar boy!'

For a second Adam had thought Nick was going to throw a punch. David and Graham were looking on silently and in that moment Adam had realized that if he and Nick had a fight they would be forced to take sides. That afterwards no matter who won or lost nothing would be the same again. He knew they wanted to see the film and it was obvious that Nick was being unreasonable, but he sensed that they would side with Nick. Even as the realization hit him David had stepped in.

'I changed my mind about the film anyway. Let's go fishing instead.'

It was meant to defuse the situation and Adam knew it. But he also knew Nick had won a subtle battle. They had gone fishing, but Adam had never forgotten how he'd felt.

Watching David's back as he threw stones from the edge of the Giant's Chair Adam knew it was pointless to push it. He went back to his book and after a few minutes David started whistling and murmuring snatches of a song. After a while he gestured to the view.

'This is great isn't it? I'm never leaving here.'

Adam looked up. 'What about if you go to university?'

'Why would I do that? I'm going to work for my dad when I leave school. What about you, Adam, what are you going to do?'

He thought about it. He wanted to be a journalist and work for a newspaper. 'Go back to London one day, I suppose.'

David shook his head. 'You're a city boy. Do you miss it?'

'Sometimes.'

'I'd feel out of place there,' David said.

The others had eventually caught up and they had spent the day rabbiting.

'Have you ever done that?' Adam asked, to which Morris replied that he hadn't. 'What happens is you find a warren and net all the holes then shove a ferret down one of them to flush out the rabbits. In theory anyway.'

He'd never really enjoyed that kind of thing. He only tagged along fishing, shooting and rabbiting with the others because that was what they did.

Nick had become frustrated that day because his ferret kept killing rabbits down the holes instead of chasing them out. Then the ferret would go to sleep and Nick would have to dig it out. The others had taken it in their stride but if it hadn't been for the satisfaction of seeing Nick thwarted Adam would have been bored out of his skull.

Late in the day they had found another warren and when they were finished Nick came and checked the last hole Adam had netted. He kicked at one of the pegs and when it came out of the ground easily he sneered.

'That wouldn't hold a bloody mouse.'

22

The others looked on without comment while Nick made a show of doing the job himself.

'He did it to humiliate me,' Adam told Morris. 'And to make a point. He was always doing that kind of thing.'

Finally Nick had sent his ferret down a hole. An hour or so passed before it was clear that once again he would have to dig it out again. He set to with a short spade, his face set in anger while Adam lay in the sun watching with quiet satisfaction.

It took Nick half an hour to find his ferret. He bent down to pluck it from the ground and Adam got up, hoping that perhaps now they could go home. But instead of returning it to the sack Nick pinned the ferret to the ground with his foot. The animal squirmed briefly under the pressure and then almost carelessly Nick raised his spade and then suddenly jerked the blade downwards and the ferret was still. Without a word Nick wiped the blood off on the grass.

Adam was silent, recalling his mingled shock and revulsion.

'A few days later David tried to explain that Nick had to do what he did because the ferret was no good. Looking back I suppose Nick's family probably ate what he caught but I didn't see it that way then.'

'But it made you feel different from them.'

Adam nodded. 'I was different.'

That night Adam stayed late at his office. He was thinking about the Mounts, both of whom he'd gotten to know while he'd been looking for their daughter. They were lucky, they had found strength in each other, but the strain was indelibly etched in their faces. A kind of haunted look. It was the not knowing, they had told him, which was the hardest thing to bear. It always was. He looked at the photographs of their daughter on the wall. He had a feeling about her, that she was slipping away as he got closer. It was always like that. The ones he found left him in peace. Those in his dreams were the ones he never found.

Louise was asleep when he got home. He went into their room and for a little while he stood inside the door watching her in the dim light that leaked in from the landing. She bore a physical resemblance to many of the women he'd been out with over the years and she wasn't the first to tell him that he worked too hard, or that there was a part of him she felt he kept locked away from her.

Quietly he closed the door and went to the couch in the living room.

His leg was aching as it sometimes did when the weather was damp. He sat down and kneaded the ridged and scarred flesh. It still looked red and inflamed after all these years.

CHAPTER THREE

'Last time we talked you told me that despite your friendship with David you felt different from the other boys. Why do you think that was?'

'Different reasons,' Adam replied from the window. It was raining outside, a fine misty drizzle that hung like vapour in the air. 'We had different experiences. Castleton was a small rural town and I'd grown up in Hampstead. The two places were worlds apart.'

'But you tried to fit in?'

'I suppose that's human nature isn't it? To belong to the tribe.'

'For most people it is,' Morris agreed. 'Generally speaking we look for others like ourselves to associate with. The friends of Arsenal supporters are usually other Arsenal supporters.'

Adam smiled. 'If you're going to use football as an analogy I suppose I felt like a reserve. When Nick wasn't around I was brought on to play, I felt like one of the team, but then Nick would turn up and I'd be back on the sidelines.'

'During our last session you said that you thought Nick was jealous of your friendship with David. Was that because you shared experiences with David, like school, that Nick was excluded from?'

'I suppose so.'

'But you felt excluded from some of the experiences that Nick and David had in common. So, were you jealous of Nick?'

Adam had never thought of it that way. 'If I'm honest I suppose the answer is yes.'

'It sounds almost as if you were in competition with each other, in a sense, for David's friendship.'

'I don't think I felt that way,' Adam said.

'How did you feel?'

'It was more like feeling a constant need to prove myself.'

'To whom?'

'I suppose to David. I wanted our friendship to be as important to him as Nick's evidently was.'

'You didn't think it was?'

'Going back to the football analogy I felt as if I was always fight-ing for my place on the team. I was looking to score the goal that would finally cement my place. I mean it wasn't simply about David, it was about acceptance in the wider sense.'

'And did you? Score that goal?'

'I thought I had,' Adam said.

Morris rested his chin thoughtfully on his steepled fingers. He sensed that this was what Adam had been leading up to.

❧

The year was 1985 and spring had been unusually warm and dry. By summer the country was baking in a heat wave. Adam had turned sixteen and had a holiday job at the *Courier* in Carlisle. The pay was terrible, and his job was mostly running errands and making coffee, but at least he got to see how a real newspaper worked, even if it was only a local daily where news meant local horse shows and reports of council meetings.

The editor was a dour Yorkshireman who spent most of his time secluded in his glass-walled office. Now and then he would emerge and gruffly summon one of the reporters. The door would close and the unlucky victim would have to sit in full view of the rest of the office while his or her work was savagely criticized. The only person who escaped these sessions was the paper's senior reporter who, alone it seemed, had the editor's respect.

Adam had been at the paper for three weeks the first time he spoke to Jim Findlay. He was standing at the photocopier feeding endless sheets of paper into the machine when Findlay paused on his way past.

'Adam isn't it?'

Findlay was rarely in the office. He did most of his work from the pub on the corner, where he habitually sat at a table in a sunny corner by the window with a pint glass and a whisky in front of him and an ashtray brimming with cigarette butts. He was Scottish and spoke with a broad accent. He looked to be in his forties, and had thinning hair that was turning grey and mournful eyes that gazed on the world with a kind of weary resignation.

'Yes it is,' Adam answered, recovering from his surprise.

Findlay nodded. 'How're you liking our wee paper then?'

'It's fine. I mean, I'm enjoying working here.'

'Is that so? I expect you'll be wanting to become a journalist yerself one day, is that it?'

'Hopefully, after university anyway.'

Findlay seemed amused. 'University eh? You'll no' want to be working at a place like this then. I'll expect you've bigger plans.'

There was something faintly mocking in his tone, though Adam didn't feel that he was the target, but rather that Findlay was mocking himself. The humour in his eyes faded and was replaced with something closer to regret. He placed a hand briefly on Adam's shoulder.

'Don't mind me laddie,' he said, and with that he wandered off.

At the end of the day Adam caught a bus back to Castleton. It was a sunny late afternoon, the heat of the day trapped in the narrow lanes between the hedgerows. In the fields the grass was drying to pale yellow. The hedgerows of hawthorn and crab apple and cow parsley were in full bloom. Towards the woods the air shimmered in a haze.

As the bus rounded a bend and crossed a stone bridge, a cluster of vehicles and caravans parked in a cut off the bridleway came into view. A grey horse was tethered to a tree stump near an ancient truck and smoke drifted lazily across the river. Back in April Adam had first seen the camp on the way home from school. David had stayed late for cricket practice and the only other person on the bus had been an old man who sat across the aisle. He had pale skin and thin wispy hair and his eyes were rheumy and red-tinged.

'Gypsies,' he'd muttered. 'Come around every few years they

do.' His mouth turned down in a grimace and he said something quietly to himself.

A little further along the road the bus had stopped and the old man got off and walked towards some cottages set back from the lane. The bus had barely moved off when it slowed again and pulled hard over so that the hedge scraped against the side. Out of the window Adam saw a brown horse carrying three figures on its back. Two were small children, and behind them was an older girl of perhaps seventeen or so. Her head was almost level with Adam so that as she passed by only the glass and a few feet of space separated them. He registered wide, dark eyes, a full mouth, and thick, unruly, almost jet-black hair. She stared back at him without expression. She wore a simple shapeless plain cotton dress. After she had passed he looked back and glimpsed her bare legs and the full rounded shape of her breasts against the material of her dress. The horse had no saddle and only a rope for a bridle. As he watched the girl kicked her bare heels into the horse's flanks, and then the bus turned a bend and they were lost from sight.

The gypsies had stayed throughout the spring and into the summer. The old women called at houses selling lucky charms and muttering curses if they found a door slammed in their faces. The rate of break-ins and petty crime in the area rose, which people generally attributed to the gypsies. Johnson's sawmill was broken into one night and a load of lumber stolen, but though the police went to the gypsy camp none of it was ever recovered. Kyle warned Adam to steer clear of them.

When the bus reached the square in Castleton, Adam crossed the street towards the newsagent's with his jacket slung over his shoulder. The bell above the door rang as he went inside. He paused, allowing his eyes to adjust to the comparative gloom. The shop smelt of sherbet and liquorice, underlain with the whiff of tobacco. Angela smiled when she saw him.

'Hello, Adam.'

'Hi.' He went to the fridge and took out a cold bottle of coke. 'Hot out there.'

'It's lovely.' Angela pulled a face. 'Not that I would know. I've been stuck in here all day.'

He handed her some money, and as she operated the register

28

her smock tightened over the swell of her breasts. His gaze lingered for a fraction of a second and then he fixed his eye on the magazine rack.

'Here's your change.'

'Oh, thanks.' He feigned distraction, hoping she wouldn't notice the flush of colour creeping into his cheeks. Her eyes were blue, but unlike any blue he had ever seen. Pale, but shimmering with light. Her long pale yellow hair was bleached in highlights by the summer sun, her arms brushed with a light tan.

'How's your job going?' she asked him.

'Fine. I like it.'

'Are you going to the disco?' She gestured to the notice board on the back of the door where a bright orange flyer advertised a disco at the church hall at the weekend.

'Are you?' he asked impulsively. He realized his question could almost be construed as asking her out and he felt his cheeks burn. He wished the ground would open up and swallow him whole. If she noticed, however, she didn't let on.

'Yes,' she answered.

The door opened. 'Well, I better go,' Adam said, relieved and disappointed at the same time.

'See you at the weekend then.'

'Right. See you there.' As he left he caught the eye of a woman coming in. She smiled at him.

He walked down through the town to the bridge and then along the path across the water meadow. On the far side Johnson's sawmill was hidden in a copse. The familiar tangy scent of cut pine and sawdust hung in the air. The gates were open and two trucks were parked in the yard outside the cutting shed. The saws were silent. On one side of the yard stood a two-storey wooden building with an outside staircase that led to the office door. Underneath was a room where the men had their tea. Every morning Adam left his bike around the back before he caught the bus to Carlisle.

As he passed the open tearoom door he almost tripped over Nick who was sitting outside smoking a cigarette in the shade. He had left school by then and was working full time at the sawmill.

'Sorry, didn't see you there.'

Nick squinted up at him, his expression managing to look like

29

a sneer, though it might have been the sun. 'Been working hard then? All that sharpening pencils and making the tea, you must be knackered.'

Adam ignored the sarcasm and stepped over Nick's legs.

'Better watch you don't get a blister on your little finger.'

'I'll try to remember that. Is David around?'

Nick shrugged unhelpfully and picked a shred of tobacco off his lip. 'Somewhere.'

Just then David appeared at the top of the stairs. He was tanned and muscular from working outdoors in the sun, in contrast to Nick, whose face remained pale beneath his black hair and who still looked like a skinny kid.

'Have you finished?' Adam asked. He was thinking that they could go down to the river for a swim but David shook his head.

'We're working late today. There's an order that needs doing.' He aimed a kick at Nick's foot. 'Come on. We'll see you tomorrow, Adam.'

Adam watched as they headed towards the shed and Nick laughed at something David said. He knew that when Nick had applied for a full-time job a few months earlier David's dad hadn't been too keen on the idea. Adam had overheard David pleading Nick's case, insisting that Nick couldn't be blamed for the way his dad was, and though in the end Mr Johnson had conceded, Adam had the feeling he'd never really been happy about it. He wondered if Nick knew about that.

It was getting dark by the time Adam and the others arrived at the disco at the weekend. A group of younger boys lurked in the darkness at the edge of the tiny car park furtively smoking cigarettes. In the entrance hall two women from the church social committee sat behind a scarred wooden table taking money and dispensing entrance tickets. One of them cast a disapproving eye over Nick's leather jacket.

'You can leave that in the cloakroom if you like,' she said.

He gave her his money without answering and held her eye until, flustered, she dropped her gaze. Inside they stood bunched near the door. The hall was about half full. The music was loud and clusters of local kids stood around the walls, boys on one side, girls on the other, except for three young girls dancing together near the stage at the front. The DJ seemed to be absorbed with his record collection. A bank of coloured lights in front of his sound system blinked on and off with the music and a single silver glitter ball suspended from the rafters cast a forlorn pattern on the dance floor. A woman and a balding man wearing a knitted tie with a brown check shirt were selling cups of orange juice and sandwiches, which nobody was buying. The woman wore a fixed smile and jigged determinedly in time to the music. Occasionally they both glanced uneasily towards a group of four teenagers standing in one corner of the hall.

They were conspicuous both by their appearance and by the space around them that set them apart from everybody else. Their clothes looked like hand-me-downs and they shared a common dark hue to their skin and eyes. If anybody looked their way they stared back with silent hostility. Adam recognized one of the two girls as the one he'd seen from the bus back in the spring, though there was something different about her. He decided she looked smaller than he remembered, perhaps because last time he'd seen her she was on horseback. She also seemed young, which he put down to the fact that all the other girls in the hall wore clothes and make-up that made them look older than they really were. She looked over as if she sensed him watching her until one of the boys with her noticed and glared at her.

'Fuckin' gyppos,' Nick muttered.

Graham nudged him and nodded towards a couple of girls who had started dancing together. 'There's Christine Abbot and that friend of hers.'

They wore high heels and short tight skirts, and when one of them noticed they were being eyed she said something to her friend and they both giggled. Nick and Graham went over to talk to them.

Adam looked around for Angela but he couldn't see her anywhere. He and David lingered by the door. A few boys plucked up the courage to approach a group of girls. They paired off and started moving to the music with blank expressions. The music seemed to get louder as if the DJ thought sheer volume would make up for what else the hall lacked. It was hot and airless and after a while Adam told David he was going to get a drink. In the toilets he splashed water on his face and then made his way to the entrance and went outside where it was cool and the sound of the music faded.

'Hello, Adam.'

He turned around and found Angela smiling at him. 'Hi,' he said and for a second or two was at a loss for anything more to say. She wore jeans and a pink T-shirt with the imprint of a pair of lipsticked lips on the front like a big kiss. With the touch of make-up she wore and her hair done differently she looked older. 'I thought you weren't coming,' he said eventually.

'Were you waiting for me?'

He wasn't sure what to say. His heart was beating faster than normal. 'Would you mind if I was?'

'No.' For a moment neither of them spoke, absorbing the fact that they seemed to have crossed some kind of invisible boundary. 'What are you doing out here anyway?' she asked.

'It was hot inside.'

She gestured towards the children's park next door. 'Shall we go over there then?'

'Don't you want to go in?'

She looked at the door. 'Not really.'

The park was deserted, lit with a single overhead lamp. Angela sat on a swing and caught the chains in the crook of her elbows. They talked for a while about nothing much, the sounds from the hall drifting over to them. He told her about his job and she told him that she liked art at school but didn't know what she wanted to do when she left.

'What about you?'

'I think I'd like to be a journalist.'

'You mean work at the *Courier*?'

'No. I mean for a national paper. Or perhaps a magazine.'

'You'd have to live in London or somewhere wouldn't you?'

'I suppose.'

'Don't you like it here then?'

'Sometimes I do,' he said, and grinned at her.

She smiled. 'Like now?'

'Yes.' Suddenly emboldened he said, 'I'm glad you came tonight.'

She reached across and found his hand. 'I'm glad too.'

They went for a walk hand in hand around the park. It was warm and the air felt thick and soft in the darkness. The sounds from the hall grew fainter.

'Shouldn't you go back inside?' Angela asked. 'Who'd you come with?'

'David and the others. I think Graham and Nick were talking to some girls though.' He frowned, looking back at the hall, thinking perhaps he should go back, though he didn't want to.

Angela squeezed his hand. 'David'll be alright. All the girls fancy him.'

He was surprised, but when he thought about it he supposed it was true. David was popular and easy-going and he made the girls laugh. He experienced a faint twinge of jealousy. 'What about you? Do you fancy him too?'

'David?' She laughed at the idea. 'I suppose I never thought of him like that. I prefer the dark serious type,' she teased. 'I remember the first time I saw you after you moved here. I felt sorry for you.'

'Sorry for me? Why?'

'You looked lonely.' She squeezed his arm and he smiled though he was slightly uneasy that she had felt sorry for him.

It was late when Graham and Nick came out of the hall with the two girls they'd been talking to. When Nick put his arm around one of them she laughed coarsely and pushed him away, but then the four of them made their way around the back of the building and vanished in the darkness.

Angela raised her eyebrows and looked amused, then looked at her watch. 'I should be getting home.'

'I'll walk you,' Adam offered.

'Alright.'

'I better just go and tell David.'

'I'll wait outside.'

It was crowded in the hall and at first he couldn't see David anywhere. He looked twice around the hall until he finally found him talking to the gypsy girl he'd noticed earlier while her friends looked on with sullen suspicion. One of them in particular stared with obvious hostility. He had the same general look as the girl and might have been her brother.

'I'm off,' Adam said when he went over.

'Alright. See you later.'

The girl went back towards her friends and David followed her with his gaze.

'Did I interrupt something?'

'I just asked how long they were staying.'

'I don't think her friends liked her talking to you.'

'They're gyppos, Adam. They don't like outsiders much.' David looked around the hall. 'Where've you been anyway?'

'Just talking to Angela Curtis.' He tried to make it sound casual, but he didn't think it worked. 'I said I'd walk her home anyway, so I better go.'

David grinned and said he would see him later. When he got outside Angela was leaning against the wall beyond the light from the door. 'I thought you'd got lost.'

'Sorry, I couldn't find him.'

She smiled. 'It doesn't matter.'

As they started walking towards the road she slipped her hand inside his.

Approaching the end of a long hot August, Castleton and the surrounding country seemed smothered in a sleepy stupor where late in the day nothing much stirred. Cows lay down in the shade of oak trees in the fields and buzzards circled lazily in the thermals high above the fells. Then something happened which abruptly shook the town from its lethargy.

One Saturday afternoon Adam was waiting outside the shop when Angela finished for the day. She wore a band in her hair and a denim skirt that ended mid-thigh. They walked along by the river where she took off her shoes, holding on to his shoulder for balance as she stood on one leg. They followed the path away from the town, past the sawmill and along the edge of Castleton

Wood. At one point they passed the gypsy camp on the other side of the river where a woman was hanging washing on a makeshift line and some grubby children were playing with an old bike. The woman stared at them as they passed.

'I wonder why they live like that,' Adam mused aloud. 'Do you think they're as bad as people think?'

'My dad doesn't like them coming into the shop. He thinks the kids will nick anything they can get their hands on. When I was young he used to tell me I should stay away from them because gypsies sometimes stole children.'

'That's a bit strong isn't it?'

She smiled ruefully. 'It's true the kids will nick from the shop though. You have to watch them like hawks. Little buggers.'

Half a mile further on there was a bend in the river where a willow tree grew and made a pleasant shady spot to sit. The water was shallow close to the bank where it flowed crystal clear over pebbles and rocks. They sat in the long rye grass that was flecked with splashes of vivid red from the poppies that grew in the field. Angela tilted her face to the sun and closed her eyes. She took a deep breath.

'I love that smell, don't you?'

It was the sweet smell of hay from a nearby field from where they could hear the drone of a tractor.

A week ago they had been to the cinema in Brampton and on the way home had taken a shortcut through the graveyard. They had paused under the big oak tree by the south wall and kissed. Adam remembered the feel of her body pressed against his, her quickening breath.

She opened her eyes and caught him watching her. The air seemed suddenly still. He didn't try to conceal what he felt sure must be evident in his eyes. She leaned towards him and kissed him briefly and then her expression grew serious. She hugged her knees, not looking directly at him.

'Adam . . . can I ask you something? Have you ever had sex?'

'No. Have you?'

She shook her head. 'Sometimes though, I feel as if I want to. With you I mean. It's just . . . I want it to feel right. I want it to be special. Does that sound silly?'

'No.'

'There are girls in my class at school who've had sex with their boyfriends. They make it sound so casual. I don't want it to be like that.'

'Neither do I,' he said.

She picked a stem of grass and began shredding it. 'Let's wait. Can we?'

'Of course.' He reached for her hand. 'As long as you like.'

She smiled and they lay down side by side. He felt closer to her somehow. They linked hands and the warmth of the sun and the drowsy hum of insects lulled them into a languorous daze.

'This is so beautiful,' Angela murmured. 'I don't think I ever want to live anywhere else.'

'Never?' he questioned.

She opened one eye. 'Why would I?'

'Don't you want to travel?'

She thought about that. 'I suppose so,' she said at last. 'I'd like to go to America.'

'What about somewhere closer? France.'

'Paris. I'd love to go to Paris. I want to see the Eiffel Tower and all the glamorous shops. And I'd like to go to Italy. But I'd always want to come back here.'

He pondered what she'd said and then abruptly Angela sat up. 'I'm hot,' she announced. She stood up and went down to the river's edge and waded into the water until it reached just below her knees while Adam sat on the bank watching her.

'What's it like?' he asked.

She turned around and grinned. 'It's freezing.'

A dragonfly skimmed the surface of the water, and the sun shining through the branches of the willow made shimmering patterns of light. Where the bottom was stony the water was clear, the colours of the stones bright and hard, sandy browns and darker reds, but further out towards the far bank the river grew deep and dark where it was shadowed by overhanging branches. As Angela bent to scoop water in her hand, her long hair fell across her shoulders and as she stood she pushed it back and splashed her face. Adam felt his throat tighten. He wanted to capture this image of her and store it away in his mind, to absorb the detail of the light and the reflections on the water, of a green weeping willow and a girl whom he thought he was falling in love with.

When she came back to sit beside him again, she gestured to the paperback he'd shoved in his back pocket and asked what it was.

'*Cider with Rosie*. It's by someone called Laurie Lee.' He showed her the cover. 'It's about a boy growing up in Gloucestershire before the war.'

'Is it good?'

'Yes.' He started to tell her about it. She sat with her knees drawn up to her chin as he described the sense of another time that the book evoked.

'Who's Rosie?' she asked.

'A girl.'

'What's she like?'

'She's nice,' he said. 'He thinks about her all the time.' An insect landed in Angela's hair, and he reached out and brushed it away. She smiled and then turned to look at the water and for a while neither of them spoke.

It was evening by the time they walked back towards town. The light had grown soft and hazy, turning purple in the dusk. They passed the gypsy camp and heard the sound of voices from behind a caravan. The smell of wood smoke filled the air. Close to town they crossed the water meadow near the now quiet sawmill. On the other side of the river Adam glimpsed two figures in the trees. He stopped.

'What is it?' Angela asked when she saw where he was looking.

The figures had gone, however, slipped back among the trees as if they didn't want to be seen, though not before Adam had formed a fleeting impression of a boy and a girl, the boy tall with thick brown hair, the girl slender and dark. For a moment he was sure it had been David. He was on the verge of saying so, but in the end he didn't.

'Nothing,' he said. 'Thought I saw something that's all.'

There had been times over the last few weeks when Adam had seen the gypsy girl in the trees across the river from the sawmill. She appeared to be waiting for somebody and she always hung back in the gloom as if she didn't want to be seen. When he thought about it he hadn't seen so much of David lately, though he'd been spending time with Angela so maybe that was it. Besides, if David was seeing the gypsy girl he probably wouldn't want his dad to know about it, which might explain why he hadn't said anything. And maybe it hadn't been David anyway.

But if it was, he wondered as they walked on, had David told Nick?

Two days later, on Monday, the *Courier* was buzzing with rumours of a big story. For once Findlay turned up and went to the editor's office where the two men were seen talking for almost an hour. When Findlay finally emerged he disappeared for the rest of the day, but he returned late in the afternoon and spent an hour at his desk hammering at his typewriter. Adam was proofing ads for the following weekend's edition when Findlay surprised him by appearing at his side.

'Working late I see, Adam.'

'I thought I'd just get this done.'

Findlay glanced at the ads. There was something different about him, a kind of gleam in his eye. 'Where is it you live, Adam? Over Brampton way somewhere isn't it?'

'Just outside Castleton.'

'Aye, I thought it was. Do you know anything about the gypsies that are camping over there?'

'I've seen them,' Adam said uncertainly.

'One of them's gone missing. A girl. She hasnae been seen for a couple of days now. Do you ever talk to any of them?'

'Nobody does much.'

'No, I suppose they don't. They're not much liked, eh? Still, this wee lassie is a good-looking girl I've heard. Mebbe she just met some local lad, eh? And the two of them have eloped.' He chuckled, but his gaze was penetrating. 'If you hear anything, will you let me know?'

'Alright,' Adam said.

'Thanks. Anyway, I expect she'll turn up. Don't work too late, Adam.'

In the morning the story was all over the front page of the *Courier*. The missing girl's name was Meg Coucesco. There was no photograph, but the police had provided an identikit and Adam recognized her as the girl from the disco. He read the story through with growing unease. She was seventeen years old and had last been seen late on Saturday afternoon when she had left the camp alone. She had never returned. There was little detail in the story other than a description of what she'd been wearing, and a statement from the police expressing concern for her safety. A search of local land had been organized for that day involving local police and volunteers, and anyone who had visited the camp over the summer, or who knew the girl, was asked to come forward and speak to the detectives on the case. The final quote was from a unnamed senior officer who said that at this stage the actions they were taking were merely a precaution. There was always the chance that the girl had simply chosen to run away of her own accord.

Adam wondered about that. If the police thought she had run away, why were they conducting a search and asking to speak to anyone who knew her?

At the end of the day he was glad to be alone on the bus, to give him a chance to think. Whenever he'd seen Findlay around the office that day he'd done his best to avoid him, though he wasn't sure why. He unfolded a copy of the paper he'd brought with him and stared at the picture of the missing girl. It was a good likeness though curiously expressionless, which made him think of the first time he'd seen her from the bus when she'd stared back at him through the window.

He kept thinking about the times he'd seen her near the sawmill and about the two figures he'd glimpsed vanishing among the trees on Saturday. He'd been thinking about it all day.

When he got off the bus Adam went to the sawmill. The saws were quiet and men were packing up or leaving for the day, though Nick was still working in the shed stacking freshly cut planks of pine. He found David outside the tearoom underneath the office and took him aside before he handed him the paper.

'Have you seen this?'

He watched as David read the headline, his gaze lingering over the identikit picture of the girl. Though he frowned slightly he didn't react in any other way.

'The police want to talk to anyone who knows her.'

39

David regarded him blankly. 'What of it?'

'Shouldn't you talk to them?'

They could hear David's father talking on the phone through the open door at the top of the stairs. David lowered his voice.

'Me? Why me?'

'Well, you talked to her that night at the disco.'

'Adam, I spoke to her for about a minute. That's all. I don't know her.'

Adam experienced a sense of relief. What had he thought anyway? It must have been somebody else he'd seen in the trees with Meg.

Just then Nick came over from the shed. He looked curiously from one to the other. 'What's up?'

David handed him the paper and after he'd read the headlines he glanced at David and gave it back. There was something in his expression that Adam couldn't put his finger on.

'So?'

The question was directed towards Adam. Suddenly his relief evaporated, though he wasn't sure why. 'I've seen her a couple of times,' he said. 'In the trees across the river. I got the impression she was waiting for someone.'

'What if she was?'

He didn't know how to answer. 'I'm pretty sure I saw her there on Saturday. She was with somebody.'

Nobody spoke. The silence seemed to press down on Adam like a heavy weight.

'Did you see who it was?' David asked finally.

There was something faintly challenging about his tone. 'Not really. I mean I'm not sure. I thought I did, but . . .' Adam broke off. He was struck by the way Nick was looking at him. That same old sneer.

'But what?' David said.

Something clicked in his brain. All of a sudden he was certain that it was David he'd seen. 'Nothing.' Adam met his eye. 'Nothing, I don't know who it was.'

The story about the missing girl remained on the front page for the rest of the week. Findlay wrote a feature about the gypsy way of life which delved into the historical roots of Romany travellers and the suspicion and distrust they encountered wherever they went. The evidence that they were involved in petty crime was indisputable but some of the other things gypsies were accused of such as illegal prostitution and gambling, along with many of the more lurid myths like baby stealing, were less common and in some cases had probably never been true.

As the days passed and despite massive searches there was no sign of Meg Coucesco. The *Courier* reported the police speculation that she had merely run away. Adam read each report with increasing unease. He kept replaying the scene in the yard with David and Nick when he'd felt compelled to deny what he'd seen. Though he asked himself why he'd done it he already knew the answer. It was for the same reason that he hadn't asked David since then to explain himself. He wanted to show David that he trusted him, that he could be trusted in return, as much as Nick. Even more.

As the days passed he found himself facing a dilemma. He knew he ought to persuade David to go to the police because he must know something about Meg Coucesco's disappearance. He didn't believe that David had done anything to hurt her, but the problem was whenever he decided to talk to David he always found Nick around, and anyway as each day went by he became less certain about what he'd seen. Sometimes he thought he had glimpsed David's face, if only for a moment, and at other times he was sure he hadn't seen anything more than a tall, indistinct shape. The fact that David seemed completely normal and utterly untroubled only added to his self-doubt. David, in fact, took little interest in the story.

One evening he questioned Angela about what she remembered. 'When we were out by the river on Saturday, did you see anything in the trees across from the sawmill?'

She looked mystified. 'Like what?'

'I don't know. Anything. I thought I saw somebody.'

'You didn't say anything. Who was it?'

'I don't know. It was probably nothing.'

The day afterwards at work he caught Findlay watching him thoughtfully and when he had to deliver some copy to the pub

41

where Findlay was again ensconced, the reporter took it without even a glance and gestured to a chair.

'Why don't you sit down, Adam?'

He wanted to refuse but didn't see how he could. Findlay lit a cigarette and studied him through a haze of smoke.

'Would you like a drink of something?'

'No thanks. I have to get back.'

'Don't be in such a rush, laddie. Stay here a minute and let's have a wee chat. The place'll no fall down without you.' He chuckled softly to himself. 'I suppose you'll be finishing with us soon to go back to school, eh?'

'In a couple of weeks.'

'Aye, you'll probably be glad to get back.'

Adam didn't reply. He had a feeling this was leading somewhere, that Findlay was interested in more than how he felt about going back to school.

'This business about the wee gypsy lassie has affected us all. It makes you think when something like this happens in your own back yard. It must have been bothering you too, eh, Adam?'

'No more than anyone else I suppose.'

'No? I thought since you live over that way . . . Mebbe you'd seen the girl around, you know.'

'I might have once or twice.'

'Is that so? What was she like?'

'I don't know. I never spoke to her.'

'But I mean, what was she like to look at? It's hard to tell from the identikit pictures, you know? Would you say she was pretty?'

'I suppose so.'

'Mebbe the police are right then, do you think? Could be she just met a lad from some other town and they ran away together. Did you ever see her with anyone?'

'No.'

'Not even with a local lad?'

'No.'

Findlay stared at him. He had the uncomfortable feeling that the reporter could see everything that he was thinking.

'Mebbe you heard something about a lad the girl might have been seeing, even if you didnae actually see them yerself.' Findlay persisted. 'There're rumours she was seeing somebody you know.'

'I never heard anything,' Adam said.

'Ah well, it was just a thought, you know.' Findlay made a gesture as if to dismiss the subject. He lit another cigarette, and smiled. 'Let's talk about something else, eh? You know I used to live in a village like Castleton myself, Adam. Did I ever tell you that?'

'No.'

'Aye, well I'm glad I'm no there any more. I don't like these wee places where everybody knows what everybody else is up to, you know what I mean? Like when I was living in this place, I knew this lad who was nicking sweeties from the shop on the corner. Him and his brother used to go in there and fill their bags with stuff, and I don't just mean they were taking a few gobstoppers and the like. They were getting away with whole boxes of chocolates. You know what they lads were doing with all this stuff, Adam? They were selling it to all the other kids around there.'

Findlay paused for a moment and emptied his glass. He studied it reflectively. 'The trouble was, the woman who owned the shop was my auntie. I knew how it was affecting her losing all this stuff, and my mother knew that I must have some idea who was responsible. You know what she wanted me to do? She wanted me to tell her who it was. Difficult decision that. 'Course, I was only a wee lad then.'

'So what did you do?'

'What would you have done, if you'd been me, Adam?'

'I don't know.'

'Well, I didn't know either. But in the end I had to decide. It was a case of divided loyalties you might say. I realized then, Adam, that we all have to make moral choices in our lives.'

He paused again and then he stood up. 'You sure you don't want something to drink?'

'I have to get back.'

Findlay let his gaze linger, then nodded. 'Aye, well, I'll see you later.'

What Findlay had said stayed with Adam throughout the day and on the bus ride home. He was still thinking about it when he crossed the water meadow towards the sawmill. David and Nick were leaving work for the day, heading along the track towards the road. He hung back watching them, and then for no reason that he could put his finger on he started following them from a distance.

He soon realized they were heading for a steep hill called Back Lane which led to the part of town known as the bottom end. He followed them past small cottages with front doors that opened directly onto the road, and then past several streets of council houses that had been built after the war, a collection of prefab bungalows with pebble dash cladding and iron roofs. At the bottom of the hill Back Lane ended in an unpaved bridle track that vanished among tall trees.

He gave them a few minutes before he followed. The houses on the edge of town were quickly lost from sight as the track curved towards a bridge over the river. Tall leafy elms and oaks filtered the light, lending a green-tinged hue. It was quiet other than for the twittering of birds and the gurgle of water beneath the old stone bridge where the river was dark and sluggish. Around the next curve the trees ended and on the edge of a meadow three cottages formed a terraced row beside the bridleway. On the other side of the meadow was the edge of Castleton Wood, which formed the boundary of the estate.

The cottages had slate roofs and stone chimneys, their gardens long overgrown with weeds and brambles. Some of the windows were missing glass and had been covered with plastic sheeting, and the paint on the doors and frames was peeling and blistered. A proliferation of junk lay in the unfenced gardens. Old car parts, rusted wire netting, and a rotting chicken house that appeared to be slowly dissolving into the ground poked out of the weeds and nettles. A battered van was parked just off the track and a skinny mongrel dog lay asleep by an open door, its leg twitching as it dreamed.

Confronted for the first time with the reality of where Nick lived, Adam realized he'd expected something more dramatic. The vague air of unspoken mystery that had always surrounded him, the sullenness and obvious results of physical abuse, had conjured dark family secrets. But the truth was simply depressing and squalid.

Adam hung back, remaining hidden in the trees until David and Nick emerged from the first of the cottages. There was something oddly furtive about them. They looked around as if to make sure they were alone and then, apparently reassured, they opened the back door of the van. David reached into his pocket and then leaned inside. When he reappeared a few seconds later he said something to Nick before he quickly turned and started walking back along the track. Adam remained hidden, pressed against the trunk of a tree as David passed by no more than eight feet away. When he peered back towards the cottages a minute later Nick had vanished and the scene was once more quiet and deserted.

In the morning it was on the news that James Allen had been arrested and taken into custody for questioning about the disappearance of Meg Coucesco. It was Findlay who told Adam that the police had found a bracelet in his van belonging to the girl.

'They were acting on a tip-off.' From the look in his eye Adam realized that Findlay suspected that he had had something to do with it.

For twenty-four hours Adam was plagued with uncertainty about what he should do but before he could reach any decision Allen was released due to lack of evidence. He learned from Findlay that the fact that there was no body made it difficult for the police to press charges, though Findlay had spoken to a detective who was convinced that Allen knew what had happened to the girl. He was known to have been to the camp regularly that summer, and he had a history of violence.

When Allen vanished after he was released Findlay was unsurprised.

'If he showed his face around Castleton again the gypsies would nae doubt take matters into their own hands, Adam,' he said.

In the event, though, they didn't need to. He was killed a few days later in Derbyshire when his van hit a petrol tanker and he was burned to death.

'Poetic justice, eh, Adam,' Findlay commented philosophically.

'She was never found,' Adam finished. He was standing by the window. The rain had stopped and the sun was struggling to break through the clouds above Islington.

Morris was thoughtful. 'What do you think happened to her?'

'I don't know.'

'Didn't you ever speak to David about it? Even after Nick's father was killed?'

Adam went over and sat down. His leg was playing up, causing him to limp slightly. 'We never mentioned it.'

'Obviously this whole event made a significant impression on you,' Morris said. 'Are you saying that your choice of career stems from this incident?'

'I suppose so.'

'Why do you think that is?'

'Aren't you the one who's supposed to come up with the psychological whys and wherefores?'

'I'm more interested in what you think.'

'I suppose I feel guilty.'

'Why?'

'Because I didn't tell anyone what I'd seen.'

'So, you think David had something to do with whatever happened to the gypsy girl?'

'Don't you? I'm sure he knew her. I think he was seeing her. It must have been him that I saw in the trees the day she vanished. And what about the bracelet the police found?'

'You think he planted it in Nick's dad's van?'

'What else was he doing?'

'I think it's all what the law would call circumstantial evidence. You're telling me that your choice of career, your dedication to your work . . .'

'You mean obsession.'

Morris smiled. 'You're saying that this all stems from a sense of guilt.'

'Maybe not guilt exactly. Partly perhaps.' Adam struggled to articulate something he'd always known, but had never confronted

46

openly even to himself. 'Maybe when I'm looking for a missing child, I'm looking for her too in a sense. For Meg.'

Morris considered this, and then gave a little smile. 'It seems very neat.'

'Neat?'

'Your extreme dedication to your work stemming from this incident when you were what, sixteen? Which results ultimately in the breakdown of your relationship with Louise. That is what you seem to be telling me isn't it?'

'I'm not telling you anything. I thought you were the one who came up with the answers.'

'If that was true, I would say that there is more.'

'More?'

'That you haven't told me everything. In my experience psychological cause and effect is never so straightforward as this.'

Adam didn't say anything. Morris was right. There was more. But none of it was relevant. Louise just needed to understand that once a girl had vanished and she remained on his conscience, rightly or wrongly. 'Time's up,' he said, rising to leave.

There was a postscript to Meg's disappearance that Adam didn't tell Morris about. During the final weekend of the summer Adam went fishing with David and the others at Cold Tarn. It was a long ride up to the fells and then through the forest to the lake. When they got there Adam wandered off along the shore and found a shady place where he cast his line out into the water and then propped his rod against a log and sat down to read *The Catcher in the Rye*. After a while he felt drowsy, lulled by the peace and the stillness of the water. He nodded off and when he woke it was getting late. He checked his line and found his bait gone as usual, but no fish on the hook so he packed up and started back along the shore to look for the others.

There was a part of the shore where he had to cut into the woods that fringed the lake to avoid a high rocky promontory that formed one side of a small bay. He would have passed by, but he saw David standing by the water's edge, seemingly deep in thought. Intrigued, Adam put his gear down and moved closer, quietly making his way out along the promontory. David remained motionless looking out across the lake. Though Adam followed his gaze there was nothing to see but the still, almost black waters of the tarn, and high above the far shore the small outline of a walkers' hostel that was open in the summer months.

As Adam watched David looked at something he was holding in his hand. He stared at it for several seconds before he suddenly drew back his arm as if to throw it into the lake, and whatever it was flashed when it caught the sun. But then he froze and after a few moments he dropped his arm again. As he did Adam dislodged a piece of loose rock that skittered down the slope and dropped to the water. David appeared startled and looked from the spreading ripples on the lake towards the trees where Adam crouched hidden. For a moment they seemed to look directly into one another's eyes, then David turned away and quickly vanished among the trees.

CHAPTER FOUR

A few weeks after what had turned out to be his final session with Morris, Adam followed a man as he made his way through the crowds at Euston and climbed aboard the six-fifteen from platform seven. They shared the same first-class compartment, the other man nodding briefly before he opened the evening paper. Alan Thomas was forty-six. He was an executive for a print firm. Adam knew a lot about him. He had three children, a boy and two girls. Adam knew their names, where they went to school, when their birthdays were. Thomas's wife, Christine, habitually wore a vaguely trapped expression that manifested itself in a kind of desperation in her eyes.

The train started moving and as it did the compartment door opened. A man with a briefcase started to come in until Adam stood up and blocked his way.

'Sorry, this compartment is full.'

The man looked startled and then puzzled by the empty seats. Adam smiled apologetically, though he didn't move out of the way. 'I'm sure there are seats further on,' he said. Eventually the man made a snorting sound and turned on his heel. There was a rustle of paper as Thomas regarded Adam warily, perhaps thinking he was sharing a compartment with a madman. Adam closed the door and returned to his seat. He weighed up the man opposite him. Thomas was heavier, but running to fat. He probably ate lunch at expensive restaurants too often, drank too much. Maybe lately he was drinking more. To help him sleep. If things went wrong then Adam thought he would come out on top. He was younger and fitter, even with a bad leg. He clenched his fist, and unclenched it

49

again and he stared at Thomas coldly. He almost hoped Thomas tried something.

'I want to know what you did with Liz Mount's body after you killed her,' he said.

He saw the reaction in Thomas's eyes. The sickening fear and perhaps a kind of relief as well. Relief that the demons he'd lived with for months finally had a face if not yet a name.

When he got off the train forty minutes later Adam went to the police and told them what he knew. He couldn't give them the name of Liz's friend who'd told him that Liz had confided that Thomas had once tried to kiss her when he'd taken her home after baby-sitting, and that he'd put his hand up her skirt. He'd said if she told anyone they wouldn't believe her and she would get into trouble. It wasn't worth it, she'd said to her friend. She just wouldn't go back.

Thomas hadn't admitted anything, but Adam could guess some of what had happened. Thomas had probably seen Liz on the train that morning and perhaps he'd followed her. When she went back later he'd been on the train with her. Somehow he'd managed to get her to his house without anyone seeing them, though Adam didn't know how. Perhaps he'd threatened her, perhaps it was just opportunist luck. Maybe he hadn't even meant to kill her.

The police would question Thomas, and they would find Liz's body somewhere near the house, Adam was sure of that, either before or after he confessed. After he left the police station he went to see the Mounts. He sat outside their house for a long time before he finally went to the door. Parents have a kind of extra sense where their children are concerned, especially mothers. He believed in the intuition of women. Carol Mount opened the door and as soon as she saw him she began to cry.

He found out later that Thomas had tried to assault Liz on the train and when she had resisted he'd pushed her out. Later he'd driven back to the spot where she'd fallen and recovered her body.

When he finished the story he wrote Adam sat for a long time in the dark. The light on the phone didn't blink. By then Louise had left him.

Part Two

Two Years Later

CHAPTER FIVE

The Reception area at Condor Publications was self-consciously trendy. Visitors were confronted with a long, curved silver counter behind which sat two young women who might have been part-time models. Having given his name and stated his business Adam was invited to take a seat. There was a choice of three couches, each a different colour. He chose the grape and idly flicked through a magazine, one of Condor's mass-market coffee-table monthlies.

The phone call that had brought him here had been slightly mysterious. Karen Stone had managed to avoid revealing exactly why she wanted him to come in, except to say that she wanted him to meet somebody she was certain would interest him. Beyond that she wouldn't be drawn. He wasn't busy, in fact wasn't working on anything at all, and so he'd agreed. He was also a little bit intrigued, he admitted to himself. The past six months had been spent ghostwriting the autobiography of a twenty-five-year-old pop star. He'd laboured to make the accumulation of obscene amounts of money by somebody who was largely uninteresting and devoid of talent sound interesting, and he was relieved to have finished. It had reaffirmed his belief in the notion that there is no justice in the world. The book had been a break from his normal work. An attempt to make some changes in his life. It had been a largely unsuccessful experiment, he decided.

'Adam.'

Jolted from his reverie he turned to find Karen Stone smiling warmly at him. He stood up and she offered her cheek to be kissed. She smelled of expensive perfume and looked, as ever, fantastic.

He tried to remember when he'd last seen her. A month ago? Longer, he thought. Too long.

'You look well,' she said. 'Thanks for coming. Come on through.'

She led the way through a set of doors and along the corridor that housed the various editorial offices.

'By the way, congratulations on the promotion,' he said.

'Thanks. It's brilliant isn't it? I still can't believe it.'

He could, however. She was only twenty-nine, but then magazine publishing was a young person's business and in her field Karen was the best editor he knew. They'd met about a year earlier when he'd first started casting around for commissions. She knew his work and though she'd expressed surprise at his change of direction, she'd been happy enough to give him the odd lifestyle piece. He'd accepted two before he'd decided that writing features about liposuction and country hotels didn't do it for him. This time she hadn't been surprised, and though they hadn't worked together since, they had remained friends.

They came to a door with a plate bearing Karen's name and her title of Publishing Editor.

'Impressive.' He ran his finger over the raised gold lettering.

She grinned. 'I think so.'

'So, are you going to tell me what this is all about now? Who's the mystery person you want me to meet?'

'Her name's Helen Pierce, she's an old friend. She came to see me a few days ago to ask for my help and after I'd listened to what she had to say I thought of you.'

He was immediately wary. 'What kind of help does she need exactly?'

'I think it would be better if she explained that herself. Come and meet her.'

He put his hand on her arm to stop her opening the door. 'I get the feeling I'm not going to like this. Listen Karen, if this is about your friend's missing child I can't help. I'm sorry but I don't do that any more.'

She regarded him steadily, searching the depths of his eyes. 'So, what are you going to do? Another hack job on some flash-in-the pan pop star?'

'Ouch.'

'I just can't believe you'd waste your energy on something so frivolous.'

He looked around with mock confusion. 'Sorry, there must be some mistake. I didn't realize this was *The Times*.'

'Very funny. Look, you're here now. At least come and meet Helen, hear what she has to say. Do it for me, please. She doesn't know who else she can turn to. And incidentally there's no missing child. Helen doesn't have children. In fact nobody is missing.'

This last part finally convinced him and he gave in, as he was sure she had known he would. 'No promises though,' he said.

'Fair enough.' She squeezed his hand briefly, then opened the door.

A woman who had been standing at the window turned to face them. She was about Karen's age and was wearing a dark-coloured suit. She was attractive, he thought, but not stunning. Her suit was well tailored, probably expensive, but not the sort of cutting-edge fashion favoured by most of the women who worked for Condor. She might have been a consultant of some sort, or maybe a lawyer.

Karen did the introductions. 'Adam Turner, Helen Pierce. Helen, this is the writer I told you about.'

As he shook her hand he had the feeling it was his turn to be appraised. Her expression was guarded. 'Karen's told me a lot about you, Mr Turner.'

'Don't believe any of it,' he joked. She offered a hesitant smile. She was nervous, he thought, and then revised his judgement. She was on edge.

They sat around a small conference table where Karen held her meetings and wielded her power. On the wall behind her desk were the framed covers of the magazines under her control, including *Landmark*, which occupied pride of place and was the prize that went with her recent promotion. Condor published mostly gossipy coffee-table monthlies, but *Landmark* was the exception, mixing arts and social commentary along with the occasional investigative piece. It was the least profitable magazine in the Condor stable, but it conferred a degree of respectability on Ryan Cummings, Karen's boss and the owner of the company.

'Karen tells me you two are old friends,' Adam said, breaking the ice. 'Are you in the publishing business too?'

'Actually, I work for a research company.'

'Helen and I were at university in Exeter together,' Karen explained. 'We shared a horrible flat for two years.' To Helen she said, 'I told Adam that it would be best if he heard what you have to say first-hand.'

'Alright, though I'm not sure where to begin, exactly.'

'Take your time,' Adam told her. He felt himself slip easily into his old persona. How many times had he sat with parents who needed his help to find their son or daughter, trying to get them to open up and talk freely about a subject that, despite them having sought him out, was inevitably painful for them. 'If I need to clarify anything I'll ask questions.'

She nodded and dropped her gaze while she composed her thoughts. 'About a month ago, at the beginning of September, I learned that my brother, Ben, had been killed in a car crash. The fact is that since then I've come to believe that his death wasn't an accident.'

She paused and met Adam's eye. She was, he knew, trying to evaluate his reaction. She would have told her story before, most likely to people who hadn't necessarily believed her, including the police. She would have been listened to politely at every level. Sympathy and condolences would have been offered, but in the end the disbelief she encountered would have become increasingly obvious. Frustration and a sense of isolation would have set in. He knew all this had happened otherwise she would not be sitting at this table now.

A year ago he had decided that he couldn't do this kind of work any more. At least not if he was trying to make up for something that had happened seventeen years earlier. After his divorce from Louise he had begun to seriously question the direction his life was taking. Louise wasn't the first casualty of the guilt he felt about Meg Coucesco. There had been others over the years, all of them eventually driven away. Maybe getting married had been an expression of a subconscious desire to change, as writing the autobiography of a spoiled pop star had been a conscious one. Neither had worked. Besides, nothing was

56

ever that simple. Even now as he listened to Helen Pierce he felt a familiar stirring of interest. He hadn't felt that way for a while.

'Why do you think your brother's death wasn't an accident?' he asked, conveying no judgement either by his tone or expression.

She took a visible breath. 'Ben was killed with two of his friends when their car left the road and rolled down a hill. The police report said that Ben was driving and the autopsy showed that his blood alcohol level was four times the legal limit. But that can't be right. Ben didn't drive. I mean he *couldn't* drive. He didn't know how. And he didn't drink either. At least not to the extent the police are claiming. I've never known him to have more than the odd beer.'

'Then how do you explain the autopsy report? Mistakes are very rare.'

She gave a quick impatient shake of her head, her eyes flashing a brittle defensiveness. 'I can't explain it. But I know, I *knew*, my brother.'

'Tell Adam *why* Ben didn't drink,' Karen prompted gently.

'Since he was a child he'd suffered from epilepsy. It was controllable though he still had the occasional seizure, but he had to take medication every day. Something called Lamictal. Drinking reacted with the drug and made him violently ill.'

'Is it possible he had stopped taking his medication when the accident happened?' Adam asked.

'No. The autopsy report showed that it was present in his blood.'

Her point, Adam thought, was interesting rather than compelling. At least from the point of view of a detached third party, which was always the role he forced himself to take, at least initially. 'How old was Ben?'

'Nineteen. He was studying at London University.'

'You said that he didn't drive. That's unusual for somebody of his age.'

'It was because of his illness,' Helen explained. 'Legally he wasn't allowed to hold a driving licence. Even though his medication largely controlled his condition he still sometimes had seizures.'

'So, what exactly made the police so sure he was driving when the accident happened?'

'He was behind the wheel when the car was found, still wearing his seatbelt. Look, I know how it looks. I can understand why the police drew the conclusions they did.'

'But you still think they have it wrong?'

'I'm certain of it. I wish there was some way I could convince you. It's here, inside, that I know that somehow this is all wrong.'

She put her hand against her chest. Her expression was intense and her eyes almost pleaded for him, for somebody, to listen to her. He felt instinctively that she was genuine. Not everybody was. Sometimes it wasn't even intentional, just a kind of self-delusion, a refusal to accept the facts. In the past he had chosen the cases he worked on not because of any revelatory fragment of information he had learned when he interviewed relatives, but because he was moved by their certainty, their instinct about what had happened to their child. Often there was nothing solid to go on. He felt Helen's instinct was true, but on the face of it the police appeared to have drawn the logical conclusion.

'Tell me this,' he said. 'If you don't believe your brother's death was an accident, then what do you think happened?'

The pleading in her eyes turned to defeat, frustration. 'That's the trouble. I just don't have an answer to that question. Believe me I've thought about it, I've looked at this from every possible angle, I've even doubted myself on occasions. I've wondered if the police were right, if it was just one of those terrible things, a momentary lapse of judgement. If something made Ben act out of character and he got drunk and then for some reason he got behind the wheel of that car. Sometimes I've even half believed that. If enough people tell you that you're wrong, Mr Turner, believe me after a while you start to wonder, no matter what your convictions are.'

'And yet despite the evidence . . . ?'

'I still can't accept it. And I can't simply stand by and do nothing. I tried to get the coroner to listen to me at the inquest, but he accepted the police version of events. The verdict was accidental death.'

'Why don't you tell Adam about the protest, Helen,' Karen interjected.

'The protest?'

'Ben had just finished his first year of an arts degree. Last year he got involved with an environmental group through some people he met at university. They lobby against habitat destruction, the use of pesticides and so on, organizing petitions and protests, that sort of thing. To be honest I don't think Ben was as committed as a lot of them. He cared about the issues like most of us do, but he was never really a political person. He got involved through a girl he met. Her name was Jane Hanson. She was a year or so older than him, very pretty, very serious type. I met her once when he brought her round to the flat. I think she'd been involved in the protest at Newbury when she was at school, she came from that way somewhere, and she was completely immersed in this sort of thing.'

Something in her tone struck Adam. Was it a faint trace of bitterness? Jealousy perhaps.

'Anyway, she was taking part in a protest during the summer,' Helen went on. 'A group of activists were trying to prevent some woodland being cut down to make way for a holiday camp and Ben decided to go with her. They'd dug tunnels and built tree huts and all that sort of thing to keep the bulldozers out. That was in June. He was supposed to come back in September, but he was killed a week before he should have left.'

'There had been a lot of bad feeling between locals and some of the protesters,' Karen added.

'Some people were beaten up, threats were made, that sort of thing,' Helen explained.

'Was Ben threatened personally?'

'I think so. He mentioned on the phone that there had been some incidents but it was nothing serious, at least not that I know of.'

'The police knew about this?'

'I imagine they did. Yes, I'm sure they did.'

'Do you think there could be a connection between the protest and your brother's death?'

He saw her indecision as she considered how to answer, and guessed that it was tempting for her to say yes, to latch onto anything that might make some kind of sense, but to her credit she shook her head wearily.

'To be honest I just don't know. I can't say that Ben ever gave me the impression that there was anything sinister going on. It was just the sort of clashing between groups you'd expect really. It's possible that he wouldn't have said too much though. He wouldn't have wanted to worry me.'

'What about this girl you mentioned, Jane Hanson? Was she in the car when the accident happened?'

'No,' Helen answered, her mouth tightening. 'She left the protest a week earlier.'

'Have you spoken to her or anybody else from the camp to see if the threats were any more serious than Ben told you?'

'I haven't spoken to Jane, but I did go to the camp. Nobody there seemed to think there was any reason why Ben would have been singled out.'

'Helen,' Karen said. 'Tell Adam about your parents.'

'Both my parents are dead, Mr Turner,' Helen said. 'Ben was my only family. He lived with me ever since he was thirteen, when my parents' car was hit by a van travelling at eighty miles an hour. The driver was drunk. Both my parents died at the scene but he survived. That's why when Ben knew he had epilepsy he decided he would never learn to drive. It's also why I know that it's inconceivable that he would have been drunk behind the wheel of that car, even if for some inexplicable reason he had decided to drive that night. Ben wouldn't even be a passenger in a car if the driver had so much as had one drink. He was almost obsessive about it.'

It was, Adam thought, the most convincing argument she had put.

'I don't know where else I can go, Mr Turner,' she said. 'I've wondered if I should let it go. Nothing will bring Ben back. But I can't. He was all I had. I loved my brother and now he's dead and I want to know what happened to him. What really happened. I can't go through life always wondering.'

Again there was a plea in her eyes. He wasn't sure yet if this was something he wanted to get involved in. He was aware of Karen watching him, trying to gauge his reaction. In fact he was intrigued, and he was moved by what Helen had said. He understood what she was going through, and he reasoned that in

60

this instance there were no obvious parallels with Meg Coucesco. But he needed time to think. He promised that he would consider everything she'd said, and she didn't press him, but took her cue and rose to leave. She held out her hand.

'I want to thank you for at least listening to me, and for not being patronizing. Whatever you decide, I'm grateful for that at least.'

He shook her hand and Karen showed her to the door, murmuring something to her quietly, and as he watched them he remembered something. 'Wait a minute. You didn't say where all this happened. Where exactly was your brother killed?'

'In Cumbria,' she said. 'Near a town called Castleton.'

He barely registered her leaving, or Karen coming back to the table. She looked at him, her brow furrowed. 'What is it, Adam?'

'Nothing,' he said. 'It's nothing.' He looked at his watch. 'Look, I have to go, can we meet later?'

He arranged a time and hurriedly left, and only paused when he stood outside again and was gulping lungfuls of air. 'Christ,' he muttered.

CHAPTER SIX

Adam sat stirring a long black outside an Italian café near Covent Garden. He saw Karen stop at the lights and wait for them to change before she crossed. She looked over and when she saw him she waved. She was tall, her short, dark hair framing fine, even features. He lost her when a bus thundered past spewing out diesel fumes into the already polluted London air, and then the lights changed and a swarm of people stepped into the road.

When she arrived he pulled out a chair and signalled to a waiter. 'I ordered you a cappuccino. Do you want something to eat?'

She shook her head. 'I can't, Nigel's picking me up to go to dinner. Some business thing. You go ahead though if you want.'

'Maybe later.'

Nigel. Tall, good-looking Nigel, who was an investment banker and whose family owned half of Shropshire. Old money, old school tie. He tried to imagine Karen being the perfect hostess on one of those country weekends, hanging out with the polo and horsey set and dressing for dinners in some great baronial hall. Somehow he couldn't see it.

'So, how is Nigel?' he asked.

'Fine. He's very busy.'

He stirred his coffee, saying nothing.

'You don't like him do you?'

'I don't know him.'

'That's right, you don't,' she said, a trace of defensiveness in her tone.

'Maybe I just don't like the idea of him taking my best friend off to live in the country.'

'Flatterer,' she said, though she smiled. 'Anyway, Nigel knows my career is here.'

Does he? Adam wondered. Nigel struck him as the type who, when he married, would expect his wife to give up her amusing hobbies, like her career for instance, and settle down to produce lots of little well-bred Nigels to continue the family line.

'Besides, it isn't as if we're engaged or anything,' she said.

Yet, Adam silently added. The waiter brought Karen's coffee and Adam changed the subject. 'I've been thinking about your friend Helen.' She looked at him over the rim of her cappuccino. 'I can't help, Karen. I'm sorry.'

She looked surprised. 'Is that because you don't want the commission, or because you don't believe her?'

'It isn't because I don't believe her.'

'Then you don't want the commission?'

'I wasn't aware there was a commission. I thought you were helping a friend.'

'I am.'

'But you think there might be a story in it for *Landmark*, is that it?'

'I'm not sure I like the way you said that,' she replied in clipped tones.

'Sorry. I didn't mean that to sound the way it came out.'

'Apology accepted.'

'But you do want to commission me professionally I take it?'

'Yes. But I don't know if I would run the story, even if it turned out there was one. It would depend on the story. If for example it turned out to be a case of police bungling I might not be interested. But if it was more than that . . .'

'Like what?'

'I don't know. That's your part isn't it, to ferret out the truth? But whatever the case I wouldn't run anything without Helen's agreement.'

'Fair enough. But as I said, I can't help. Sorry.'

'But you still haven't told me why.'

'I'm busy at the moment.'

'I thought you'd finished the book you were working on.'

'I have.'

She waited, saying nothing, levelling her intelligent gaze on him, and he knew he'd have to do better than that.

'Alright. The truth is I'm not sure this is the direction I want to take.'

'Oh. So it's that again. Sorry, I must have mistaken you for somebody I knew who had a mission in life.'

'I wouldn't say it was a mission.'

'Wouldn't you? Righting wrongs. Helping people like Helen who don't know where else to turn. That girl you wrote about in Suffolk, the one who was pushed off a train, she'd never have been found if it wasn't for you.'

'Liz Mount. That was her name. Perhaps it would be better if she hadn't been. At least her parents could have clung to the hope that she was alive and well somewhere.'

'I don't think you believe that,' Karen said.

'Well, maybe not.'

Karen sipped her coffee thoughtfully. 'So, what's the real reason you don't want to do this? I get the feeling you're not telling me something.'

'You're wrong.'

'Then at least promise you'll think about it.'

She had pricked his conscience, as of course she had intended. She gave no quarter, Karen, which was probably why he liked her so much. 'Alright. I'll think about it.'

'Thank you, Adam.' She reached across the table and briefly put her hand over his.

Just then a taxi drew up by the kerb. The rear door opened and Nigel poked his head out. He was wearing a dark pinstriped suit with a red handkerchief in the breast pocket. His dark hair was smoothed back over his aristocratic forehead. 'Come on, darling, we'll be late.'

Karen withdrew her hand. 'Sorry, I have to go. Will you call me tomorrow?'

'Yes.'

She bent to kiss his cheek as Nigel looked impatiently at his watch. 'Hurry up, Karen. You know what the traffic's like at this time of day.' He held the door for her, and then belatedly remembered Adam. 'Sorry to drag her off like this. You weren't discussing anything important were you?'

'No, not really,' Adam answered, but it was a rhetorical question and Nigel was already turning away.

He watched the taxi pull away from the kerb, and for a moment he experienced a faint regret.

Karen sat back as the taxi negotiated rush hour traffic. Nigel was telling her about the people they were having dinner with, giving her tips on whom she ought to be especially nice to. Or perhaps instructions would be a better term. Like when he'd taken her home to meet his parents and he'd lectured her on etiquette for the entire journey, as if he was afraid she'd embarrass him by using the wrong cutlery at dinner. She tuned him out, turning her thoughts instead to Adam.

She wondered why he was reluctant to take on this commission. If Helen was right about her brother here was a possibly innocent victim whose death might not be what it appeared to be, a police force who wouldn't listen, and apparent discord between a bunch of protesters and locals. It was exactly the sort of thing that would normally interest him. She sensed there was something he wasn't telling her. She remembered a year ago, shortly after they'd met when Condor had put on a launch bash and she'd invited him to go along with her. Sort of a date. The truth is she had been interested in him. He was intelligent, and quite good-looking, and there was something else about him that appealed to her. He was a loner, slightly mysterious in some fashion. Maybe that was it. The lure of mystery.

Somebody had organized a karaoke machine and Adam, quite drunk, had got up to do a rendition of 'Bohemian Rhapsody', spoofing Freddie Mercury's camp antics. To her surprise he was funny, hilarious in fact, and when he finished it was to loud applause and calls for an encore, which he'd declined. At two in the morning they'd found themselves sitting together outside, watching the lights reflected on the Thames at Kew, sharing a bottle of Heineken. She had looked at him lopsidedly and directed a playful punch to his arm.

'You're a dark horse, Adam Turner. Who would have thought you could take off Freddie Mercury?'

'That's me. Dark horse from way back,' he'd agreed.

'But you really are, aren't you?'

'Absolutely.'

She'd regarded him solemnly. 'You know what? I don't really know anything about you.'

'There's not much to know.'

'There must be something. I don't even know where you're from.'

'Hampstead.'

She'd frowned. 'I thought you mentioned once that you went to school in Scotland or somewhere. Up North anyway.'

'Did I?'

She'd pointed to his knee, which he'd absently begun massaging the way he did sometimes. 'And what about that? How did that happen?'

'An accident.' He passed her the Heineken bottle. 'Look at the lights on that boat out there. See the way they're reflected on the water, like a mirror image. The water looks like oil.'

'It probably is fifty per cent oil,' she'd said, and then sighed. 'There you go. You always do that. Change the subject whenever we start talking about you.'

'Bad habit. Sorry.'

'Tell me about Louise.'

He'd looked surprised. 'My ex-wife? What about her?'

She wasn't sure why she'd brought the subject up, except that she was curious, she supposed. He'd mentioned her once and then abruptly steered the conversation in another direction. 'What went wrong between you two?'

'Long story.' He'd stood up and offered her his hand. 'We should look for a taxi.'

She'd sighed. 'Dark horse. That's what you are.'

There were no taxis around so when they did finally flag one down they decided to share, but since they lived in opposite directions she'd suggested he should stay at her place. When they got in she put on some music and said she was going to get ready for bed. When she came out of her bedroom wearing her Dodgers T-shirt he was flaked out on the couch, with his shoes off. She'd given him a pillow and a blanket.

'Here you go, Freddie.'

He'd looked up at her, and somehow he'd seemed vulnerable. Or maybe she was just drunk, or maybe a lot of things.

'I had a good time tonight,' she'd said at last.

'Me too.'

Another silence. Then she'd said, 'That couch is lumpy.'

'It is a little.'

'So ... perhaps you should sleep in there.' She'd gestured vaguely towards her bedroom, and he'd pondered that gesture for a while before he agreed that yes, he could do that.

They got into bed from opposite sides, and after a few seconds they slid together. He was wearing his shorts and she still had the T-shirt on. Tentatively they'd wrapped their arms around each other. She'd rested her head on his chest. In the darkness the alcohol had seized her brain again and everything was spinning a little.

'Wow, I feel a little woozy,' she'd said.

'Me too.'

'Can we just lie here like this for a little while?'

'Of course.'

It felt kind of safe and pleasant. Like being with a friend, and yet not quite. 'I'm sleepy now,' she'd murmured.

'Yes.'

She'd nuzzled closer, her leg over his, and felt his breathing become deep and regular. 'This is nice,' she'd murmured.

'It is.'

'Night, Freddie.' Then she'd drifted off into a happy oblivion.

In the morning when she woke she had a massive headache. She'd sat up groaning, and only then realized that Adam was gone. She saw the depression in the pillow beside her, and fuzzily recalled the previous night. A minute later he'd appeared, already dressed, carrying orange juice. He'd sat on the end of the bed and from there it was all downhill. They'd talked chiefly of feeling terrible, and commenting with wonder on how much they'd had to drink, recounting moments from the previous night, laughing, shaking their heads. It all had a hollow ring and went on for too long, as if each of them was desperate to avoid mentioning the most glaringly obvious of all the evening's developments.

In the end, their conversation withered into silence and he'd said he should be getting along, inventing, she was sure, some urgent task. She wasn't sure how to feel. She hadn't wanted him to go, but she was uncertain about whether to say anything. Perhaps he regretted what had happened. Or nearly happened anyway. Perhaps he was trying to let her know he didn't feel that way about her. In the end it was a relief of sorts when he did leave.

Two days later she'd arrived at his door, and when he'd answered she'd launched into her prepared speech.

'I don't want this thing to come between us, Adam. I like you and I feel we've become friends. I value that.' She'd thought he looked relieved.

'I don't want it to come between us either.'

'So, we're still friends?'

'Friends.'

'Great.'

And in fact their friendship had survived intact, though it had taken several months before they were completely easy again in each other's company, before that shadow dissipated. It wasn't really until Nigel had arrived on the scene. Perhaps that was partly why she'd started seeing him, because she'd sensed it was a way to finally clear the air between herself and Adam.

And yet, sometimes, she wondered at the way Adam looked at her. Christ, she had to stop thinking about him like this. They were friends weren't they? Wasn't it supposed to be men who couldn't handle a relationship with a woman on that level?

Abruptly she realized that Nigel had stopped talking and was looking at her strangely. Guiltily she came to. 'Sorry, what did you say?'

'Karen.' He sounded exasperated. 'I said perhaps it might be a good idea not to have more than a glass or two of wine tonight. What do you think?'

'You mean instead of my normal bottle and a half, is that it?' she said testily.

'Actually,' he said huffily, 'I was talking about me. I'm still taking those antihistamine tablets.'

Contrite, she put her hand on his arm. 'I'm sorry, Nigel.' She looked away, suppressing a giggle.

CHAPTER SEVEN

Adam's flat was on the second floor of a converted Victorian semi in Wimbledon. It was cluttered but comfortable. He rarely ate there, avoiding all forms of cooking unless they were ready-made meals from Marks & Spencer that he could put in the microwave. After the break-up of his marriage he'd given up the office he used to rent in favour of working at home. At first he'd converted the spare bedroom for use as an office but after a while he'd moved into the living room where he felt more comfortable. When he and Louise had split up, she had taken the TV, and he had never replaced it. His work and the remains of his life outside of work had merged.

He sat at his desk, which was actually a long table that occupied the wall space on one side of the room. He was slowly drinking a glass of Scotch, and thinking about Helen Pierce and the way fate intervenes in life sometimes. Earlier he'd posed the question to himself that had Helen's brother been killed in say, Devon, would he be willing to help her? The absolute truth was that he wasn't sure. He liked her, he wanted to help her, but he wasn't certain on the face of what he knew whether he could. Beyond her own conviction that her brother's death hadn't happened the way the police said it had, there was little to support her. But then there never was. He received letters from people all the time whose children or sisters or brothers had vanished or died. They all believed something had happened that didn't tally with the official version, and they all asked for his help. Of course he couldn't help them all, though he did reply to each and every one of them. But of the ones he did look into the truth was never obvious. Normally it was only the conviction of the family that convinced him to investigate.

He knew he wasn't going to ghostwrite another book, and he wasn't about to go back to doing lifestyle pieces either. The thing that really bothered him was the idea of going back to Castleton. Who knew what can of worms that would open up? But a quickening in his chest belied his reluctance.

His thoughts drifted back to the summer a year after Meg had vanished. Throughout the intervening year he and Angela had continued seeing each other though their relationship had stalled on the knowledge that he would eventually go away to university and from there would probably move to London to begin his career. For the same reason they hadn't had sex. The commitment to one another that step seemed to entail foundered on the looming presence of the future.

In August the country was assaulted by a sudden heat wave after a long damp July. A crowd of them had gone to a pool in the river where the water was deep and clear. He recalled lying in the grass as he dried off, warmed by the sun, watching Angela climb the bank towards the bridge which some of them had been jumping from. Nick was smoking, wearing wet cut-off jeans, his body skinny and pale. He wore a familiar faintly contemptuous expression. He no longer suffered any outward scars or bruises, but whatever damage had been inflicted inside by a father who'd been dead nearly a year would probably always remain.

In the river David and Graham were encouraging people to jump from the bridge. A girl leapt out and shrieked as she hit the water and when David helped her up the steep bank she laughed flirtatiously. He grinned. He was tanned with a lean muscular build, his thick hair lightened by the sun.

Angela stood on the edge of the bridge and looked down. She stretched out her arms to the sides and balanced on her toes.

'I'm going to dive,' she announced.

Her hair was wet, and droplets of water glistened on her skin. She wore a one-piece black swimsuit cut high on her hips that emphasized the flat plane of her belly and the swell of her breasts. She grinned and raised her arms above her head and slowly tipped her weight forward. As if in slow motion she fell forward, entering the water with a muffled splash to emerge moments later in a cascade of spray. She swam smoothly to the bank where David took her hand and helped her up. In that moment they looked at one another and with a jolt of awareness Adam saw something unspoken pass between them. She smiled uncertainly and as she walked away David followed her with his eyes. Sensing somebody watching him Adam turned to find Nick looking on with an amused, sardonic light in his eyes.

After that the rest of the summer seemed fraught with unspoken currents and subtle tensions. Angela was prone to long silences, and sometimes he would watch unnoticed when she and David were together. The smallest gesture or an intercepted glance seemed loaded with meaning.

It all came back with a sudden vivid clarity that surprised Adam. It was strange, he thought, how long dormant memories could return, bringing with them the smell of hay drying in the fields, the sound of laughter in the air, and the sense in her silence and her startled smile when he spoke, that Angela had been drifting from him.

His knee was aching. He rolled up the leg of his jeans and massaged the bare ridged and curiously misshapen flesh. It hurt when the weather was cold or damp, like rheumatism, but sometimes the pain just came unexpectedly. He sometimes wondered if it was just a way of reminding himself. Of making sure he didn't forget.

A little after nine he called the number Karen had given him for Helen, and asked if he could come and talk to her the following day after she had finished work. He said there were some things he wanted to clarify. She agreed, and gave him her address in Hammersmith.

Adam arrived just after six to find that Helen lived in a flat on the fourth floor of a converted building overlooking the Thames. He looked out of the living-room window at the view, comparing her flat with his own. Research must be rewarding, he mused. Helen must have guessed what he was thinking.

'When our parents died Ben and I inherited their farm. Ben's

71

share was held in trust until he was twenty-one. I used mine to buy us somewhere to live.'

She handed him a drink and led the way to her brother's room, where she lingered in the doorway. It was orderly, everything in its place. A life packed away.

'When did you say he went to Cumbria?' he asked.

'June. The beginning of the month.'

'The other two boys in the car, did you know them?'

'Not really. I don't think Ben had known them long.'

'Who did the car belong to?'

She went to a dresser and picked up a framed photograph. 'This one. His name was Simon Davies. The other one was Keith Frost.' There were four people in the picture, which was slightly out of focus. Three young men and a young woman sat on a stone wall smiling at the camera, with trees in the background. 'Ben sent this to me not long after he went up there. This is him.'

The colours in the picture had a vaguely washed-out look. A cheap processing shop, Adam thought, one of those one-hour places. Helen's brother had short brown hair, and wore jeans and a T-shirt with some logo on the front. Next to him sat a girl with long reddish-coloured hair and a slightly more reserved smile than the others. She wore glasses, which gave her a slightly studious look, though she was undoubtedly attractive. Her hands, Adam noticed, were clasped in her lap, while Ben's arm was around her shoulders. There was something about their body language that the picture had caught. They were out of balance.

'Do the families of the others know how you feel about what happened?' Adam asked.

'No, I haven't said anything. I spoke to them on the phone but I got the feeling they didn't want to talk. I didn't realize until later it wasn't just because they were upset.' There was an echo of anger in her tone. 'I can't entirely blame them,' she said. 'It's just . . . I don't know. They don't have any reason to doubt the official version, do they? They think their sons were killed because Ben was drunk.'

Adam looked at the picture again. 'I assume this is the girl Ben was going out with. Jane something?'

'Hanson. Yes.'

Again he thought he detected the faint bitterness he'd noticed in Karen's office. 'You said you hadn't spoken to her at all since Ben died?'

'No. The last time I spoke to Ben he told me that Jane had left. This was about a week before he died. I gathered they had broken up, but he didn't want to talk about it so I didn't press him. I always got the impression that he was more interested in her then she was in him. Perhaps if Ben had a fault that was it. He wore his heart on his sleeve a bit.'

'When you spoke to him then, did he say anything that struck you as out of the ordinary? Did he sound worried at all?'

'He sounded a bit down, which I put down to Jane leaving him.' Helen looked away. 'She never even phoned me, you know. I didn't really expect her to be at the funeral. She may not even have known about it, but she must have heard about what happened sooner or later. I thought she would have phoned.'

Adam didn't say anything. What could he tell her? Who was to say what the girl's reasons had been for leaving? Maybe she and Ben had split up because after a couple of months living in the woods together she couldn't stand the sight of him any more, but he didn't want to tell Helen that. Neither did he want to say that for somebody who lived with his heart on his sleeve, as she'd said Ben did, losing a girlfriend might be enough to make a person act out of character. Perhaps get drunk and get behind the wheel of a car he didn't know how to drive.

'What about the protest, did he say anything about that when you talked?'

'No. I asked him when he was coming home, and he thought about a week or two. He was vague.'

'Nothing else?'

'No.'

He questioned her some more about the protest itself, but she really didn't know much about it. He asked if he could keep the picture.

'I'll scan it into my computer and print you a copy. Would that be okay?'

'Fine.'

She hesitated. 'Does this mean you'll be going there?'

Up until then, he hadn't really decided, but once she'd posed the question he knew the answer. 'Yes, but I can't promise anything,' he told her.

Relief and gratitude jostled in her eyes. Finally somebody was taking her seriously. 'Thank you,' she said quietly.

A vague unsettling guilt niggled at his conscience. He wished he was more certain of his motives.

Later he called Karen at home, and told her what he'd decided. 'Before you say anything I have to say I'm really not sure about any of this. Helen told me that Ben had just broken up with his girlfriend. You know how it can be. Heartbroken young guy gets drunk and kills himself. It could well be that the police have got it right. When you talk to her, try to dampen her expectations a little could you?'

'Alright. But I'll fax you a contract in the morning, anyway.'

'I'll be in touch.'

'Adam,' she said quickly, before he could hang up. 'Tell me something. You must have a feeling about this, an instinct if you like. I mean you wouldn't be taking this on otherwise.'

He heard an underlying probing note to her tone. He was sure she was wondering what had changed his mind. 'If I find anything I'll let you know,' he said.

She accepted the gentle rebuff. 'Goodnight then.'

That night he dreamed. The images were confused. He was in a forest in the dark, the moon occasionally glimpsed overhead. Ahead of him a figure materialized and as he drew nearer, his heart pounding, fear tightening his insides, he saw that it was Meg. She was pale, her hair matted, her clothes ragged, and he knew that she had been dead a long time. Her wide eyes beseeched him, but he didn't know what it was she wanted. And then it wasn't Meg, but Angela. She was laughing, her head tipped back, and David was with her. Then suddenly a flash accompanied by a roar of sound and he woke with a cry escaping his lips and his body soaked with sweat.

CHAPTER EIGHT

The M6 cut a swathe through the industrial north midlands past Stoke-on-Trent. Adam stopped occasionally for petrol or to stretch his legs. The weather continued to be uncharacteristically warm, the whole country basking in a kind of Indian summer. It was a good day for driving and this was the first really long run he'd made in the Porsche he'd recklessly bought six months earlier. It was a 911, with muscular flared arches and a whale-tail. Metallic green with tan leather trim. His pride and joy. He'd always wanted a Porsche, and when he'd finally realized he would never be able to afford a new one he'd considered going the classic route. He'd bought a magazine and thought about it for a couple of weeks, pondering the upkeep and the fact that he didn't know one end of a spanner from another, then decided what the hell and started making phone calls anyway. Eventually he'd bought a 'seventy-eight model from a man in Lewes who'd owned it for ten years, during which time the car had been fully restored and treated with the respect of an enthusiast. Adam hadn't even haggled over the asking price.

She rumbled like a big cat, with a throaty growl, and when he put his foot down the power pressed him back against his seat. The insurance was a killer, but some things in life you just have to have.

Beyond Preston vistas of the countryside opened up, and after Morecambe he had the Yorkshire Dales on his right and the Lake District on his left and Ocean Colour Scene on the CD player. The quickest route was to follow the motorway all the way up to Carlisle and then it was less then forty minutes to Castleton through Brampton. An alternative, more scenic route was to turn off at Penrith and follow minor roads along the valley through the villages that huddled beneath the fells, and that was the way he chose.

The sun was going down as he plunged into the countryside. He opened up the throttle along the deserted roads and the sound of the engine echoed back from the dry-stone walls. In the hollows where the sun had already fled he switched on the headlights. Trees and fields flashed by on either side, the bleak high fells looming to his right. He slowed as he passed through villages where the old houses and buildings were built from local red sandstone, his memories stirred by familiar sights; the churches with their squat, square towers topped with battlements like castles; high hedgerows where cow parsley grew profusely among the hawthorn and crab apple and pink soapwort; village pubs and a local garage with two old-fashioned pumps outside that looked as if they belonged to another age.

He crossed stone bridges spanning rivers and streams and took arbitrary turns as he came upon them to delay his arrival, wanting to savour the last of the journey, and the odd mixture of apprehension and exhilaration he experienced at the prospect of his return. Finally, as he drove through Halls Tenement he pulled over outside a pub, its windows lit in yellow squares, a couple of Land Rovers and a handful of cars in the car park outside. He got out to stretch his leg, which was aching after the drive. The sun had vanished and dusk had taken over the countryside, casting villages, fields and woods in eerie purple half-light.

He drove the last few miles at a sedate pace and when he arrived in Castleton it was almost dark. As he crossed the bridge over the river he glanced across the water meadow to the dark line of trees that hid Johnson's sawmill, if it was still there. Further on the main street narrowed as he passed the newsagent that was once owned by Angela's father. The shop looked the same but the name above the door was no longer Curtis. He emerged into the partly cobbled square and turned through the gates of the New Inn, which was a pub and hotel and hadn't been new since 1745 when the coach house had burned down and a new one had been built. The barns at the rear had been converted into extra rooms, four on ground level, four above, with steps leading up the outside and a walkway past the doors.

He hadn't booked, but the tourist season had ended and there was no problem getting a room. He chose a new one in the conversion, and as he signed the register the young woman who checked him in asked if he would like to have dinner in the restaurant across the hall, which when he looked was empty. The hum of voices emanated from the bar, however, along with the smell of roast beef and gravy.

'I'll get something at the bar,' he said. She smiled and asked how long he would be staying. 'I'm not sure. Say a week.'

On the way past the bar he heard a woman laugh and when he looked inside and saw her standing among a group with her back to him his heart skipped a beat. For an instant time confused him and he thought at first it was Louise. She was slim with long blonde hair that shone in the light, but then he remembered where he was and it was no longer Louise he thought of but the person she had reminded him of the first time he'd seen her. He stood transfixed but then the woman in the bar turned and she wasn't Angela after all.

He went to his room and sat down on the bed. His heart was still beating too fast and he experienced an odd sense of revelation. All these years he had harboured a memory of her, but it was like something covert and hidden. Only now did he begin to sense the force of everything he had kept shut inside himself all that time.

He went to bed early and woke at six-thirty as it was beginning to get light. The hotel was quiet other than the first sounds of stirring from behind the kitchen doors when he looked in the restaurant. He decided to go for a walk before breakfast, partly from curiosity and partly to loosen up his leg, which had stiffened overnight. The town was deserted, the sky purple, beginning to turn blue as the sun crept up over the hills. When he reached the river he followed the public footpath across the meadow and as he approached the trees on the far side he detected the familiar, tangy scent of cut pine and sawdust. As he drew nearer he could see that the sawmill was still there. He paused, flooded with memories of riding his bike this way in the holidays before catching the bus into Carlisle

77

and his job at the *Courier*. Other memories crowded and jostled in his mind and when he turned and walked back the way he'd come crows flapped from the trees and mocked him.

At the hotel he ate breakfast alone in the restaurant, though next to him a table covered with the litter of empty cups and egg-smeared plates was testament to the fact that others had also been up early. Afterwards he drove along the valley towards Brampton and took the main road to Carlisle where he followed the signs to the new hospital. Inside he followed directions to the pathology department and asked to speak to Dr Keller.

'My name's Turner,' he told the receptionist. 'I have an appointment.'

Dr Keller, when she arrived, didn't fit the mental picture Adam had already formed of her based on their brief phone conversation when he'd called from London. He was expecting somebody older than the woman in her mid-thirties who approached him. Her smile was friendly as she offered her hand.

'I'm afraid I can't spare you more than half an hour,' she said, speaking with a soft Scottish accent as she led the way along a narrow corridor.

Her office was large and untidy. Files in brown folders that hadn't made it to the filing cabinets were stacked on every available surface. She made space for him on a chair beneath a framed certificate from Edinburgh University on the wall.

'On the phone you mentioned a road accident.' She sat behind her desk and opened files she had already retrieved. 'Three young men. Pierce, Frost and Davies?'

'That's right.'

'And you're a journalist?'

'I'm a freelance writer. I specialize in investigative features.'

'I see. Well, I've checked with the police and there's no investigation pending. The coroner's verdict was accidental death, but I take it you're aware of that.'

'Yes.'

Dr Keller laced her fingers together on her desk. 'So, how can I help?'

'When we spoke you said autopsies were performed on all three victims. Did you examine the bodies yourself?'

'Actually, yes.'

'Can you tell me if you found anything unusual at all? Anything to indicate this could have been something other than an accident.'

She furrowed her brow. 'I'm afraid I don't follow you.'

He explained briefly that Helen Pierce maintained that her brother, who was supposedly the driver of the car, not only didn't know how to drive, but didn't drink either. 'I understand the autopsy results showed that his blood alcohol level was several times above the legal limit.'

She listened without comment, and then began to scan the contents of the files in front of her. 'That's correct.' As she leafed through the pages she laid out some photographs on the desk. They were black and white prints, each of the naked body of a young male, Ben Pierce among them. He lay face up on the autopsy slab, the channels designed to carry away body fluids clearly visible.

'Judging from the contents of his stomach and by measuring the rate of alcohol absorption in his blood and brain I'd say this young man had consumed the equivalent of a large glass, or about a quarter of a bottle of spirits prior to the accident.'

'Enough to make him drunk?'

'People react differently when they drink, but I'd say so, yes. In his case the reaction might well have been worse.'

'Oh? Why is that?'

'He also had traces of a drug called Lamictal in his blood. Do you know what that is?'

'The medication he took to control his epilepsy?'

'That's right.'

'His sister claims that he didn't drink much because of his medication. Apparently more than a beer made him sick.'

Dr Keller met his eye and though she didn't look entirely unsympathetic she shrugged slightly. 'That's quite possible. The side-effects people experience from drugs like Lamictal can vary, but certainly for some mixing it with alcohol could make them quite ill. However, there is no doubt that this young man had been drinking.'

'There's no chance of some kind of error I suppose? Perhaps his results were mixed up with somebody else's.'

She shook her head, and smiled a little wryly. 'I'll disregard the implied slur on my professional conduct, Mr Turner. There is absolutely no chance of a mistake having occurred.'

'No offence intended, Doctor.'

'Then none is taken.'

Somehow it was this one thing, this anomaly that Helen Pierce had been so adamant about that had struck Adam most of all. If she was wrong about that, then perhaps she was wrong about everything else too. Maybe she simply hadn't known her brother as well as she thought.

'You said that this young man's sister claims that he couldn't drive,' Dr Keller said.

'He never learned because of his epilepsy. Apparently their parents were killed in a car accident. By a drunk driver.'

'Have you considered the possibility that that fact in itself may very well explain what happened here? A young man whose judgement is impaired by alcohol gets behind the wheel of a car. His inexperience leads to the accident.' She shrugged. 'It's tragic, but I'm afraid not unusual.'

On the face of it, her logic made sense, Adam had to admit. Except that Dr Keller hadn't known Ben Pierce the way Helen had.

'Anyway, I don't see anything unusual here,' Dr Keller said at length. 'The injuries are consistent with those I would expect to see with victims of a road accident.'

Adam examined the picture of Ben, looking in particular at a black mark between his neck and shoulder. Other than this blemish he appeared uninjured. 'What is that, a cut?' Streaks of what he assumed was blood ran away from the wound and down across his shoulder and ribcage.

'Yes.' Dr Keller referred to her notes. 'There were traces of paint in the wound that matched samples from the vehicle. The wound itself is around six inches long, and penetrates to a depth of almost an inch. About half of it appears to be a clean cut, the edges are more or less neatly severed. The rest is messier, more jagged.'

'What does that mean?'

'My guess would be that it was caused by a section of metal from the wreck. It was forced in like so.' She demonstrated what she meant by pointing her hand and thrusting downwards towards the space between her own neck and shoulder. 'The angle of entry suggests it might have come from the roof. Then, forced by the momentum of the crash it cut through the flesh towards the base of the neck.' She slashed towards her own neck with the tips of her fingers. 'That would have produced this jagged section of the wound. It was this that killed him by the way. The artery was partially severed. Other than that this young man suffered only a few minor abrasions, apart from a blow to the head, which very likely rendered him unconscious. Though it wouldn't have killed him.'

'So, you're saying cause of death was what exactly?'

'He bled to death. Probably over several hours.'

Adam thought about that. 'He was found in the driver's seat, I believe, still wearing his seatbelt. If it took so long for him to die, why didn't he get out of the car? Wouldn't you expect him to go for help?'

'As I said, he was probably already unconscious. With the amount of blood that he lost, I doubt that he ever came around.'

'But it took several hours before he died?'

'I would say so.'

Adam looked at the photographs of the other two bodies, and something about them struck him. Both Keith Frost and Simon Davies appeared to have suffered more visible injuries than Ben. They were each marked with a mass of what looked like bruises and abrasions. He pointed it out. 'Isn't that odd?'

'Actually there is a logical explanation. They were both found some distance from the car. My guess is that neither of them was wearing a seatbelt. The first time the car rolled the doors probably popped open like the ends of a can and they were thrown out. It happens all the time. That partly accounts for their more obvious injuries. Both were killed almost instantly by the way, and both from a massive trauma to the head.'

'You said partly,' Adam said. 'Partly accounts for their injuries.'

'Yes. Some of these injuries occurred prior to the accident. About two or three days earlier I'd say. Mostly bruising and abrasions, some minor facial cuts, though one of them had a cracked rib.'

'Any idea how they might have happened?'

She pursed her lips. 'If I had to guess? I'd say they were probably in a fight. Quite a violent one.' She paused for a moment, her brow furrowed in a puzzled frown.

'What is it?'

'It's probably nothing. But I did wonder at the time why one of these two young men hadn't been driving. Perhaps then we wouldn't be sitting here now.'

'I don't understand.'

'Well, neither of them showed any trace of alcohol in his blood,' she said, and then saw his expression. 'I thought you knew that. I suppose these injuries could be the explanation. Perhaps neither of them was up to it.'

He pondered her theory, but it didn't make a lot of sense. It looked as if Frost and Davies had taken some punishment, but hardly enough that they'd allow someone high on a cocktail of drugs and booze to get behind the wheel. Especially if that person didn't know how to drive.

'You look sceptical,' Dr Keller observed.

'It's my nature. But you said yourself that these older injuries on the other two were mostly cuts and abrasions.'

'Yes.' She looked again at the pictures. 'As I said, it did strike me as unusual at the time. An anomaly shall we say.'

'But not enough to raise in your report?'

'No. The facts are inescapable. Ben Pierce was found in the driver's seat. Both of the others were thrown clear before the car came to rest. The evidence at the site, and the injuries I recorded during my examination of the bodies both there and here confirm that.'

'There's no chance any of them were moved?'

Dr Keller frowned. 'Moved?'

'Perhaps they were switched. Perhaps one of the others was driving.'

'Why would anyone do that? Besides, it isn't possible. As I said, the evidence is clear. Both of these young men were in the back seat before they were thrown clear. I found fragments of tissue and clothing away from the wreck that clearly showed where each of them had fallen. I'm afraid there's no mistake.'

Nevertheless, Adam thought, he had come looking for answers and instead had found one more thing that didn't make sense. He thanked Dr Keller for her help, but as he left the hospital he was beginning to think that perhaps Helen's misgivings were justified. Something about this didn't feel right.

The police station in Castleton occupied a plain, purpose-built building behind the town's only supermarket. On one side a metal gate opened to a small area where a police Range Rover with the Cumbrian police insignia on the door was parked. Adam went inside and pressed a buzzer on the counter and a few moments later a young police constable appeared.

'Can I help you, sir?'

'My name's Adam Turner, I'm a journalist and I'm looking into an accident that happened near here in September. Three university students were killed.'

'Yes. I remember that.'

'I was hoping I could speak to the officer who attended the scene.'

'Just a moment.'

The constable disappeared and a few minutes later a man wearing the uniform of a sergeant appeared. He wore a curious, uncertain expression and there was something familiar about him, which it took Adam a moment to place. He was heavier than when Adam had last seen him, more solid, and his once rosy cheeks were more ruddy and weathered now, but it was unmistakeably Graham. For a moment he gaped in surprise. It was Graham who spoke first, extending his hand across the counter.

'Hello, Adam.'

They shook hands. Of course Adam had expected to run into them all sooner or later. Graham and Nick, and of course David. Somehow he'd known they wouldn't have moved away. But he hadn't been prepared for this. 'Sorry,' he said, realizing how he must look. 'It's the uniform that threw me there for a minute.'

'I joined when I was eighteen,' Graham said. 'I didn't know what else I wanted to do really. It was either this or an apprenticeship.'

'Looks like you did the right thing,' Adam said, gesturing to the stripes on Graham's sleeve.

'I got these a year or two ago when they moved me back here from Brampton. It's not exactly Scotland Yard, but it's not a bad life. We don't get the sort of problems they have in the city, thank God. Not yet anyway.' He looked around, perhaps pondering the surroundings where he could probably expect the rest of his career to be played out. 'What about you, Adam, where are you living now?'

'London.'

'And you're a journalist. When I heard the name I wondered if it was you. You always knew what you wanted to do. How long have you been back?'

'I arrived last night.'

'I don't suppose it's changed much.'

'No, not really.'

'So, what brings you back here anyway? Gordon said something about you wanting to know about the lads that were killed in that accident last month?'

'I'm looking into it for the sister of one of them. She has some questions about what happened.'

'Helen Pierce,' Graham said, frowning.

'You spoke to her?'

'A few times. Ben, wasn't it, her brother's name? He was driving but she said he couldn't have been. Something to do with his illness. He was epileptic.'

'According to Helen her brother never learned to drive because of it. She said he didn't drink either.'

'Because of the medicine he was taking. Yes, she told me that too.' Graham opened a flap in the counter. 'Look, why don't you come inside where we can talk properly?'

They went through to a small inner office and Graham gestured to a chair at his desk. 'Have a seat, Adam.' He went around the desk and settled himself in his own chair. 'Is Helen Pierce a friend of yours, or is your interest in this professional?'

'A bit of both, I suppose you could say.'

'You know there's been an inquest already? There's really no doubt that Ben Pierce was driving the car when it crashed, and the autopsy results proved he'd been drinking.'

'I know. I talked to the pathologist this morning.'

'So, how can I help?'

'I don't know exactly. I'd like to find out more about how the accident happened,' Adam said.

'Hang on.' Graham got up and went to a row of filing cabinets where he dug out a copy of the accident report. 'It was the fifth of September. A woman reported seeing the wreck from the Geltsdale road when she was taking her kids to school. I went up there straight away.'

The Geltsdale road crossed the fells and wound down to the valley in a series of curves, passing through the forest for a good part of the way. From what Adam could remember it was pretty steep in places. Graham pushed the report across the desk.

'It's all there if you want to see it. Ben Pierce was in the driver's seat just as you see him in the photograph; the others had been thrown clear. They were all dead when I arrived. The accident happened some time the night before.'

Adam scanned the report. Everything had been measured and recorded, including the skid marks on the road, and the contents of the car, which had been recovered. Mostly clothing and other belongings, including three backpacks. 'It looks from this as if they were going somewhere,' Adam said, reading through the list.

'Probably back home to London. They were part of a load of protesters we had here over the summer. A lot of them were leaving about then.'

'What time did the accident happen?'

'Between about nine and ten as far as we can tell.'

'Funny time to be leaving,' Adam said, to which Graham made no comment.

An empty half-bottle of supermarket brand whisky had been found, which might seem a little convenient to a suspicious mind, but Adam couldn't see anything in the report that looked obviously wrong. The car itself was found to have worn tread on one of the tyres but was otherwise mechanically sound. The logical conclusion anyone could draw was that the driver had been drunk while travelling too fast along a dangerously steep road at night. He'd lost control and skidded over the edge. End of story.

'What were they doing there?'

Graham got up to file the report away again. 'What do you mean?' he asked over his shoulder.

'They were packed up as if they were planning to leave, and they were travelling towards Castleton. But it's a long way from anywhere up there.'

'Perhaps they'd been to a pub somewhere.'

'But there are no pubs up there, unless you go right over the fells,' Adam reasoned. 'You didn't check?'

'There was no reason to.'

That was true, Adam acknowledged silently. 'What about this protest they were involved with? Where was that?'

'On the estate at Castleton Wood, at the northern end.'

'Castleton Wood?'

'Didn't you know? The estate is for sale. A company called Forest Havens wants to buy it. The woods have been full of bloody protesters since the spring. They've got a camp up there.'

A definite trace of rancour had appeared in Graham's tone, which Adam wondered about. But something else struck him. 'The wood is nowhere near where the accident happened. In fact it's the other way, so they couldn't have been coming from there.'

'Perhaps they'd been to Alston.'

Maybe they had, Adam thought, though that was a twenty-mile drive over the fells. 'You didn't try to find out then?'

'Like I said, I had no reason to.'

'Not even after Helen Pierce expressed misgivings?'

'I listened to what she had to say, but facts are facts, Adam.'

Adam glanced through the report again, looking for something out of place, but if there was anything there he couldn't see it. He thought about the injuries on the bodies of Ben's friends. 'I gather from what you said a minute ago that you don't have a lot of sympathy for the protesters?'

'They're bloody troublemakers, a lot of them. All kinds of hippy types sitting on their arses collecting the dole all summer. Half of them on drugs.'

'Is that the prevailing opinion?'

'You could say that.'

'Has there been trouble between them and local people?'

'Not to speak of.'

'Helen Pierce thought her brother might have been threatened.'

'There might have been a few scuffles, but nothing serious.'

'When I spoke to the pathologist she said that she thought two of the boys, Frost and Davies, might have been in a fight a few days before the accident. One of them had a broken rib among other things. What do you make of that?'

'What do you mean?'

'Well, did you know about it? It must have been in the autopsy report.'

'I don't know what you're getting at,' Graham said, sounding suddenly defensive.

Adam pressed the point. 'Maybe the accident and the protest might be linked somehow.'

'Linked, how?'

'I don't know. Why would anybody beat them up? People get worked up about these things. It seems to me it would have been worth looking into anyway.'

Adam knew that he was implying criticism of the way Graham had handled Helen Pierce's concerns and it was clear from his expression that Graham didn't appreciate it.

'There's nothing to suggest that those three lads being part of the protest had anything to do with this,' Graham said. 'What happened was an accident, plain and simple. Young lads out drinking, happens all the time. Take my advice, Adam, don't start trying to make something out of this that isn't there.'

'But you said yourself you didn't really investigate any other possibility.'

'There was nothing to investigate.'

'Maybe on the face of it,' Adam insisted doggedly. He knew that based on the evidence he was being unreasonable, but he pushed the point anyway. 'After Helen Pierce talked to you didn't you at least wonder why her brother was driving? You know neither of the other two had been drinking. Even the pathologist wondered about that.'

'But she also said both of them were in the back of the car when it left the road,' Graham said flatly. 'So what was I supposed to do?'

'You might have tried to find out where they had been. Perhaps to see if anybody had seen Ben drinking, maybe in a pub in Alston. It could be that somebody even saw him get behind the wheel when they left. At least that would have proved the point to Helen Pierce.'

'I could have done those things, yes. But I didn't, because there was no need,' Graham said angrily. 'It might not be like London here, but that doesn't mean I have time to run around all over the country asking questions I already know the answer to. Nobody doubts that lad was driving except his sister. I feel sorry for her loss, but it doesn't alter the facts. I can't tell you any more than that.'

There was nothing else Adam could think of to ask for the moment, and it was clear that Graham was losing patience so Adam thanked him for his time and rose to leave. Graham showed him to the door.

'That accident had nothing to do with the protest, Adam,' he said. 'There's already been a lot written in the papers about that, and most of it bloody rubbish. Some people around here have had enough of journalists. You might want to remember that before you go around stirring things up.'

'I'll bear it in mind,' Adam said, thinking that if he didn't know better, he'd have thought Graham's warning had sounded almost like a threat.

CHAPTER NINE

Angela parked her car in the driveway outside the large red sandstone house that had once belonged to David's parents. It had a walled garden, and was on the edge of the town. Behind it there was a paddock where Kate, their ten-year-old daughter, kept her pony. Across the fields the River Gelt cut a path through the valley from the fells, which rose up behind the house. In the summer the hills were a patchwork of pale greens and browns and the purple of the heather. In the winter they were grey and barren, shrouded with cloud and often covered with deep snow. In bad years the blizzards could rage for weeks.

She went inside the house and put away the groceries. When she was done she went upstairs to the attic room that had been converted for use as her studio and checked her email. She loved this room, with its big roof window that looked out towards the river and the fells. There was a message from Julian Crown, who was her publisher. He wanted her to call him.

As she stood in front of her drawing board looking at the illustrations for the story that she was working on, she wondered what he wanted. The books that she wrote were very simple, aimed at two- to four-year-olds. It was the accompanying pictures that breathed life into her words. It was a career she'd stumbled into almost by accident, when she'd answered an ad in one of the Sunday papers. After Kate was born the doctors had told Angela she wouldn't have any more children, so when Kate started going to kindergarten she suddenly had the house to herself again and she was bored. David had said she could help out with the office work at the sawmill if she wanted to, but the business was doing well enough without her, and he already had Mollie as his personal assistant-cum-secretary-cum-administrator. Besides which, the sawmill was David's passion. She wanted something for herself.

She had phoned her old boss at the mail order company in Carlisle where she'd worked after she'd finished art college, and he'd offered to give her back her old job, but seeing the old office again, and many of the same faces, had made her hesitant. While she was thinking it over she saw an ad inviting people interested in a career as an illustrator for children's stories to submit samples of their work.

Believing she had nothing to lose she'd gone to the library and pored over a stack of books like the ones she'd read to Kate when she was younger. Then she had gone home and written one herself, basing it around Castleton and the fells and surrounding countryside, and including a few whimsical watercolours. She'd posted it off quickly, before she changed her mind, not really expecting anything to come of it.

The publisher, it turned out, liked her work. His name was Julian Crown. Over the phone he told her that her pictures evoked a strong sense of childlike innocence that was, in his words, 'really quite charming'. She went down to London on the train to meet him, suspicious that there would be a catch, half expecting him to ask her to pay for the production of her book herself. In fact he turned out to be a likable and genuine man who wore a suit with a buttonhole flower. He took her to lunch at a restaurant in Poland Street and told her that if she listened to his advice he thought he could sell her work. She had, and he did. Since then on average she'd produced a book a year. She wasn't about to retire to the South of France on the proceeds, but she enjoyed the feeling of independence and the sense of purpose it gave her. She only worked a couple of hours a day, usually in the mornings after Kate had left for school. She could have done more if she wanted. Julian was always trying to persuade her that she should.

She picked up the phone and called the number for Kimberley Books and was put through to Julian.

'Angela, you got my message.' He sounded pleased to hear from her.

'Hello, Julian, how are you?'

'Marvellous. Couldn't be better. How's life in the wild open spaces?'

'It's Cumbria, Julian. It isn't exactly the Russian Steppes.'

He laughed, but to him it might as well have been. On one of her occasional visits to London he'd taken her to meet his wife. They lived in a three-storey Georgian terrace house in a leafy street near Belsize Park. The world of publishing apparently involved an endless round of social events. In between cocktail parties and book launches Julian and his wife, who Angela had thought was beautiful and sophisticated, went to the opera and the theatre and ate at fine restaurants. Their house was tastefully and expensively furnished. Angela had showed Julian on a map exactly where she lived and she recalled his expression of surprise.

'My dear, it's practically in Scotland.' He seemed to think civilization ended somewhere just north of Hampstead, and Hadrian's Wall hadn't been built for nothing.

Now, as they chatted, and he asked how her current book was progressing she wondered what he really wanted. She told him the book would be finished on time.

'Excellent,' he said, and there was a significant pause.

'Was there something specific you wanted to talk about, Julian?'

'Actually there is, now that you come to mention it. An American firm is interested in publishing you.' He paused to allow a moment for that to sink in. 'They like your work, but they want you to do a series specifically for their market.'

'You mean, set them in America?'

'Actually, they want you to make them more English. Or at least more like the average American's idea of England. Put in a few teashops and the odd m'lord perhaps. There is a catch,' Julian added.

'A catch?' She should have known there would be. The excitement she'd begun to feel rapidly dissipated.

'The thing is they want nine books over the next three years.'

'Nine?' she echoed.

'And they would want you for a publicity tour.'

Suddenly she realized exactly what would be involved. What had begun as an interest, something she found personally rewarding, would become a full-time career. Three books a year would mean taking on a commitment way beyond her current contract with Julian. She understood that it wouldn't end there. It would just be the beginning. A tour would mean she would have to go away, perhaps for weeks. Her life would change. 'I don't know, Julian. There's Kate to think of.'

He sighed. 'I was afraid you'd say that. This kind of opportunity doesn't often come along, Angela. It may never happen again. Before you turn it down, at least think about it. Will you promise me?'

She hesitated before she agreed. She owed him that much. 'Of course I will.'

'That's all I ask.'

He then spent another fifteen minutes reiterating what was at stake. He kept repeating that it was a once-in-a-lifetime opportunity. If things went well perhaps other countries would publish her books too. The Americans would launch her with a tour of their major cities. New York, San Francisco, Chicago. When he finally let her go her head was spinning with the thought of all those places she had only ever read about. After they hung up she gazed out of the window at the fells. Once she had thought that this was the only life she ever wanted; herself and David and Kate, this house. They had been happy. Her expression clouded with sadness.

Downstairs Angela paused in the doorway to David's study. The room smelt vaguely musty so she opened the window to let in some air. She glanced at some papers on the desk. A recent bank statement for the sawmill revealed that there was more money going out of the business than was coming in. She opened the drawer where she knew David kept his Scotch and the bottle she found was only two-thirds full. Yesterday it had been unopened.

She looked around at the hunting and fishing prints on the wall, the clutter of male effects. Three or four fishing rods in one corner, an old leather shotgun case that he kept behind the bookcase. The room had David's stamp all over it. It was a man's room. She used to think she knew him. For most of their married life together they'd been happy. They had the occasional argument and there were things about David that irritated her, but they weren't important. No doubt he felt the same way about some of her habits. But these last few months he had changed. At first she'd put it down to worry about the sawmill. The local economy, which was so reliant on farming, had taken a battering in successive years, and uncertainty over the estate hadn't helped matters. But it was more than that. She had the disconcerting feeling that this was the room of a stranger. These days when David was at home he sat in here brooding and drinking. He wouldn't talk to her any more, though she knew there was something eating away at him. She couldn't remember when he'd last slept in their bed. A month? Six weeks? It was affecting Kate as well. She avoided her father and these days hardly ever brought friends home from school.

For the first time in thirteen years Angela faced the possibility that her marriage was in trouble. How much longer was she prepared to go on like this? Briefly she envisaged a new life for herself and Kate. It was just a momentary speculation, prompted in part by her conversation with Julian, partly by an increasing sense of hopelessness. Almost immediately she banished the thought. What was she thinking? Guiltily she left the room.

CHAPTER TEN

As Adam went into the newsagent's the bell over the door rang. He paused, savouring the mingled smells of tobacco and sugar confectionary. A middle-aged woman behind the counter looked up and smiled. He didn't recognize her. He went over to the counter and picked up some chewing gum.

'Wasn't this shop once owned by George Curtis?' he asked casually. 'I noticed the name over the door had changed.'

'I couldn't tell you,' she said. 'I haven't lived here long.'

Her accent, he realized, wasn't even Cumbrian. She sounded as if she was from Newcastle. He smiled, feeling foolish, and went back outside. As he walked back towards the square he watched people pass by, searching for a familiar face. Across the road a woman came down the steps from the bank. She was fishing in her bag, perhaps looking for her car keys because she stopped beside a Renault parked by the kerb. He watched her, his heart beating hard in his chest. At that moment she looked up, and their eyes met.

Her hair was still long and pale blonde. She wore jeans and a dark jacket, and his secret fear that the years would have changed her was swept away. She broke their gaze and found her keys, but then as she was about to get into her car she looked again, and this time her brow creased in a puzzled frown. All at once her expression slowly dissolved. She gave a small, disbelieving shake of her head and smiled uncertainly. She began to cross the road, and as he went to meet her, her smile broadened.

'Adam? My God. Is it you?'

'Hello, Angela.'

She was momentarily lost for words. Her eyes were startling. Vivid blue, but paler than he remembered.

'This is incredible. What are you doing here?'

'I'm, uh, visiting for a few days.'

A few feet and fifteen years separated them. Neither of them knew quite what to do. In France they would have embraced and kissed, but bound by the reserve of the English they were briefly awkward. Then Angela grinned and stepped towards him.

'Adam, it's so good to see you.' And at last, they hugged one another.

They went to the New Inn for coffee, and sat at a table in the corner of the bar. As they chatted, catching up on the main events of their lives, he had to force himself to concentrate on what she was saying. He knew he was staring. Until they'd hugged he hadn't really understood how much he'd wanted to see her. Maybe he'd never allowed himself to acknowledge what she had meant to him. He had put away his feelings all those years ago, closed the door and turned the key on some inner sanctum. Now, seeing her again had let loose emotions he hadn't felt for a long time.

As she talked he compared her with the mental image he'd preserved. Of course she was older, but when he'd left she'd been a girl. Now she was a woman, and more beautiful than ever. Her skin was smooth, though there was a tiny scar on her jaw that he didn't remember being there before, and her voice had altered, having lost the girlish inflection of youth. It was richer, and when she laughed, as she did often, it produced a yearning in him that was almost physical. He wanted to touch her. He also experienced an echo of bitterness that he had ever lost her.

He learned that she had a daughter, and she mentioned David's name. Somehow he wasn't surprised that they had married. He kept his expression carefully neutral, though he noticed the hesitation in her voice, and when he steered the subject towards other things she happily asked him about his work. She wasn't surprised that he'd become a journalist. When she told him about her own career there was a note of pride in her voice.

'That's fantastic. Mind you, I always thought I would become the writer,' he said.

'Well, it's not exactly Harry Potter, but I do love it.' She told him about her conversation earlier with her publisher.

'What will you do?'

She frowned. 'I don't know.'

He sensed there were undercurrents, considerations that he didn't feel he could ask about. Her expression became clouded for a moment, and then she changed the subject.

'You haven't told me if there's a Mrs Turner yet.'

'There's an ex-Mrs Turner.'

'I'm sorry. Do you have children?'

He shook his head. 'We weren't together long enough for that.'

As they skipped over the years, filling in the gaps, she told him her parents had sold the shop and retired, and mentioned the names of people he remembered.

'What about Nick, is he still around?' he asked.

She nodded. 'And Graham too. You'll never guess what he does now.'

'Let me try. He joined the police force and runs the local station.'

She pulled a face, her surprise spoiled. 'How did you know?'

'I saw him earlier.'

He explained how they'd met and she looked suddenly thoughtful. 'What were you doing visiting the local police station? Does it have something to do with why you're here?'

'I'm working on something.'

'A story?'

'It could be.'

She looked intrigued, but before she could ask any more questions she noticed the clock on the wall. 'Christ! Look at the time. I'm sorry, Adam, I have to go and pick Kate up.' She hesitated, weighing her thoughts. 'Look, why don't you come for dinner tonight? If you're not doing anything of course.'

'I didn't have anything planned.'

'Great. Let's say about eight? You know where we live, it's David's parents' old house. We moved in after they died.'

Suddenly, confronted with seeing David again, seeing them together, he wasn't sure it was a good idea. He sensed Angela's own reservations, no doubt wondering as he did if they could forget the past. But he wanted to see her again, and it was that and perhaps curiosity that made his decision. 'I'll be there.'

'Good.' She stood up then leaned over to kiss his cheek. 'See you later.'

He watched her go, his senses filled with her scent, his emotions in turmoil.

Adam sat in his room aware that he ought to leave otherwise he'd be late. Was this a good idea he wondered? Of course it wasn't. So why was he going? He got up and went to the door and when he opened it a blast of freezing cold air hit him. It was dark. He could have stepped back into another dimension, cast back through time. Only it had been early morning instead of night.

He remembered looking out of the kitchen window, though he couldn't see much. It was dark outside, and cold. Summer had ended and he was in the last year of school. The idea of freezing his nuts off waiting to blast a few ducks out of the sky was definitely unappealing. He looked at the clock on the wall. It was only three in the morning.

When the kettle boiled he poured hot water into his thermos. At least he'd have hot soup. He tasted it, and grimaced as he examined the packet. It was supposed to be chicken but it tasted of salt.

Outside it was even colder than he'd thought. The moon appeared briefly through a gap in the clouds then vanished again. Kyle had said he could borrow the Land Rover and as he drove into town Adam turned the heater on full blast, shivering while the cab slowly warmed.

'You're late,' David said, when he arrived. 'We thought you weren't coming.'

'I wasn't sure we'd still be going. It feels as if it might snow.'

Nick threw him a contemptuous look. 'A bit of snow won't hurt anyone.'

'Fine,' Adam said, unwilling to argue.

The others threw their gear in the back and they started off. It was normally a half-hour drive up to Cold Tarn but it took them longer because as they climbed towards the fells it began to snow. Adam stared glumly into the swirling flakes that blew out of the darkness. When they reached the forest they turned down a rutted frozen track and drove as far as they could. Where it ended they had to leave the Land Rover to walk the final half-mile or so.

Adam had borrowed Kyle's shotgun, which he carried in the crook of his arm, with the barrel broken and unloaded as they began to follow a trail towards the lake. Within five minutes the snow started really to come down, turning the forest into a hushed and eerie, almost otherworldly place. The ground beneath the pines was quickly covered, and the air was filled with softly falling flakes, acting as insulation, deadening sound. The moon had vanished and all around there was only the black of the trees and the white of the snow.

It took them twenty minutes to reach the edge of the lake. Beyond the trees they sensed rather than saw the open space above the water. David picked out a place in the cover of a holly bush where Adam could wait and gave quiet instructions.

'Remember, don't make a sound. Stay here until it's light. You'll have a clear shot.' He pointed to the invisible reeds that fringed the shoreline where the ducks would fly in to feed in the morning. 'I'll be further along the shore.' He turned and in a few seconds he and the others were swallowed by the darkness.

'Great,' Adam muttered quietly. He loaded the shotgun and stood it against the tree beside him. It was a little after five-thirty, which meant it wouldn't begin to get light for at least another hour. He thought wistfully of the warm bed he'd left behind.

By six-fifteen it was still dark and the snow was falling even more heavily. Adam's feet were numb, his hands felt clumsy and unresponsive. He resisted the urge to flap his arms and stamp some feeling back into his feet, knowing he was supposed to keep quiet. The hot soup was all gone and he was hungry. Beyond the holly bush the snow made everything look strangely unfamiliar and it was still falling. He couldn't see the way they'd come any more, their tracks had vanished along with the path. He wondered whether he ought to go and look for the others. How was he even supposed to see a duck let alone shoot it? He was reluctant to move, however, because he didn't want to be the first to pack it in. But after another ten minutes the cold had convinced him. He picked up the shotgun and cradling it in the crook of his arms he started back through the pines away from the lake so he wouldn't cross in front of anybody's line of fire.

After a couple of minutes he thought he ought to head back towards the water to find the others. The snow made the ground appear uniformly smooth and hid rocks and fallen branches, making for difficult going. He walked with his head down and after a while he paused to get his bearings. He couldn't hear a thing, and he couldn't see where the lake was any more. He reasoned that if he got lost he could always retrace his steps, but how could he lose a whole lake so quickly? From his tracks he saw that somehow he'd managed to weave in a curve left, which meant the lake had to be somewhere on his right.

He paused on the edge of a small clearing beneath a pine laden with snow. He was sure the lake must be just ahead. He wondered if he should call out. But maybe he shouldn't. It had almost stopped snowing, and perhaps by the time it was light there would be ducks after all. He began to think he should have stayed where he was. He started forward again and as he did he brushed against a branch and dislodged its burden of snow, which thumped to the ground. At almost exactly the same moment he registered a bright flash in front of him and a roar of sound and then he was falling. He felt cold snow on his cheek and somebody was screaming. It seemed to go on for ever.

The branches of huge chestnuts overhung the narrow lane that led to the house. Adam and David had gathered conkers here that first year he had had moved to Castleton. Filled their pockets with the biggest they could find, then soaked them in vinegar and dried them slowly in the oven in David's mother's kitchen, before drilling holes in them through which they threaded knotted string. It seemed like a lifetime ago.

They would have been fourteen then, both going to Kings. When he thought of those times it seemed like a happy childhood. It was always different when there were only the two of them. He'd felt accepted, a part of everything. Only with the others, especially

Nick, had David been different. But over time he'd come to think of it as a kind of conspiracy between himself and David. Something only they understood. He remembered David saying once, in an uncharacteristically serious manner, that Nick had a rough time at home. For David it was tantamount to a speech. The implication was that Adam should understand that if David appeared less obviously his friend sometimes it was only because of Nick. In a way it had deepened Adam and David's friendship.

Or at least he had always thought so.

As Adam turned through the gate the headlights swept over fallen leaves blown up against the wall in drifts, and the tyres crunched on the gravel driveway. The lights in the windows and the porch lent the house a warm, welcoming feel. The back of Angela's Renault was visible in the garage, and a Land Rover that he assumed belonged to David was parked outside. Clutching a bottle of Côte de Rhone from the supermarket in town, he went to the door and rang the bell.

It was David who answered. For an awkward moment or two they regarded one another before David held out his hand and they shook hands.

'Hello, Adam.' His grip was calloused and firm. He was heavier in the arms and shoulders and his hair had darkened over the years, though traces of grey showed at his temples. His face was weathered and lined, and there were dark smudges beneath his eyes, which Adam was surprised to see bore the spider web red veins of a drinker. Despite the changes, however, the boy Adam remembered remained clearly visible. Until this moment he hadn't been sure what he would feel but the rush of bitterness that suddenly engulfed him took him by surprise. He struggled to keep his feelings from showing, though David hesitated as if he'd seen something in Adam's eyes, then he stood aside.

'Come in, Angela's in the kitchen.'

As they passed through the house Adam had time to recover his composure. Through open doors he caught glimpses of rooms that he remembered. When they reached the kitchen Angela turned from the sink at the sound of their voices, wiping her hands on her apron. Her welcoming smile failed to conceal a shade of anxiety. She offered her cheek, which Adam duly kissed.

David busied himself opening wine and passing around glasses. 'Old friends,' he said, raising his own.

'Old friends,' they echoed, their smiles a little forced. Adam began to think that coming here had been a big mistake.

A young girl appeared at the door and David called her over. 'Come and meet Adam. This is Kate, our daughter.'

'Hello, Kate,' Adam said, not the only one he thought who was grateful for the diversion. She could have been Angela at the same age. But as he looked more closely he saw the differences. She had the same hair and the full mouth, the same colour eyes even, but she had her father's height and there was a trace of him in the shape of her jaw.

'Kate, help me finish dinner, will you?' Angela asked. 'Why don't you two go and sit down and I'll call you when it's ready.'

They went through into the lounge and covered the years as Adam had with Angela earlier, only this time every sentence seemed to be mined with reminders of the past, which they both avoided mentioning with glaring obviousness. They should just get it out in the open, Adam thought. Clear the air. Remember how you almost blew my leg off and then while I was in hospital you started seeing Angela?

All at once Adam realized David was looking at him with an odd expression, and for a second he thought maybe he'd spoken out loud. But then he realized it wasn't that. David was looking at his knee, which unconsciously he'd begun massaging.

'It aches sometimes,' he explained.

David nodded uncomfortably and held up his empty glass. 'How about a refill?'

Over dinner, to their daughter's embarrassment, her parents made her the focus of their conversation. Adam heard all about her school, her friends, holidays they had taken when she was younger. They might have been obsessively devoted parents, except that they all knew that Kate was a safe and neutral topic. When she was excused she went gratefully, like a shot, probably relieved to escape subtle tensions she could sense even if she didn't understand them.

'So, tell us what brings you back to Castleton, Adam,' Angela said, when Kate had left the room, and clasped her hands beneath her chin, her eyes reflecting the flickering candles on the table. 'You said something about a story earlier.'

'I'm looking into an accident that happened a month or so ago. Some boys were killed in a car crash.'

'I remember that. It was terrible.' She turned to David. 'Weren't they involved with the protest?'

'I don't know.'

'I'm sure they were. Did you know about that, Adam? There's a plan to sell the estate to a company that's going to turn it into a holiday park.'

'So I heard.'

'What about those lads?' David said suddenly. The abruptness of his tone was startling. He emptied his glass and refilled it. 'You said you were looking into the accident,' he added in a more normal voice.

'Yes, the sister of one of the boys who was killed doesn't accept the official version of what happened.'

'I don't understand,' Angela said.

'The police say it was an accident. A case of drunk driving. She isn't convinced.'

'But how does that involve you? I thought you said you're a journalist.'

'I am, but I'm freelance. I sort of specialize in this sort of thing.'

Adam was aware of the intensity with which David was watching him from the other side of the table.

'What sort of thing?'

'Usually it's missing people. Kids. The police have them down as runaways, which a lot of them are. But then now and then somebody, usually a family member, refuses to accept the official version. It's more common than you'd think. Sometimes their convictions are groundless. Other times not.'

'And when they're not?'

'It depends,' Adam said. 'Once I did a feature on a girl in Devon who simply vanished one day. The police were convinced she had run away. She'd been having problems at home, and she'd taken off a couple of times before, though she'd always come back in the end. This time she didn't.' He paused, and when he went on, he met David's eye. 'It turned out she had been seeing a local boy, someone her parents didn't know about. They'd had a fight and he killed her. Her remains were found in a field three years after she vanished.'

'My God,' Angela said quietly. 'I think I remember that now. I even read the story in one of the weekend papers. I didn't even look at the writer's name. That was you? That girl's poor parents.'

'Like I said, it happens more often than you'd think.'

David picked up the wine bottle on the table, but it was empty. Wordlessly he got up and went through to the kitchen. When he came back he was carrying a bottle of Scotch. 'Anyone else want one?'

'No thanks,' Adam said, 'I'm driving.' Angela flashed a look at her husband. He felt unspoken tensions between them that had nothing to do with his presence. 'Anyway, you mentioned the protest these boys were involved with. Tell me about it.'

'It was in the news quite a bit over the summer,' Angela explained. 'Last year the estate was put up for sale after Lord Horsham died. The trouble is nobody wanted to buy it as a whole, so the plan was to split the estate into parcels. A German company wanted to buy the house and turn it into a conference centre for their managers. They were going to bring in all their own staff. The rest of the land was going to be divided up and sold to neighbouring farms, and worst of all, especially from David's point of view, the wood was going to be sold to a big Northumberland firm. They already have most of the forestry commission contracts in the area, so it would have meant the end of the sawmill.'

'It would have finished the whole bloody town, as good as,' David cut in.

'Quite a few people rely on the estate for work one way or another,' Angela said. 'Farming's practically dried up after BSE and then foot-and-mouth. We don't get as many tourists these days. People don't come to walk the fells the way they used to. So, when Forest Havens proposed buying the estate intact to turn it into a holiday park, a lot of locals were relieved.'

'It will mean a lot of new jobs,' David said.

'The company plans to turn the Hall into a four-star hotel with a golf course and an artificial lake. And David would continue to manage the wood, which saves the sawmill and the jobs of the men.'

'Presumably there's a catch,' Adam said.

Angela nodded. 'Part of the plan is to build lodges and cabins in the woods. There would be bike and walking trails and some ponds stocked with fish, that kind of thing. It only affects the northern part of the wood, about a quarter of it all up, but of course it means a lot of trees would have to be felled.'

'And that's the part the protesters object to?'

'As soon as they heard about it back in May, they started arriving,' David said. 'Hundreds of them. Most of them aren't even from the area. A bunch of wannabe eco-warriors and dropouts. I doubt they give a toss really, half of them.'

'I don't think that's fair,' Angela said. 'They believe in what they're doing, and they have as much right to their opinions as anyone who lives around here.'

'As you can see, Angela sympathizes with them,' David said scathingly.

'I can see both sides that's all,' she said tightly.

'It's alright for them isn't it?' David said. 'Dammit! When they've finished here they'll just clear off back to wherever they came from. Won't matter to them if people lose their jobs and have to move away. It's hard enough keeping young people here as it is for Christ's sake.'

There was a brief awkward silence after David's sudden outburst.

'I'm sorry,' Angela said to Adam. 'You can see it's a touchy subject. To be honest I'll be glad when it's all over.'

'When will that be?'

'The court has issued an eviction order against the protesters. If they don't leave soon they'll be forcibly removed.'

'They won't leave,' David said. 'Not voluntarily. The bloody media will be back with their cameras. And all people are going to see are a bunch of kids getting dragged out of their tree huts and tunnels yelling their slogans about oppression and fascists. Everybody will think they're the bloody victims. Nobody cares about us. Companies like Forest Havens don't like that kind of publicity. It isn't good for their image. Next thing you know they'll pull out and go somewhere else. And the bloody protesters know it.' He emptied his glass again and poured another.

'Nobody gives a bugger about us though. Least of all the journalists who make it sound as if we don't care about the environment, so long as we're all making money. Have a look around, Adam, before you start sympathizing with the protesters. See how many millionaires you find around here.'

'Don't try and drag Adam into this. He isn't even here because of the protest,' Angela said.

'Isn't he?'

They were both looking at him, expecting an answer. Adam felt as if he was being asked to take sides. 'My only interest in the protest is if it has a bearing on the accident.'

'What do you mean?' Angela asked.

'I don't know exactly. Maybe nothing.' He told them about the injuries on two of the bodies. 'Perhaps they were beaten up. It could be significant.' He shrugged to indicate it was only speculation.

David stared at him and then emptied his glass before reaching for the bottle again.

Adam helped clear the table before saying he ought to be going. When Angela showed him to the door she started to apologize for David's outburst.

'He's been under a lot of pressure. If Forest Havens did pull out, he would lose the mill. He's struggling as it is.'

'I understand,' Adam told her.

She ran a hand back through her hair in a gesture of weariness. 'Perhaps this was a mistake. I didn't mean for you to have to listen to our troubles.'

'I'm glad I came.'

'Are you? I think you'd say that anyway.'

'Look, if you need a friendly ear,' he offered. 'I mean if you want to talk, you know where I am.'

'Thanks. I might take you up on that.'

'Any time.'

She smiled and hesitated, then reached out and touched his arm lightly, a brief gesture of intimacy. 'Adam. It's so nice to see you.'

'And you.'

'Goodnight.'

*   *   *

As he drove back to the New Inn he thought about the evening. At first he'd put their early awkwardness down to a hangover from the past, only to be expected, but obviously David and Angela had problems of their own that had nothing to do with him. He'd sensed the tensions between them, and David had been drinking heavily. Maybe some of it was stress related to the sawmill, but he thought it went deeper than that.

At the New Inn the car park was empty save for two other cars parked next to each other. A door to one of the ground-floor rooms was open spilling light onto the covered walkway. As Adam made for the stairs he glanced inside. A middle-aged couple were sitting at a table drinking beer and watching TV. There was a bowl of crisps in front of them. As he went by a second woman appeared from the room next door carrying another packet of crisps and a bowl of dip. She smiled and nodded, and was followed by a short fat man who paused to close the door.

'Lovely evening.'

'It is,' Adam agreed, pausing to look at the clear sky. The man spoke with a thick Birmingham accent.

'I saw that car of yours earlier. It's an old one isn't it? Nice condition though. Drive alright does it?'

'Pretty well.'

'That's mine there, the Rover,' the man said. 'Always driven Rovers, I have. Used to make lovely cars once, they did. That un's not bad, but it's not the same.'

'I suppose,' Adam agreed, feeling obliged to make some comment.

'We're up here to do some fishing. Me and me mate and the ladies. You fish at all?'

'Not a lot.'

'Some nice rivers up here. Better than the canal. Nice change too.'

'I expect so.'

'Well, 'night then.'

'Goodnight,' Adam said.

He went upstairs to his room and lay down on the bed, but he couldn't sleep. He could hear the TV below, and the murmur of voices and even after they had fallen silent he remained staring wide-eyed into the darkness.

CHAPTER ELEVEN

As the sound of Adam's car faded, Angela turned out the porch light and went back inside. She turned off the lights and went down the passage towards the study. The lamp was on, casting a dim yellow light through the partially open door. David was sitting at his desk, a bottle of whisky and a glass in front of him. She started to go past, but then changed her mind. Too often lately she had left him to his thoughts and his drinking. Every time she tried to talk to him it turned into a fight. She supposed that she was hoping he would snap out of whatever it was that was eating away at him, but she saw now that by allowing things to go on like this she was destroying their marriage as surely as he was. She pushed open the door.

'Adam's gone.'

David's face was half hidden in shadow. 'You shouldn't have invited him here.'

'Why? What was I supposed to do? Just say, "Nice to see you again after all these years, perhaps we'll run into each other again some time"? He's an old friend.'

'He was a bit more than that for you wasn't he?'

She stared at him, amazed by what she thought she heard in his voice. 'David, are you jealous?'

'Should I be?'

'For God's sake I only met him again this afternoon.' She watched him reach for the whisky bottle to refill his glass. 'And don't you think you've had enough?'

His paused and met her eye, then dropped his hand. Suddenly he looked vulnerable. Fatigue was etched into his features and uncertainty filled his eyes. There was something in his expression that was almost . . . she searched for the right word . . . almost a plea, and it touched her though she didn't understand it. She went over and crouching down took one of his hands between her own.

'What is it, David? What's happened to us?' He shook his head. Was it defeat? A denial, or simply an expression that he didn't know any more than she did? 'You're not really jealous of Adam are you?'

'I saw the way he looked at you.'

'What?' she said, with genuine surprise.

'And you. You looked different tonight,' he said. 'I didn't know what it was at first. Even before he got here you were running around, checking everything, I don't know.'

'I just wanted everything to be right.'

'You were worried, Angela. Admit it. You were worried about what he would see.' He gestured to the whisky bottle. 'Would I drink too much, what would I say?'

She couldn't deny it and didn't try. 'I thought this might be a chance to forget everything for a while, just for a few hours. He's just an old friend, David. Somebody we haven't seen for a long time.'

'Come on, you can't believe that, Angela. We can't just pretend none of it happened. For Christ's sake did you see the way he limped? I did that to him.'

'It was an accident. He never blamed you for that.'

'But what about what happened afterwards, while he was laid up in a fucking hospital bed? Do you think he's forgotten?'

'Nothing happened between us.'

'It didn't have to. He saw what was going on. He knew what we were thinking.'

'We couldn't help the way we felt.'

'Maybe not. But if it was all so innocent why did we both feel so bad about it? Why did I stop going to see him?'

He was right. She remembered how guilty she had felt sitting on the bus with David after they had been to the hospital. Nothing had happened, nothing had even been said for a long time, but she'd felt guilty nonetheless. She had known, they had both known long before the accident that they were attracted to each other. Neither of them had expected it. It had just been there, that inexplicable something, a chemical chain reaction that neither of them had any control over. At first, though she had found herself thinking about David all the time, she'd tried hard to suppress her feelings. She'd been confused because she'd had feelings for Adam too. Once she had believed she loved him, and knew he'd felt the same way about her. But had they really been in love? They were young, but then she'd been young when she'd fallen in love with David too. Perhaps if there hadn't always been the knowledge that Adam would one day leave things might have been different. Though perhaps that wasn't really the issue. Maybe it was just that they were different people with different ideas and plans and ultimately his leaving was a reflection of that. She had never really known. The accident had prevented their relationship from running its natural course.

'It was a long time ago, David,' she said. 'And Adam has nothing to do with what's been happening to us.'

'Until now maybe.'

'What does that mean?'

'Nothing, forget it.'

'Forget it?' She shook her head in frustration. 'Don't you think it's time we talked? Sometimes I feel we're not the same people that we were. That you're not the same. You don't even sleep in our bed any more.'

'You know how things have been, Angela. I've been under a lot of pressure.'

'Don't tell me that!' she said angrily. 'Don't tell me this is all about the sawmill.' She waved a hand at the half-empty whisky bottle. 'This! The drinking, never talking, the way you sit in here all the bloody time, brooding. Dammit David, this is about us. Us!'

'It isn't just the sawmill.'

'Then what? What is it?'

'It's everything. Those protesters could still make Forest Havens pull out.'

'No,' she said, suddenly knowing there was more to this than he was trying to have her believe. 'There's something you're not telling me.' She saw immediately that she was right. Some expression flashed in his eyes. What was it? Whatever it was it vanished, and he became guarded.

'There's nothing else.'

'I don't believe you. I know how much the business means to you and I've tried to be understanding. I knew you were worried when the estate was first put up for sale, and afterwards when you didn't know if Forest Havens would get planning permission. But they did, and soon the protesters will be evicted and I don't understand why you're like this.' She gestured to the whisky in his hand. 'Every night you lock yourself away in here. You shut me out, you shut out your own daughter, and you drink yourself into a stupor. So what is it, David? What is it really? And don't tell me you're afraid the deal will fall through because I don't believe that any more!'

She thought she had finally got through to him. For a moment he seemed on the verge of something, and then the moment passed and a veil slid down over his eyes. He turned away from her.

Angrily she went from the room, slamming the door behind her in frustration.

Upstairs in their bedroom her anger ebbed and left her feeling only empty and alone. An hour later he hadn't come to bed, and she knew that he wouldn't. She lay in the darkness, fighting back tears of frustration and helplessness.

CHAPTER TWELVE

For the second day in a row Adam was the only guest at breakfast. A waitress was clearing another table and as there was no sign of the Rover in the car park he assumed the two couples from Birmingham had made an early start.

After breakfast he drove out to the northern edge of Castleton Wood. He left his car on the verge at the edge of the road and followed the track that led through the trees. The day was sunny but cool enough to remind him that it was October. The oaks and the beech trees had lost many of their leaves, and what remained reflected the sunlight in a blaze of yellow. Coloured signs printed on laminated paper were nailed to trees along the edge of the track. SAVE OUR WOODLAND. EVERY TREE WE CUT DOWN IS ANOTHER GASP FOR OUR PLANET. Occasionally there were flashes of ironic humour. CUT DOWN A TREE, WE NEED MORE JUNK MAIL. Other signs asked for donations of food, clothing or money.

The track passed by a small clearing where a young woman watched as he approached. He raised a hand and called out a greeting. 'I'm looking for the protest camp.'

She pointed along the track. 'If you keep going you'll come to the communal area.'

Her hair was long and matted, and when she smiled she revealed heavily stained teeth. Some logs had been arranged around an open fire for use as seats, and a blue tarpaulin slung over some low branches formed the basis of a crude tent.

'Have you been here long?' he asked.

'About six months.'

He couldn't imagine living this way for that length of time. He asked about her camp, and why she was there.

'They want to cut down the trees,' she told him.

As they talked he thought she seemed friendly enough, though her smile was a bit vacant, and the answers she gave him to his questions were simple to the point of bordering on the naïve. A sign had been nailed to a tree, a kind of New Age exhortation to protect mother earth, nourish her, life is a cycle, a rhythm to become attuned to, and so on. The girl gazed at him. Her clothes looked handmade. She reminded him of the kind of pictures of medieval peasants found in school history books.

He thanked her and moved on, passing other camps back in the trees, often with shelters made of plastic sheeting or tarpaulins. There were also a few tree houses here and there, sometimes connected with rope walkways. Some looked sturdier than others, and when he went to take a closer look at one he was confronted with a notice fixed to the tree warning trespassers away, which he found mildly ironic. He encountered a few other people like the girl he'd talked to, but most of the camps were empty.

The track led eventually to a fairly large clearing where thirty or so people, mostly young, sat or stood around several pit fires. Over one a large pot of rice was cooking and another was filled with some kind of greenish stew. A half-dozen beaten-up vans and cars were parked on the grass, and some washing lines had been strung between the trees. A dog started barking, an ugly grey terrier tied by a rope lashed to a tree. A bizarre-looking figure wearing a battered top hat and dishevelled morning coat teamed with tartan trousers patted the dog until it quietened. He went back to his place among a group sitting around a smouldering fire and watched Adam approach with an expression of mild enquiry.

'Morning,' Adam said. 'Nice day.'

'Good morning,' the young man replied, his accent surprisingly public school. He appeared to be in his mid-twenties and had begun rolling a joint. The others around him passed around some cans of lager. Some had dreadlocks, others shaven heads, and most had pierced various parts of themselves. All of them wore an unconventional assortment of clothing. Unlike the girl Adam had spoken to earlier, these people looked less like throwbacks from another century and more like refugees from the punk era of the seventies and eighties, except that they weren't old enough. Though there was nothing untoward in their manner, their appearance was vaguely threatening

A young girl asked if he'd like a cup of tea, which struck him as incongruous. 'No thanks. I'd like to talk to you if I could, though.'

'Have a pew,' the one wearing the top hat said. 'I'm Peter. What can we do for you?'

They shook hands. 'Adam Turner. I'm a journalist.'

'Right. Make sure you get my surname right then. Fallow.' He spelt it out. 'Which paper do you work for?'

'I don't. I'm freelance.'

Fallow looked disappointed. 'Well, you're a bit early anyway.'

'Early?'

'Aren't you here for the eviction?'

'Not exactly. When is it going to happen?'

'Aha, the question on everybody's lips. If only we knew the answer.' He grinned and lit up his joint. The sweet smell of cannabis laced the air. After he'd taken a couple of good tokes he passed it on, and accepted his turn for a swig of lager.

'You don't seem too worried by the prospect of getting kicked out,' Adam said.

'That's because it's our chance to let people see the fascist state at work. They'll probably come at night hoping to get us all out before anyone sees what's going on, but it won't work. We'll be ready.' He tapped his nose, hinting at secrets.

'You mean you'll resist.'

'Not in the way you mean. We've got friends on the inside, they'll tell us when it's about to happen and we'll have the press here waiting. Lights! Cameras! Action!' Gleefully he gestured to the surrounding woods. 'They'll have to drag us out. But first they'll have to get us down from the trees and dig us out of our underground burrows. It'll be on the nine o'clock news.'

'Publicity for the cause,' Adam guessed.

'In a word, precisely.'

'Isn't it a bit late for all this? I assume the council have already approved the Forest Havens plans.'

'True, but companies like Forest Havens hate bad publicity. They want everyone to think they're nature-friendly. Have you seen their brochures? Lots of happy smiling families enjoying their holidays in the countryside. Pictures of bike trails through leafy woods and rolling fields, foxes playing in a meadow and all that sort of thing.'

'It doesn't sound too bad,' Adam said.

'Of course it doesn't. Of course they never show the acres of trees they cut down, all the habitat they destroy to create their artificial natural wonderland with its man-made lakes and rustic kiosks selling ice cream and hamburgers. The last thing they want is this place all over the nine o'clock news as we're dragged out by our heels.'

'So, the more media, the better as far as you're concerned.'

'Exactly. If you want to know when it's all happening leave us your number and we'll send you an invitation.'

'Thanks,' Adam said. 'I'll bear it in mind.' A frightening-looking youth with rings through his eyebrows and a shaved head offered him a toke of the joint, which he declined. 'Actually, I'm interested in the three boys who were killed near here in a car accident a month or so ago. They were part of this protest weren't they? Did you know them?'

'Hmm, a little. I know Jane better.'

'Jane Hanson?'

'Yes. The others came up with her, but I didn't have much to do with them. There were more of us here then and people tend to split into their own groups. Anyway they left when all the others did.'

'All the others?'

'About a hundred of them, mostly students. They all decamped after some of the local heroes turned up here one night. I think they'd decided not to wait for the official eviction.'

'What exactly happened?'

'The usual. They surprised us one night and started pulling camps apart and beating people up.'

'The usual? You mean this had happened before?'

'Not here, but I've seen the same kind of thing at other places. Sometimes it's just local thugs with nothing better to

114

do, out for a bit of fun. Sometimes it's people trying scare us off.'

'And which was this?'

Fallow looked grim. 'These weren't just troublemakers, they meant business. They were organized and most of them had clubs. It was the students who got the worst of it. We get a lot of them coming to these things in the summer. They bring their tents and treat it like a scout jamboree. A jolly lark. Anyway, like I said, after that most of them left.'

'You reported what happened to the police I take it?'

'The next day. They came and took statements.'

'Was anybody arrested?'

Fallow looked sceptical. 'The local plod came to see us a few days later. He made noises about the descriptions being vague and so on.'

'You don't think the police took what happened seriously?'

'Let's just say that we find the constabulary generally think we ought to regard a few bruises and bloody noses as a natural hazard.'

Maybe what Fallow said was true, but as he had said himself, this had sounded more sinister than just some local troublemakers, Adam thought. Now he understood how the boys with Ben had come by their injuries. 'So, this was before the accident? How long before?'

'A few days,' Fallow said.

'And afterwards, Jane Hanson left as well?'

'No, she'd already gone by then,' a voice piped up.

'This is Ellie,' Fallow said, gesturing to a girl sitting nearby. 'She knows Jane as well as anyone.'

She was perhaps eighteen or nineteen. One of her ears was pierced by at least a dozen rings, and she wore another through her nose. Her hair had been shaved to a uniform quarter-inch length and was dyed bright red.

She smiled. 'Hello.'

'Hi. So, when exactly did Jane leave?'

'A few days before the camp was attacked. Ben and the other two stayed on. Poor Ben. He was nice.'

'You knew him?'

'A little. He was too nice for Jane. I don't mean that in a horrible way, but he wasn't strong enough, you know? Jane needs somebody who can stand up to her. Ben was besotted with her. He'd have done anything for her. I think that was partly why she decided to finish it. She asked me to keep an eye on him, before she went. I didn't do a very good job did I?'

'Where did Ben and the others go after they left here?'

Ellie looked at Fallow who shrugged. 'No idea. We never saw them again.'

'But they definitely didn't come back here?'

'Definitely.'

Adam wondered where they had been for the next few days until the accident happened. Why hadn't they gone home? 'What about Jane? She went back to London?'

'I think so. I know she was supposed to be starting a job down there,' Ellie said.

'Deserted us,' Fallow cut in cheerfully. 'I always knew she would in the end. She's probably got some corporate job in the City, sold out to the fascists.'

'Don't mind him,' Ellie said. 'They never saw eye to eye those two. Jane doesn't think this kind of protest works any more. She was always saying we have to play them at their own game.'

'She thinks our image works against us,' Fallow added, and looking around Adam thought she had a point.

Ellie grinned and dug Fallow in the ribs. 'She just had different ideas that's all.'

'What kind of ideas?' Adam asked.

'I don't know. She and the others were up to something though. It started after she talked to that reporter, didn't it?'

Fallow shrugged. 'I think so.'

'Do you know the reporter's name? Or the paper?' Adam asked.

'The *Courier* I think. It's a local paper. I can't remember the reporter's name, but she was a woman. Youngish. About twenty-three or -four I should think.'

'You don't know what Jane and this reporter talked about?'

'Not really. Jane did mention one thing, though. It must have been before Forest Havens got planning permission, or around that time anyway. She overheard some people talking in a pub or somewhere. She was pretty worked up about it.'

'Worked up as in angry?'

'Partly. Excited I think as well.'

'But she didn't say why?'

'No. I definitely got the impression she thought it was important though.' She shrugged. 'But obviously it didn't work out, whatever it was, because she left, didn't she?'

'But Ben and the others didn't.'

'No. Not until the camp was attacked anyway.'

'You said you knew Ben a little. Did you know that when he and the others were killed it was Ben who was driving?'

'Yes, his sister told me. She came here one day before the inquest.'

'So, you probably know that she doesn't believe the police version of what happened. What do you think about that?'

'I don't know. I remember Jane telling me once that he didn't drink much because he was taking some sort of medication. I never saw him have more than a can of beer.'

'Did you ever see him drive?'

Ellie thought for a moment and shook her head. 'But it could be that I just didn't notice, you know.'

'Did the police ever question you about it?'

'No.'

Adam wasn't really surprised. He asked if there had been any other trouble besides the night they were attacked, but aside from minor harassment and a bit of name-calling there was nothing really.

'Ben's sister said he'd been threatened,' Adam said. 'Do you know anything about that?'

Both Fallow and Ellie shook their heads. 'Sorry.'

He wondered why Ben and perhaps the others had been singled out, but they didn't have any ideas, unless it had something to do with what they'd been doing. 'I don't suppose you know where I can find Jane?' he asked Ellie finally.

'Not really. She lives in London somewhere, that's all I know.'

'Okay. Thanks. If you think of anything, let me know.' He gave her a card with his mobile number on it.

'Okay,' Ellie promised.

Before Adam left Fallow asked for his mobile number and added it to a list of other media contacts he had in a notebook. He also gave Adam a badly photocopied flyer meant to educate people to the cause. It was full of exclamation marks and exhortations to action.

He left them to go back to whatever they were doing, which as far as he could see wasn't much. As protests went it seemed like a fairly harmless one. A bunch of society's misfits, full of the idealism of youth, taking the opportunity to camp out in the woods and protect Mother Nature. At least that was probably how some of them viewed what they were doing. Maybe for others it was just a change from sleeping by the canal in some northern city. How bad could it be? Collect the dole, live off donations and spend their days drinking lager and smoking dope. No wonder Jane had thought there was a better way to elicit public support.

As he went back along the track towards the road Adam tried to imagine what would be left of the wood if the development did go ahead. He remembered walking here when he was young. In the spring, the bluebells came up and made a stunning carpet of colour beneath the trees. There had been the sound of cuckoos in the early morning, and the echoing staccato hammering of woodpeckers. He stopped beneath a massive purple beech, the lower branches of which trailed against the ground in a wide circumference around the trunk. There were trees here that must be hundreds of years old. For generations the wood had been carefully managed. Parts of it were still coppiced and as mature trees were harvested new ones were planted, the mixture grown for timber carefully planned. The flyer claimed it was one of the largest ancient woodland sites left in England. Incredible to think such places weren't protected, and yet, apparently, they weren't. But as David had said, without the development the estate would be broken up and local people would lose their jobs. The economy would take yet another battering. There were always two sides to an argument, though rarely did either see the opposing point of view.

He emerged from the wood by the road. From there, looking towards the town he could follow the edge of the wood towards the river, where the two were separated by a meadow and a copse that grew near the bottom end of the town. In a hollow of the fields the sun flashed on the grey slate roofs of the cottages where Nick had once lived. Drawn by curiosity he started down that way following the perimeter of the wood. The cottages were lost from sight, and didn't come into view again until he reached the edge of the meadow. It was overgrown with weeds and thistles and the bridleway that cut through it looked little used. The cottages on the other side looked even more dilapidated than he remembered, and the roof of one was partly missing, exposing a gaping black hole and the skeletal rafters underneath. He doubted that anyone lived there any more.

The last time he'd been here was the day when he'd seen David put something in James Allen's van. That same night, as he'd later learned from Findlay, the police had found a bracelet belonging to Meg Coucesco. Had David and Nick put it there and then tipped off the police? He'd always thought so. But if they had, then why? Had they known something about James Allen? He supposed that was what he'd thought later. But where did they get the bracelet and what exactly had they known? He supposed nobody would ever have the answers now. Allen was long dead, and Meg too probably. He had wondered often enough what would have happened if he'd told somebody what he'd seen the day Meg had vanished when he'd glimpsed her with somebody in the trees near the sawmill. Perhaps when he'd first heard she was missing she was still alive and if he'd spoken out she wouldn't have died. It was the guilt he would always carry with him.

He found he was clenching his fists. When he looked at his hands there were deep marks where his nails had dug into the flesh of his palms. He rubbed them together.

He would have turned away then, but once again curiosity drew him across the field towards the cottages. When he was twenty yards away he was startled when the door to one of them opened and a young woman came outside. She carried something that looked like kitchen scraps to the edge of the overgrown garden and tossed them into a thicket of nettles and blackberries. As she turned around she saw him and stopped dead. She paled visibly and stifled a gasp.

He held up his hands in a gesture to show he meant no harm. 'Sorry, I didn't mean to startle you. I wasn't sure anybody lived here.'

She looked to be in her twenties, or maybe thirty. Her brown hair was dull and pulled back from her face and she wore faded jeans and a shapeless sweatshirt, beneath which he had the impression of a skinny body. The look she'd worn, which he would almost have described as one of terror, changed to one of wariness. It was enough to stop him from going any nearer. She seemed to cower and her eyes darted nervously towards the open door she'd emerged from. He wondered if she was simple-minded. He saw now that the cottage she'd come from was the only one that had glass in the windows and one of the others even lacked a front door.

The woman continued to watch him, saying nothing. He smiled, trying to put her at ease. 'I used to know somebody who lived here.' He heard himself adopt the kind of tone he might have used to speak to a child. There was no response. 'His name was Nick,' he added. This time he thought there was a flicker of recognition. 'Does he still live here?' he asked, surprised.

She didn't answer. He waited uncertainly, not sure what to do next, then took half a step closer. She flinched and he stopped, alarmed by the look of fear that sprang into her eyes. He took a step backwards, sure there was something wrong with the woman. He didn't want to be responsible for frightening her so he raised his hands again and continued to back off.

'Look, I didn't mean to scare you. I'm going to leave.' He hesitated. 'Are you alright? Is everything okay?' Again she didn't respond. Slowly he turned and began to walk away. When he'd gone twenty yards he looked back. The woman had vanished and the cottage door was now firmly closed. He stood there for a minute or so, a little bemused by his experience, wondering who she was. Something caught his attention, a movement he glimpsed from the corner of his eye. But when he looked there was only the other empty cottages, and then a crow flapped from a tree behind the roof and he thought that must have been what he'd seen.

Then there was only silence, and once again the cottages appeared deserted. As he walked back towards the wood he had the feeling he was being watched, but he didn't turn around.

CHAPTER THIRTEEN

The *Courier* occupied the second floor of a grey stone Georgian building on Hardwick Street. The entrance hall had a high ceiling and a chipped tile floor. There was a single lift, but it had always been slow and noisy so Adam used the staircase. The polished wooden banister was dark and scratched with age, and his steps echoed faintly as he climbed. The building had once housed a tea merchant and would have been impressive when it was built. Now it was faintly seedy and smelt of the disinfectant used to mop the floors.

The offices hadn't changed much. A dozen or so desks occupied the main work area beneath the high ceilings with their patterned plaster mouldings. One new feature was the IBM computer terminal on every desk, and thick tangles of cabling that snaked around the edges of the room. A middle-aged man wearing a jacket that was too small for him sat staring morosely at his screen. A young woman with short spiky bleached hair emerged from what had once been the stationery room. She moved with brisk purpose, sat down at a desk and started tapping at her keyboard frowning with concentration. At the back of the room the editor's glass walled office was still there, where Jim Findlay sat at his desk.

Adam was more surprised by the fact that Findlay didn't appear to have changed much than he was to find that he was now the editor. He'd filed a memory of Findlay as being old, but even now he couldn't have been more than sixty at most. He supposed that at the age of sixteen anyone over twenty-five was practically decrepit.

He gave the receptionist his name and she picked up her

phone and spoke into it briefly. In his office Findlay looked over in surprise. 'He says to go ahead,' the receptionist said as she hung up.

'Adam,' Findlay said, as he emerged shaking his head. One or two people looked up from their work. 'As I live and breathe. Now what are you doing here?' He smiled warmly and held out his hand. The smell of cigarette smoke and beer clung to his clothes, along with a whiff of malt whisky.

'I wasn't sure whether I'd find you here or at the pub on the corner,' Adam said, as they shook hands.

Findlay smiled ruefully. 'Times change, Adam.' He gestured to his name on the door. 'The things we give up in the pursuit of power, eh? Sometimes I wonder if it's worth it.'

Turning towards the rest of the room he raised his voice and addressed the few people busy at their work. 'See here, all you lot. This fella here started out on this very paper when he was just a lad at school. Now he's a big shot journalist all the way from London. He's worked for all the big papers, isn't that so, Adam? Just remember that when you're complaining about covering the next meeting of the Women's Institute.'

A number of faces gazed at him with expressions ranging from mild curiosity to bored resentment. He caught the eye of the young woman he'd noticed earlier who looked up from her screen, smiled briefly and went back to her work.

'How do you know so much about me?' Adam asked when they were sitting in Findlay's office.

Findlay lit a cigarette, inhaling deeply. 'I read a feature in one of the Sunday papers a few years ago. When I saw the name I had a feeling it must be you. I've kept an eye out since then.' Through the haze of cigarette smoke his gaze was shrewd. 'I've always found it interesting, the field you chose to specialize in. What would you call that?'

'Investigative journalism?'

Findlay smiled. 'Aye, it is that. But it seems to me a lot of what I've seen has some common themes, Adam. Like the story you did about the wee girl that disappeared down in Suffolk a few years ago. I've often wondered what started you down that particular path.'

'Who knows?'

'Aye, who indeed?' Findlay echoed thoughtfully. 'Anyway, I take it this is no' a social call. What can I do for you?'

'I'm looking into something,' Adam said, grateful for the change of subject. 'To do with the protest at Castleton Wood.'

'I wouldnae've thought there was much there to interest you. That kind of thing happens all the time these days.'

'It's for a human interest feature, bit of a change.'

Findlay studied him for a second. 'Is that so?'

Ignoring the faint scepticism Adam said, 'I'm trying to track down somebody who was involved in the protest during the summer, and I heard she may have talked to a reporter from the *Courier*. I was hoping to speak to whoever it was. I imagine you've covered what's been going on over there.'

'We have, though not for a wee while now. I expect we'll send someone out there when the eviction starts though. I had a lass by the name of Janice Munroe on that one. She's from Dumfries. Hold on a minute.' He went to the door and called out to somebody. 'Janice? Would you come in here?' Turning back to Adam he said, 'She's good this one, Adam. I don't expect I'll be able to keep her long.'

The young woman with bleached hair that Adam had noticed earlier appeared at the door. Findlay did the introductions and they shook hands. She was in her early twenties, with a sharp inquisitive gaze that matched her features.

'Adam here would like to talk to you about the protest over at Castleton Wood.'

'If you can spare me some time?' Adam added, smiling.

She looked him over coolly. 'What is it you want to know?'

'I heard you might have spoken to somebody there called Jane Hanson?'

'Really? And where did you hear that?'

'From a girl at the camp.'

'I see. And what if I did speak to this Jane person?'

Findlay chuckled. 'Janice doesnae like to give away her secrets, Adam, as you can see.'

Janice shot her boss a sour look and stuck her chin out obstinately. 'Listen, I've spent a lot of time on that story. I'm no' about to just hand it over to some guy from London I never met before.'

'Er, look,' Adam said, getting the feeling there was something going on that he was missing. 'All I'm interested in is what you spoke to Jane Hanson about. If you're worried that I might muscle in on a story you're working on, you needn't be.'

She rolled her eyes. 'And I'm supposed to just take your word for that am I? Do I really look that gullible?'

Adam turned to Findlay in an appeal for help, but Findlay held up his hands. 'Don't look at me, Adam. She doesnae listen to me.'

'At least let me buy you a drink? So we can talk about it,' Adam said.

She thought it over, wondering, it seemed, what advantage there was to her. 'Alright,' she said finally. 'I'll come, but I can't do it just now. About an hour? Do you know the pub on the corner?'

He said that he did. When she had gone, he said to Findlay, 'What was that all about?'

'Youth, Adam.' He sighed. 'Enthusiasm and a burning sense of justice. Qualities that at my age have to be tempered by hard facts. I'm too old to risk losing my job, you might try explaining that to her. It's her story so I'll leave it to Janice to tell you about it, if she decides to trust you.'

Findlay showed him to the door. 'If it turns out that your interest and hers are mutual, you won't forget her if you make anything of it?'

'Of course not.'

'It was good to see you again, Adam. Come and see me again before you go back to London. We'll have a drink together.'

'I'll do that,' Adam promised. 'And thanks.'

Janice Munroe arrived at the pub an hour and thirty-five minutes later. She peered around the mostly empty room and when she saw Adam at a table by the window she came over and sat down.

'Sorry if I'm late,' she said, though she didn't sound it. 'I had to get something finished for tomorrow's edition.'

'Anything interesting?'

She pulled a face. 'Depends if you call a fish and chip shop fire interesting.'

'I get the feeling you don't.'

'Let's just say it's no' the sort of thing I had in mind when I decided to spend three years at university.' She grinned then, and her face changed. Suddenly she didn't seem quite so defensive. 'The guy that owns it forgot to turn off the fat fryer. At least that was his story. I think he just wants the insurance money so he can leave his wife.' She shook her head. 'This woman kept telling me what an idiot her husband was and the poor guy was standing right there beside her. I felt sorry for him. I sort of hope he gets away with it.'

Adam smiled, not sure if she was kidding. 'And will he?'

'I doubt it. I talked to the insurance investigator this morning. He said the guy waited until the fire was properly alight before he called the fire brigade. A neighbour said he was standing in the street watching.' She shook her head again. 'Mebbe his wife's right. Mebbe he is an idiot.'

Adam decided that despite her prickly exterior, he liked Janice Munroe. Her blend of humour and cynicism appealed to him. He asked what she'd like to drink, and went to the bar where he told the barman to make the whisky she'd asked for a large one.

'Thanks,' she said when he came back, and raising her glass took a sip. 'So. You used to work for the *Courier*?'

'Only in the holidays when I was at school.'

She looked surprised. 'You're from this area?'

'Not really.' He explained his history briefly. 'And what about you? What brings you here?'

She shrugged. 'This job for a start. I did media studies and journalism at university then I came here eighteen months ago as a general dogsbody. Now I get to cover the big stories, like chip shops that burn to the ground.' She made a wry face. 'Which paper do you work for?'

'I don't. I'm freelance. I do mostly in-depth features.'

'Really? And what are you doing in this neck of the woods, Mr Turner?' She fixed him with her gaze, and he knew if he was going to get anything out of her at all he was going to have to be straight with her.

'I talked to someone called Ellie at the protest camp who thinks Jane Hanson was working on some idea that could stop the development there going ahead. An idea she got from talking to a journalist from the *Courier*. Which I assume was you. I'd like to know what that idea was.'

'That tells me *what* you're interested in, but not why.'

'It's complicated.'

'It's lucky I've had a university education then, isn't it?'

'You know that's not what I meant.'

'Then what did you mean?'

Adam grinned despite himself. He wondered where Janice had grown up and pictured her in some high-rise flat in a grim area of Dumfries where if you didn't learn to stand your ground fast you quickly became a victim. 'Okay, does the name Ben Pierce mean anything to you?'

'Aye. He was the young guy Jane was going around with. He was killed in an accident a while back.'

'Right. Well, Ben's sister isn't convinced the accident happened the way the police think it did.' He outlined what Helen Pierce had told him about her brother, and also what he'd learned since he'd been in Castleton.

'So, you think the sister is right?'

'I think it's strange that Ben was driving. If what Helen says is true, why didn't one of the others drive? I'd also like to know where they'd been that night, and why they didn't leave the area after the attack on the camp.'

Janice took a packet of cigarettes out of her bag and lit one. 'Do you smoke?'

'No thanks. So, the bottom line is I need to know what Jane and the others were doing because it might have some bearing on what happened that night.'

'What kind of bearing?'

'I don't know yet,' he admitted. 'At the moment I'm just digging around.'

Janice tapped her cigarette ash into the ashtray, her expression deeply thoughtful. 'Are you suggesting that what happened wasn't an accident at all?'

'I'm not suggesting anything.'

'You might though, if I tell you what I know.'

'Which is?'

'If I tell you, what happens then?'

'You mean if there's a story? What do you want?'

'I want first dibs on an exclusive.'

'What?' he said incredulously. 'And why should I do that?'

'Because I have something you're going to be very interested in, that's why.' She leaned forward across the table, her expression suddenly animated. Her tone became persuasive. 'Look, it doesnae matter to you. You said yourself you only do in-depth features. I just want the headlines. Something like this could be big.'

'Hold on. Something like what?'

'Listen, Mr Turner. I'm no' stupid. We wouldnae be sitting here having this conversation if you didn't suspect that Helen Pierce was right about her brother. And if she was, then mebbe that crash wasn't an accident. Mebbe somebody wanted it to look like it was. Somebody with a motive.'

'And you think you know who that might be?'

'I could give you a list.'

She picked up her glass and sipped her Scotch, and he knew he wouldn't get another word out of her until they agreed terms. He couldn't blame her; she was looking for the break that would get her out of Carlisle, off the *Courier* and maybe onto a national paper.

'Okay,' he agreed. 'It's a deal. You get the exclusive headline.'

'There's one other thing. You can't mention any of this to Findlay.'

That much he'd already figured out. 'Alright. At least I won't without your okay.'

Suddenly she looked wary. 'How do I know I can trust you?'

'The same way I know I can trust you.'

She considered that and smiled wryly. 'Fair enough. Okay. I did talk to Jane a couple of times. We had an agreement, which is partly why I'm being so cagey here. As you know, she wanted to stop the development, and I told her I thought we might be able to help each other. She was supposed to tell me everything she found out in return for the information I gave her. Only she went back to London without keeping her end of the bargain.' She gave him a sardonic smile. 'It's no wonder they say we journalists end up being cynical is it?'

'Constant exposure to human nature. So, how did you meet her?'

'At the camp. I was doing a story on the protest back in July and we got talking. You've been there, so you know the type up there. Eco-warriors and dropouts and the like. Well Jane wasnae like that, you know? She sort of surprised me that way, which is probably why I liked her. She thought they were wasting their time building tree houses and digging tunnels. Like it was only delaying the inevitable. She had a point too. That kind of protest hardly ever succeeds in the end.'

'Too many images of odd-looking people with rings through their noses and long hair living in burrows?' Adam said.

'Aye, something like that. Jane thought there had to be other ways of getting the public to back them. It just so happened that I thought I could help.'

'How?'

'Well, my boyfriend works for a guy called Frank Henderson, do you know who he is?'

Adam shook his head and took out his notepad. 'You mind?'

'Go ahead. Anyway, Frank Henderson used to be a building contractor. He owned one of the biggest firms around here. He's also a big fat bastard, and a member of the district council, plus he's on the planning committee.'

'Aha,' said Adam, beginning to see where this might be leading. 'Let me guess. This would be the committee that approved the Forest Havens development?'

'Aye. That was at the beginning of August, but I met Jane before then. Henderson has his finger in all kinds of pies these days. Earlier this year he broke his foot and couldn't drive himself, so my boyfriend Danny was working as his chauffer for a while. He has actually got a business degree, by the way, but he took the job because he thought it might be interesting being around someone like Henderson. And it was, though not for the reasons he'd imagined. This was back in June, around the time when Forest Havens made their initial planning application. Findlay had assigned the story to me so Danny knew all about it. So anyway, one day he drives Henderson to a hotel in Haltwhistle, where he meets a man for lunch, and later Danny overhears Henderson on the phone talking to his brother-in-law, who's another fat bastard by the name of Harry Cooke, and from this conversation it's clear that if the Forest Havens plan goes ahead Cooke's building company, which, surprise, surprise, used to belong to Henderson, will get part of the building contract.'

'And this is what you told Jane?' Adam asked.

'This was only the beginning. You see about a week later Danny and I were in a pub and we saw two men having a drink. I recognized one of them as the guy from Forest Havens who was handling negotiations with the estate. The other one was the guy Danny had seen having lunch with Henderson. I did some checking. It turned out this same guy had been lobbying all the members of the planning committee on behalf of Forest Havens.'

'Only you thought he was doing more than just lobbying?'

'Aye, that's the way it looked to me.'

'Had you talked to Findlay about all of this?' Adam asked.

'Of course. It was taking up a lot of my time, so I had to, and by then there was a lot of opposition to the scheme from various environmental groups so he let me go ahead to see what I could dig up.'

'Which was?'

'It turned out that if the committee passed the Forest Havens plan, apart from Henderson one other member of the committee had an interest in a firm that stood to win contracts, though it wasn't a provable interest. Of the other four on the committee two who'd started off opposed to the plan had suddenly changed their minds.'

'Meaning?'

'Meaning it seemed funny to me.'

'You thought they'd been bribed?' Adam suggested.

'Let's just say it was convenient.'

'Did the *Courier* print any of what you found out?'

'Uh-huh.' Janice shook her head. 'I didnae have any proof, and Findlay said I hadn't enough for him to stick his neck out. By then people knew I'd been nosing around and I think somebody put pressure on him to call me off. I cannae blame him I suppose.'

'So, when you met Jane, you saw your chance. You told her your suspicions and gave her everything you had.'

'Aye.'

'And the deal you made was that if she found proof of what you suspected she would share it with you? What made you think she could do any better than you?'

'Because it didn't matter who she pissed off. Nobody could fire her.'

'And did she find anything?'

Janice nodded sombrely. 'That's what really gets me, you know. I think she did. Only she wouldnae tell me what it was. Not until she had the evidence, which I'm pretty sure she believed she would get. And then, one day she up and left. Just like that. I went to the camp and somebody told me they thought she'd gone back to London. She was meant to be starting a new job there or something.'

'But Ben and the others stayed?'

'They'd gone too by the time I went there. At the time I assumed they'd gone back to London.'

'So, this was after the attack on the camp?'

Janice nodded. 'That's the last I heard from any of them. A couple of days later Ben and the other lads were killed.'

'What about Jane? Did she return your file?'

'No, and before you ask I didn't make a copy. I should have, but I didn't.'

'Pity,' he said. He wondered if this was a dead end. If Jane had found any kind of evidence of corruption, why had she returned to London? Perhaps in the end proof had eluded her. But, he reasoned, Ben must have known what she was doing. Was it possible that he and the others had stayed behind to continue the search? He told Janice what he was thinking.

'I suppose it's possible,' she said. 'There's another possibility of course.'

'Which is?'

'Jane found proof, and then somebody bought her off.'

'That would explain her sudden departure wouldn't it?' Adam agreed. 'What was the final planning committee vote by the way?'

'Four in favour and two against.'

'Give me the names of the committee members. Maybe I should talk to them myself. See what I can turn up.' He wrote down the six names that Janice gave him. 'Which ones voted for the development?'

Janice ticked them off on her fingers. 'Henderson of course.

Campbell. His daughter-in-law owns a painting firm, and I'll give you odds of ten to one she gets part of the contract when work starts up there. Then Carol Fraser and George Hunt. They're the two that were originally against the plan.'

'Do you know if Jane talked to any of these people?'

'I expect so. Their names were in the files I gave her.' She paused, frowning in thought. 'I wouldn't waste your time with Hunt. He's that rare breed in my opinion, a man of principle. He's just no' the type to take a bribe. He's a bit of a greenie at heart when it comes to this sort of thing.'

'But he voted for the development?'

'True. But I think in the end he decided the pros outweighed the cons as far as the local community's concerned.'

Adam put a question mark next to his name. 'What about Carol Fraser?'

Janice pursed her lips thoughtfully. 'I'm not sure about her. I've met her a few times, and to be honest I like her. She's always struck me as the sincere type, you know. She weighs up the issues and stands up for what she believes is right, and usually I'd agree with her. She stood as an independent at the last election and politically she's moderate, she's no' hung up on party dogma.'

'But?'

'At first she was dead set against the development. Her argument was that they could buy the estate and have their holiday park without building in the wood. Fair point too, everybody wins. But Forest Havens weren't interested. They insisted that all their parks are built in natural woodland or forest and this one had to be the same. In other words, our way or no way.'

'So, Carol Fraser gave in.'

'Aye. Somebody had to, I suppose. But it surprised me the way she did it. She didnae just give way. She started actively promoting the development.'

Adam put a question mark next to her name. He wasn't particularly surprised at the idea of corruption on the local council. Such things went on all the time one way or the other, but in this case if it could be proved it would certainly put an end to any plans for development. Clearly with a development of this size some people had plenty to lose.

They finished their drinks and Adam promised he'd stay in touch, and he also gave Janice his number in case she thought of anything else. 'I'll get somebody in London to see if they can track Jane down.'

Outside the pub Janice said, 'Supposing Jane did find some kind of proof of what was going on and she was bought off. Do you think Ben and the others might have found out, and that's why they stayed on?'

'Maybe.'

'Which could give somebody a motive for killing them to stop it getting out?'

'People have been murdered for a lot less.'

'But how does that explain the fact that Ben was driving? Or that he was drunk?'

Adam shook his head. He didn't have a clue what the answer was. 'First the why, then maybe the how will fall into place. One more thing before you go, the man who was acting as an intermediary between Forest Havens and the planning committee, what was his name?'

'A guy by the name of David Johnson. He owns a sawmill that has the contract for Castleton Wood, so he's no' exactly a disinterested party himself.' She stopped when she saw Adam's expression. 'What is it?'

'Nothing.'

'Do you know him?'

'I did once,' he admitted. 'But it was a long time ago.'

He promised again that he'd be in touch and left Janice on the corner watching him go, her expression deeply thoughtful.

When he reached his car Adam used his mobile to call Karen in London.

'I was wondering if I was ever going to hear from you,' she said, when she came on the line. 'How was your trip?'

'It was fine.'

'You found the place alright then?'

'Uh-uh,' he responded vaguely.

'And?'

'And I need you to do something for me.'

'I might have known this wasn't a social call. What is it?'

'You remember Helen said her brother came up here with a girl called Jane Hanson. I think they were at university together, but Helen should be able to fill you in. See if you can get hold of her can you, and get me her phone number. I need to talk to her.'

'Okay. Any particular reason?'

He told her about his visit to the protest camp and his conversation with Janice. 'If Jane was onto something, I'd like to know what it was.'

'If she was bought off she's hardly likely to tell you is she?'

'No, but maybe she wasn't bought off. Maybe she had to start a new job and she ran out of time.'

'But at any rate you think Helen is right about Ben?' Karen asked.

'Too early to say.'

She promised she would get back to him as soon as she had a number. There was a brief silence, and then she said, 'Are you okay? You sound strange.'

'I'm fine.'

Another silence, and then as if she'd just remembered she said, 'By the way, I've got news of my own. Nigel proposed.'

It took a second for what she'd said to sink in. 'You mean he asked you to marry him?'

'That's generally the idea. It's normal to offer congratulations, by the way.'

'Sorry.' He struggled to order his thoughts. 'You took me by surprise. Congratulations.' He tried to sound sincere, though even to his own ears there was a distracted ring to it. He was still thinking about what Janice had told him. That was partly it anyway.

'Actually, I haven't accepted yet. Not that you asked.'

'Oh.'

Neither of them spoke. It was a curious silence, as if each of them was waiting for the other to say something else.

'I'll let you know about Jane,' Karen said abruptly.

He started to thank her, but she had already hung up. He stared at his phone, and almost called her back, but what would he say? Perplexed, he gazed out of the window.

133

CHAPTER FOURTEEN

The lounge bar at the New Inn was quiet. A couple of old men sat over a table playing dominoes, occasionally sipping their pints, and the two couples from Birmingham were studying menus by the fireplace. Adam ordered a Scotch and picked up a bar menu, trying to decide if he was hungry. The man he'd met the night before joined him and ordered two roast specials and two fish and chips. He nodded to Adam and gestured to the menu he was looking at.

'Alright there. The food's not half bad here, you know.'

'I might get something later,' Adam said, unable to find anything to tempt him. 'How was the fishing today?'

'Not bad.' He turned towards his companions. 'Caught a few didn't we?' They nodded and murmured their agreement. 'There's a lake up on the fells. Thought we might try up there tomorrow.'

'Cold Tarn.'

'Eh?'

'It means Cold Lake. Tarn is lake.'

'Oh. You know it then?'

'I used to. I haven't been there for years though.'

'Tarn. I must remember that. The name's John, by the way. John Shields.'

'Adam Turner.'

Shields introduced his wife and the other couple, though Adam knew he'd struggle to remember all their names. He was invited to join them if he felt like it, but he thanked them and said he thought he'd go for a walk and work up an appetite, though he stayed and chatted while he finished his drink.

When he got outside he wondered if he should have taken them up on their offer and almost went back. The alternative was a solitary meal somewhere, and a cold wind blowing across the square made him rethink taking a walk. For a moment he toyed with the idea of phoning Angela but he didn't know what he would say to her, and besides what if David answered the phone? Instead he turned up his collar and with his shoulders hunched against the wind started across the square.

Halfway along the main street he paused outside a small pub called the Ship. A sign outside promised home-cooked food and through the thick glass of the window he could make out a room with a low ceiling and a blazing open fire at one end. He went inside and ordered a Scotch at the bar. The light was dim and a low hum of voices from the dozen or so people in the room added to the cosy atmosphere. He nodded to a man next to him and as he scanned the room he saw David sitting at a corner table with Graham and another man who had his back to the room. With a small shock of recognition Adam noted the black hair grown over the man's collar, the way he slouched in his chair with his legs splayed out in front of him and the curl of cigarette smoke rising around his head.

'Christ,' he muttered under his breath, which attracted a glance of mild surprise from the man next to him at the bar. For a second Adam considered leaving, but before the idea had even properly formed David glanced over and their eyes met. He looked even worse than he had the previous night, the shadows beneath his eyes making it look as if he hadn't slept much. The others, alerted by David's expression, turned towards him, and knowing he had no choice Adam made his way over. As he drew nearer a fleeting look of discomfort, guilt almost, flashed in Graham's expression and suddenly Adam had the feeling that they had been talking about him.

'I was just out for a walk,' he said when he reached their table. 'I thought I'd try the food here.' He nodded to Graham and David, annoyed that he'd felt he needed to explain himself, and then lastly turned to Nick. He hadn't changed much. He was still slightly built but wiry with it, his dark eyes narrowed and veiled in the smoke of his ubiquitous roll-ups so that he

135

appeared to wear the same faintly amused sneer that Adam remembered.

Adam started to offer his hand but changed his mind and nodded instead. 'Hello, Nick.'

The response was a barely perceptible nod in return. 'Never thought we'd see you back here again.' His tone carried an unpleasantly mocking innuendo.

'Never thought I'd be back.' He was struck by the tableau the three of them made. Still together after all these years, still united by not only friendship but by the bonds of a common experience that went even deeper. They had lived in this town for all of their lives. Nobody made a move to invite him to join them and Adam was suddenly conscious of his status as an outsider. He was reminded of the day when he'd first met them when they had stopped him on the road to the estate. He had never felt so alone as he had at that moment. The overwhelming sense of isolation that came from not belonging, and the threat that entailed as a consequence. He suddenly realized that he'd spent the years afterwards trying to become one of them, to fit in, and though he'd always thought it was Nick who'd barred his true acceptance, he was wrong. It had in fact been David, because he could have overruled Nick if he'd chosen to.

A sour taste rose in Adam's throat and he took a gulp of whisky to dispel it. A flash of old resentment flooded to the surface to replace his sense of discomfort. He turned to Graham.

'I'm glad I ran into you, I was planning on coming to see you in the morning anyway.'

'Oh?'

'There's something I wanted to ask you. I talked to some of the protesters up at the wood this morning. They told me their camp was attacked at the beginning of September. Some local vigilantes paid them a visit one night.'

'That's right, there was a bit of trouble about then.'

'A bit of trouble? Men with clubs beating the shit out of a bunch of kids in the middle of the night is a bit more serious than that isn't it? When I spoke to you yesterday didn't you say there had been the odd scuffle?'

136

'Maybe some of them did get carried away,' Graham admitted, looking uncomfortable.

'Odd choice of phrase for a policeman,' Adam noted. 'Sounds as if other than a bit of overenthusiasm you endorse that kind of thing.'

'That isn't what I meant,' Graham said angrily.

'No? So, were any of them arrested, these people who got a bit carried away?'

'We didn't hear anything about it until the next day.'

'But you must have had descriptions of them.'

'It was dark, Adam. And it all happened quickly. The descriptions we got were vague.'

'Was anybody even questioned?'

Graham stared at him, one hand clamped tightly around his pint glass. 'Like I said. The descriptions were vague.'

'But surely in an area like this you'd have some idea of who might do something like that,' Adam persisted. 'Or is beating kids up with clubs common around here these days?'

Up until then David had been listening without comment, but suddenly he broke in. 'For Christ's sake, Adam, don't believe everything they tell you.'

'What? You think they were making it up?'

'I'm just saying they know how to make a story interesting for the media, that's all.' He said the word media as if it brought an unpleasant taste to his mouth.

Adam turned back to Graham. 'Two of the boys who were killed in that car accident had injuries that they didn't get in the accident. According to the pathologist they happened a few days earlier. One of them had a cracked rib. She thought they might have been in a fight.'

'What of it?'

'Didn't you think it was likely they got those injuries when the camp was attacked?'

'I suppose they could have. I didn't really think about it.'

'Yes, the same thought had occurred to me,' Adam said scathingly.

'What the hell are you getting at?'

'Well, surely when Helen Pierce came up here and started asking questions it was enough to make you wonder, wasn't it? I mean, first two of those boys get beaten up by local thugs, then they end up dead because Ben, a kid who never got drunk, was off his face behind the wheel of a car he didn't even know how to drive. It's just a little strange, don't you think? Did you know they weren't living at the camp? They left after the attack. Weren't you even curious about where they'd been for the three days before they were killed? Or what they were doing on that road that night?'

'Dammit, Adam, I told you! There was no reason for me to wonder about anything. It was an accident!'

'And the vigilantes were just a coincidence were they? Seems to me that maybe whoever organized that little event could have been specifically trying to scare Ben and his friends away.'

'Why would anyone do that?'

'That's a good question. Maybe it has something to do with this Forest Havens development plan I've been hearing so much about.'

'What does that have to do with anything?'

'The company had to get planning permission before they went ahead didn't they? There are rumours that some of the planning committee members took a bit of persuading.'

The atmosphere around the table altered perceptibly. David paused in the act of lifting his whisky glass. 'Who the hell have you been talking to?'

'Actually it was a local journalist.'

'Janice Munroe,' David said bitterly. 'I forgot, you used to work at that bloody rag didn't you?'

'You know her then?'

'I know she was trying to make trouble, running around with a lot of half-cocked ideas that didn't hold water.'

'I thought she was pretty genuine. She had a lot of interesting things to say about some of the people with a vested interest in wanting the development to go ahead.'

'I take it by that you mean me.'

'Your name came up.'

'There's no law against lobbying for a point of view, as far as I know.'

'True. If that's as far as it goes. But if council members benefit personally from contracts associated with the development, it goes a bit beyond lobbying.'

'So that's what she told you was it? Did she also happen to mention that the paper hasn't printed a single suggestion of her bloody theories? And do you know why? Because there isn't a single shred of proof to support it, that's why! But then I don't suppose that would worry you, would it, Adam?' he added.

'Meaning?'

David lifted his pint and emptied it. 'Meaning I wonder what you're really doing here, Adam. Are you really here because of those kids, or did you come for some other reason?'

'I take it you're trying to make some kind of point here. Are you going to give me a clue or do I have to work it out for myself?'

'I think you know what I mean. I think you must be enjoying this. A chance to write something that'll make us all look like right bastards. Make it look as if the people who've lived around here all their lives don't give a sod about the countryside or the wood. Not like all your hippy friends, eh, Adam.'

'And why would I want to do that?'

David stared at him and shrugged. 'Maybe you've got an axe to grind.'

Adam emptied his glass and set it down. He hoped it didn't show that David's accusation about his motives had hit home more than he cared to admit. 'You think I'm here because of some kind of grudge, is that it? A chance to settle old scores?'

David's eye flicked towards Adam's leg. 'Am I right, Adam?'

'I hate to disappoint you, but there are more important issues here. Like what happened to those three boys for instance.'

'Nothing happened except they were in an accident. They drank too much and ran off a road they didn't know. For Christ's sake it happens all the time!'

'Except that in this case the boy who was supposed to be behind the wheel didn't either drink or drive.'

'According to who? Not the coroner.' David shook his head. 'But it doesn't matter what the coroner said does it? Or what anybody says come to that. Not if you're determined to pursue some conspiracy fantasy that bloody woman at the paper has fed you.'

'If it is a fantasy then nobody has anything to worry about, do they?' Adam said. 'By the way, since we're on the subject did you ever meet somebody called Jane Hanson?'

The question took David by surprise, as it was meant to. Adam watched his reaction, and for an instant he was sure the name had registered but then David met his eye with a blank look and when it was evident that he had no intention of responding one way or the other Adam shrugged.

'Just a thought.' He looked at them each briefly in turn, then nodded generally. 'Nice catching up with you all again.' As he went to the door he was conscious that he was limping slightly and when he glanced back he saw that Nick was watching him with a sardonic gleam in his eye.

'Welcome home, Adam,' he said.

CHAPTER FIFTEEN

He remembered waking up in hospital after they'd operated to save his leg. He remembered the agony of the drive back to town, the blood that soaked everything and the numbing cold that had seeped into his bones and made his teeth chatter. He'd faded in and out of consciousness, convinced in his few lucid moments that he was going to die.

He had survived though, and a week after emergency surgery he'd gone back into theatre for a second operation to repair his mangled knee. Two weeks after that he lay in bed with his leg hoisted in the air and covered from thigh to toe in plaster. David stood beside the window.

'How much longer will you be in here?' he asked.

'I don't know. Another week or two I think.'

David looked at his leg and shook his head. 'Christ,' he said.

'It wasn't your fault,' Adam told him, as he had a dozen times already.

'Of course it was my fault. I shot you for fuck's sake! I could've killed you.'

'Well, you didn't, but now I know what it feels like to be a deer I don't think I'll eat venison again.'

'I should have made sure,' David insisted.

'Listen,' Adam said. 'It was an accident.'

David, however, couldn't meet his eye. He stared out of the window for ten minutes before he spoke again. 'Nick and Graham said to say hello, by the way.'

Yeah right, Adam thought. Graham had been in to visit once, but Nick hadn't, and never would.

The doors at the end of the ward swung open and Angela came back with fresh water in a vase for the flowers she'd brought with her. She wore jeans and a thick rollneck sweater and her cheeks were still pink from the cold.

'Got some,' she said. Through the window the city huddled under a leaden sky. The snow that had fallen a few days ago had partially melted and then frozen again and was now banked beside the roads in dirty piles. 'I was talking to the nurse. The young one. She said you've been sleeping much better this week.'

'Sometimes I wake up, but they give me something for the pain if I need it.'

She fished in her bag and produced some magazines and fruit she'd brought from the shop. 'Did you finish that book I brought you?'

'Yes. Thanks. It's over there.'

She looked in the cupboard where he pointed. 'I'll take it back to the library. Do you want me to get something else?'

'Thanks.'

She started talking about school and the shop, and he half listened to her, but mostly he just watched her. He could have reached out and held her hand, but something held him back. Perhaps it was David looking on from the other side of the bed.

'We should think about going,' David said eventually. 'We'll miss the bus.'

'I suppose so.' Angela picked up her coat. 'I'll see you next week. I'll ring your mum and she can tell me if there's anything you need. Is she coming today?'

'Later, I think.'

'Okay. Well, we better go.' Quickly she bent down and kissed his cheek. 'Bye.'

'Bye.'

David glanced away. 'See you later, Adam.'

Adam watched them leave. The doors at the end of the ward swung closed behind them. They would take the lift down, and then cross the entrance hall to the main doors. He imagined them stepping outside into the cold grey afternoon, and hurrying to the bus stop. Then sitting together on the bus for the ride home.

The young nurse on duty came by and smiled at him. 'Everything alright then?' She straightened his bed and moved the chairs back into place. 'She's nice. Is she your girlfriend?' He didn't answer, but the nurse didn't seem to notice. She smoothed the covers on his bed. 'Won't be long and you'll be home again.'

Adam kept thinking about the first time that David had come to visit after the accident. Like today he'd kept repeating that he was sorry and that it had been an accident. He'd said it often enough, and with the same insistent note of desperate persuasion that Adam had begun to wonder exactly which of them David was trying to convince.

Kyle and his mother came later, and asked the usual questions about how he was feeling, unloading books, taking ones he'd finished. More fruit. There was a short silence and his mother glanced meaningfully at Kyle, who took his cue.

'We spoke to your doctor yesterday, Adam. The last operation hasn't been a great success, I'm afraid. Your leg's healing quite well, but left the way it is you won't have a great deal of mobility.' He paused. 'You might never walk again without crutches, or at least a cane.'

It didn't come as a total surprise. He'd seen enough huddled doctors and nurses to be able to read their expressions. At least they weren't going to amputate, which had been his secret fear.

'There is an alternative though,' Kyle went on. 'I'm afraid it wouldn't be very pleasant for you. But the outcome could be much better in the long run. It would mean another operation, perhaps several over time.'

'How long?'

Kyle and his mother exchanged glances. 'Perhaps six months to a year.'

That long. He tried to hide his dismay from them. 'I'd have to stay here?'

'No,' his mother said quickly. 'You'd only be in hospital for the operations and for a little while afterwards. But you'd have to come in for physiotherapy every day. Of course you couldn't manage that on your own, and there's school to think of.'

They had thought it all through. He listened as they outlined their plan, which was that he and his mother would stay in Carlisle

143

close to the hospital during the week. The physio would be for several hours each day and travelling backwards and forwards wasn't practical. At weekends they would go back to the Forge. He tried to listen to it all, but after he'd gotten the gist of it he couldn't concentrate.

'Do you want some time to think about it, Adam?'

He came to with a start. Kyle and his mother were looking at him with concern etched in their expressions and he realized they had been waiting for his answer. For how long? He wasn't sure. A minute? Ten?

'No, it's okay,' he said. 'I'll do it.'

Kyle offered a stoic 'Well done'. His mother kissed his forehead. 'It's the right decision, Adam. In the long run. You'll see.'

His life during the next eight months altered completely. Each day between operations, he went from school to the room on the ground floor of the hospital to undergo physio. He grew to hate the final walk on crutches down the long corridor with its green walls and brown polished tile floor. He passed eighteen doors along the way. Ten on one side and eight on the other. The rubber tips of his crutches made a squeaking sound with every laboured step he made. His physiotherapist was a woman from Glasgow called Amy. She began every session by ordering him to lie on the rubber mat where she manipulated his leg in a series of bends and stretches that lasted for twenty minutes. He had to clench his jaw against the pain. All the time she talked in a matter-of-fact manner about what they were doing. Now and then she glanced at his face and if she saw beads of perspiration on his forehead and tears in his eyes she offered soft words of encouragement, but she never, ever felt sorry for him or allowed him to feel sorry for himself. She asked him once how the accident had happened, though she must have known. After that she never mentioned it again.

After the stretches came the parallel bars, where he tried to walk their length while taking some of the weight on his arms. And then there were machines designed for resistance training to strengthen his muscles. Progress was achingly slow and by the end of every session he was exhausted from the effort of both the exercise and trying not to give into the pain.

'That's good,' Amy used to say. 'I think we've made a wee bit of progress today, Adam.' Then she'd smile and say she would see him again the next day. And so it went on, day in day out. School and then physio, and then back to the flat where he and his mother were living for something to eat, followed by more schoolwork and another hour of exercise before bed and an exhausted sleep.

Sunday was his only day off and the day when Angela came to visit. She came alone. David came during the week, though his visits grew steadily more infrequent.

In the spring Adam took his exams at school. In July Amy told him his physio sessions were finished. She advised him to walk as much as possible. He still needed a cane, but in time, if he kept up the stretches and walked every day, his leg would heal. A week later he and his mother moved back to the Forge.

He'd been home for three weeks when Kyle said that he had to go into town for a few things and suggested Adam go with him. They were in the kitchen, sitting at the breakfast table on a Saturday morning. Kyle was looking over the top of his paper, while Adam's mother cleared the table.

'Yes, why don't you, Adam?' she said.

'I don't think so. Thanks anyway.' He saw the glances they exchanged, though they didn't press the issue. He hadn't seen David for weeks.

Angela came the following day after she'd finished at the shop. He walked along the road to meet her, partly for the exercise and partly because he wanted to be away from the house. He was sitting on the fence when she came riding her bike between the rows of chestnuts that flanked the road through the estate. She didn't see him at first and as he watched her he was reminded of the day two years earlier when he'd sat on the bank of the river as she walked barefoot in the water.

She smiled and waved when she finally saw him. 'I didn't see you there.'

'I was waiting for you.'

As they looked at one another, her smile faltered uncertainly. He suggested they go for a walk.

'Alright.'

They climbed the fence and walked through the wood towards one of the main paths. He spent a lot of his time walking there now. He'd learnt to recognize the trees. The smooth grey trunks of the beech, the gnarled oaks and huge spreading limes along with alder, holly and elm.

They chatted for a while, and then fell silent. The wood was full of the sound of twittering birds and sunlight filtered through the leaves and splashed on the ground in grassy glades.

'I've been accepted at Warwick University,' Adam said eventually.

Angela was quiet, thinking about this. 'When do you go?' she said at last.

'In a few weeks.'

She looked at him in surprise. She must have realized that he'd known for months.

'There are facilities there I can use. A pool and gym,' he explained.

He stopped, and as they faced one another he sensed that she was struggling with something she wanted to say. He went on quickly with what he'd rehearsed earlier. 'Listen, we might as well accept that it isn't meant to be, don't you think? Between us, I mean.'

Her eyes widened. 'What do you mean?'

'I mean I'll be at Warwick and you'll be here. And afterwards I'll probably try for a job in London.' He shrugged. 'Not a great basis for a relationship is it?'

He looked into her eyes, trying to gauge her reaction. He still harboured a faint hope that he was wrong. He saw confusion, and surprise. Though he hadn't planned what he said next, he couldn't let her go without being certain.

'Unless you've changed your mind about staying here for ever that is.'

She smiled sadly. 'Adam . . .' she began.

He cut her off. 'It's alright. I didn't really think you would. Do you mind if we go back? My knee's starting to hurt and I haven't got any pills with me.' Before she could object he turned and started back the way they'd come.

A week later he was out walking when he stopped to sit in the grass near the river. His knee was aching and he leaned with his back against a tree and massaged it the way Amy had taught him, listening to the faint sound of gurgling water. After a while he must have dozed off and when he woke it was to the murmur of voices. On the far bank Angela and David came into view, walking hand in hand. He couldn't hear what they were saying but he was struck by how at ease they appeared together. As he watched them, Angela laughed at something David said and punched his arm. He caught her hand, and pulled her around to face him. His hands slipped to her waist and he pulled her close.

Adam didn't move until they had passed by and were lost from sight. By the time he got home his knee was swollen and he was in severe pain. His mother took one look at him and ushered him into a chair.

'Adam, you're pale. What is it?'

'Nothing. I just overdid it a little.'

She fetched his pills but he shook his head.

'I don't want any.'

'But they'll help you.'

'No. I'll be fine, I just need to rest,' he insisted.

Upstairs in his room he lay down. The pain in his knee grew worse, so that it felt like a hot blade cutting through flesh and bone. It filled his mind, mercifully preventing him from thinking about anything else.

CHAPTER SIXTEEN

In the morning Adam was up early and for once he didn't eat alone. John Shields and his wife and friends were already sitting at a table that was practically groaning under the weight of enormous cooked breakfasts.

'Grand day,' Shields said, forking half a sausage into his mouth, which he washed down with a gulp of tea.

Outside it was, as he'd said, a grand day. The sun was rising into a pale clear blue sky, and a light frost dusted the grass. Adam chatted with the four over coffee and toast, offering the occasional comment as they discussed the local scenery and fishing. When they rose to leave he wished them luck. 'Try the southern end,' he advised when Shields said they were heading for the lake. 'There's a kind of rocky promontory that sticks out from the shore. You can't miss it. It used to be a good spot.'

'Right then. Southern end you say? We'll give that a try.'

After breakfast Adam phoned the district council offices in Brampton. Neither George Hunt nor Carol Fraser was available, their council roles being part time, however, the woman he spoke to gave him a contact number for each of them. He tried Hunt first, who agreed to see him the following morning if he could arrive early, but when he spoke to Carol Fraser she told him she would be in the council offices that morning and if he could be there by nine-thirty she could spare him half an hour. Before he left he looked up Angela's number and called her. After his run-in with David the night before he was half expecting her to hang up on him, but in fact she sounded pleased to hear from him.

'Adam, I was just thinking about you. I still feel bad about dinner the other night.'

'Well, you could make it up to me if you like.'

'Oh, how?'

'You could let me take you to lunch somewhere today.' Though he tried to make the invitation sound as casual as possible, just one old friend to another, he wasn't sure either of them entirely believed it. She hesitated before she agreed.

'Great, I'll pick you up around one.'

The district council was housed in a red sandstone building behind the main street of Brampton. Adam asked for Carol Fraser at the desk and when she appeared a few minutes later his first impression was that she was younger than he'd expected. He put her at around his own age, somewhere in her mid-thirties. When they shook hands her smile was friendly and direct.

'Thanks for seeing me at such short notice,' he said.

'I'm normally in for an hour or two, so it's no problem. Easier to meet here than for you to come all the way out to the farm.'

'You live on a farm?'

She opened the door to an office and flipped on a light switch. 'My husband and I.' She pulled a face. 'Not that we have much to do these days. We lost our herd in a foot-and-mouth outbreak two years ago.'

'I'm sorry. That must have been tough.'

'You could say that. It's not an uncommon story around here I'm afraid, but we're luckier than some. I know of people who'd begun to restock only to lose their herd again. At least that hasn't happened to us. But of course without animals we're not much of a dairy farm.'

'How long before you can start again?'

She shrugged. 'Perhaps another year. Of course we were compensated, but the money doesn't last for ever.'

She gestured for him to take a seat and she went around one of two desks in the room. 'Sorry it's a bit crowded. We share offices. So, how can I help you? On the phone you mentioned the development at Castleton Wood.'

Briefly he explained that he was a journalist and he was doing a story on the protest. 'I'm interested in the background to the original proposal. I understand that prior to planning permission approval being granted you were opposed to it?'

'Initially, yes,' she agreed.

'But you changed your mind?'

She regarded him with faint suspicion. 'If you mean did I wake up one morning and simply switch horses on a whim, Mr Turner, then the answer to your question is no.'

'But you did change your mind,' he said, unbowed by the reproof in her tone. 'In fact, didn't you become an outspoken supporter of the plan?'

'Yes, and that was because I eventually realized that to vote against it would not be in the best interests of the community.'

'But you didn't feel that way initially?' he insisted.

'Look, Mr Turner, I was never opposed to the plan per se. How could I object to something that would create jobs and indirect employment in an area that's quite frankly had the arse kicked out of it in recent years? I had hoped that Forest Havens could be persuaded to amend their plans to exclude building cabins within Castleton Wood. I argued strenuously for that change, unfortunately I was not successful.'

'So, that's when you decided to support the plan?'

'It is. Much as I deplore the destruction of part of the wood, sometimes it's necessary to compromise.'

'And no doubt the people lobbying for Forest Havens put their case strongly.'

'Of course.'

'And you met with these people?'

'Naturally.'

'Was David Johnson one of them?'

'Yes, as a matter of fact.'

Up until that point Adam would have gone along with Janice Munroe's assessment of Carol Fraser. She had a direct and open manner that he liked, and nothing she'd said had carried even the suggestion of a false note. But at the mention of David's name he sensed a reaction. Maybe it had been nothing more than a fractional narrowing of her eyes that made her seem at once more guarded, though in an instant it was gone.

'Councillor, are you aware of rumours that were circulating

earlier this year that certain members of the planning committee may have had a personal interest in wishing to see this development go ahead?'

Adam watched her carefully, but she only offered a wry smile. 'There are always those kinds of rumours in local politics, Mr Turner.'

'Do you give them credence in this case?'

'In terms of brown paper envelopes stuffed with cash? I don't think so.'

'In some other way then?'

'These situations aren't always black and white,' she said. 'Who's to say that two people sitting side by side at a masonic dinner don't discuss a particular issue, and without anything being said, a kind of understanding is reached.'

'Are you saying that happened?'

'I'm saying that I'm sure it does happen. I doubt that anyone could be so naïve as to think it doesn't. As to whether it's corruption or not, who can say?' She shrugged philosophically. 'I can tell you one thing though.'

'Which is?'

'I'm not a freemason.' She smiled disarmingly. 'You know the media have tended to take the side of the protesters, but I think it's a little unfair. The people in this district are used to tough times but there's a limit to anyone's endurance. I sympathize with the protesters but believe me, local people care about the environment in a way that many city people never seem to be able to understand. After all, the countryside is their way of life.'

In other circumstances, Adam thought, he might have taken exception to this rosy view of country folk. If they cared so much, he wondered privately, how come that prior to foot-and-mouth wiping out their stock some of them had no qualms about chronically overgrazing the fells in pursuit of European subsidies. But he kept his mouth shut and a smile on his face, and when the councillor asked if he had seen a model of the planned development he said he hadn't but that he would like to.

Carol Fraser led the way up the stairs and into a large room domi-nated by a long table surrounded by chairs. The model stood on a separate table at one end of the room. It had been commissioned by Forest Havens, she explained. It depicted Castelton Wood much as it had always looked, except that in the northern part where the protest camp currently was there was a series of rustic buildings and cabins nestled snugly among the trees. To the east the Hall stood in pristine grounds, and much of the farmland was converted to rolling fairways and an artificial lake. What remained was depicted as petting farms with sheep and goats and rabbits. Carol Fraser pointed to another cluster of buildings.

'This will be a working dairy farm where people can spend their holidays learning what it's like to really live in the country.'

Her eyes danced merrily with sharp-edged amusement. Small figures in the farmyard created a sunny, idyllic scene. There were people forking hay, having picnics in the grass, bringing in the cows for milking. Even the animals seemed to be smiling. There wasn't a speck of cow shit in sight.

'Very impressive,' Adam commented drolly.

'Compromise, Mr Turner. Life is all about compromise.'

He thought he detected a faint wistful note in her tone. He looked at the model again. At the northern edge of the wood where it ran close to the river something struck him as wrong. It took him a moment to realize what it was. The boundary of the development appeared to be marked by the river itself, separating it from a copse and the bottom end of town. The cottages where Nick had once lived and where he'd encountered the strange girl the day before were missing. In their place another rustic-type building stood by the river and small model boats were tied up against a jetty.

'What's this?' he asked.

'The boathouse. The plan is to have canoes and rowing boats for the holiday-makers to take on the river.'

'But that land isn't part of the estate is it?'

'No, the company negotiated separately to buy that, I believe.'

'Do you know who the owner was?'

'A local man I think. I don't remember his name.'

'Allen? Nick Allen?'

'Actually I think that was it.' She looked at him questioningly. 'Does it matter?'

'It might,' he answered, but despite her evident curiosity, he didn't elaborate.

When they left, Councillor Fraser walked with him down the stairs. He thanked her for her time and she told him that if he needed anything else he should contact her.

'There is one other thing I wanted to ask you,' he said. 'Have you ever met somebody called Jane Hanson? She was at the protest camp during the summer.'

She creased her brow in thought. 'No, I don't think so.'

She held his gaze, and shook his hand, but she couldn't conceal a subtle change in her eyes. He left with the definite feeling that Jane's name had struck some chord with her, though evidently it was something she preferred to keep to herself.

He drove the long way back from Brampton taking the Geltsdale road, which cut through part of the forest above the valley before descending towards Castleton. He'd vaguely recognized a description of the spot where the accident had happened from the police report. It was at the bottom of a hill that ended in a deceptive curve. The road had originally been built by cutting into the hillside, and later the forestry commission had bought the land. Now, pines towered over the road on one side while on the other there was a steep drop.

He parked and got out where the car had left the edge. A trail of broken saplings marked its passage down the hill and further on a mature tree bore a deep gouge in its trunk and beyond that, perhaps a hundred feet further, he thought he could see where the wreck had finally come to rest.

Adam stood there for several minutes, trying to imagine being trapped in a car as it plummeted off the road at night. For a few seconds it would have been airborne, a deceptive sense of defying gravity before the jolting crash as it hit the ground.

He started to climb down. It was even steeper than it looked from the road and the thick layer of pine needles on the ground was slippery underfoot. After a couple of minutes he paused and peered back towards the road. It seemed like a long way. He started down again, but as he found a foothold and reached towards a low branch for support he started to slide. The branch whipped through his fingers as he scrabbled for purchase, his weight precariously balanced. He saw a vision of himself tumbling head over heels in a headlong plunge to his certain destruction. What a stupid way to go, he thought, and then instinctively leaned his weight backwards to try and slow his inevitable fall. He dug his heels in and reached out for handholds as he flew past. They whipped through his fingers and lacerated his palms. He bumped and slid over roots and rocks and thin branches whipped across his face. The ground tore at his nails and it felt as if he was picking up speed with every moment. The world became a blur of green and brown. Rocks pounded his kidneys and fear welled up in his throat. It occurred to him that he could easily plummet onwards for hundreds of feet until eventually he smashed his skull. At almost that instant the ground began to level and he felt himself slowing down. He renewed his efforts to control his fall until finally his heels dug into the soft ground and then with a jarring thump he collided with a half-rotten stump. A sharp pain knifed through his knee and made him yelp with surprised agony.

He sat up slowly and probed the old injury, wincing at each stab of pain. Looking back towards the road he saw that he hadn't fallen as far as he'd thought. The premonitions of death had been premature, though when he tried to stand he had to hang onto a tree for support. He tested his weight, relieved to find that his leg wasn't broken. He'd expected blood and torn tissue, but when he examined his knee the old scars were intact.

He'd ended up where the ground briefly flattened before falling away again in a gentler slope. Shards of glass among the pine needles and the odd piece of debris proved this was also where the car had come to a stop. A large tree where it had finally come to rest bore faded blue paint marks, and when he poked around in the undergrowth he found a sock and a pair of broken silver-rimmed spectacles, from which one lens was missing.

He sat down with his back resting against the tree, his knee throbbing painfully. There was something poignant about the glasses, he thought, perhaps because they symbolized a kind of vulnerability. He turned them over in his hands. It was quiet. Sunlight filtered through the trees except where it beamed down in slanting shafts through the gloom. It was cool and dim, a kind of permanent forest twilight. He wasn't sure why he'd wanted to come here. It wasn't so much in the hope of finding something the police had missed, but maybe because he was looking for a sense of feeling. He tried to imagine the last few moments of the accident. The headlights piercing the night, then illuminating the trees below as the car tipped nose forward. The sudden scream of the engine as the wheels spun without resistance. The three people trapped inside would have been disoriented, flung about as the car hit the ground and rolled. He imagined their cries of terror and pain as flesh met unyielding metal, as the doors popped open and the two boys in the back were flung out to their deaths.

And afterwards, there would have been silence. Perhaps the ping of metal from the cooling engine. Maybe an unconscious groan from Ben as he slowly bled to death, his friends already staring sightless into the night sky.

Why had Ben been driving that night? Despite everything his sister had said the evidence was clear. Perhaps the question he ought to be asking himself, Adam thought, was what could have made Ben act in a manner that was so out of character? Had it in fact been the combination of alcohol and his medication distorting his judgement? It was possible. But then why had he been drinking in the first place? His mind wandered. What had they known? Where had they been the night they were killed, and where were they going? Had they found proof that would have exposed corruption in the council and stopped the development?

Lots of questions, and amid them all he kept seeing David's face. He had lobbied the planning committee. Personally he had a lot to lose. The other night at dinner he had lost his temper, and he'd been drinking heavily. He had a drinker's face and also the shadowed eyes of the insomniac. A man troubled by his conscience perhaps?

Adam began to get a sense that there was something here, something right in front of his eyes that was crucial to his understanding of what had happened that night, and he hoped that if he waited long enough it would be revealed. But whatever it was eluded him. There was only the gloomy twilight world beneath the pines, a few splinters of glass and a broken pair of glasses.

In the end he got painfully to his feet and started to make his way back to the road.

*　　*　　*

The climb was slow and painful. He was forced to practically crawl, putting most of his weight on his good knee. Every few minutes he paused and when he peered towards the road it seemed he'd made no progress at all. By the time he'd reached halfway he was sweating and dazed with pain. Once again he looked up, and this time he realized with a start that there was a figure standing up there, silhouetted by the light behind.

The figure didn't move, and it occurred to Adam that he hadn't been seen. 'Hello,' he shouted. 'I'm hurt. Do you have a rope?' His voice seemed to be muffled, swallowed by the trees around him. There was no response, so he tried again. 'Can you hear me up there?'

He waited, then raised an arm and waved, but he already knew the gesture was futile. Whoever was there remained eerily still, watching him. Adam experienced a tiny prick of unease. Suddenly without having said a word or made a gesture, the figure turned and vanished. Adam waited for him to come back but when he didn't he wasn't surprised. Then he heard a sound he couldn't identify, two sharp cracks a few seconds apart, followed perhaps twenty seconds afterwards by the sound of an engine. In a few moments it faded and was gone.

It took him another forty minutes to finally emerge onto the road and when he hobbled over to his Porsche he stared at the smashed headlights, understanding now what the sound he'd heard was. His first reaction was anger at the senseless vandalism, but as he thought about it he decided that perhaps it wasn't senseless. He looked again at the headlights. The intended message took on an ominous tone.

CHAPTER SEVENTEEN

Adam gave a couple of quick blasts on the horn to announce his arrival. The door opened and as Angela came out of the house she noticed the broken headlights.

'Sorry, I can't get out,' he said, and leaned over to open the door.

'What happened?' she said, when she got in.

'Somebody trying to tell me something, I think.'

'Tell you what?'

'That I'm not welcome perhaps.' He explained what had happened earlier. 'I suppose it could have been worse. I've been thinking about it. There was something about the way whoever was up there just stood watching me. I get the feeling he was thinking about doing more than smashing up my lights.'

Angela stared at him as she struggled to make sense of what he was saying. 'Why would anyone do that? What were you doing up there anyway?'

'I wanted to see for myself where the accident happened. As to why, I don't know yet.' He told her briefly about his visit to the protest camp, and also about Janice Munroe's suspicions of council corruption, though he didn't mention David's name.

'I can't believe this,' she said. 'You're saying that those lads had some kind of proof of all this?'

'I'm saying it's a theory, nothing more. I think they were probably asking questions and nosing around. Did you know a bunch of people armed with clubs went to the camp one night and started beating people up?'

'Yes, of course. It was terrible.'

'Maybe whoever attacked the camp was trying to scare them off. Ben's sister said she thought he'd been threatened. Maybe somebody was worried about what they'd find out.'

Angela thought about what he was saying. 'And you think all of this had something to do with the accident?'

'I don't know. Maybe.'

'My God.' She shook her head in disbelief. 'Adam, are you sure about this? I mean it seems so, I don't know, unreal I suppose. Things like this don't happen around here. At least they never used to.'

'But now?' he asked, picking up on the inference.

She looked troubled. 'The development has changed people. Or maybe it's brought out what was already there. I've heard people say that they should just send in the bulldozers and if the protesters don't move that's their problem. When the camp was attacked some people were saying whoever it was didn't go far enough. What scares me is the hate you hear in their voices. They really mean it. And now this.'

'Like I said, it's just a theory.'

'But what about what happened to your car? That's more than a theory. Have you been to the police?'

'No. I don't think there's any point. I couldn't give them a good description so there's not much they could do.' He didn't add that he didn't have a lot of confidence in the local police. 'Anyway, let's forget about it for now. What about lunch?' He looked at his watch. He'd arrived an hour late and it was almost two.

Angela was distracted, still mulling over what he'd told her. 'I was going to suggest going to a place in Alston. It's a bit of a drive though, over the fells towards Hexham.'

'Will it be open by the time we get there?'

'It's open all day I think.'

He knew the road, and the idea of driving over the fells with Angela appealed to him. From what he remembered of Alston it was a nice little town, built on a steep hill with partly cobbled streets. He turned around and headed towards the square and from there he took the road south. At the bridge they passed a group of four people walking into town. One of them had a shaven head and wore shapeless dungarees, another was dressed in an old-fashioned dress that trailed along the ground. She smiled and waved as they went past.

'Protesters,' Angela commented.

'When I was up there I got the impression they're quite a mixed bunch,' Adam said. 'Overall they struck me as pretty harmless.'

'You wouldn't think so the way some people react,' Angela said. 'Some of the shops in town refuse to serve them.'

'So, the general feeling is more against them than for them.'

'You heard David the other night. People are worried about their jobs and businesses. Without the development a lot of people are going to find it hard.'

'What would happen, really, in David's case?' he asked.

'It would put the sawmill out of business.'

'But you'd be alright. I mean I know the sawmill means a lot to David, but you've got this American publishing deal haven't you?'

'I haven't told David about that yet.' Angela stared ahead out of the window for a while. 'It's not just the sawmill. It's the town, everything here. David has never wanted anything else.'

'And you, Angela, what about you?'

She glanced at him. 'I don't know.'

'I remember once you said you'd like to see Paris.'

She looked astonished. 'Did I?'

'Have you ever been?'

She laughed. 'No.'

'That's a shame.'

'What about you, Adam, have you travelled much? You always seemed to want to get away. You had plans, you always knew where you were going.'

'Well, I wasn't born here. And I've travelled a bit. Even to Paris.'

'Is it as beautiful as everybody says? It can't be.'

'I think it depends who you're with. It's a city for lovers they say and I can see why. I think you'd like it.'

She smiled uncertainly, as if there was a vague inference in his comment. He hadn't meant there to be. At least he didn't think so. But then maybe he had. He glanced across at her. She was beautiful, he thought. Truly beautiful in a natural, unselfconscious sense. They lapsed into silence and drove the rest of the way without speaking much, though Adam felt their silence was a comfortable one. Once or twice he caught her eye and she smiled. Green fields and stone walls bordered the road, with the fells rising on one side in stark profile against a glorious autumn sky. At Edenhall they turned east and rapidly climbed above the valley. The landscape changed quickly. Fields and trees gave way to open windswept vistas that had a kind of stark, empty beauty of their own. The clutter of towns and the populated lowland fell behind, and a feeling of space overtook them. The sky seemed to expand overhead.

At Alston they drove halfway up the steep cobbled main street and walked back down past the butcher's and greengrocer's to a little pub opposite the library. There were only a handful of other customers and the smells coming from the kitchen promised better than average food.

They sat at a table by the window, where Adam was glad to be able to take the weight off his leg. He'd been limping badly, and now his knee was aching. It was like somebody had taken up residence with a saw. A dull blade gnawing at the bone.

'Are you alright?' Angela asked, seeing him wince as he sat down.

'I think I twisted it or something when I fell earlier.'

'Does it bother you much normally?' she asked hesitantly.

'It comes and goes.'

She regarded him steadily from her wide blue eyes. 'Do you think about it much, Adam? What happened I mean?'

He wasn't surprised by her question. In fact it was inevitable that they would talk about the past. Perhaps especially because they'd so assiduously avoided any mention of it over dinner, which maybe had been due to David's presence.

'Do you mean the accident?' he asked. 'Not really.'

'What about afterwards?'

'You mean us?' he said, with a prick of malice, which he regretted almost immediately.

'Yes.'

'Sometimes.' He thought of Louise, and the way she had

resembled Angela, though now he could see it was in type only. So many of the women he had been out with over the years shared common characteristics. Blonde, sometimes blue-eyed. Jesus, what would that psychologist he and Louise had been seeing have made of that?

Angela dropped her gaze for a moment. 'It's funny isn't it?' she said, when she looked up again. 'I mean, it was such a long time ago, but in a way it feels like yesterday. I've always felt badly about the way things ended. You knew about David and I didn't you? That day when we went for a walk in the wood and you told me you were leaving for university?'

'Yes,' he admitted.

'How long had you known?'

'I'm not sure. I suppose I sensed something before the accident. The way you used to look at each other. Then when you started visiting the hospital together it was sort of obvious.'

'I knew you did. I wanted to tell you but it seemed such a lousy thing to even think with you in hospital. You know, nothing ever happened between us.'

'It was a long time ago, Angela. It doesn't matter any more.'

'It does to me. I've always regretted not telling you that. Even though I knew you'd guessed, I wanted you to know that we hadn't done anything about the way we felt. I mean, I felt bad enough just thinking it, knowing. We both did. I've always hoped you didn't hate me, Adam. I suppose even that's selfish isn't it?'

'I didn't hate you,' he said. 'And I don't think you were selfish.'

'What did you feel then?'

'I don't know if I remember exactly. Hurt I suppose. My ego took a bit of a battering.' He smiled, hoping he had managed to conceal what he was really thinking. How could he tell her he'd never really forgotten her? She was the first girl he had ever loved, and the emotions were far more powerful because their relationship had ended before familiarity bred pragmatism. Idealized through distance. He recognized this, but it didn't change anything. Maybe she was the only woman he'd ever loved in a way, because how could he have really loved any of the others if he had even subconsciously compared them with her. Or because he'd always felt their relationship was unfinished and as such he'd held back. He knew it was this as much as Meg Coucesco which had fuelled his self-destructive work habits.

He saw that her brow was furrowed slightly as she looked at him, as if she sensed something of his thoughts.

'What about David?' she asked. 'How did you feel about him?'

'Like anyone whose friend just stole his girl,' he said. 'I struck him off my Christmas card list.'

She smiled, but he knew she must have picked up on the underlying bitterness in his voice.

'He really did feel badly, Adam. That's why he stopped going to see you. He just didn't know what to say. He couldn't face you.'

'Look, Angela, it really doesn't matter. Like I said, it was all a long time ago.' He picked up his empty glass. 'Another?'

He thought she would say something else. Try again to persuade him how badly David had felt. Poor David. She didn't know it all. She didn't know the half of it. She didn't know that he'd always suspected that David had meant to shoot him. Perhaps he hadn't planned it. In fact he was certain he hadn't. But David had known better than to shoot at something before he'd properly identified it. She didn't know the things David was capable of. She didn't know about Meg.

Over lunch they kept to strictly neutral topics, but they couldn't escape an air of tension that had developed between them. Or perhaps it wasn't tension, more a slight unease. As they started back towards Castleton, Adam thought about the question she'd asked him earlier, about how he'd felt about David. There was an occasion when they were at school that stuck in his mind. The results of an early set of exams Adam had sat had been posted on the school notice board. He'd achieved the highest score in the school, but his achievement had been eclipsed by the school rugby team, captained by David, beating Penrith in the inter-school league final. During assembly the Head had heaped praise on the team, and the exam results, which might ordinarily have gotten a mention, were forgotten. In the hall afterwards he and David were walking to class when a junior had asked David for his autograph.

'My hero,' Adam had said sarcastically.

David had grinned with embarrassment and then a minute later had produced a small package. 'I nearly forgot. This is for you.'

It was a boxed pen. The kind David's dad used to give to his good customers, but this one was inscribed with the words:

FOR ADAM, CONGRATULATIONS

'What if I hadn't passed?' he remembered asking through his amazement, to which David had shrugged.

'I knew you would.'

The following year the gypsies had arrived. After that nothing had ever really been the same.

'Adam, what is it?'

He turned to Angela, startled. He realized he was gripping the wheel so hard his knuckles were white and his jaw was clamped tight. 'Nothing, it's okay,' he said. 'Just my leg.'

When they were near Castleton again, he said, 'Can I ask you something? You can tell me it's none of my business if you like, but the other night I got the feeling that things are a bit strained between you and David.' She looked away, avoiding his eye, and he thought maybe he'd overstepped the mark. 'Look, forget it. It really isn't any of my business.'

'No, it isn't that. You're right, things have been difficult lately. I suppose I've been trying to convince myself that it's just the business.'

'I meant what I said the other night, if you need to talk. Sometimes it's easier to talk to someone who's removed from the situation.'

'That sounds as if you're speaking from personal experience.'

'I was.'

'You were married once weren't you?'

'For a while.'

'What was she like?'

How had the conversation swung around to him, he wondered. 'I thought we were talking about you?'

'Sorry. Anyway, to be honest I wouldn't know where to start. David has changed. I suppose you must have noticed how much he was drinking.'

'He did seem to be knocking it back. I saw him in the pub last night, did he tell you?' He could tell from her surprised look that he hadn't. He wondered about that. If somebody he hadn't seen for almost twenty years practically accused him of bribing council officials, wouldn't that be something to mention when he got home?

'He doesn't tell me much these days,' she said.

She looked both sad and angry at the same time. 'Nick was there too, and Graham. Actually I went by the cottages where Nick used to live yesterday.'

'He still lives there,' Angela said.

'I wondered if he did. I ran into a girl there, a young woman anyway. She seemed a bit strange.'

'Mary. She and Nick live together.'

'Is there something wrong with her?'

'I think she has some kind of mental illness. She doesn't go out much. How was David anyway when you saw him?'

'He was alright. We had a bit of a disagreement actually. Seems that the media poking their noses in aren't too popular with some people.'

'Was he drinking? I mean did he seem drunk?'

'Not especially.'

'He's been drinking a lot lately,' Angela said. 'He never used to be a heavy drinker at all. He might go to the pub with Nick or somebody once a week and have a few pints, but that's about it. He hardly touched spirits before, but you saw the way he was hammering the Scotch the other night. I don't even know how much he's getting through now.'

'Is it the business? I suppose he's been worried about it?'

She shook her head, a gesture of what he wasn't sure. Was it frustration, or did it mean there was more to it than worry about the business?

'He won't talk to me. That's the whole bloody problem.'

'Communication breakdown. Sometimes there are things one partner can't tell the other.'

She looked at him curiously. 'Is that what happened to you, Adam? Is that why your marriage broke up?'

'Partly.'

'Sorry, now it's my turn to say it's none of my business.'

'No, it's okay.'

'What was your wife's name?'

'Louise.'

'Do you still see each other?'

'No,' he said. 'The truth is we should never have married in the first place. We only lasted a couple of years anyway. Not like you and David.'

Angela frowned. 'I suppose that's what I don't understand. I used to think I knew him so well, that we knew each other. But none of this is like David. Sometimes I wonder if I really know him at all. I can't help feeling that there's something eating at him. Something he won't tell me about. He doesn't even sleep in our bed any more.' She stopped short, and he had the feeling she was surprised at herself for revealing such a personal detail, even embarrassed. 'Anyway, all marriages go through this sort of thing at some point I expect,' she added.

There was a note of closure in her tone, and he got the impression she didn't want to talk about it any more so he let the subject drop. They were almost back in Castleton anyway and ten minutes later he pulled up outside her house. She thanked him for lunch, and leaned over to kiss his cheek.

'Don't get out. And thanks for listening.'

'Any time. Look, before you go, there's something I meant to ask you.'

'Yes?'

'The journalist I mentioned earlier who works at the *Courier*? She said that David was lobbying the council on behalf of the Forest Havens development, is that right?'

'Yes, as a representative of the local small business association. He worked hard to get support for the development. Why do you ask?'

'No particular reason. It just surprised me when his name came up, that's all.'

'Right,' she said, though she wore a slight frown as she got out. He watched her go to the door, and returned the brief wave she gave him.

As he drove away her scent lingered in the air.

CHAPTER EIGHTEEN

Angela turned out the kitchen lights. Outside the window it was dark. She had been sitting at the kitchen table, thinking about her lunch with Adam. As she went along the passage to the stairs she paused outside the partially open study door. A single lamp cast a dim yellow light that left the corners of the room in darkness. David's profile was heavily shadowed, giving his eyes a strangely hooded appearance. He didn't even realize she was there until she tapped on the door.

'Do you want something to eat?'

He looked startled. 'I'm not hungry.'

She glanced at the bottle on the desk, thought to say something and then changed her mind. What was the point? She turned to leave.

'Where's Kate?' he said suddenly.

'She went to bed an hour ago.'

He looked at the time and appeared surprised that it was so late. 'She didn't say goodnight,' he murmured, almost to himself.

'She probably didn't want to disturb you.'

He looked up, and they both knew that wasn't the reason. Wearily he ran his hand back through his hair.

'I saw Adam today.' His expression changed at the mention of Adam's name. He looked suddenly what? Defensive perhaps? Wary; maybe that was a better word.

'What did he want?'

'We had lunch together.'

'Lunch?'

Her temper flared. 'Yes, you remember that, David. When two

167

people sit down and have a meal. Perhaps even talk.' She took a breath. 'He said he'd been talking to a journalist at the *Courier* about the development. She told him there are rumours that some members of the planning committee might have been bribed to vote for the Forest Havens plan.' She watched him carefully, and noted that he didn't seem surprised. 'Did you know about it?'

'I know who he's been talking to. Her name is Janice Munroe.'

'Is it true?'

'Of course it isn't! If it was true they would have splashed it all over the front page.'

'Adam said she couldn't prove it. That's why the story never ran.'

'Well, there you go then.'

She lingered in the doorway. Something about his reaction bothered her. It was partly the knowledge that he must have already known about the rumours but had never mentioned them to her, but also the way he dismissed the subject without looking her in the eye. 'How do you know it isn't true?' Angela asked. 'After all, you weren't on the committee.'

'I know Janice Munroe is a troublemaker. She'd say anything if she thought it would do her career some good.'

'You were lobbying for Forest Havens,' Angela said, almost to herself.

He stared at her. 'Of course I was! Without that development the mill is bloody finished.'

She'd been thinking all evening about the way Adam had almost casually mentioned David's name. Of course it hadn't been casual at all. She had known he was hinting at something.

'It's true isn't it?'

'What is?'

'Oh, for God's sake, David, don't treat me like an idiot!'

'Does it matter what I say?'

'Yes, it matters. I want to know if you were involved. I want to know if you promised anybody on that committee something in return for their vote.'

She saw the answer to her question in his hesitation, it was written all over his face.

'It doesn't matter what I say, does it,' he said. 'You've already made up your mind. For Christ's sake Angela, life isn't always so fucking black and white. Do you really think this kind of thing doesn't happen all the time? So, some builder wins a contract. Maybe he gets a look at his competitors' tenders before he does his own. Compared to the kind of stuff you read in the newspapers every day is it really such a big deal?'

She shook her head in disbelief. She was angry, angrier than she could remember being for a long time. Her hands were trembling.

'What was I supposed to do?' he said. 'Was I supposed to just stand by and do nothing? What if the plan had been turned down? Think about all the people who would be out of work.'

'So, you did it for them, is that it?'

'Alright, I admit I was thinking of myself too. Of us.'

'How can you say that? How can you say you were thinking of us? For weeks now you've barely spoken to me, or your daughter. All the time you said it was because of the strain you were under. The truth is you were worried you would be caught!'

He looked away, reaching for the bottle.

'That's it, David. Have another bloody drink. Salve your guilty bloody conscience.'

'Look, the only reason I didn't tell you is because I knew you'd react like this.'

'Is it David? Is that the reason?' She stared at him, trying to read what she saw in his eyes. It was partly the truth, but not all of it. Maybe he'd been afraid she would talk him out of it, but the committee had passed the plan now. There was something else, something he wasn't telling her.

Later, as she lay in the darkness of their bedroom she couldn't sleep. She was angry. If David had been involved in some sort of corruption, was that really so bad? She didn't approve of it. She didn't condone it. And yet as David had said, that kind of thing must go on all the time. A contract awarded. An agreement reached quietly over drinks between associates. She wasn't so naïve as to think any differently. So why was she so angry?

Was she angry with David, or was it Adam? Both of them, she thought. David because of what he'd done, and how she'd learned of it. Adam for what? Being the messenger? No, that wasn't it. What had he told her earlier when he'd picked her up from the house? That somebody had sent him a message when they had smashed his headlights, to warn him off. He had talked about the accident when those lads had been killed as if perhaps it wasn't an accident. That maybe somebody had wanted to stop what they knew from getting out. Whom had he meant? He'd asked about the sawmill, what would happen if the development didn't go ahead. Had he been suggesting that David had something to do with what had happened to those lads? She couldn't believe that he had. But why mention it otherwise?

Christ! A gnawing unease kept her awake. She was restless, unable to stop her mind working. There was an unfamiliar sensation in the pit of her stomach. A kind of clenched feeling. She was afraid, she realized.

But afraid of what exactly?

CHAPTER NINETEEN

In the morning Adam looked for a car breaker in the local phone book. He knew from experience that these were the best places to find affordable parts for his car. It turned out the closest one was just off the A69 outside Brampton.

It was still early by the time he arrived. A chain-link fence ran along the edge of a little-used road, behind which piles of rusting car bodies were stacked. At regular intervals signs warned intruders to beware of the dog. He drove through the open gate and followed a dirt track to a wooden barn-like building outside which a four-wheel drive was parked. A figure inside looked over his shoulder at the sound of the car and came towards the door wiping his hands on a rag. It wasn't until Adam got out that he realized that it was Nick.

He watched as Adam limped over with what seemed like a glint of amusement in his eye, then his gaze flicked towards the Porsche. 'Have an accident then, Adam?'

'Not exactly. I wasn't expecting to find you here; is this your place?'

'Yeah.'

'You were working at the sawmill last time I saw you.'

'Well, that was a long time ago, wasn't it? I still do a bit there now and again.'

Gesturing towards his car, Adam said, 'I was looking for some headlights.'

The old antipathy between them was as keenly felt as it had been the first day they'd met, and the same sullen contempt he remembered was still present in Nick's expression. It occurred to

Adam that Nick could well have been the figure he'd seen on the road, which made the irony of their present situation something Nick would no doubt find amusing. He thought maybe he should try somewhere else, but before he could say anything Nick turned and went towards the rows of wooden racks that filled the barn.

'Wait there, I'll see what I've got.'

He vanished for a few minutes and when he came back he was carrying a headlight unit, which he put on a wooden counter near the door while he examined the connections. 'It's a bit rusty, but it should be alright. What year is your car?'

''Seventy-eight.'

'Should fit then. I might have another one. There's a wreck somewhere I haven't finished stripping yet. Not a lot of demand for Porsche parts, around here,' he added pointedly.

Adam ignored the comment. Nick picked up a heavy wrench and grabbed a sack that clinked with a metallic sound and slung it over his shoulder. 'You can wait here if you want.' He brushed past and headed out to the yard.

Because he didn't have anything else to do Adam followed through a desolate landscape. During the night it had rained, and in the early morning light, under a heavy grey sky, wrecked cars rested like abandoned carcasses in the mud, their paintwork rusting, most of them stripped of anything that might be remotely saleable. Where windscreens had once been only dark, gaping holes remained. Along a muddy avenue minor oil slicks shimmered on the surface of puddles, and the ground was littered with all kinds of rusting discarded junk. In the heart of the yard the scene was reminiscent of a sepia toned photograph. It felt as if the sun never penetrated. The colour was all leached out of the landscape, leaving only black streaked mud, and the reddish-brown rusting bones of old cars under a grey sky. The air was tainted with the heavy cloying stench of dirt and oil.

Apparently having found what he was looking for Nick started clambering up a pile of old cars towards what Adam recognized as the remains of a Porsche like his own, only this one lacked a roof.

'It was hit by a cement truck,' Nick said, as he started working on the light. 'The bloke driving it was showing off to his girlfriend. Her head was ripped clean off. They found it in a field.' He grinned with grim amusement.

Adam left him to it and wandered off among the piles of old cars. By the time he went back to the barn Nick had the headlight and was examining it outside.

'Do you get all the accident wrecks around here?' Adam asked.

'Depends. Most of them.'

'What about the car those three boys were in when they were killed?'

Nick glanced at him, then gestured vaguely. 'Yeah. That one's around somewhere.'

Nick said the light would fit and offered to fit them both. 'It'll cost another thirty quid mind.'

Adam agreed, having long since become used to paying other people for repairs that most old Porsche owners would have happily done themselves, but which he lacked the knowledge or inclination for. 'By the way, I went by your house the other day,' he said casually, as Nick went to work. 'At least it used to be your house. The cottages near bottom end?'

Nick paused and gave him a thoughtful look. 'That was you Mary saw? She said somebody had been around.'

'Is she your wife?'

Nick picked up a screwdriver and grunted a reply. 'We're not married.'

'I might've scared her unintentionally.'

'She's not used to people.'

'Well, tell her I'm sorry.' He let a few moments pass then said, 'So, have you found somewhere else to live?'

Abruptly Nick stopped what he was doing and looked up. 'What makes you think I'm looking?'

'I heard you were selling up.'

'Who told you that?'

'I'm not sure now. Why, are you trying to keep it quiet?'

'Just wondered how you knew.' Nick feigned indifference and went back to the light he was trying to remove.

'Actually, I heard you'd sold to Forest Havens,' Adam remarked,

173

but this time Nick gave no response. 'You must have got a good price for that bit of land.'

'What of it?'

'Just making conversation.'

Nick smiled sardonically. 'You always were a talker, Adam.'

After that Nick wouldn't be drawn by anything Adam said, so he left him to it. He heard a sound from behind the barn, and curious to see what it was he went around there, but as he got closer to the corner he heard the clanking of a chain and glimpsed the edge of what looked like a doghouse. The clanking stopped, and he heard a low throaty growl. He remembered the warning signs on the fence and decided he didn't need to get any closer. Slowly he backed off.

He followed a track through the yard instead, and once he was sure that Nick couldn't see him he followed one of the avenues through the piles of wrecks back to the one he'd found earlier. He hadn't been sure then, but now as he surveyed the blue Vauxhall like the one in the photographs from the police accident report he was certain it was the one Ben Pierce was supposed to have been driving. It was still relatively intact, standing on all four wheels, though the tyres were flat and the roof was partly caved in. Above the windscreen was a jagged hole where a chunk of metal had been torn free, and every other panel on the rest of the body was dented as if somebody had taken a sledgehammer to it.

Adam yanked open a door. The upholstery and dash were smeared with mud and dead leaves and other debris, and a dank smell of decay rose from the interior. At first there appeared to be nothing to see, though the glove compartment was closed despite the lock being missing. Out of curiosity he tried to open it but it was jammed solid, so he looked around and found a metal rod beside the remains of an old Land Rover, which he used to pry the lid open. He saw then why it had been jammed. The back of the compartment had been crushed leaving only a narrow space inside. He squeezed his hand in and pulled out the damp remains of a service manual and what was left of a chocolate bar. Further back he felt something else graze the tips of his fingers. It felt soft and slightly damp but before he could get it out he was startled by a voice behind him.

'What are you doing in there?'

He turned around and found Nick watching him. He was holding a heavy wrench in a vaguely threatening manner.

Adam stood up and wiped his hands on his jeans. 'Isn't this the car those boys were killed in? I thought I saw something.' He held up the remains of the chocolate bar he'd found. 'I think it's past its sell-by date though.' He tossed it back inside and started back towards the barn.

Nick stared at him suspiciously, then followed. 'Your car's ready.'

When they got back to the barn Adam wrote out a cheque for the amount he owed, though he was taken aback when Nick told him how much it was. 'That's a bit steep isn't it?'

Nick shrugged. 'I can take them off again if you like. New ones'll cost you four times that.'

It wasn't worth arguing about, so he tore out the cheque and handed it over. 'Thanks.'

Nick put it in his pocket without looking at it. 'Any time.' He watched with a gleam of amused satisfaction in his eye as Adam got in behind the wheel and when he was about to leave leaned down to the window. 'Drive carefully.'

After leaving the yard Adam drove to a small village a few miles north of Brampton where he drove around looking for the address George Hunt had given him over the phone. It turned out to be a small cottage at the end of a row opposite a duck pond. It was a little after nine-thirty by the time he arrived. He went down the short path, through a neat little garden bordered with flowers, and as he reached the door it was suddenly opened by a late-middle-aged woman who was struggling to put her coat on. Her eyes widened when she saw Adam and she uttered a small gasp of surprise.

'Sorry, I didn't mean to startle you,' he said.

For a second she stared at him uncomprehendingly. 'Who are you?'

'My name is Adam Turner. I arranged to meet your husband.' He glanced at the number on the door, wondering if he'd got the wrong house. 'Councillor Hunt?'

'Oh yes. Yes. That's right. George mentioned it I think. I'm sorry, I'm running late.' She glanced at her watch and finished shrugging on her coat. 'Look, I really have to go. I'm going to miss my bus. He's in the kitchen.' She gestured vaguely behind her. 'I'm sorry. I have to run.' As she edged past him she looked at her watch again. 'Sorry about this.'

'That's okay,' he assured her.

'Just go through.' The woman hurried to the gate where she stopped and looked inside her bag as if she'd forgotten something, then apparently satisfied she started walking quickly along the street with her coat flapping about her as she tried to button it with one hand and search in a pocket with the other.

Adam watched her go and then contemplated the open door and the quiet hallway. He noted the prints on the wall, several line drawings of nudes that had a classical feel and reminded him of pictures from books on Greek mythology. A narrow staircase led to the upper floor, and a door on the left led to what appeared to be a lounge. He glimpsed the corner of an upright piano. From somewhere towards the back of the house, where he assumed the kitchen was, came the murmur of voices.

'Hello?' He debated whether to ring the bell or simply go in. In the end he rang the bell, but when nobody came he went tentatively along the passage. From behind a closed door the murmured voices grew louder. It was, he realized, the sound of Radio Four. He pushed the door open, and a man with a grey close-cropped beard looked up in surprise.

'Councillor Hunt? I'm Adam Turner. Your wife let me in. I think she was in a bit of a hurry.'

Understanding dawned and George Hunt smiled and rose to his feet, hand extended. 'Come in, sit down.' He looked along the hallway. 'I'd better just close that door. My wife gets a bit flustered in the mornings. Hang on a minute. There's tea in the pot if you'd like some. Help yourself.'

Adam sat down, taking in the plate with a half-eaten piece of toast and the folded newspaper. The kitchen was cramped but homely. A small garden was visible through the half-glass back door. The radio on top of the fridge was an old-fashioned Roberts and beneath it a number of notes and some photographs were stuck to the door with colourful gnome magnets.

When Hunt returned Adam apologized for interrupting his breakfast, but Hunt waved his apology away.

'That's alright.' He turned the radio off before he sat down again. 'Sorry about Judith. My wife. She was always late for everything, even when we were courting. Can I offer you some toast?'

'I'm fine thanks.'

'One of life's small luxuries when I have a late lecture. A leisurely breakfast,' Hunt explained.

'You work at the college?'

'Hmm,' Hunt said. 'For my sins.' He glanced towards the fridge where Adam had been looking. 'Those pictures were taken last year in Spain. That's my daughter Elizabeth.'

Between a chubby-looking Hunt and his pale wife, stood a slim smiling teenager. She was a pretty girl of around seventeen or so, her youth emphasizing the age of her parents, both of whom must be approaching sixty at least, Adam thought. Not far from retirement. A time when many people these days were under huge financial pressure.

'You're a journalist you said?' Hunt asked.

'That's right.' Adam explained that he was doing a piece on the protest and was interested in background on the development. He asked the same questions he had of Carol Fraser, questioning Hunt's change of position. The answers Hunt gave echoed what his fellow councillor had said inasmuch as Hunt claimed that though he'd initially been opposed to the plan he was convinced to change his mind by the potential benefit to the local community. To Adam's mind, however, Hunt sounded less as if he was quoting from a policy document. Reservations seemed to resonate through his reasoning.

'Couldn't the same case be made by almost any developer?' Adam questioned, playing devil's advocate. 'I mean, there's always going to be an upside to these things. Another factory gets built on a green-field site, but the factory means jobs, a stronger local economy and so on.'

'True,' Hunt answered reflectively. 'But this is a particularly depressed area. As I'm sure you're aware, the economy here is rural-based, and farming has taken a beating in the last few years.'

'And you believe the answer is to turn the Castleton Estate into a holiday park?'

Hunt smiled ruefully. 'What I believe personally is not the issue. My job as an elected official is to represent the view of the people who voted for me.'

'But as I understand it you have a record of defending the environment.' Adam recalled Janice's description of Hunt as being something of a greenie. 'Wouldn't the people who elected you have done so because they shared your views?'

'The correlation between people's beliefs and their actions is not always as clear as one might expect, Mr Turner, depending on circumstances. Offer a starving vegetarian a tasty lamb chop and see for yourself.' He smiled ruefully. 'A crude analogy perhaps, but true nevertheless.'

'So, you voted in favour of the plan, though in fact you remain personally opposed to it?'

'Correct.' Hunt gestured around. 'I have a simple and comfortable home, a loving wife and daughter, and I get a great deal of satisfaction from my work. I have a secure pension plan that will allow me to live comfortably until I die. Not everybody is so fortunate. Many people in this area are suffering great hardship. Personally I decry this kind of destruction to our countryside. Castleton Wood is a unique habitat. It's all that remains of a landscape that has long since vanished from most of the country. I fight against this kind of thing whenever I can, but principles have to be balanced against human needs. Besides, if I go against the desires of the electorate I risk being voted out at the next election, and then there would be one less person to oppose people like Frank Henderson. Sometimes it's better to lose the battle in order to win the war, you might say.'

'Compromise,' Adam said, echoing the term Carol Fraser had used.

'If you like. It's a part of life. Though you might also term it a strategy.'

'You mentioned Councillor Henderson. I assume that you and he don't see eye to eye on these issues?'

Hunt didn't answer, merely regarded him thoughtfully.

'This is off the record, Councillor.'

'In that case, you assume correctly. Henderson cares only for himself, in my opinion. If he happens to make a decision that benefits the electorate he serves, it's purely coincidental. Again, my opinion only.'

'Councillor, and this is also off the record, are you aware of rumours that Councillor Henderson and perhaps others might have been offered certain inducements to vote in favour of the Forest Havens development?'

Hunt clasped his hands beneath his chin. 'Off the record, I'm aware of such rumours,' he replied carefully.

'Do you give them any credence?'

'Let's just say, Mr Turner, that in the case of Councillor Henderson, very little would surprise me.'

'But you don't have any personal knowledge of them?'

'No.'

'Were you personally ever offered any kind of inducement to vote in favour of the development?'

Hunt smiled. 'Notwithstanding the fact that if I had been I would hardly admit as much, the answer is no. I must add, however, that it's unlikely that anybody would attempt such a thing. I think after fifteen years on the council my ethics are well established, and my record speaks for itself.'

'Did you ever speak to David Johnson or anybody else lobbying for Forest Havens?'

'Spoke to him, yes. He was persuasive.'

'But he didn't make any kind of offer?'

'No.'

'One last question. Did you ever meet somebody called Jane Hanson?'

'The young lady from the protest camp? Yes, I met her on several occasions. As a matter of fact she asked me the same kind of questions that you are asking now.'

'Do you know if she spoke to any of your colleagues on the planning committee?'

'I assume she spoke to all of them. I know Henderson was complaining about her, and I saw her with Carol, that's Councillor Fraser, once or twice.'

'You're sure of that?' Adam asked. 'You saw Jane Hanson with Councillor Fraser?'

'Absolutely sure.' Hunt paused, regarding Adam quizzically. 'I take it there is a point to all of this?'

'There is,' Adam said, recalling how Carol Fraser had specifically denied having met Jane. 'I'm just not sure what it is yet.'

When Adam arrived back at the New Inn early in the afternoon something was going on. John Shields's Rover was parked in the car park along with several police vehicles and a small knot of curious onlookers had gathered outside the lounge room door where a uniformed constable prevented anyone from going inside, including Adam.

'I'm a guest here.' Adam produced his room key as proof. He could see Shields with his wife and their friends inside talking to Graham.

'I'm afraid nobody's allowed inside for now, sir. If you could come back in ten minutes or so I think we'll be finished.'

'Finished with what?' Adam asked, but he couldn't get anything more out of the constable. His first thought had been that there had been some kind of accident, but there was no sign of damage to Shields's car, and nobody appeared to be injured.

In his room he stood by the window where he could keep an eye on what was happening outside while he phoned the *Courier* and asked for Janice Munroe.

When he was put through he told her about his meeting with Carol Fraser the day before. 'When I mentioned Jane, the council-lor said she'd never met her. I think that's unlikely don't you?'

'Yes,' Janice admitted.

'So, I was wondering if you could do a little digging for me. Councillor Fraser told me that she and her husband own a farm. Is there any way you could find out more about it? Get some kind of fix on their financial situation.'

'I'll try,' Janice said, though she sounded reluctant.

'You never really know what people are capable of when their backs are against the wall,' Adam said.

'Yes, I know. I like her that's all.'

'I liked her too. But I'm sure she wasn't telling me the truth when she said she hadn't met Jane. I talked to Councillor Hunt this morning. He was quite open about the fact that he'd met her, and that she was asking questions about the committee.'

'Alright, I'll see what I can do.'

'Thanks.'

Outside the window the whoop of a police siren sounded and died. Down in the car park the two couples from Birmingham had appeared with several uniformed police officers, including Graham. Another car had arrived with a man and a woman who looked like detectives.

'Where are you?' Janice asked.

'In Castleton at the pub where I'm staying. Something's happening here.'

'Anything I should be interested in?'

'Could be. I'll call you back.'

He went downstairs and practically bumped into Mrs Shields. He tried to remember her first name. 'Is everything alright? It's Pauline isn't it?'

'Yes, that's right.' She looked flushed and what at first glance he'd thought was worry he now saw was a mixture of confusion and excitement. 'It's been quite a day I can tell you,' she said. 'I don't know what to make of it.'

Just then one of the detectives opened the door of an unmarked car and John Shields and his friend got in the back. 'Where are they taking your husband?' Adam asked.

'Back up there. To where we found it.'

'Where you found what?'

She looked at him wide-eyed. 'Don't you know? I thought you knew. Our John pulled something out of that lake where we went fishing today. We went where you told us, down the end where that rock is.'

'What was it?'

'A bone,' she said, then dropped her voice, her eyes dramatically wide. 'A human bone. Looked like it was a bit of somebody's leg. It had bits of stuff still stuck to it. You know.' She shivered at the thought.

She explained what had happened, though there wasn't much to tell, really. After Shields had realized what it was he'd hooked they'd packed up and come back to the pub where he'd called the police. They'd had to wait for some other officers to arrive and now Shields was going to show them exactly where they had been fishing.

'I said I didn't want to go back there,' she said. 'Not me. Gives me the creeps it does.'

As the cars started to leave Graham glanced over and saw Adam. He frowned when he saw Pauline Shields and then came over.

'Mrs Shields told me what happened,' Adam said. 'Is it true that it was a human bone they found?'

'We don't know what it is yet but chances are it's just an animal bone. Probably a sheep or something.'

'Seems like a lot of police interest for a dead sheep,' Adam observed sceptically.

'It was too big for a sheep,' Pauline Shields said indignantly.

Graham frowned at her. 'Well, whatever it was we'll find out soon enough, but we don't need any journalists jumping to conclusions before we do.' He threw a warning look at Adam and then went back to his car.

Excusing himself from Pauline Shields, Adam went back to his room and called Janice again.

'A human bone?' she echoed when he related what was going on. 'And there was me thinking nothing would ever happen around this bloody place. Do you know where they're going?'

'Yes. Actually I was the one who told them where to fish.'

'Would you take me there if I meet you at the pub?'

He hesitated, but he didn't see how he could refuse. She told him she'd be there as soon as she could.

Adam sat on a rock out near the end of the promontory in a patch of late afternoon sunlight. Down below in the small crescent-shaped cove John Shields was talking to the police. The area had been cordoned off by a constable who'd run a police tape through the trees, though for now there was nobody else there. Janice climbed up to join him. When she got there she was breathless.

'What did you find out?' he asked.

She pulled a face. 'Not a lot. There's no' much they can do until the morning. They're bringing divers in tomorrow.'

'Did they tell you anything about what they found?'

'Not really. That sergeant wouldnae let me near those fishermen.' Down below Graham glanced up as if he'd heard her, though in reality he was too far away. Janice looked at Adam curiously. 'Do you two know each other?'

'Why do you ask?'

'I get the impression he's no' exactly thrilled about you being here.'

'I used to know him when I lived here.'

'I take it you weren't friends then?'

'No, not really.'

They sat in silence for a while, watching what was going on, though in fact there was nothing much happening. Adam was aware of the curious looks Janice gave him every now and then, and he could almost hear her thinking. Findlay had said that she was a good reporter, which he could believe. He'd often thought that women made better journalists than men. They were more attuned to the subtleties of human behaviour. He guessed that she'd sensed something underlying whatever Graham had said to her about him.

He looked across the lake. The surface was still and dark. What secrets would be revealed in the morning he wondered? It wasn't far from where he sat that David had shot him all those years ago. Everything had looked very different then, shrouded in snow, the lake all but invisible. But he was thinking of another occasion a year before that when he'd watched David standing on the narrow strip of beach where John Shields now stood talking to Graham. David had been about to throw something into the lake. Whatever it was had flashed in the sun when he drew back his arm, but then he'd hesitated and evidently changed his mind, because whatever it was in his hand he'd put back in his pocket.

He came to, realizing that Janice had spoken to him. 'Sorry, what did you say?'

'I said I wonder how long it's been in there. I mean how long does it take for a body to decompose to just bones?'

'I don't know.'

'It must be years though. Especially in cold water. What do you think? Ten? Twenty maybe?'

'Nearer twenty I'd say.'

She looked at him strangely, perhaps struck by his tone.

*   *   *

In his room at the New Inn Adam brooded on the events of the afternoon. He was thinking about Meg Coucesco, wondering how long it would be before somebody connected the find in the lake with a gypsy girl who went missing seventeen years earlier. There was nothing to say it was her, of course, but he didn't think it was a sheep either, and how many people around here had vanished the way Meg had?

Some intuition told him that it was her. In a curious way he wasn't even surprised, rather he felt that the discovery had about it a kind of fatalistic inevitability. He had even been instrumental in it, since had he not told Shields where to fish the bone might never have been discovered.

What he felt chiefly was a kind of numbed shock. Like somebody rudely jolted from their own self-deception. He supposed a part of him had always wanted to believe that she was alive, that she had simply run away. But deep down he'd known that wasn't true. He'd been at war with his own conscience over the years, and the direction his career had taken had ultimately been an effort to make amends. Perhaps his obsession had also been about subconsciously destroying relationships with women whom he had chosen because they reminded him of Angela, but Meg and Angela were all part of the same mixture, all connected to him through David. He felt he was at the centre of a web of interconnected relationships and events, and that circumstances had brought him to this point, this place, for a reason. He didn't know what had really happened to Meg, but had he spoken out about the things he'd seen, the truth would have come out. That much he was certain of.

He stood up and paced the room. The broken glasses he'd found half-buried in the pine needles where Ben Pierce and his friends had been killed lay on top of the photograph Ben's sister had given him. He picked them up and turned them over in his hand, the one remaining lens with its spidery cracks catching the light. When he'd found them he'd been struck by the notion that they were symbolic of a kind of vulnerability. He could feel the sharp ridge of glass from the cracked lens beneath his thumb. Ben and his friends were young when they died, as Meg had been when she vanished, and what was youth if not innocence, and what was innocence if not vulnerability? He felt as if Meg had risen from her watery resting place to remind him of an obligation he owed her. A debt he was being asked to fulfil dating from a long-lost summer of his youth.

CHAPTER TWENTY

Adam killed the engine and switched off the lights. He remained in the car for a while to allow his eyes to become accustomed to the darkness. He was parked on the grass verge beneath a tree through the branches of which a yellowing moon was occasionally visible between breaks in the clouds. When he got out a cold wind rattled the turning leaves. He shivered and pulled up his collar and started back towards the gate that barred the entrance to Nick's yard. In one hand he carried a torch, and at his waist he'd tied two plastic bags containing several pounds of steak and sausages. The knife he'd used to cut the meat up, both of which he'd stolen from the kitchen of the New Inn, was tucked in his belt. As he walked along the edge of the chain-link fence that surrounded the yard the torch beam flashed on one of the signs warning intruders to beware of the dog. He touched the handle of the knife for reassurance.

Through the gate he could make out dark stacks of rusting cars. There was no sound, other than a frog croaking somewhere nearby. He shook the gates so that the chain clanked, expecting at any second to hear the rush of paws across muddy ground as some half-starved and demented beast flew out of the darkness. However, there was nothing. He wasn't sure if this was a good or a bad thing. Did it mean the dog, for whatever reason, wasn't in there? Or worse, was it being cunning and even now was lying patiently in wait? Reluctantly he tucked the torch inside his jacket and started to climb.

Getting over the gate wasn't in itself a problem. He dropped the last couple of feet on the other side, taking care to favour his good leg and fall into a roll. Picking himself up he grabbed a chunk of meat with one hand and the knife with the other, his heart thumping as he searched the darkness. Twisted shapes rose from the ground and threw deep shadows where it would be easy for something to hide. The muddy avenues that led through the stacks of wrecks were black as pitch.

Adam had a plan. It depended on his reasoning that a guard dog's basic drive for food would override whatever training it had been subjected to. If it came after him he was going to keep it at bay with chunks of meat, at least temporarily. Somehow it had seemed like a better plan when he'd conceived it in his room.

He whistled, a low beckoning note, though it took him a couple of attempts to actually produce a sound because his mouth was as dry as sand. If the dog came he wanted to be close to the gate when he tested his theory. His palms were sweating. Fear oozed from his skin in what he was sure must be a heady chemical brew. There was no sound, no response at all.

'Here, boy,' he croaked.

His muscles began to cramp from the tension. There was no dog, he concluded. Perhaps the signs were a bluff. Perhaps Nick took it home at night.

Even so, as he began to make his way towards the corner of the yard where the Vauxhall was, he paused every few steps to listen and look around. Once or twice when he thought he saw a movement he froze, but each time nothing happened and he decided it must have been either a rat or else his mind playing tricks on him.

When he reached the wreck he shone his torch inside. It looked the same as when he'd left it. The knife went back in his belt and then he climbed in and closed each of the car's remaining three doors. They creaked loudly, sounding like a shriek in the stillness of the night. None of them had windows but at least he had the illusion of protection. Working by torchlight he squeezed his hand into the narrow space at the rear of the glove compartment until he felt something back there. As he had earlier that day he formed an impression of something damp and pliant. Gradually he worked his hand in far enough to get a grip on it. He tried not to think about the dog coming now, rushing out of the darkness while his hand was stuck fast.

Getting it out again was painful. He scraped the flesh of his knuckles against the broken edges of a chunk of plastic inside, gritting his teeth as he slowly shredded his skin. His prize was a damp wad of papers, which in the light of the torch he could see were covered with writing, though the ink had run and it was mostly illegible. He folded them and tucked them in his pocket. Just then he heard a sound and froze.

He strained to listen, his heart thudding, barely breathing. A gust of wind moaned softly through the abandoned wrecks as if they themselves were some hunched, stirring beast. Then it was silent. He began to breathe again, and reached for the door handle, and then he heard it again.

This time he knew what it was. A low bubbling snarl getting rapidly closer. His heart leapt in his chest. He flicked the torch beam into the darkness between two piles of wrecks and glimpsed a blurred black-and-tan shape thirty feet away hurtling straight at him.

'Shit.'

Desperately, he grabbed for a piece of meat from one of the bags at his waist. At the same time he dropped the torch and scrabbled for the knife. He heard the sound of breaking glass and the light went out, but by the light of the moon he could still see the dog. It was almost on him. He registered a broad muscular chest and lips drawn back over yellowed teeth. It scared him half to death that it had moved so fast. Ten feet away it leapt towards the open window that framed Adam's head. He reacted instinctively, propelling himself into the back seat with feet and hands like a terrified crab. He felt fur brush his hand as the animal's front paws landed squarely inside the car and its head and shoulders filled the open space of the window. The snarling grew frenzied accompanied by the sound of claws scratching frantically against the side of the door. He heard his jeans rip and felt fangs rake his ankle, but he was moving fast, still scuttling backwards out of the missing rear door. The dog came after him through the window and lunged for his face, teeth bared, eyes maddened by rage, and then Adam was out and rolling to get to his feet. He was on his knees but the dog was already there. It burst from the door with terrifying speed. He felt its hot breath against his skin and instinctively raised an arm to protect his face. A scream formed in his throat as the dog slammed into him and the force of its momentum knocked him off balance. He sprawled on his back expecting the crunch of its jaws and agonizing pressure as teeth ripped through flesh and splintered bone.

But suddenly the weight was gone. When he looked the dog had retreated a step or two and was wearing an almost comical expression of surprise.

It shook its head and swallowed. A single hungry gulp. He realized then that it had inadvertently seized the chunk of steak he'd been holding rather than a piece of his face. The respite lasted about two seconds before the dog lowered its head and growled menacingly, its purpose in life recalled. It took a stealthy step towards him.

Adam grabbed another piece of meat and tossed it a couple of feet away. 'There, boy, go get it.'

The animal hesitated, torn between its duty to rip out his throat and the lure of prime fillet. The fillet won. The dog sniffed it out and swallowed it.

Shakily, Adam rose to his feet while the dog fixed him with a baleful glare and a low threatening rumble escaped its throat. He fed it another chunk, tossing it further into the darkness, and then another while he quickly checked himself over. He was relieved to find he'd suffered no more than a few scratches, though he'd lost his torch. Warily he edged his way around to the front of the car with the dog following, its eyes never leaving him and its growling growing louder.

'Good boy. Want some more? Here you go.' He threw another handful of meat and while it was occupied retrieved his torch, which turned out to be broken, and started back towards the gate.

The dog followed, getting bolder and more threatening all the time as its stomach filled. Thirty yards from the gate the steak was gone and he was down to sausages. He fought the impulse to turn and run, and instead cut the bag free and heaved what was left as far away as he could.

'There you ugly bastard, go and make yourself sick.'

The dog stood its ground, seeming to sense this was its last chance to kill him. Its head twitched in the direction of the sausages but then it fixed its eye back on him, snarling, its legs quivering.

'Fuck.' Adam gripped the knife. His legs felt like jelly and his heart was pounding fit to burst.

Then abruptly the dog fell quiet, its posture relaxed. Defeated, it cast him a final, almost reproachful look before it turned and trotted into the darkness. Adam turned and ran. He scrambled up the gate and quickly dropped over the other side where he collapsed on his hands and knees, shaking all over, and was violently ill.

It was past midnight by the time he got back to his room. He felt drained. He took out the wad of papers he'd found in the wreck and put them on the bed. For this he had almost got himself killed.

Though they were damp and the ink had run on all of them, he managed to separate them into three identifiably separate documents, two of which were clearly photocopies. The first was a copy of some kind of certificate that was too far gone for him to have any hope of deciphering. The other was made up of seven sheets, each covered with handwritten notes in the same left-sloping hand with tight loops and curls. Four of the sheets were almost completely illegible, and of the rest only the occasional phrase could be made out. For the time being Adam laid them against the heater to dry them out while he turned his attention to the final document.

It was a single sheet. The weight and texture of the paper was different from the others. The ink had smeared in a haze of colours. Whereas the others were all black print on white, this one had red, green and blue at the top, all of which made him think that it was an original rather than a photocopy, and possibly a letterhead of some kind.

He removed the shade from the lamp by his bed and examined it under the bare light bulb, and after a while he put it down and fetched a pen and on a separate piece of paper he tried to copy down letters that he could read, and so isolate them from the smudges and faded characters that only distracted him. When he was done he looked at the result and was certain that it was a letterhead. The first letter looked like an L, but the rest of the word he couldn't make out at all, except for the final letter, of which only part was clear; a single horizontal line. The other words were the same, letters and parts of letters. He did his best to isolate each one. He thought there were two on the first line, the first with four letters, the second with five and possibly also beginning with L. The next line had four words, and then something beneath that in much smaller letters he couldn't make out at all except that perhaps it ended in a set of numbers.

A phone number, he wondered?

He went to work on the second word at the top starting with L. It was L something and then D and then what looked like an O. The O was strange though. It seemed to be the wrong size. Not an O, part of another letter. P? No, that wasn't right.

'What is it?' he murmured aloud.

He put it down for a moment, and walked around the room before he went back to take another look. At first there was nothing, then it came to him. G. It was a G. LblankDGblank. It didn't make sense. DG? And then suddenly it did make sense. He filled in the blanks. LODGE. He stared at the word he'd formed, his heart quickening.

A lodge. Something Lodge. Where Ben and his friends had stayed for two nights after they left the camp the night it was attacked. He grabbed the phone book and flicked through the Yellow Pages. It had to be somewhere close, he thought, and probably somewhere inexpensive. He found it almost immediately.

LAKE LODGE

CAMPERS' AND WALKERS' ACCOMMODATION
Peaceful Chalets with Views of Cold Tarn and the Fells

Though it was late he picked up the phone and dialled the number in the advert. After a few rings an answering machine cut in and a voice informed him that the lodge was closed for the season and went on to give details of when it would reopen, but no other contact number.

Adam hung up. A small map in the advert showed that the place was off the Geltsdale road high on the fells. He vaguely remembered a building visible from Cold Tarn, which had once been a hotel.

It was almost three in the morning when he called Karen's number in London. The phone rang endlessly, and then finally she answered, her voice heavily blurred with sleep.

'What time is it?'

'Late. Early. Sorry.'

Suddenly she sounded more awake. 'Adam? Is everything alright?'

'I'm fine. I nearly got my leg chewed off earlier, but I'm okay.'

'What?'

'I'll tell you some other time. Listen, have you found Jane Hanson yet?'

There was a pause. 'Are you calling me at . . . what? Two a.m.? Jesus, Adam!' He heard her take a deep breath. 'No, I haven't found her yet, but I will let you know when I do.'

'I'm sorry, Karen.' He passed a hand wearily through his hair. He shouldn't have called, but he needed someone to talk to, and it was Karen he'd thought of. 'Listen, go back to sleep, I'll speak to you tomorrow.'

'Great. Thanks for waking me, Adam.'

He was perplexed at the edge of anger in her tone until he recalled the way she had practically hung up on him the last time they'd talked.

'Are you still there?' he asked, thinking suddenly that she had done it again.

'Yes.'

'I should apologize,' he said. 'About the way I reacted to your news about Nigel. I'm sorry.'

'What are you sorry *for* exactly, Adam?'

'For being distracted by other things. For not being happier for you. I am. In a way anyway.'

'In a way?'

'Well, I have to admit it took me by surprise. I mean, I'm used to you being not married I suppose. Or being around or something.' He heard himself talking, and thought he wasn't making any sense at all. 'I think what I'm trying to say is I'll miss you.'

192

The truth was he'd experienced a vague twinge of jealousy at her news. He'd always felt there was something special about their friendship. It stemmed at least partly from the night they'd spent together a year or so earlier. Even though it had been a mistake, it had lent their relationship a kind of intimacy. Okay, they hadn't had sex, but they had slept entwined in one another's arms. He remembered watching her as she slept in the morning, and the confused tangle of emotions he'd felt. A kind of protectiveness and tenderness, along with a healthy dose of lust that only a cold shower had prevented him acting on. That and the fact that he liked her too much to screw their friendship up, literally or otherwise.

There was a moment of two of silence. 'Life moves on, Adam.'

'I know,' he said. The real truth here, he suddenly saw, was that they might have made a go of it together, but then he had thought that about other women at other times, and he'd always been wrong. He hadn't wanted that to happen with Karen, but he couldn't have explained that then, any more than he could now.

He heard her sigh at the other end of the line, a sound of weary resignation. 'Look, let's just forget it shall we? Apology accepted.'

'Right.'

'Since I'm awake now, I may as well tell you about Jane Hanson.'

'You did find her?'

'No, it seems that she's moved, and at the moment I don't know where to.'

Karen explained that she had managed to get Jane's address from the university, but that when she had left London for the summer she had also left her Battersea bedsit. 'I talked to a neighbour who remembered Jane saying something about starting a new job in September. She's been sending mail to an address she thought was a friend of Jane's. A flat in Clapham. I went there too, but there was nobody home. The woman next door told me the girl who lives in the flat works for an airline and she's often away, but she hadn't seen anyone who looked like Jane around and she didn't think anyone else was living there.'

'Great. What about the job she was starting? Any ideas about that?'

'No. Her neighbour thought it had something to do with PR, but that's all she knew.'

'Makes sense,' Adam said. 'So, that's it?'

'Not quite. I called the university back and managed to get an address for her parents. It's in Brighton. So far I haven't had any luck calling them, but I'll keep trying. I'll let you know if I make any progress.'

'Okay, thanks.'

'You still think it's important to talk to her?'

'Yes.' He looked at the documents he had spread out on his bed, reminded of why he had called Karen in the first place. 'I found something tonight which she might be able to explain.'

'What is it?'

'I'm not sure. From what I can make out it's somebody's medical records, or doctor's notes or something.'

'Medical records? Where did you get them?'

'In the wreck Ben was meant to be driving. I've been trying to decipher them. The patient was somebody called Marion Crane. From what I can make out she was in some kind of hospital for a period of several weeks. There are dates beside each entry. The first I can make out is T/27/4, which I assume is Tuesday the twenty-seventh of April. The last is M/22/5. Monday the twenty-second of May. There are a few more before and after that I can't make out. The notes mention medications and dosages and observations about her condition, but I can only read fragments so it's hard to put it all together. As far as I can tell she was suffering from some kind of illness, but she seems to have slowly recovered. I've found the phrase, "the patient's condition has improved" several times.'

He gave up and put his notes down. The long night and the hours staring at faded handwriting had taken its toll. His brain wasn't functioning properly any more and he had sharp pains in his temples. He should have left this until the morning, except that he couldn't escape the feeling there was something there, right in front of him, staring him in the face. But he couldn't see it.

'What does this have to do with the accident?'

'I don't know,' he said wearily. 'That's what I'm hoping Jane can tell me.'

'Can you find the doctor's name anywhere, or the hospital?'

'No. At least if there is I can't make it out.'

'What about the medication? What are the drugs mentioned?'

He brightened suddenly. Why hadn't he thought of that? He searched his notes, and then went back to the photocopies. 'There's one here. Clopalmazine. Fifty milligrams.'

'That's an antipsychotic I think. Hang on.' There was silence and then he could hear a tapping sound.

'What are you doing?'

'I'm in the other room. Wait, I'm just hooking up.'

He heard the sound of a modem, and then more tapping, which he realized was the sound of her typing into a computer keyboard. 'I'm starting a search,' she told him.

Adam cast his eyes over his notes again, his brain slowly clearing. It was starting to make sense.

'Here you go,' Karen said. 'Clopalmazine. A drug used in cases of acute depression. Blah blah and so on. The rest is technical stuff mostly, but it looks as if your mystery patient might have been in a psychiatric ward or hospital. Apparently Clopalmazine was superseded by more effective treatments in the late eighties.'

Adam looked back to the dates that appeared beside each entry made on the original sheet. 'You said Clopalmazine was superseded in the late eighties?'

'That's what it says here.'

'Can you get a twentieth-century calendar on your screen?'

'Don't see why not. Wait a sec.' He heard the tapping of keys. 'It's downloading now.'

'See if you can match the dates here to a year before the nineties. When does Tuesday the twenty-seventh of April first appear?'

'Hold on.' He heard tapping again. 'First hit before the year 1990 is 'eighty-five.'

'And the next?'

'Nothing then until 'seventy-eight, and then we're into the sixties. 'Sixty-nine. Do you want me to go on?'

He finished writing them down. 'No, it's okay.'

'You think your mystery patient could have been treated in one of those years?'

'It's a reasonable deduction. Somewhere to start anyway.'

He apologized again for waking her, and Karen promised to call as soon as she found Jane. After they'd hung up he stared at the dates he'd written down. 'Eighty-five. He had lived in Castleton that year. He would have been sixteen, and that summer he'd worked for the *Courier* during the school holidays. Something else had happened that summer too. 'Eighty-five was the year Meg Coucesco had vanished.

It was coincidence, he told himself. And yet intuitively he felt it was more than that. He had learnt over the years that life works in curious ways. Fate. Coincidence. A grand plan. Who knew? But maybe past and present were separated by little more than the blink of an eye. Perhaps every significant event had repercussions that resonate continually through life, affecting everything that follows.

In the end, defeated and exhausted, he fell into a deep and troubled sleep.

Part Three

CHAPTER TWENTY-ONE

The room where Mary lay on the big old-fashioned bed was lit by a single small lamp that stood on a scarred three-legged table. She had covered the shade with a red scarf, so that the light was like a heart. Warm, red, pulsing with blood. Sometimes she imagined that she could actually see it beating. As if it really was a heart, and she was in a womb surrounded by the pulsing flow of blood, of life. Safe and protected.

She heard the sound again, a muffled thump.

It's coming for you, Mary.

The voice in her head was both frightening and oddly comforting. She had lived with it for so long now that when it was absent she almost missed it. Without the voice the silence was like a vacuum. She remembered learning at school that nothing could live in a vacuum.

It's getting nearer, Mary. It won't be long now. The waiting is almost over.

She didn't know whom the voice belonged to. It didn't matter. When she was young, before she had started to become ill, she had read books about crazy people who heard voices in their heads. They gave their voices names. The Watchers or something like that. Those stories had made her heart thump under the covers at night, and sometimes she'd been afraid to turn out the light, but she knew in her heart that they were only stories, they weren't real. She didn't think that any more. The voice spoke in a sibilant dry whisper like something slithering through the grass.

She heard another thump, and then the creaking of floorboards, very faint, almost undetectable. The sound ceased. A mewing sound like that of a newborn kitten escaped her lips. A whimper of fear. She could feel a presence nearby. She wished Nick would come home. He knew how much she hated being here alone at night.

He's not coming.

The voice chuckled. It liked to taunt her, it liked her to be afraid. But she was not afraid of *it*. The voice could only take her fears and twist them, magnify them, parade them before her even when her eyes were screwed shut, but it couldn't hurt her. Sometimes she spoke back to it. She told it she wasn't afraid. It laughed, but she sensed its impotent anger, knowing that she had uncovered its Achilles' heel. But now the voice was enjoying itself, because what she was afraid of was real, it was not inside her head, it was real.

Mary opened her eyes. She heard the wind outside and felt the movement of air through the ill-fitting window frame. The thin cotton curtains flickered, and the scarf over the lamp lifted fractionally and fell like a breath, like the beat of a heart. Mary could see her reflection in the mirror above the dressing table. She was curled up in a foetal position, her thin, pale arms like those of a child. Her hair was lank and stringy and needed washing, her eyes stared wide, accentuated by dark smudges underneath.

I am a mess, she thought. Twenty-seven years old. Hard to believe. Much of her life was lost to her. She recalled it in fragments, as if viewing a jigsaw puzzle, the pieces of which had been scattered haphazardly on the floor. Her thoughts, her inner self, veered crazily between extremes. At times she understood a great deal about herself, at times she hardly knew who she was. Sometimes the voice in her head seemed more like the real her, and she, what she was now, faded and paled into the background. She thought this was the real goal of the voice, to dominate her, make her so afraid that she would just go away and then the voice would control her body. The voice was, she thought, only herself. Another part of her. The crazy part.

When she had been taking her medication the voice almost went away. She had felt as if she was waking from a kind of sleep, during which she had been conscious the whole time, immersed in a world her brain manufactured and that she was unable to escape from. But the other world, the one she knew everybody else lived in, slipped in and out of her own allowing her glimpses of reality, though it remained out of reach. The medication changed all that. She began to get better. The problem was that the medication made her shake, it made her feel sick and it left an unpleasant metallic taste in her mouth that wouldn't go away. When she looked at herself in the mirror she saw somebody with the slightly slack-jawed, vacant appearance of the heavily drugged. She moved through her days as if they were a swamp, she felt listless and tired. Eventually she'd made the decision to stop taking the medicine.

Mary rose from the bed and went to the window. She pulled the curtain aside a fraction and peered into the night. There was a moon, and the meadow was softly lit with grey light. Something moved to her left, close to the cottages, a shape merging with the wall, then with a piece of junk rotting in the long grass. It moved quietly, silently, and paused. It was lost in the depths of shadow beneath a twisted beech that had been struck by lightning years ago and now stretched bony dead branches to the sky. She stared at the black place where she thought it was, willing it to materialize until her vision swam. She couldn't see it, but she knew it was there. She could feel it.

It's watching you, Mary. Soon it'll come.

'Fuck off,' she muttered under her breath. Her heart was thumping, fear wrapped its sinewy limbs around her throat. She gripped the edge of the window frame and the tendons stood out hard on her thin wrist. The dark, almost purple scars underneath showed in sudden relief and as they caught her eye the voice chuckled. She ignored it, focusing on the movement outside. And then it was gone, for now, slipping away among the trees.

She went back to the bed and lay down, curling herself up again. There was a gun underneath the bed that Nick had put there. He'd told her that when she was frightened she should think of it. But she couldn't bring herself to touch it.

Her thoughts flowed like a river, churning and twisting over rocks, forming rapids, slipping away too fast for her to catch sometimes. The voice was trying to speak to her but the sound of the water drowned it out. She allowed herself to float, to be carried, and she fell into a restless sleep.

꙳

When she awoke she knew instantly that she wasn't alone. Terror seized her and she fought the urge to cry out.

It's here, Mary. It's come for you. I told you it would, you little bitch. Now you're going to be sorry. Now it's going to hurt you.

The voice chuckled and goaded her. It wanted her to be frightened. It wanted her to try to run. It came to her that the voice wanted her to die. *It* wanted to die. But she wasn't ready to give up. She remained still, controlling her breathing, pretending to be asleep.

It was at the door. She sensed the door was open because the flow of air across her body had altered. She could feel it across her bare thigh and buttock. She knew her skirt had ridden up, exposing her knickers. It was standing at the door staring at her. She could hear its breathing. Shallow. Watching. Thinking.

Please leave me alone. She said the words in her mind. Please. Please. Please. She thought about the gun under the bed. Where was Nick? Why wasn't he home? He left her alone too much. She was frightened. She couldn't prevent a pitiful sob escaping her lips. Her body trembled and she screwed her eyes shut.

Won't do you any good, Mary. It's going to get you. Now you're really going to get what you deserve.

She heard something move closer. Her eyes were tightly shut but she knew it was there. Time passed. How long? She didn't know. Slowly she opened her eyes. Something swam into her vision. Something not human, its shape changing, fluid. She wanted to scream but she couldn't make her voice work. She was paralysed with terror.

Then it moved away and she heard the door close, the click of the old-fashioned latch. Not this time. It had left her. Not this time. But it would be back. She knew it would be back.

CHAPTER TWENTY-TWO

The discovery in Cold Tarn made the breakfast TV news. Adam watched as reporters speculated about the bone, which the police were now confirming was human. Comparisons were drawn with the case of a woman's body that had been discovered in Ullswater a few years earlier, but in the absence of any real facts there wasn't much to report. John Shields was interviewed, enjoying his fifteen minutes of fame.

When Adam arrived at the lake he found a different scene from the day before. The promontory had been cordoned off and uniformed police were on hand to keep back the crowd of reporters and the merely curious. Janice was talking to somebody, but when she saw him she came over.

'Hello. Where've you been?'

'I had a late night,' he said drolly. She looked at him curiously but didn't ask anything more. Towards the lake a group of police officers, among them Graham, and several other people were standing around watching two people in a small boat fifty yards out on the lake. 'What's going on?'

'They've been sending divers down all morning, but they havenae found anything yet,' Janice said.

They watched the boat for a little while. A diver surfaced briefly, and there was a ripple of interest among the people on the shore, but when he vanished underwater again the murmur of voices returned.

The man that Janice had been talking to earlier passed them as he walked around with a phone glued to his ear trying to pick up a signal. When he smiled at her briefly she saw Adam's questioning look.

'He's a reporter from the *Mail*,' she said. 'They ran a story this morning.'

'About this?' Adam was surprised that they had heard about it in time to make the first edition.

'Hmmm.'

Janice avoided his eye, and then he understood. 'Did you tip them off?'

Guilt flashed across her expression. 'I know, I know, you don't have to say anything. I'm a terrible person.'

'I wasn't going to say that.'

'Aye, mebbe not. But you think it.'

Adam avoided commenting directly on what he thought. 'Does Findlay know?'

'He knows about the story, but I don't think he knows it was me that gave it to them.' She glanced at him. 'I'd appreciate it if you didnae say anything.'

'I think he'll work it out for himself.'

She frowned. 'Aye, I suppose he will. Listen, I know how it looks, but I don't want to be stuck here all my life, you know. Findlay should have stood by me when I wanted to do a piece about the planning committee. A story like that could've gotten me noticed.'

'You had no proof,' Adam pointed out.

'Oh, come on, you know as well as I do I could've written it so there was just enough to make people start asking questions. Findlay was just covering his arse.'

Adam didn't say anything. He had the feeling her defiance was more about justifying what she'd done to herself rather than to him.

'How else am I going to get out of here?' she said. 'I don't think the *Mail* are going to be impressed by my erudite coverage of the local flower show, do you?'

He was saved from having to answer by a shout from one of the men in the boat. A diver surfaced holding something up and suddenly all around them conversations ended and cigarettes were hurriedly put out as reporters and onlookers pressed forward for a better look. The journalist from the *Mail* hung up his phone and trotted over to join the others. The boat started back towards the shore, towing a line that was attached to something partly submerged and guided by two divers. At the beach it was immediately surrounded by a knot of people.

'What is it?' someone shouted, but the police took no notice.

Adam caught sight of a woman huddled in a thick coat. 'Isn't that the pathologist from Carlisle? Dr Keller?'

Janice nodded. Up on the promontory some photographers had slipped through the police tape and had positioned themselves in the hope of getting a good picture. A constable went after them and started herding them back again and as Adam watched a movement further back in the trees caught his eye. Someone was back there, hidden in the gloom among the pines high up on the top of the ridge. For a moment he couldn't make out who it was, then the figure moved into a patch of light and Adam saw that it was David. For a second it seemed as if their eyes collided, then abruptly David turned and vanished.

'What is it?' Janice asked, seeing Adam's expression.

'Nothing,' he said. He turned back to watch the group huddled on the beach.

Nick learned about the find in Cold Tarn when he stopped at the newsagent's to buy tobacco on the way to the yard. His eye caught the headline as he was handing over his money.

The old man behind the counter saw what he was looking at. 'We'll be swamped by the buggers now. There's been cars going up that road since before it was light. Says in there they're going to send divers down.'

Nick grabbed a paper and put it on the counter and the old man took his money and rang up the sale.

'Wonder who it was?' the old man said, eager to talk, but Nick took his change and left the shop without saying a word. The old man watched him go and shook his head. 'Surly bugger,' he muttered. He went back to unwrapping the bundles of papers the way he did at this time every day. He shivered; it was getting colder in the mornings. He glanced at the sky, which was flecked with harmless fluffy white cloud. This weather couldn't last. He could feel a change in the air, making his rheumatism play up.

When he reached the yard Nick unlocked the gate, whistling through his teeth for the dog. It appeared at the corner of the barn, its tail between its legs. 'C'mere,' he called and dug in his pocket for the chunk of dog roll and the handful of biscuits that comprised its daily meal. With barely a look he tossed them on the ground and swung open the gates. When he turned around the dog hadn't moved. Fucking animal! What was wrong with it? 'Suit yourself then.' He kicked the food to one side as he went back to his Landcruiser. Even when he stopped by the barn the bloody animal hadn't moved. He thought there must be something wrong with it.

It was only when he got out that he noticed the dog's swollen belly. As he started round the back to chain it up it trotted meekly ahead of him with its head down. The stink around there was terrible. Bloody dog had been sick. He chained it up and looked around, wondering what the hell it had eaten. It lay with its head on its paws looking half dead. He hadn't noticed if the barn door had been forced. Someone had poisoned a dog once so they could break into the yard. Kids probably, looking for money, but he never kept any around. They'd wrecked the office though, the little bastards.

He went back around to the front of the building but the door was secure and when he opened up there was no sign of disturbance inside. Maybe the dog had caught a rabbit with myxie or something. He put the kettle on to make coffee and rolled a cigarette. Then he sat down at the table and took the rolled-up paper out of his pocket. When he'd finished reading he looked at the phone. He hesitated before he dialled David's number at the sawmill. There was no answer. Too early. After a while he went outside and rolled another smoke. He needed to think. Everything was coming apart. Everywhere he turned. For a while he'd thought it would be okay. Then Adam turned up, sticking his bloody nose in. Jesus. Now this. And Mary. Mad Mary. She thought something was going to get her. Maybe she was right.

He couldn't think. He needed to work. He picked up his tools and went down through the yard. He'd finish stripping that Jag. He could think better when he worked.

He might not have noticed the Vauxhall, except for the foot-prints in the mud. Dog and man. The dog never strayed far from the barn. He paused. The door was shut, and as he stared at it he saw the scratch marks, long thin scrapes. He knew what they were instantly. The bloody dog made the same marks when it scratched against the barn door. He went over and looked inside the car. Something glistened on the floor and when he picked it up he saw it was a piece of glass. Thin, not like glass from a window. The glove compartment hung open. Hadn't it been jammed shut when the car had come in? He remembered catching Adam here, the look on his face.

Shit! He turned and went back towards the barn.

David sat in his Land Rover at the bottom of Back Lane where he'd parked after leaving the tarn. He'd been there for more than an hour, and he was cold though he barely noticed it. He caught a movement in the rear-view mirror and glancing up saw a woman standing outside one of the council houses across the road. She had her arms folded across her chest and was staring in his direction with a frown of open disapproval, almost hostility. Wondering what he was doing there. Nosy bloody bitch!

He was surprised by the vehemence of the thought. He looked in the mirror at his bloodshot eyes. Christ, he was cracking up. He looked liked shit. He hadn't been home the night before. After Graham had phoned to tell him about what had been found in the tarn he'd stayed at his desk in the office, drinking steadily as it grew dark. He hadn't wanted to face Angela again. Especially not now. He knew he wouldn't be able to look her in the eye. Perhaps he wouldn't ever be able to again. But then maybe he wouldn't get the chance because she wouldn't be there. He smiled grimly at the thought. No doubt Adam would be happy.

Adam! Fucking Adam! Sometimes he thought that name had been a curse to him ever since that day they'd waited by the road for him when they were kids. Somebody new on the estate they'd heard, a kid from London. Some snotty Southerner. He tried to remember whose idea it had been to make him pay to pass. But of course it would have been Nick's. His was another name that had become a curse. Where the hell was he? He tried calling the yard again, but like every other time that morning there was no answer.

It was funny how a person's life could be changed by something that at the time seemed insignificant. And that one thing shaped your life for ever. Take that day on the road. Adam had given him a bloody nose, but he'd still helped him up. Why had he done that? He supposed he'd felt bad about making him fight. He'd liked him too for some funny reason. Maybe because even though it was obvious he'd been scared he'd tried not to show it and he hadn't backed down. He remembered seeing Adam on the first day of term at Kings and feeling guilty about what had happened so he'd gone over and offered to shake his hand. Nothing was ever simple again after that. He'd known from the start that Nick and Adam would never mix. They were like oil and water. If it had been just Graham it would have been okay, Graham had always been easy-going, but Nick, he was a different matter.

David leaned forward and rested his head on the wheel. He had a headache. It felt like something tightening around his skull. Squeezing his brain. He hadn't even known why he'd liked Adam. Always with his nose stuck in a book, didn't know one end of a fishing rod from another hardly. He supposed it was partly that they went to the same school, not that he'd ever wanted to go to Kings. That had been his dad's idea, and he'd only just scraped in. Not like Adam. It was obvious from the start that he was smart and maybe that's why he'd liked him. He was different. The trouble was Nick. Or maybe it was both of them. He'd never really understood it himself. It was like they both wanted something from him. He knew Nick was somehow threatened by Adam, as if he thought Adam would take his place or something and so he'd always had to make sure he didn't make Nick feel he was being pushed away, but at the same time he had to be a friend to Adam. And he'd always felt as if Adam needed him somehow. It seemed as if he was always trying to work this balancing act between the two of them but somehow he couldn't do it and when it came down to it he'd known Nick his whole life.

Jesus. It was all so long ago and now it was such a fucking mess.

It had felt strange up at the tarn earlier. When was the last time he'd been there? Years. More than he could remember. That place held nothing but bad memories. He'd watched Adam while the boat came back to shore. For a few seconds he wasn't thinking about what the divers had found, instead he was thinking about an early morning years ago when the ground had been covered in snow. He could picture what had happened as if it was just a day or two ago. He'd been thinking about Angela. Wondering what he was going to do. He'd known he couldn't go on the way he had been for much longer. He was starting to think about them together, wondering what they did. Sometimes he'd found himself watching them with his fists clenched and he'd had to turn away so they wouldn't see what he was thinking. Then he'd heard a movement behind him, something glimpsed underneath a tree across a small clearing. He'd lifted his gun because he needed the distraction and he was bored because there weren't going to be any ducks anyway. He'd thought at first that it was a deer. Then the voice of caution reminding him never to shoot at anything until he was certain of the target. He remembered peering into the grey half-light and starting to form a shape but it had moved again and before he could properly consider what he was doing he'd pulled the trigger.

His hands had been numb, his fingers clumsy. He remembered the roar and flash mingled with a scream that didn't come from any deer. But there had been an instant. An instant when he'd seen. Seen what? Fuck! Fuck! He banged his forehead on the wheel. Thud. Thud. Thud. Repeatedly until he thought he felt the skin break. Jesus Christ! What was happening to him?

He was breathing heavily. Taking great gasps of air, his whole body shuddering. He should have known that day when he'd watched Angela dive from the bridge. He should have known then, when he felt something tighten in his throat, when he felt the muscles in his belly clench, that it would all end in fucking disaster. And maybe now, finally, it would. In a way he was almost grateful. All of his life since Adam had left he'd been waiting for him to come back. No, that couldn't be true. But maybe he'd felt as if he'd been living a life he didn't deserve. That someday it would all come down around his ears.

What if he'd noticed Angela before Adam had? He'd asked himself that question a million times. He didn't know why he hadn't, except that she was just Angela. He had known her so long she was just there. But what if it hadn't been like that? What if he had been with her the night of the disco? Then he would never have talked to Meg. Then he wouldn't be sitting here now. Christ! What was the point of torturing himself? What was the fucking point?

He felt something wet on his face, and for a second he thought it must be raining, but the window wasn't open and anyway it wasn't rain. He looked at his wet fingers. His vision was all blurred. Tears. For fuck's sake he was crying! He laughed, but it was a harsh choking sound that caught in his throat. He was falling apart, cracking up. He'd end up like the girl Nick lived with, Mary, who was completely crazy.

He got out of the car, stumbled into the road and slammed the door behind him. He looked back to see if the woman across the street was still watching him, but he couldn't even see through the tears swimming in his eyes. It was happening to him more and more. He thought it was partly the booze. Partly. Wasn't it supposed to make you melancholy? He supposed that was true. It stopped him from thinking too, that was why he did it. It allowed him to sleep. He didn't think about dead people.

He stumbled along the bridleway, wiping his eyes, pulling himself together. There was worse to come, he knew that now. Adam would make sure of that. His conscience, his fucking tormentor. He would bring it all down. He didn't understand the town, he didn't understand any of it and he never had, and because of that he would destroy it all.

At the bridge he paused to look at the cottages on the other side. He didn't come here much, couldn't remember the last time he had. It was strange that Nick had lived here for so long, a place that couldn't hold many happy memories, if any. But Nick was odd, you never really knew what he was thinking. He supposed that was why Nick and Mary lived together. They were suited in a peculiar way. One thing he'd never thought was that Nick would sell the cottages. He'd always said he wouldn't, though he wouldn't spend a penny to fix them up either. Even when Forest Havens had said they wanted this land to build their boathouse, and offered him more than it was worth, Nick had said he wouldn't sell. But then the offer had been increased, several times, and finally Nick had agreed. Who wouldn't? But even then it seemed Nick was reluctant. Funny how everybody has their price. And once it's reached, funnier still the things that people are capable of to protect what they cherish. Ha-ha. Fucking hilarious.

He crossed the bridge. He hadn't been here in over a year. Maybe two. The sun was on the roofs. The cottages looked unlived-in, forgotten and abandoned. He emerged from the trees as the sun slid behind a cloud and shadows raced across the meadow. He felt suddenly cold. But he was often cold these days. He shivered. Somebody walking over his grave. He wasn't eating properly. He'd lost weight lately. He could feel his bones grind. Nick's car wasn't there. He wondered where the hell he could be. Maybe Mary would know. He went towards the door and as he did a curtain twitched in the bottom window. He raised his hand to knock but before he could the door was flung open and he found himself staring down the barrel of a twelve-bore shotgun.

He heard the click and felt a massive rush of fear like a physical blow. It took his breath away. He knew his life was about to end. Somewhere behind the fear he felt a tiny glimmer of relief.

CHAPTER TWENTY-THREE

Adam was the last to leave the lake. The area around the shore remained cordoned off with police tape, and a single unlucky constable had been left to ensure the scene wasn't disturbed; he was sitting on a log near the water's edge, smoking a cigarette and idly skimming stones. Across the other side of the lake, high up on the fells a building was visible. That, Adam thought, must be Lake Lodge. Funny how Ben and his friends should have stayed there of all places after leaving the camp. In view of the lake, from which invisible strands seemed to radiate, linking past and present. And now something had been found out there, beneath the dark cold water. Possibly Meg Coucesco, or what was left of her after all this time. He wondered about David being there earlier. There was a kind of symmetry to it all.

He pulled up the leg of his jeans. His knee was aching and it looked red and inflamed. One day he was going to have to see a specialist and find out if anything more could be done or he would be crippled with arthritis by the time he was fifty. He kneaded the flesh and began massaging it in a circular motion.

'You alright?'

Startled, he looked up and found the police constable he'd been watching earlier standing in front of him. 'I'm fine. It's just an old injury.' He rolled down his jeans, embarrassed in some way by the exposed scars.

'Thought you'd have gone with the others,' the constable said.

'Oh, I'm not one of them.'

'I wasn't sure. So, if you're not a journalist how come you're here?'

The question, Adam saw, was asked out of simple friendly curiosity. He didn't correct the assumption that he wasn't a journalist. 'I'm staying at the same pub as John Shields. The one that found the bone.'

'The fisherman? Is that his name?' The constable took out his cigarettes and offered one to Adam before lighting up. 'I only heard about it this morning,' he explained. He stared glumly across the water. 'I'll probably be here all bloody day.'

'You're not based in Castleton then?'

'No. Carlisle. I think there's only a couple of lads in the town. So, what are you doing around here then? Holiday is it?'

'Sort of.'

'Well, give you something to tell everyone when you get home, won't it?'

'I suppose it will,' Adam agreed. 'What was it they bought out of the lake earlier then?'

The constable sucked on his cigarette. 'I shouldn't really say anything.'

'I understand. I expect I'll hear about it on the news tonight anyway.'

The constable thought about that. 'Well, I don't suppose it matters. That was a body they pulled out before. What was left of it anyway.'

Adam looked impressed. 'Really?'

'Wrapped up in something it was,' the constable added with the air of somebody privy to confidential information. 'Know what that means?'

'What?' Adam asked, though he did know what it meant.

'Somebody must have done it. Wrapped the body up I mean.' He adopted an expression of authority. 'That means it was murder, see. I mean, it couldn't be an accident or suicide, could it?'

'I see what you mean. Do they know who it was?'

'Not yet.' The constable flicked his butt towards the water. 'They might never know. And I don't suppose they'll ever find who did it.'

'Why's that?'

'Stands to reason doesn't it? Whoever it was has been in there a bloody long time. No evidence see.'

'I suppose you're right.' Adam stood up. 'Well, the crowd should be gone now, so I better get going myself.'

The constable suddenly appeared to regret having said so much, as if Adam was betraying his confidence by leaving.

'On holiday you said?' His tone was a little more officious.

'Sort of.'

'What did you say your name was?'

'I didn't.'

He left the constable looking vaguely worried about having said more than he should have. He started off through the trees heading back towards the road where he'd left his car. His knee still ached, and he was conscious of limping.

His mobile phone rang as he was driving towards town and when he picked up it was Angela.

'Did you hear what they found at Cold Tarn?' she asked.

'Yes, I've just come from there.'

'I've been watching it on the news; they think it's a body.' She paused and then as if it had just occurred to her said, 'What were you doing there?'

'The people that found it are staying at the pub. I was curious.'

'Oh.'

The line went silent, and he thought he'd lost the connection. 'Angela?'

'I'm here. I was thinking about something.'

'You sound tired.'

'I didn't sleep well.' Another long pause, and then she said, 'David didn't come home last night. I called the sawmill earlier but nobody's seen him since yesterday.'

'I saw him this morning. He was up at the lake.'

'David was?' She sounded puzzled. 'Did you speak to him?'

'No.' She was silent again, no doubt wondering why not. 'Look, what are you doing today?' he asked impulsively.

'I don't know. Nothing specific I suppose. I've asked the mother of one of Kate's friends if she could stay for a few days.'

'I've got a few things to do, why don't you come with me,' he suggested.

'I don't know,' she answered uncertainly. 'I don't want to get in the way.'

'You won't. I'd be glad of the company.'

'What are you doing anyway?'

'There are a few things I have to check on.'

'Is this to do with the story you're working on?'

'Yes.'

He could sense her thinking about it, and he also sensed some underlying conflict in her. In the end she agreed though, and he told her he'd pick her up in half an hour.

Carisbrook Hall had been built in 1825. Renovations were under way but it would be some time before the building would appeal to the kind of upmarket buyer the developer was hoping would be lured by the old red brick façade. The giant billboard adjacent to the main road promoted period features and a chance to own a slice of history as well as a secure investment. The interior of the building was to be gutted and the new apartments would be state of the art. An artist's rendition of the finished landscaped exterior made the place look like part of a country estate. At the moment though, the building, which was all that remained of the original hospital, looked dark and grim. The windows were mostly broken, the brickwork stained and blackened by a hundred years of grime, and the towers that topped each wing gave it a gothic, fortress-like appearance. High brick walls flanked the remains of the huge wrought-iron gates that had once barred entry to grounds that were now overgrown and littered with abandoned waste. Adam wondered about the people who had once been incarcerated here. What had they thought when they first viewed the place? It must have been a forbidding and terrifying sight when they passed through the now broken gates.

'What are we doing here?' Angela asked.

They hadn't spoken much on the way to Carlisle. Angela had seemed distracted, caught up in her own thoughts. He thought he sensed a trace of coolness towards him. He showed her the papers he'd recovered from the wreck in Nick's yard. 'I think they're the patient records of somebody called Marion Crane, who was being treated for some kind of psychiatric illness in the mid-eighties. Possibly here, since it was the main psychiatric facility for the area at the time.'

After making a few phone calls Adam had discovered that Carisbrook Hall had been part of the old general hospital then.

Angela frowned as she read what was still legible. 'How do you know it was in the mid-eighties? I don't see any date here.'

He explained about the use of Clopalmazine mentioned in the notes, and how the days and months corresponded to the year 1985.

'I don't understand. What does this have to do with the accident?'

'I found these notes in their car in Nick's yard.' He explained how he'd broken in the night before.

'Why did you have to break in? Why not just go when Nick was there?'

'Because somehow I didn't think he'd want me nosing around. The other day I was at the district council offices. They have a model of the Forest Havens development there. Did you know they're going to demolish the cottages where Nick lives to build a boathouse?'

'Yes, I think I remember hearing something like that,' she said.

'I'd love to know how much Forest Havens paid for that land. I wouldn't mind betting it was a hell of a lot more than it was worth six months ago.'

She thought about what his tone implied. 'What exactly are you saying, Adam?'

'You remember what I said about the rumours surrounding the planning application? And maybe Ben and his friends had proof of something that if it got out could have stopped the development?'

'You think Nick was involved?'

'He had a motive for wanting the development to go ahead.'

'So, when you broke into his yard you were looking for proof?'

'I didn't know what I'd find. But if they did have some kind of proof it has to be somewhere.'

'And this is it?' Angela held up the photocopied records.

'I have no idea,' Adam admitted.

Angela was silent. She avoided looking at him directly. 'The other day,' she said after a while. 'When you mentioned the rumours about some of the committee being bribed, you were hinting that David was involved too, weren't you?'

'You have to admit he has a motive for wanting the development to go ahead, and he doesn't deny that he lobbied the council.'

'I asked him about it.'

'What did he say?'

She shook her head, a gesture of frustration and disenchantment. 'We had a fight. He denied it at first.'

'At first?'

'Then he started trying to justify himself. He said nobody had been bribed, I don't know, he was making it sound as if this kind of thing goes on all the time.'

'What kind of thing?'

'I'm not sure. Tenders leaked, contracts agreed with a nod and a wink I suppose.'

'So he admitted it?'

'In a way.'

He knew she had to have guessed what he was thinking; that if David was involved with corruption, and if that had anything to do with the accident that had killed Ben Pierce and his friends, then perhaps he was involved with that too. She didn't say anything, however. Instead she seemed to withdraw from him.

He parked the car outside the new unit that had replaced Carisbrook Hall. It consisted of a number of smallish square buildings built around a central grassy mound where seats had been placed for the patients so that they could sit outside when the weather was fine. Though the design of the buildings themselves was drab and generally uninteresting, the flowerbeds and a few trees gave the place a feeling of normality. Perhaps that was the whole point, Adam thought, comparing it to the old Hall. Maybe the buildings had been deliberately designed to be unimposing and functional. Certainly the unit looked more like a collection of council offices than a facility for the treatment of the mentally ill.

At the reception desk Adam asked to speak to somebody senior on the staff and the woman he spoke to asked them to take a seat in the waiting area. A woman, who was perhaps in her early forties, eventually approached them. She introduced herself as Dr Grafton, the assistant director, and led the way to her office.

'Now, how can I help you?' she asked, when she was sitting at her desk.

'I'm trying to locate somebody who might have been a patient at Carisbrook Hall before it was closed,' Adam said. 'I was hoping that perhaps somebody here might be able to help.'

'I see. The person you want to locate, this would be a relative?'

'No.'

Dr Grafton folded her hands on her desk. 'Then I'm afraid that you've had a wasted journey. You see even if we did have the information you want, I wouldn't be able to give it to you. It's a matter of patient confidentiality.'

Adam had expected this and, unable to think of a way around it, he'd decided simply to play it by ear. He seized on a phrase she had used. 'You said even if you did have the information? Does that mean you don't keep the records from the old hospital here?'

'Actually, there was a fire at Carisbrook the year it closed. Almost all of the administration records were destroyed.'

'I remember that now,' Angela said. 'It must have been about four or five years ago.'

It was a setback Adam hadn't expected. 'You mean all of the patient files prior to that time were destroyed in the fire?'

'Yes.'

'So, there's no way of telling whether somebody was treated there or not?'

'Unless their files were sent on to another facility or to a patient's own doctor, as sometimes happened, yes.'

Adam took out the copies of Marion Crane's files and passed them across the desk. 'Doctor, I understand your point about patient confidentiality, but could you at least tell me if these notes could have come from Carisbrook?'

She picked them up and scrutinized them. 'May I ask where you got these?'

'I found them among the effects of somebody who recently died,' he said, simplifying the truth.

She put them down. 'There's nothing here to indicate which hospital they might have come from. If indeed they came from a hospital at all. What makes you think they were from Carisbrook?'

'Only that it was the main facility here during the time that Marion Crane was treated.'

Dr Grafton looked again at the documents and Adam anticipated her next question. 'The use of Clopalmazine and the dates there suggest the year 1985.'

'I see,' she said, and Adam took her barely perceptible nod as agreement.

She folded her hands on the desk and regarded him thoughtfully. 'What precisely is your interest in the patient referred to here? I believe you said you were looking for her?'

'That's right.' He struggled to come up with a plausible explanation, but off the top of his head he couldn't think of anything that he thought she would believe. 'The truth is it's possible Marion Crane, whoever she is, may have information that I'm interested in. More than that I can't say, because frankly I don't know any more.'

Dr Grafton considered this before she commented. 'You know, it's curious but you're the second person to come here recently with questions about Carisbrook Hall.'

'Why curious?'

'That person was also interested in a specific year: 1985 in fact.'

Adam's pulse quickened. 'When was this?'

'It must have been in August sometime. Near the beginning I think.'

'And was the person you spoke to a young woman by the name of Jane Hanson?'

'Yes, I believe that was her name.'

'Did she also ask about somebody who had been a patient at Carisbrook?'

'No. Actually she wanted to know where she could find Dr Colin Webster.'

'Is he somebody who works here?'

219

'No. But he used to be the director of Carisbrook. He retired when it was closed down.' She gestured to the document that still lay on the desk. 'I suppose there's no harm in my telling you this much. This is indeed, as you'd guessed, a copy of part of a patient file from Carisbrook.'

'How can you tell?' Adam asked.

'For two reasons. The first is that I worked at Carisbrook myself for several years.'

'And the second?'

'I recognize the handwriting. It's Dr Webster's.' She smiled enigmatically. 'I assume you'll want to speak to him. You'll find his number in the phone book. He lives in a village just north of the city. Though I should warn you he'll probably tell you the same thing I did, that patient confidentiality prevents him discussing any specific case. And another thing, it might be better if you didn't mention that I sent you.'

'Do you mind if I ask why?'

'Let's just say that Dr Webster and I didn't always see eye to eye.' She smiled and rose from her seat. 'And that's really all I can tell you.'

She showed them back out to the reception area, where they shook hands.

'One other thing,' Adam said. 'Do you know why Jane Hanson was looking for Dr Webster?'

'I'm afraid you'll have to ask him that,' she said, and with a faintly enigmatic smile added, 'Good luck.'

Outside they fastened their coats against the bitter wind and walked towards Adam's car. Angela was deep in thought, her chin buried in the upturned collar of her coat, her eyes on the ground. When they got in the car Adam turned the heater on full.

'Who is Jane Hanson?' Angela asked.

As he pulled out of the car park Adam explained her link to Ben Pierce and told her about the arrangement Jane had with Janice Munroe at the *Courier*.

'Which is why you think those lads may have had some kind of proof of council corruption?'

'Basically, yes.'

'But why don't you just ask this Jane Hanson herself?'

'Because she's somewhere in London, but I don't know where yet, and I can't wait to find out. Besides, there's no guarantee she'll talk to me. Hang on a sec.' Adam called Directory Inquiries on his phone and asked for a number for a Dr Colin Webster in the Carlisle area. After a moment the operator said she had a listing for that name in Staveton. When he hung up he asked Angela if she knew the place.

'Yes, it's a village not far from the airport. Just go back out the way we came in and then turn north at the big roundabout.'

Adam headed back towards town and followed the road around past the castle.

'So, why do you think Jane Hanson didn't ask about Marion Crane directly?' Angela asked.

The same question had occurred to Adam. 'Maybe we're working from opposite directions. It could be that she knew something that eventually led her to Marion Crane's patient file. We have the file, but we don't know what it means.'

He picked up his phone again and called the number Directory Inquiries had given him and when a woman answered he asked for Dr Webster.

'My husband isn't here at the moment,' she said. 'He won't be long though, he's just taken the dog for a walk. Can I take a message?'

He asked her if she thought her husband could spare him a few minutes of his time. He was vague about his reasons, saying only that he was interested in Carisbrook Hall. She seemed quite happy to agree.

'To be perfectly honest I think Colin gets a little bit bored with my company every day.' She laughed. 'I expect he'll be glad to talk to you.'

He thanked her and hung up. They passed the airport and a little further on a sign indicated a left turn to Staveton, though Angela didn't even notice. She was absorbed with her own thoughts. He had the feeling that she had withdrawn from him again. He took the turn anyway and when half a mile further they came to a small pub on the edge of another village he pulled over. Angela looked at him questioningly.

'Let's get something to eat,' he said.

She nodded, but didn't say anything. Inside she sat at a table while he ordered sandwiches and drinks at the bar but when he brought them over she didn't touch hers.

'Something's bothering you. What is it?' he asked.

She fixed her gaze on him. 'What do you think happened to those three lads, Adam?'

'I don't know yet.'

'But you suspect something. You think somebody killed them because of what they'd found out.' Her voice rose angrily. 'Dammit! You think David is involved don't you? Is that why you told me about the rumours surrounding the committee? Were you hinting at more than just bribery?' She stared at him, shaking her head at the answer she saw in his expression. 'You wanted me to confront him! Christ, I feel like an idiot. All morning I've been thinking about it. I kept hoping I was wrong. But I'm not am I?'

'Wait a minute, I didn't want you to do anything,' he protested.

'No? I don't believe you. Why did you hint at David's involvement then?'

'Look, maybe it's true I wanted to see how you reacted, to see if you knew about the rumours, I probably even wanted you to think about it.'

'And now you want me to think about whether my husband is capable of murder, is that it? Is that why you asked me to come with you today?'

'No, of course it isn't,' he said, though she was partly right.

'Then why?'

'I just wanted to see you.'

Her eyes widened fractionally, a reaction not so much to what he'd said as to something she detected in his tone. For a few seconds they were both silent and then she started to get up. When she spoke she didn't sound angry any more, but her voice was coldly controlled.

'You're wrong, Adam. You're talking about *murder*. How could you even think David is capable of something like that? You don't even know that it wasn't just a terrible accident. And even if it wasn't then there are hundreds of people who want that development at least as badly as David. What about Nick? Or the people at Forest Havens or somebody on the council committee? For God's sake, why would you think it could be David?'

She stared at him uncomprehendingly. He wanted to stop her from leaving, but he didn't know what he could say to her. She didn't believe David was capable of what he was suggesting. She couldn't. But then why should she? David was her husband. It was clear they had problems, and so what if he was drinking heavily? That didn't mean she could stop loving him, didn't mean she could suddenly see the man who was the father of her child as capable of taking another life. And she was right, David wasn't the only one who had a motive. Apart from anyone else there was Nick of course. Not forgetting Nick. Well, maybe David didn't act alone.

She left without saying another word, and he didn't try to stop her. He watched the door swing closed behind her, aware of the curious glances from a couple at the bar.

What could he say? She thought she knew David, but she didn't know about Meg. Nobody did. Nobody except him.

When he went outside she was nowhere to be seen. As he drove into the village he passed a taxi parked outside a garage. He glimpsed a figure through the garage window and slowed when he saw that it was Angela, but even as he stopped she came out and climbed into the back of the taxi. As she did she glanced along the road, perhaps seeing the Porsche out of the corner of her eye, and for a moment she hesitated, but then the door closed and the taxi pulled away.

CHAPTER TWENTY-FOUR

The Websters lived in a large stone house surrounded by a wall and within a stone's throw of a squat church with a square tower. Adam assumed the house was the old rectory. A wild cherry tree grew in the middle of the lawn. The gates were open so he drove in and parked next to a Mercedes estate. When he climbed the steps and rang the bell a woman with short grey hair opened the door. She wore a tweedy skirt and a string of pearls and greeted him with a polite questioning smile. He introduced himself and told her he had phoned earlier.

'Oh, yes. Do come inside. It's rather cold today isn't it? We've had such lovely weather too. Let me take your coat.'

'Thank you.' He shrugged it off and she hung it on a stand in the hall.

The woman introduced herself as Cecilia Webster and told him that her husband was in the front room.

'He likes to read in front of the fire after lunch,' she said, and then leaned a little closer with a conspiratorial air. 'He usually falls asleep actually, so you've come just at the right time. Follow me and I'll take you through.'

She led the way past open doors, through which he glimpsed large well-furnished rooms, the walls of which were painted in traditional deep reds and greens, the carpets thick and luxurious. The front room was in fact on the southern side of the house. French windows opened onto a stone flagged terrace with steps that led into a formally laid out garden.

'Colin. This is the young man I told you about who phoned earlier.' She turned slightly towards Adam. 'Mr Turner, this is my husband.'

Colin Webster rose from a comfortable-looking wing chair on one side of the fireplace in which some huge logs burned fiercely. He had the kind of thin, refined features that lent him a slightly aloof and vaguely aristocratic air, an effect that was heightened by the fact that he wore a greenish-coloured suit with a dark striped tie. His smile was polite, but lacking in warmth. It was easy to imagine him wearing a white coat over his suit, striding the wards of Carisbrook Hall with the detached manner of an intellectual observer, issuing instructions to subordinates who trotted along in his wake. He shook Adam's hand and gestured to a chair.

'Please, do sit down, Mr Turner.' He turned to his wife. 'Are you going out Cecilia?'

'Yes, I'm just going into the village to get a few things.'

'Perhaps we could have some tea first?'

'Of course.' She smiled at Adam. 'Do you drink tea, Mr Turner?'

'Yes, thanks. That would be nice.'

'Right. I shan't be long then.'

She left the room and closed the door behind her, and only then did Webster sit down again. He crossed his legs and steepled his fingers. 'My wife tells me you phoned earlier. You mentioned that you wish to discuss Carisbrook Hall?'

'That's right.' Adam said that he was a journalist from London covering the protest at Castleton Wood. 'You're aware of the development plans for the estate?'

Webster made a small gesture, both of acknowledgement and dismissal. 'Only in the vaguest terms I'm afraid.'

'Well, anyway, during the course of preparing some background material I learned that one of the protesters, a young woman, had come across some information that might throw the development into question. I believe it may have had something to with Carisbrook Hall.'

Webster raised his eyebrows in mild surprise. 'Really?'

'I understand this young woman may have been to see you? Her name is Jane Hanson.'

Webster thought for a moment and then raised one finger in recognition. 'Yes, now that I think about it I do recall a young woman by that name. She telephoned once.'

'Did you ever meet her?'

'No. In fact I only spoke to her briefly.'

'Do you mind if I ask what you discussed?'

'Not at all. As I recall she was, as you say, interested in Carisbrook Hall.' Webster frowned slightly as he sought to remember their conversation. 'I recollect that she asked me some questions about patient numbers, the kind of complaints that were commonly treated, that kind of thing. It was really very general information.'

'She didn't ask to meet with you?'

'No. Actually, I was rather surprised that she had phoned me at all, to be frank. The things that she wanted to know are readily available in far more comprehensive form than anything I could tell her. There have been several books written about the history of Carisbrook Hall that are available in the local library. In fact, I told her as much.'

'She didn't ask you anything else? Nothing about a specific patient for example?'

'No,' Webster said, his tone stiffening. 'And of course if she had I would not have been able to answer her questions anyway. I'm sure you're aware of the rules of patient confidentiality, Mr Turner.'

'Yes, of course. What about a particular period? Did she mention a specific date or period that she was interested in?'

'No. As I said, her enquiries were of an extremely general nature.'

Just then the door opened and Cecilia Webster wheeled in a tea trolley. She bustled about pouring for them both, while her husband ignored her presence other than to murmur a faint thank you when she passed him his cup. Dr Webster, Adam thought, was a man used to having people attend to his needs. Cecilia Webster told Adam that it had been nice meeting him.

'I'll be back soon,' she said to her husband.

Webster barely acknowledged her. After she had left he picked up his cup and saucer and stirred methodically, his spoon clinking against the china cup. Then he sipped his tea and put his cup and saucer down on the table. He offered Adam a biscuit from some arranged on a plate before choosing one himself. The entire sequence was like a well-practised ritual that never varied.

'You said that this young woman you mention had information

pertinent to the development on the Castleton Estate,' Webster said at length. 'But I don't understand what that has to do with Carisbrook Hall.'

'Frankly, Doctor, neither do I,' Adam said. 'In fact, that was what I was hoping you could help me with.' He decided not to mention Marion Crane specifically, since Webster had already made it clear where he stood on patient confidentiality.

'I see. I take it there is a reason that you can't ask Ms Hanson directly?'

'At the moment I don't know where she is, other than some-where in London.'

'Ah.' Webster nodded and picked up his cup and saucer again. After a few moments he said, 'Tell me, how exactly did you know that Ms Hanson had contacted me?'

'Actually, somebody at the new clinic told me that Jane had been there asking where she could find you,' Adam answered, not mentioning a specific name, though Webster guessed who it had been.

'Dr Grafton I imagine. Yes, of course.'

After that Webster seemed even more remote and answered Adam's questions in clipped, almost curt tones. He could well imag-ine this man clashing with Dr Grafton. Webster's style would have been autocratic, the type who expected unquestioning obedience from his staff.

Adam asked a few general questions about Webster's time at the hospital in the hope that something would turn up. It turned out that Webster had been in charge there from the late seventies until the Hall had closed, at which point he had retired. It was clear though that whatever had led Jane Hanson to find Marion Crane's records, and what their significance was, he wasn't going to find the answers here. Over the years he'd become used to dead ends and disappointments, to leads which at first appeared promising vanishing like smoke. But the feelings he was left with remained the same. A sense of frustration and the ever present question, where to next? And sometimes there was nowhere else. Sometimes the trail went cold and eventually he was forced to admit defeat. He hoped this wouldn't prove to be one of those times.

He finished his tea and thanked Webster for his time.

'I'm sorry that I couldn't be of further help, Mr Turner.'

He drove back through the village the way he had come, stopping on the way at the garage to fill up. He didn't pay any attention to the blue Mercedes on the other side of the pumps until Cecilia Webster appeared from the shop door putting her purse away in her bag. She smiled brightly when she saw Adam.

'Hello again. Did you and Colin have a nice chat?'

'I'm afraid I wasted your husband's time, Mrs Webster.'

'Oh, don't worry about that. He has plenty to waste these days. He misses his work you know. He used to spend more time at that horrible old place than he did at home.'

Adam smiled. There was a faint wistfulness in her tone that made him think that she had preferred it that way. He supposed it was natural enough. People spent their entire working lives living partly independent existences, and then suddenly were forced together during retirement. For some it must be a difficult transition.

'Personally I loathed the place. Such a dreadful atmosphere,' she went on. 'I think the new clinic is much nicer. Colin fought against the closure of course. If they hadn't shut it down I expect he would still be there.'

Perhaps that was the root of the rancour between Dr Grafton and Webster, Adam thought. The old and the new. It was a familiar enough story. Changing times bred deep resentments.

'I suppose now that it's empty people have become interested in it again.'

'Sorry?' Adam said.

'Carisbrook Hall.'

'Oh, I see, yes.'

'You're the second person in as many months.'

'The second?'

'Yes. A young woman came to see Colin, in August I think it was.'

'Right. Actually, your husband mentioned her. Jane Hanson wasn't it?'

'Yes, that was her name. Do you know her?'

'Not really. You say she came to the house?'

'Yes. A pretty girl. Anyway, I must be going. Goodbye, Mr Turner.'

'Goodbye,' Adam said.

As she drove away he finished filling his tank. For some reason it hadn't occurred to him that Webster would have lied about Jane, but now that he knew that he had, he found he wasn't surprised. The question was: why had Webster lied?

Instead of driving directly back to Castleton, Adam took the road towards Haltwhistle and then turned off to climb the fells. High up above the forest he found the turn-off that he was looking for. A wooden gate barred the way across a rutted track, and a painted sign announced LAKE LODGE, though another that had been nailed over it announced that the lodge was closed for the season. The gate wasn't locked, so he opened it and drove carefully down the track. It was rough and potholed in places, not exactly ideal terrain for a Porsche. He winced every time he felt a thump against the floor.

The lodge consisted of a main wooden building the size of a large house which was surrounded by a number of small cabins connected by a network of pathways through overgrown grass. Adam got out of his car. A stiff easterly wind blew across the fells and chilled his bones. From the lodge he could see the forest and Cold Tarn far below. It looked small and black and seen from this perspective was much more obviously hardly a lake at all. Overhead, clouds raced across the sky pursued by shadows that flew over the barren landscape of the hills where a few hardy sheep grazed here and there. A bunch of crows wheeled and flapped around a solitary pine nearby.

He approached the main building and found the doors were firmly locked and secured with chains, the ground-floor windows shuttered against the elements and vandals. There was no sign indicating a contact address or number for the owner out of season, though clearly whoever it was didn't live on the premises year-round. It wasn't difficult to understand why. In the winter this would be about as desolate and windswept a place as you could hope to avoid. The pervading air that clung to the cabins and the unkempt grounds they sat in was of slow disintegration. The repairs done at the start of each season were probably inadequate, the revenue from hikers and the like insufficient to pay for what was really needed. Several of the cabin's roofs sagged alarmingly.

He guessed that Ben and his friends had chosen to come here after the attack on the camp because it was both cheap and out of the way. He assumed the letterhead he'd found in the wreck was the remains of their bill, but other than the name of the lodge it hadn't told him anything else. He'd been hoping to speak to somebody who remembered them, but once again it seemed he'd hit a dead end. The cold wind eventually drove him back to his car.

For a while he considered his next move. The lake down below appeared deserted again. He wondered why Dr Webster had lied about having met Jane Hanson. It seemed likely that however Marion Crane figured in all of this it had to do with the time she'd spent at Carisbrook in the mid-eighties. But who was she? And what had Jane Hanson learnt that had set her on a path that had at some point led to these medical records? And how did any of it fit with the development in Castleton Wood? Questions, plenty of questions but no answers.

Again he experienced a sense of events turning full circle. He thought about Angela and was tempted to call her, but he had no idea what he would say to her. Outside the wind picked up, rocking the car when it gusted down from Cold Fell. The sky seemed close enough to touch, a heavy leaden mass that turned the afternoon into a kind of semi-dusk. Even up there surrounded by open space he felt oppressed and enclosed. The long sunny days of autumn were coming to an end it seemed, and winter was approaching with a vengeance.

He started the car and drove to the tourist information office in Brampton. The woman he spoke to told him the owner of Lake Lodge was somebody called Gordon King. The bad news was that Mr King spent the winter each year in India.

'There used to be a caretaker until two years ago, but he retired. Apparently he wasn't replaced.'

That made sense, Adam thought, judging from what he'd seen of the state of the place. He thanked the woman for her help and went outside. Another dead end. But then maybe not. It was almost six. In a lane off the square the Border Raiders pub was open for business. It was as good a place as any to kill some time while darkness fell. He was contemplating a second night of illegal breaking and entering.

The lounge bar was warm and cosy, a coal fire glowing hot in a fireplace that dominated one side of the room. The polished wooden bar gleamed softly in the dim light, and the brass beer pumps were buffed to a faultless shine. Several groups of suited men stood around drinking and talking. Apparently the Border Raiders was the favoured hangout of Brampton's professionals, small-town accountants and bank managers drinking pints of dark bitter in a fog of cigarette smoke.

Adam ordered a Scotch and as the barman poured a Grants there was a loud laugh from across the room where three men stood by the fire. One of them clutched a pint glass in one hand and a fat cigar in the other. He was florid-faced and overweight, a bluff, imposing figure. His face looked familiar, but Adam couldn't place him.

'Do you know who that is over there?' he asked the barman. 'The big one?'

'That's Councillor Henderson.'

Suddenly Adam recalled where he'd seen the face before. It had been on a pamphlet at the district council offices. It seemed that Henderson liked to be the centre of attention. He talked loudly and laughed at his own jokes.

'Who're the men with him?' Adam asked, as the barman polished glasses with a soft white cloth. He glanced over.

'The one in the blue suit is Councillor Campbell. The other gentleman is Mr Kirk.'

Campbell was wiry and thin-faced. He had a hawkish, sharp-eyed look about him but both he and the other man deferred to Henderson. They laughed when Henderson did and agreed with everything he said. When Henderson drained his glass the others quickly followed suit. Henderson collected their glasses and came to the bar.

'My round, Arthur,' he said.

The barman obediently began pouring while Henderson stuck out his belly and puffed on his cigar, surveying the room with the air of a fat potentate secure in his own kingdom. He glanced at Adam and nodded briefly.

'Councillor Henderson?'

'Aye, that's me.'

'Adam Turner. We've met. I was with David Johnson.'

Henderson searched his memory and like a good politician smiled with false recognition, though his eyes were shrewdly appraising. 'Oh, yes, I remember now. Turner. How are you?'

'Fine. Glad to see that Forest Havens got the go-ahead, by the way.'

'Yes,' Henderson said, but now he sounded cautious. 'This area needs more schemes like that. What did you say your name was again?'

'Adam Turner. Actually, I was just having a drink with David last night.'

'I take it from your accent you're not from round this way, Mr Turner?'

'Not any more. Used to be though. David and I went to school together. Kings.'

'I see.'

The barman put the last of Henderson's pints on the bar, and Henderson hesitated for a second then gestured to Adam's own glass. 'Can I buy you a drink?'

Adam drained the last of his Scotch. 'Thanks.'

'Same again, sir?' the barman asked.

'Make it the good stuff this time.' He gestured to a twenty-year-old malt on the counter behind the bar. 'A large one.' He smiled at Henderson, whose expression hardened a fraction as he put a twenty-pound note on the bar.

'One for yourself, Arthur.'

'Thank you, sir,' the barman murmured.

Henderson nodded to Adam. 'Give David my regards next time you see him.' He started to turn away.

'I will. Funnily enough he mentioned your name last night come to think of it. We were talking about the development.'

Henderson hesitated. 'Oh?'

'I said I was interested in the tenders for the building work. David thought in my business I should talk to you.'

'I'm not sure I follow you,' Henderson said, definitely on the defensive now. 'When did you say we'd met before?'

'To tell the truth I might have exaggerated that slightly.'

What remained of any pleasantness vanished from Henderson's expression. 'Turner you said didn't you? Exactly what business are you in, Turner?'

'Sewage, you might say. That's my speciality. Rooting around in the shit. I'm a journalist actually.' He extended his hand, which Henderson pointedly ignored. Adam shrugged and withdrew it. 'Anyway, now we're having this cosy chat, would you care to comment on the rumours of irregularities over the approval for Forest Havens' plans?'

Henderson stared at him coldly. 'If you'll excuse me.'

'I understand your brother-in-law owns a building firm, Councillor. Will he be putting in a tender for part of the development work do you think?'

Henderson leaned close. The smell of cigar smoke was ingrained in his clothes, and his breath was beery. 'I should be careful of the things you say if I were you, Mr Turner.'

Adam smiled blandly and made a show of looking over Henderson's shoulder. 'That's Councillor Campbell over there isn't it? Perhaps I should come over and talk to you both at the same time. Kill two birds with one stone so to speak.'

Wordlessly Henderson turned away. 'Thanks for the drink by the way,' Adam said to his back.

He stayed for a while, making a show of sipping the Scotch, which was actually pretty good. Henderson glanced over now and then and at one point left the room through a door that was marked as the way to the toilets. When Adam followed he saw Henderson standing outside, talking animatedly into a mobile phone.

It was dark when Adam walked back to his car. The square was deserted except for a few cars. Somebody threw a cigarette butt from the window of a four-wheel drive parked along the street which exploded in sparks on the pavement and some youths came out of the chip shop laughing and shoving each other. Adam started the Porsche and headed out of town. The Scotch had settled with a pleasant knot of warmth in his stomach and he was actually looking forward to the night ahead.

CHAPTER TWENTY-FIVE

Voices drifted from the yard below the window. From snatches he overheard David knew they were talking about what was going on at Cold Tarn. Everybody was talking about it. He'd stopped in the town after he'd left the cottages to buy a bottle of whisky and people were talking about it in the supermarket. Not surprising really.

He sat down behind his desk again. He'd been thinking all day about those few seconds that morning when he had found himself staring down the twin barrels of a shotgun. He remembered looking at Mary and her eyes were crazed and wide and whatever she saw it wasn't him. She hadn't snapped out of it until he'd spoken her name. He supposed he would think about those seconds for a long time, perhaps for as long as he lived. They said that your life was supposed to flash before your eyes when death was imminent. Had that happened to him? He didn't think so. Parts of it perhaps. He remembered fear. Not the kind of fear he could describe to anyone so they would really know what it was like. Everything was sucked out of him. As if he had a hole in his guts through which his insides had been vacuumed. The sensation was something like a fairground ride that plunged you into a too rapid descent. After that had come a sort of numb acceptance. It happened too fast to think, but funnily enough he remembered a very brief moment of calm. It was then he'd seen bits of his life flicker across an internal screen.

He had been trying all afternoon to remember what those images had been. It seemed important. In those few moments when he'd believed he was going to die an automatic switch had tripped in his brain. He thought that was what had happened. It was some sort of built-in response to distract him. Something to make dying less traumatic. He wanted to know what parts of his life his subconscious had considered the most pleasant distraction before the blast of a shotgun shell disintegrated his brain into a million bloody fragments. But he couldn't remember much. He'd seen Angela and Kate. Kate riding her pony for the first time, and Angela was laughing at something, but that was all.

He became aware that the door to his office had opened, and belatedly he realized that somebody had knocked. He looked up and saw Mollie looking at him uncertainly.

'I was just about to leave for the day. Is there anything else before I go, David? Can I do anything?'

She had worked for his dad before him. He remembered that she'd given him sweets when he was a little boy.

'No, I'm alright, Mollie. Thanks.'

She started to go, then hesitated.

'Shut the door on your way out, Mollie,' he told her before she could say anything else.

'Yes, alright,' she said, her expression filled with something almost like grief. For an instant he regretted speaking sharply, but then his regret drifted away from him, like a small boat bobbing on a strong current. In the space of a few seconds he'd forgotten about her.

He glanced towards the clock on the wall. Where the bloody hell was Nick? He hadn't been at the yard all day. There was a space on the wall below the clock, a bright square patch where the mirror had hung before he'd taken it down. He couldn't stand to see himself any more. He didn't want to be reminded of what he looked like. Bloodshot eyes, haggard flesh. He reached for the bottle and poured more whisky into the chipped enamel mug he was drinking from.

When Mary had put the gun down he'd collapsed. It was comical really when he thought about it. His legs had given out and he'd simply folded up, sat on his arse on the ground.

'Jesus,' he'd breathed, when he could talk again. 'What are you doing with that thing?'

She'd looked blankly at the gun. 'I thought it had come.'

'It?'

235

She hadn't answered though, and he could tell from her eyes that she was as mad as a hatter. Eventually he'd managed to stand up and had taken the gun from her and leaned it against the wall. As he led her back inside the house something occurred to him and he'd checked the barrels to see if the thing was actually loaded. It was.

He'd sat Mary down in the kitchen. There was an unpleasant smell in the house, and unwashed dishes were stacked in the sink. He'd looked around at the squalor, wondering when was the last time anyone had cleaned the place. Mary herself was a mess and her hair was greasy. She'd watched him as he poked around looking for the things to make some tea but she hadn't said anything.

'Mary,' he'd said gently when he sat down. 'Where's Nick?'

She'd stared blankly.

'Have you seen him this morning?'

Nothing.

'Did he come home last night?'

'He leaves me alone too much,' she'd said, speaking at last.

There was nothing else he could get out of her. She rambled about 'it' coming for her, but didn't seem to have any idea where Nick was. In the end he'd left her, not knowing what else he could do. He couldn't worry about her when he had so much to think about.

He stayed at his desk as the light faded outside, and even when it was quite dark he didn't turn on the lights. He kept waiting for Nick to phone or turn up. Finally the phone did ring, its shrill tone startling him. He stared at it with his heart pounding before he picked it up.

'There you are. I talked to a bloody friend of yours earlier.'

It was Henderson. He sounded angry. 'What friend?' He didn't know what Henderson was talking about.

'Adam bloody Turner, that's who. What the hell is going on, Johnson?'

Why was Adam talking to Henderson?

'He came into the bloody pub. Started going on about the development. Talking about contracts and such. He said he's a fucking journalist for Christ's sake! What have you been telling him?'

'Nothing. I haven't told him anything,' David said. Bloody Adam! Dammit! 'Don't worry, he's just trying it on. He doesn't know anything.'

'You better bloody well hope not. Can't you do something to stop him? You know what's at stake here.'

What was he supposed to do, David wondered? 'Leave it with me,' he said. But Henderson wasn't about to let it go so easily. He was still talking loudly as David hung up. On the way out he pulled the phone cord out of the wall. The office door slammed shut behind him and the cold wind felt like the whip of a tree branch across his face.

He drove home, but didn't pull into the gate. Instead he sat in the lane and watched the house. The yellow squares of the windows spilled light into the darkness outside. Every now and then he saw Angela moving around inside. He wished he could go over, put his key in the door and step inside. He closed his eyes, remembering what it had felt like going home at the end of the day, having Kate run to him, and then kissing the back of Angela's head as she made dinner. It had been a long time since he had done those things.

The other night, when she had asked him about the planning committee she had looked at him in a way he'd never seen her do before. As if she was seeing something in him she hadn't known was there until then.

He started the engine and headed back towards town. He kept looking in the mirror as he drove down the lane watching the house get smaller and more distant.

The sound of a car outside drew Angela to the window in her studio that overlooked the front of the house. At first she thought it was somebody turning through the gate and her heart raced. She thought of David and Adam almost simultaneously. She both wanted it to be one of them and at the same time hoped it was neither but when she pulled the curtain back the sound was already fading and she only glimpsed red tail-lights through the horse chestnuts along the lane.

Damn. Her mouth tightened as disappointment and relief jostled for dominance. She knew it had to have been one of them, and felt suddenly sure that it was David. She crossed quickly to the phone and started punching in the numbers to call his mobile but it was turned off and she only got a recorded message. After a moment she hung up. Adam. Damn him and his theories. She wished she had never gone with him today. She knew he was wrong about David. It was ridiculous. No, wrong word. That made his suspicions sound comical, something to be dismissed and ridiculed, but there was nothing even faintly amusing about this. The things he'd said were madness. Unbelievable.

All the way home in the back of the taxi she'd stared out of the window, seeing nothing. The driver had talked for a little while, chatting about the weather and asking if she'd lived in Castleton long. She answered in monosyllables if at all. Once she'd caught his eyes on her in the mirror before he'd quickly looked away. After that he'd put the radio on and they'd driven in silence the rest of the way. When they'd arrived at the house she had tipped him generously and tried to smile. Bad day, she'd told him.

She went upstairs and sat down in front of her computer screen. She felt drained. There was an email message from Julian reminding her tactfully that they needed to respond to the American offer. Without too much delay. She managed a faint smile. In other words don't take all bloody month about it. For a few moments she allowed herself to contemplate an existence where she and Kate moved away, and she became a celebrated author of children's books. They would go and live in a rambling cottage somewhere. Perhaps in Oxfordshire, on the edge of the Cotswolds. Away from all of this. She looked around her. But it wasn't the house she wanted to escape, or the town. It was the feeling she had that everything she had built her life on had turned to sand and was shifting beneath her feet. Her marriage was crumbling, and she was afraid.

She tapped a quick reply to Julian, asking for a few more days, and clicked on the Send icon before she could change her mind, and in an instant it was gone, then she disconnected from her provider.

What was she afraid of? She switched out the lights and went downstairs. The house was quiet without Kate. In the kitchen she poured herself a glass of wine. Rationally she went over everything

Adam had told her. He hadn't tried to stop her when she'd left the pub. He hadn't tried to convince her that she was wrong.

She was afraid partly because David had changed. Or perhaps to say he'd changed wasn't accurate. He'd revealed parts of himself she hadn't known existed. He had secrets from her. His drinking was a symptom, as were his moods. Of what? Stress? She didn't think so. Yes, he'd been preoccupied, overworked and worried for a long time and that had taken its toll. But this was more than that. Guilt then. Was that what was eating him? How long had he been this way? A few months? It was hard to pin down a precise time. Certainly throughout September. A thought occurred to her.

Those three lads had been killed around the beginning of September.

As the pub door swung closed behind him David peered about the room. He'd decided to try the Crooked Man in Halls Tenement because he knew that sometimes Nick drank there. There were only half a dozen vehicles outside and Nick's had been among them. He was sitting alone with his back to the window, slumped forward with his arms resting on the table. He didn't look up. An almost empty pint glass was in front of him.

'Scotch,' David said to the barman. 'Make it a large one.' He gestured towards Nick. 'Has he been here long?'

'Most of the day.'

David paid for the Scotch and emptied the glass. He couldn't bring himself to go over to Nick. Not yet. Now that he'd found him he wasn't sure what he was going to do. In the end Nick must have sensed somebody watching, and he looked up. His eyes focused. It was clear he'd had plenty to drink, but he wasn't drunk. He didn't look surprised. Finally David went over.

'I've been trying to find you all day. You weren't at the yard.'

'I've been here.'

What now? What was he going to do now? For a second the room swam in front of David's eyes and he put a hand on the table to steady himself. He was aware of an old man with a dog at his feet watching him curiously. He took a deep breath and focused on

Nick again. He felt as if somebody had shoved a blade in his guts and ripped it through his body.

'What did you do?' he said. His words came out in a croaky whisper. 'What did you do?' he repeated, clearer this time.

It was impossible to read what Nick was thinking. He grabbed his glass and stood up. 'I need a drink. Want one?'

David didn't answer and he kept looking at the empty place where Nick had been sitting a moment before. 'What did you do?' he repeated. His vision was blurring. His cheeks were wet. He imagined himself cracking up. Like a statue. Cracks appearing, spreading cobweb-like from head to toe. Then small chips dropping off, followed by bigger chunks. Nick went towards the bar and David reached out to stop him. He wiped his eyes and repeated his question.

'I said, what did you do?'

His voice was loud. Murmured conversations around them died away. People were watching.

'I need a drink,' Nick said again.

He heard a sound that he knew he'd made himself. It was like a shout of rage or pain or both mingled together. But a part of his mind remained detached, as if it wasn't really him. There was a sensation of release, as if a tightly stretched cable had snapped and the heavy weight it had been holding back was gathering momentum under its own force. He felt his fist connect with something and saw Nick's head snap back and then abruptly, like a switch had been flipped, it was over. He stood listlessly as people rushed forward and held his arms even though it must have been obvious he wasn't going to do anything else. He didn't hear their voices, only noise, and he barely felt their restraining hands. From the floor where he'd fallen Nick wiped blood from his nose and looked up with a pained expression. Not physical, but something deep which tugged at David inside as Nick got to his feet and made for the door.

They only let him go when the lights of Nick's Landcruiser flashed by the window.

Adam, David thought. This was all because of Adam.

CHAPTER TWENTY-SIX

The moon appeared now and then, seen hazily through thinning cloud. As the road climbed towards the fells a set of head-lights appeared in Adam's rear-view mirror, and stayed there. It would vanish every now and then when he rounded a bend, but reappear shortly afterwards. When he reached the gated turn-off to Lake Lodge he pulled in and switched off his lights and engine. Silence and darkness closed around him as he waited for the vehicle to pass. About half a minute went by and then headlights lit the road behind him, and a few seconds later swept by. Darkness fell again and the sound of an engine faded and was gone. Only then did he get out and open the gate, and once he was through he closed it again though he didn't replace the chain.

He drove at walking pace with only his parking lights on and when he reached the lodge he drove around the back and switched them off. When he got out he took the new torch he'd bought earlier, along with a long-handled screwdriver.

It was cold and quiet, though as he became accustomed to his surroundings it wasn't so quiet after all. The night was full of a hundred small sounds. The hoot of an owl, the spooky shriek of a deer from the forest, the rustle of something moving through the grass close by. The breeze rattled in the branches of a nearby solitary pine and water dripped from a leaky gutter.

He tried a door at the back of the building, testing his weight against it, but it was locked and felt solid and unmoving. He moved along to a window and though it too was locked there was a gap between the shutter and the window frame. He worked the screwdriver into the gap and after several good jerks the wood splintered and the lock snapped off. He peered through the window to see if he could get at the catch but in the end had to resort to smashing the glass. The noise it made was alarmingly loud and seemed to go on for ever as fragments fell inwards, sounding like the high notes on an out-of-tune piano. When it was over he waited for several long seconds before he felt for the catch and climbed inside.

He bumped his hip painfully against a sharp edge. It was even darker inside and the air was stale. Casting his torch beam around he picked out boxes and chairs, a battered desk shoved up against a far wall. He was in a small storage room. He tried the door, which led out into a passage. Directing the torch towards the floor he made his way to the front of the building where there was an entrance hall and to one side of a counter a door marked OFFICE. On a desk inside there were some brochure holders, a primitive-looking phone system and a computer terminal. Several filing cabinets stood against the wall.

Adam closed the door and pulled the curtain over the window before turning on the light. He sat down at the desk, wondering where to begin. Gordon King certainly hadn't gone to a great deal of trouble to square things away before he'd closed up the lodge and bolted for the beaches of Goa, or wherever it was he'd gone to. A cardboard box minus its lid appeared to serve as a repository for the last of the incoming mail. It was overflowing with a mixture of bills, junk mail, the occasional reservation query, which appeared not to have been answered, and a complaint from a customer about the misrepresentation of the lodge facilities in a magazine it had been advertised in, along with several demands for payment from creditors King owed money to.

He opened a drawer and found the mouldy remains of what might have been a Bounty along with the May issue of *Penthouse* magazine. A search of the remaining drawers produced several fishing magazines but not much else. Abandoning the desk Adam scooted the chair over to a filing cabinet. On top there was a large desk diary where King appeared to record his bookings. It seemed business had been slow that year, and a quick search around the beginning of September revealed nothing relating to Ben and his friends.

He turned his attention to the filing drawers. If the accumulated bills and accounts he found inside had been filed according to some logical system it was a mystery to Adam. He heaved several bundles out onto the desk and began going through them. There were copies of guest receipts dating back three years, but they were arranged haphazardly. It took an hour of searching before he finally found what he was looking for. He shoved the rest of the stuff back in the drawer before he began to examine the account that bore Ben's name.

They had stayed at the lodge for two nights, sharing a single cabin between them, arriving on what must have been the day following the attack on the camp and leaving on the fifth of September, the night of the accident. What was interesting was that they had been charged for two and a half days, which Adam pondered for a while. The only other charge listed was for phone calls that came to a total of nine pounds twenty-seven, which seemed a lot. Unfortunately there was no breakdown of individual calls and with a groan Adam turned back to the cabinet. He found the phone accounts but nothing for September. He checked the box containing incoming mail and it wasn't there either. He thought for a few moments and his eye flicked from the phone system to the computer monitor. Judging by the way Ben's account was printed the lodge used some kind of rudimentary hotel accounting software, and it was logical to assume that phone calls were automatically itemized on some background program. It was worth looking anyway so he turned on the computer and waited for the screen to come to life.

The system was old with limited memory capacity and the billing program staggered to life. He found the software operating the phone system easily enough, but it took a little longer to bring up the itemized calls. When he did eventually find what he was looking for he entered the dates he wanted isolated in a field box that appeared and brought up a list of every outgoing call made from the lodge during that time. He assumed there must be a way to figure out which one applied to which room, but he couldn't see how to do it, so he printed off a hard copy list of every number that had been called. A quick glance revealed that there were seventeen local calls in all, one to a mobile phone and one to a number with an international prefix. He ran his eye down the list until one caught his attention. It was the only number he recognized. He stared at it for several long seconds, then folded the printout along with the room account and tucked it inside his jacket pocket.

As he did a sound alerted him to the fact that he was no longer alone.

At first he wasn't sure what it was that he'd heard, but whatever it was had started a shrill insistent alarm ringing in his head. He waited to see if it would be repeated but when it wasn't he got up and switched off the light before opening the door to the hallway a fraction. There was nothing there. He crossed to the nearest window and peered between the crack in the shutters. As his eyes adjusted to the darkness again he wondered if the sound he'd heard was simply a rat or merely the settling timbers of an old building. When he still couldn't see anything outside he returned to the office and working by the light of his torch put everything back the way he had found it. When he was finished he paused to take a final look around, and just then he heard the unmistakeable sound of a car door closing outside.

He flicked off the torch. The car door had been closed quietly, the sound a muffled clunk. He went to the window again and peered outside but he still couldn't see anything. He wondered if the Porsche had been discovered, and as if in answer he heard the splintered crunch of broken glass from the back of the building as somebody climbed through the window he had broken. A few moments later he heard stealthy footsteps coming along the passage towards the hall.

Quickly he crossed to the front door but it was locked so he went back to the window and snapped the catch to raise the sash. It opened smoothly but the sound it made was unmistakeable. The footsteps in the passage stopped and then almost immediately started again, only this time whoever was there was running. Adam flipped the catch on the shutters and pushed but nothing happened. He felt in the dark for whatever was holding them while behind him the sound of running footsteps reached the hallway. Taking a few steps back Adam hurled himself at the window with his arms crossed in front of his face. He hit the shutters and felt a momentary resistance before they flew open with a crash and his momentum carried him over the ledge. As he hit the damp grass he rolled and a second later was on his feet and running. A sharp pain knifed through his knee and his run became a clumsy limp. From somewhere behind he heard a muffled curse followed by a thump and then he was around the corner and fumbling for the keys to his car.

The engine exploded into life and dropped to a growl as he shoved the stick into first gear. In his haste he let the clutch out too fast and for a moment the wheels spun for traction then he eased off a little and the car shot forward, the back end slewing around as he fought the wheel. The end of the building rushed towards him and he swung hard left towards the track. He winced as the car hit a dip and the floor and the ground connected with a bone-shuddering crash. As he felt the wheels hit the track he changed up and put his right foot down, throwing dirt into the air, then eased off again and aimed the car towards the road. As it straightened he glimpsed a flash in the mirror from the corner of his eye. Instinctively he ducked as the rear window exploded into a million fragments. There might have been a second shot but he wasn't sure. The car leapt forward bouncing over potholes at speed and when he switched on the lights the gate was suddenly there and thankfully it was open. He hit the brake and turned hard to the left then floored the accelerator again. The back slid around and then the wheels connected with the tarmac and the Porsche was suddenly in its element, behaving the way it was designed to do. In moments he was hurtling down the hill.

A bend curved round to the left; a line of trees stood out in the white light ahead. Adam changed down, the engine note dropping to a rumble before he touched the throttle again. The Porsche held to the road as he pulled it through the bend and as he did he glanced in the mirror and glimpsed a gleam of light. He grinned to himself, adrenalin surging in his veins. The seat held him snugly and the wheel was light in his hands. Catch me if you can, he thought.

The lights lit a long downhill stretch ahead, at the end of which was the edge of the forest. Overconfidence made him take the first curve at dangerous speed and cold sweat popped on his brow as the back of the car began to slide towards the edge. He overcorrected, instinctively hitting the brake too hard, and the wheels locked. Rubber screeched and a pungent stench rose from underneath the car. The lights swung wildly out into the void beyond the road. He took his foot off the brake and even though it went against instinct he touched the throttle and the car leapt towards darkness. For an instant it seemed as if he'd acted too late but a fraction of a second before oblivion the car responded and came around. It was over in moments, but he'd been a foot and a half away from plunging off the road.

He glanced in the mirror but there was nothing there. At the approach to the next curve he dropped a gear and braked smoothly, then powered out the other side, hugging the tarmac with room to spare. A long straight opened up and he put the pedal to the floor. Still no light behind. He was in control and nothing short of another Porsche was going to catch him now.

He wondered if this was a scene that had been played out before; only then it had been three kids in a beat-up old Vauxhall on this same stretch of road. The straight ended in a long curve left which was sharper than it looked. He passed by the place where the Vauxhall had gone over the edge and it was easy to see how it could have happened. He experienced some echo of what Ben and his friends must have felt. The gut-wrenching inevitability of impact following a brief illusion of weightlessness. Headlights plunging down, lighting the tops of trees as the car began lazily to turn. They would have known they were about to die. They had probably screamed in terror. In his mind's eye he saw the doors pop open as two bodies were flung against the trees with bloody ferocity. He saw the wreck bounce and roll and a shaft of metal pierce Ben's body like a sword. When it came to rest there would have been silence, the ticking of hot metal, the smell of petrol and the ebb of warm thick blood from a ruptured artery. And above, on the road, had a vehicle stopped? Had somebody climbed out and stood watching and listening?

Adam came to and realized he'd taken his foot off the throttle. The engine note changed as the Porsche slowed. He rounded the bend and changed down through the gears, and then barely idling he waited, his eyes on the rear-view mirror.

Half a minute passed and then headlights appeared behind. The Porsche was captured and held in a growing beam of light. He heard the sound of the approaching engine made louder by the missing rear window and as it drew closer he kept his eyes glued on the mirror until the lights dazzled him as the angle changed. He glimpsed a dark shape, a big vehicle and an indistinct figure behind the wheel. It was a dark-coloured four-wheel drive but he couldn't see the make. He squinted as it headed straight for him, showing no sign of slowing. He looked back over his shoulder trying to get a better look and suddenly it was almost on top of him. Another second or two, that's all he needed. The lights grew rapidly into a blinding glare. Just one more second. Then suddenly he didn't have any time left and he jammed his foot down hard but he already knew he'd timed it too finely. The Porsche responded. The acceleration pressed him back against his seat as he changed into second gear but at the same time he felt the impact behind and heard the crunch of metal on metal. The wheel was wrenched from his hand. He shot forward and was brought up by the belt across his chest and his head snapped back against the rest. A tree loomed in front and he grabbed the wheel. The smell of rubber and hot oil filled the air. For a second the other car was alongside, seeming huge beside the little Porsche. He glimpsed a figure behind the wheel, a blurred pale shape as their eyes met. The driver swung hard right meaning to shove him over the edge but the Porsche leapt clear.

This time Adam didn't slow down. He took the curves fast, braking hard as he had done before and powering out the other side. Whatever damage had been done to the car it still handled responsively and the engine seemed unaffected. Trees and dry-stone walls flashed past in the white beam of the lights.

By the time he was down in the valley the vehicle behind had vanished. A mile from Castleton he pulled over and switched off the engine. He didn't move for several minutes. Then his hands began to shake and sweat flowed across his body.

It was past midnight by the time Adam pulled up outside the house. There were no lights on inside and the garage door was closed. He went over and shone his torch through the gap. He could see

Angela's Renault but not David's Land Rover. When he went back to his car he used his mobile and eventually she answered.

'Angela. This is Adam.'

'Adam? What time is it?' She sounded groggy.

'Where's David?'

'What?' Her voice was clearing. 'Where are you?'

'Outside the house.'

She didn't say anything, then a light went on in an upstairs room and he saw the curtain twitch before she came back on the line. 'He isn't here.'

'I know that. What I want to know is where he is.'

'I don't know where he is. Do you know what time it is? For Christ's sake . . .'

'Let me in.'

'What? Why should I let you in? I told you . . .'

He cut her off. 'Let me in Angela. I want to show you something.'

'You can show me in the morning.'

'I'm not waiting until morning. Somebody just tried to kill me for fuck's sake.'

His voice broke and shook. When he looked at his hands they were trembling. He thought it must be shock and he leaned forward and rested his head on the wheel. His neck was aching and he had a piercing pain in the back of his skull. 'I'm sorry,' he said. 'I didn't mean to do that.'

He thought she had hung up. He wished he hadn't called her. What he wanted to do was rest. Light spilled out into the yard as the front door opened. Angela was clutching a robe about her body with both arms. She came towards him, her face pale. 'You better come inside,' she said.

His neck ached badly and a lacework of pain extended upwards into his skull and down across his back from the impact against the headrest. He was limping again. 'Do you have anything to drink?' he asked.

Angela brought a bottle of Scotch and a glass and they sat at the kitchen table. He poured himself a measure, clinking the bottle against the glass. He felt strange, light-headed. 'Delayed shock,' he said, as Angela watched him. The Scotch helped, burning its way down into his gut. He glanced at the clock on the wall and remembered Angela's daughter, though for a second her name eluded him. 'It's late.' He glanced towards the door and the stairs beyond. 'Did I wake Kate?'

'She's staying with a friend.'

He thought she had already told him that, and nodded.

'Are you alright? Do you need a doctor?'

He was rubbing the back of his neck. 'I'm fine, just a bit of whiplash I think. Have you got any aspirin?'

She went to a cupboard and came back with a packet of Panadol. He swallowed three.

'Are you going to tell me what happened? You said somebody tried to kill you.'

He told her about the lodge, how he'd thought Ben and the others might have stayed there, but when he went to see what he could find out it was closed for the season.

'The owner spends the winter in India apparently. So I went back there tonight.'

'You broke in? Why? What were you hoping to find?'

'I wasn't sure. A record of their account. At least then I'd know where they went after they left the camp.'

'And did you find it?'

'Yes. They arrived on the third of September, the day after the attack, and stayed for two nights. They left on the fifth. The night they were killed.'

Angela looked away. He couldn't tell what she was thinking. 'You said that somebody tried to kill you.'

He told her what had happened. When he mentioned the gunshot she almost flinched. 'Somebody must have followed me there.' He told her whoever it was had come after him. 'He caught up with me in the forest. He rammed me. Tried to shunt me over the edge.'

'Did you see who it was?' There was a note of dread in her voice as if she was afraid of the answer.

'Not clearly. A dark-coloured four-wheel drive, that's all I can say for certain.'

There was a glimmer of relief in her eye, though a dark-coloured four-wheel drive could mean a black Land Rover like the one David drove. He knew she was thinking about that, and about the fact that he had come here looking for David.

'And then you came here?'

'After a while. I stopped for a few minutes. I was shaken up.'

'But the other car?'

'Must have turned off somewhere.'

She got up and went to the kitchen window, keeping her back to him while she thought.

'What happened tonight,' he said. 'Maybe the same thing happened before. Only Ben and his friends weren't so lucky.' It didn't explain why Ben was driving, or the fact that he'd been drinking, but it was a theory. 'The account shows that they were charged for two and a half days. I wondered about that. It could mean they left late on the fifth, instead of staying the night. Why would they do that? What was the big hurry all of a sudden?' He had his own ideas. Maybe they had been scared.

There was something else he had to tell her. He reached inside his jacket pocket and produced the phone record he'd printed off and smoothed it down on the table. 'I found this. It's a record of every phone call that was made from the lodge during the time they stayed there.'

She came back over to the table. He pointed to a call made to a local number on the fifth. He didn't say anything. He didn't need to. Her eyes widened when she recognized it as her own.

He was awake when she knocked softly on the door later. At her insistence he'd agreed to stay the night and she had made up the bed in the spare room. They had said goodnight an hour earlier, but he hadn't gotten further than removing his jersey and shirt and sitting down on the edge of the bed. Since then he'd been staring at the shadows cast on the wall by the single bedside lamp. He'd been lost in thought when she knocked. He got up and opened the door and she stood on the darkened landing, still clutching her robe tightly around herself.

'I saw the light under the door. I couldn't sleep.'

'I was thinking,' he said. They faced each other awkwardly for a moment before he opened the door wider and gestured that she should come in. He went back to the bed and sat down and she came inside and sat in a chair against the wall, her face half hidden by shadow.

'Were you thinking about what happened tonight?' she asked.

'Partly.' He paused. He was unused to talking about himself. But for once he wanted to. 'I was thinking about Helen Pierce. When she first told me about her brother I said that I couldn't help.'

'Why?'

'A lot of reasons, but mainly because it happened here. Because I have a lot of memories associated with this place. I was seeing a psychologist a while ago.' He saw her surprise. 'It was when my marriage was falling apart. It was meant to be counselling but we ended up talking about a lot of other stuff too. All the clichés about them are true, you know. They want to know about your parents and if you were happy as a child.'

She managed a smile. 'And were you? Happy I mean?'

'I don't think I was unhappy exactly. I suppose I never felt sure of myself after we moved here. I never really fitted in.'

'But you had friends. David . . .' She broke off uncertainly, seeing his expression. 'Look, whatever you feel about him now, whatever happened after your accident, you were friends once.'

'I used to think so.'

'Until you were in hospital and you realized he was trying to steal your girlfriend?' She leaned closer, her expression intent. 'Adam, it really wasn't like that, you know. Neither of us knew what to do about the way we felt. I told you before that nothing ever happened until after it was over between you and me. You shouldn't blame David, it was both of us. We couldn't help the way we felt. If you hate him for what happened, then you should hate me too.'

He was surprised. 'Who said I hate him?'

'Alright resent, or whatever. But you do don't you? Isn't that why you want to believe he had something to do with what happened to those lads? And what about tonight? Somebody tried to run you off the road and you came here looking for David, because you assumed it was him.'

Had he assumed that? He wasn't sure. It could have been David, though Angela wouldn't admit the possibility. She thought she knew him, knew that he wasn't capable of hurting anyone. But she didn't know about Meg and Adam knew if he told her now she would think he was crazy, making it all up.

'Why did you come back, Adam?' Angela asked. 'If you weren't sure at first, what changed your mind?'

She was watching him intently, unaware that as she had leaned forward her robe had come apart revealing her nightdress and a glimpse of her thigh. He could lie to her about his reasons, but he was certain she would see it in his face.

'The truth is I wasn't sure how I felt about seeing you again. I wasn't sure it was a good idea. I assumed you would be married, had a life. I didn't know you were married to David of course. The point is I didn't think I had a right to butt in.'

She was silent for a while, absorbing what he'd said. 'But you decided to come.'

'For all kinds of reasons, yes. But I'd be lying if I said you weren't among them.'

He thought she would be angry, that she'd feel certain now that his suspicions about David were rooted in what had happened between the three of them. Instead she looked sad. 'Adam. It was such a long time ago. We weren't much more than kids . . .'

He could guess what else she'd been about to say. They hadn't ever done anything more than kiss and hold hands, aware that they had always had different plans. But it didn't matter. He'd loved her.

'You know I said I was seeing a psychologist? His name was Morris. Louise, my wife, thought that I used my work to shut her out, and that I felt it was more important than our marriage. Anyway, I came to realize that she was right in a way. I've always done that with the women I've known, driven them away effectively. I remember the first time I saw Louise in a bar. She had her back to me but she had long pale blonde hair. She reminded me of you.'

Angela's eyes widened in surprise. She shook her head slowly, a small movement that was an expression of incomprehension, though her eyes remained full of sadness, regret for him perhaps, for the things in his life she sensed he had missed. She couldn't understand why he had been so affected but she could appreciate the result.

He stood up. 'I know it's crazy, if that's what you're thinking.'

She stood and touched his cheek. 'I don't think it's crazy. I've always felt badly about what happened. The way it did anyway. I didn't know you felt that way about me then. So strongly.'

She was so close. As she dropped her hand from his face he caught it without thinking and they stood motionless staring into one another's eyes. Without thinking about it he began to draw her towards him. She hesitated and then moved closer. They embraced, not as lovers, but in some instinctive need for comfort each felt. She put her head against his shoulder and he stroked her hair, remembering instantly the feel of it between his fingers. He could smell the mingled scents of her skin and some lotion she used and he had to force himself to resist the sudden impulse to kiss her neck. Their bodies touched briefly and then he felt her draw away very slightly and he let her go. She smiled, a little embarrassed.

'I should let you get some sleep.'

He nodded, not trusting himself to speak. At the door she paused.

'He isn't a bad person, Adam.'

Then without waiting for him to respond she quietly closed the door behind her.

CHAPTER TWENTY-SEVEN

Warm autumn sunlight slanting through the window woke Adam early. For a short time he lay in the unfamiliar surroundings of the room. When he glanced at his watch he saw it was still early, though he could hear sounds of activity from downstairs and guessed that Angela was already up.

He sat up and swung his legs over the side of the bed. His knee was sore and his neck ached. He was going to feel stiff for a few days but he didn't think there was any serious damage. When he went through to the bathroom he found Angela had left out a towel for him with a toothbrush on top still in its wrapper. He took a shower, turning the temperature up as high as he could bear and directed the jet onto the back of his neck.

When he went down to the kitchen the smell of coffee hit him and he realized he was hungry.

'Sit down,' Angela said. 'I'll do some eggs.'

He did as he was told. There was something different about her. She moved with new purpose and he detected a kind of resolve about her. He watched her against the window, her hair pulled back tightly from her face, her skin clear and free of make-up. She was beautiful.

Outside the sun lit the fells, but there was an icy paleness to the colour of the sky. The fields were frigid with early frost. Angela brought coffee and plates of scrambled eggs. When they'd finished eating she got up and fetched a calendar that was hanging on one of the kitchen cupboards.

'I thought about that phone call from the lodge,' she said. She turned the calendar back a page and traced her finger to the beginning of September. There was a red circle around the fifth, and the letters JC were scrawled beside it. 'The fifth was a Saturday. I remember it because Kate was staying over at a friend's house. I'd planned to cook a meal and open a decent bottle of wine. I wanted David and I to have a nice evening together for once. Just the two of us. I wanted us to forget about the problems he was having with the business, about the protest. But it didn't happen. He got a phone call, it must have been around seven or eight, and said he had to go out. Something had come up at the sawmill. I made a sandwich and drank most of the wine myself in front of the TV. I don't know what time David came home.'

The accident had happened around nine that night, but he didn't say anything. He sensed she hadn't finished yet.

'There were no other calls that night,' she said. 'So, the one he took must have been from somebody at the lodge.' She fixed him with a level gaze, her eyes startlingly clear. 'Look, I don't know what happened that night. I can't believe that David is capable of the things you suspect him of but I'm not a fool. I'm not going to bury my head in the sand and ignore all of this. I want to know the truth. I know something is eating at David. He won't tell me what it is. So, I'll have to find out my own way.'

'Alright,' he said, uncertain what she was getting at. 'I'll tell you whatever I find out.'

'No, I want to help. There must be something I can do.'

'Maybe there is.' He told her about his meeting with Dr Webster the day before, and about running into his wife at the garage. 'He lied about Jane Hanson. He claimed he never met her. Whatever Jane was on to, it led her ultimately to Marion Crane's medical records, whoever she is or was. You could try to find her. It's a long shot but you could start with the phone book.'

'You still haven't found Jane Hanson?'

'Somebody in London is looking, but I haven't heard anything.' He glanced at the time. Karen was an early starter and he knew she would be in her office. He took out his mobile and called her direct line. When she answered he got up from the table and stood at the window with his back to Angela.

'Karen, it's Adam here. I wondered if you'd had any luck finding Jane.'

255

'Well, good morning to you too. And yes I'm fine, thanks for asking.'

'Sorry,' he said, chastened by her sarcasm.

'You're forgiven. And the answer to your question is both yes and no. Yes, I managed to get an address from her father, though I gather they're not close and he hasn't spoken to her since earlier in the year, but no, I haven't managed to speak to her yet. She's an elusive girl. I've talked to her neighbour who tells me she's hardly ever home. And I've left messages, but she hasn't answered.'

'What about a phone number? A work number perhaps?'

'No such luck. There's a young guy who lives in the flat above her. I think he fancies her actually. He thinks she's got some kind of high-powered job. Says she wears expensive-looking suits and every time he's seen her she's climbing in and out of taxis, but he has no idea where she works or even what she does. She's not very forthcoming apparently. Either she's secretive as well as elusive, or she just doesn't fancy him. Can't imagine why. He's quite a hunk.'

'I'm glad there's some compensation for all the time you're spending on this.'

She laughed. 'If you were a girl I'd say that sounded like bitchiness. Anyway, you needn't worry, I'm beginning to see our Ms Hanson as a bit of a challenge. But it is starting to look as if you might have been right about her. Perhaps she was bought off; that would explain why she seems to be avoiding me.'

'True, but keep trying, would you? Maybe you can threaten her or appeal to her sense of guilt or something.'

'I'll do my best,' she promised. 'So, what's been happening up there anyway? I heard about what they found in the lake. That's near where you are isn't it?'

'Yes. I haven't seen the news,' he said. 'What's the latest?'

'Nothing much. Whoever it was has been there a long time. That's all they've said so far.'

'No speculation from the media? Nothing about who it might be?'

'Not that I've heard.'

'Not even confirmation of the sex?'

'Nope.' There was a pause. 'You seem very interested in this,

Adam. Is there something you're not telling me? You've got that tone in your voice.'

Karen's journalistic radar was as sharp as ever, Adam thought. 'I don't know any more than you do,' he lied smoothly.

'Well, I suppose I'll have to believe you,' she said, sounding as if she didn't at all. 'So, what else have you discovered?'

'I'm not sure yet. Nothing definite.'

'Alright. Call me when you can.'

He promised he would, and as they were about to hang up he remembered to ask about Nigel. Yet for some reason he was reluctant to talk about it with Angela listening. In the end he settled for a more general, how are things with you?

'You mean with work?' she asked.

'That too.'

'Adam, is there somebody with you?'

'No,' he lied, wondering how she saw through his minor deceptions so easily.

Her tone altered, taking on a subtle hint of offence. 'If that's your way of asking about Nigel, which I assume it is, then nothing is settled yet.' She broke off when there was a sound in the background and when she came back on she sounded rushed. 'Look, I have to go. Call me. Bye.'

'Bye,' he said, but she had already hung up. He disconnected, feeling as he always did lately, that he had let her down in some way. When he turned around Angela had begun clearing the table.

'Any luck?'

'No. And it looks as if we shouldn't count on getting any help from Jane Hanson either.' He related briefly what Karen had told him.

'Who is she, this Karen?'

'She's a friend. She edits the magazine I'm working for.'

'Oh.'

Angela carried their plates to the dishwasher. He wondered why he felt vaguely guilty.

He left Angela to pursue Marion Crane through the phone book, and also gave her the phone print-out he'd taken from the lodge. Maybe if she tried all the numbers something would turn up.

He borrowed Angela's car, and left his own in her garage. When she saw the shattered rear window and the crumpled rear wheel arch where he'd been rammed her composure faltered. Confronted with hard evidence of the reality of what had happened doubt flickered in her eyes.

'I'll call you later,' he promised.

He went to the New Inn first and changed his clothes, then called the hospital and asked to speak to Dr Keller in the pathology lab. The woman who answered the phone told him crisply that Dr Keller was unavailable, but asked if he wanted to leave a message. He realized she'd probably been besieged with reporters for the past twenty-four hours.

'Would you tell her that Adam Turner called, tell her that I think I have something which might help her identify the body from the lake.'

There was silence, at first surprised, but when the woman repeated his name she sounded simply dubious. 'Adam Turner?'

'That's right.' He could almost read her thoughts. Another bloody journalist who'll try anything to get a scoop. Nevertheless she said she would pass the message on and he left a number.

Half an hour later as he was leaving Castleton his mobile rang and to his surprise when he answered he was speaking to Dr Keller.

'Mr Turner,' she said coolly. 'I understand you have something I may be interested in?'

'I think so, but I need to talk to you in person.'

'I see.' She didn't try to hide her scepticism.

'I know what you're thinking Doctor, but I promise you I'm not calling as a journalist. This is personal.'

'Personal?' She thought about that for a few seconds. 'Alright,' she agreed, 'I'll see you. But if this turns out to be some kind of trick to get access to the lab, you're going to be in very big trouble.'

He didn't doubt her. 'I can be there in half an hour.'

'Fine, I'll leave word to admit you.'

In the event it took him a little longer than that and when he arrived he had to make his way through a loitering group of journalists. They regarded him with brief interest, until they concluded he was neither a doctor nor a policeman, and then they ignored him.

When he announced himself at the desk he was shown down-stairs and along a corridor before passing through a set of doors where a uniformed policeman was on duty.

'Dr Keller's expecting you.' The woman who'd brought him indicated a door and went back the way they came, evidently not keen to go any further. A sign announced that he was outside the autopsy room.

When he went inside Dr Keller and her assistant were busy on either side of a steel mortuary table. There was a smell in the air, but not of decaying flesh. Instead it was the almost metallic odour of lake water and dank mud.

Dr Keller looked up from the remains she was examining. 'Mr Turner, come in.'

He glimpsed ribs and a skull though much of what he could see was covered in what looked like mud and debris, perhaps the remains of clothing. He stared at the empty eye sockets. Rather than being clean and bleached the way people expect to see such things, the skull was grey. A shred of matter clung to the side and what looked like silt filled the gaps between the teeth. Somehow this struck him as an unnecessary indignity. He was drawn to the hole in the crown, slightly to the rear.

'Are you alright?' Dr Keller asked. 'It's quite normal for people to feel queasy.'

He shook his head. 'It's not that.' In fact, he had suddenly remembered Meg Coucesco as he had first seen her. A dark-haired girl staring at him solemnly through the windows of a bus on an unseasonably warm spring day. She'd been sitting astride a horse with two small children in front of her. He was struck by the clarity of the image. He could even remember the shapeless cotton dress she wore and the hint of a womanly body beneath it. It was this face, this image of her that haunted his dreams, he realized. The look in her eyes, a mixture of accusation and a mute plea. He reached out to a nearby bench for support.

Dr Keller was watching him with real concern now, and also curiosity. Somehow he couldn't reconcile this pile of bones with the living, breathing girl he remembered. Had she lived she might have married, had children, a home, a life, instead of being reduced to what lay in front of him. He felt sadness for her, but also a resurgence of guilt. He wondered what her last moments had been like. Had she been frightened?

'How did she die?' he asked.

Dr Keller regarded him with an appraising frown. 'Have you had any medical training, Mr Turner?'

'No. Why do you ask?'

'You said she. How did she die. How do you know these are the remains of a female?'

'Am I right?'

'Yes,' she said at length.

'How did she die?' he asked again.

'I'm not at liberty to disclose that kind of information. In fact you shouldn't be here at all.'

'I promise you that nothing you tell me will leave this room. The truth is I think I know who she may have been.'

She looked long and hard at him, then sighed. 'Alright, but I hope my faith in your word isn't misplaced.' She moved to the end of the table closest to the skull. 'After this length of time it's impossible to determine the cause of death with any certainty. However, it's a reasonable assumption that this trauma to the skull was the cause. I can't say whether the damage occurred postmortem, but my guess would be that it happened before she was put in the water.'

'Do you know what caused it?'

'A blow with a heavy blunt instrument. Beyond that it would only be conjecture.'

'Then she was definitely murdered?'

'It's highly likely. Unless you can think of another reason why she was wrapped in a tarpaulin and then weighted with chains before she was dumped in the water.'

He conjured an image of the lake at night, a figure bent over a prostrate form wrapping her body in chains. 'How old was she?' he asked when he found his voice again.

'More to the point, how old would you say she was?'

'Eighteen or thereabouts.'

She nodded her agreement. 'Certainly she was between fifteen and twenty years of age. So eighteen fits.'

'Do you know how long she was in the lake?'

'It's hard to say with any degree of accuracy. At least ten years. That much we can determine from the advanced degree of decomposition. Probably no more than thirty years.'

'How about seventeen years?'

'Yes. She could have been there for seventeen years.'

'Was there anything found with the body?'

Dr Keller held up her hand. 'Wait a minute. So far you've asked a lot of questions to which I've given all the answers.'

'Please,' he said. 'Did you find anything else?'

She hesitated, then said, 'If I find out you have a tape recorder running in your pocket I personally guarantee that you will regret this.'

He spread his hands. 'No recorder. I swear it.'

She evidently decided to believe him. 'So far we've collected various samples of fibres and so forth, some of it no doubt the remains of clothing, some of it the tarpaulin she was wrapped in. But I doubt we'll be able to tell much from them. The chances of recovering DNA material which might help to identify her killer are practically nil.'

'Nothing else? What about jewellery for instance?'

'As a matter of fact we do have some jewellery, yes.'

She led the way to a stainless-steel bench where various samples had been placed awaiting further analysis. His heart was beating faster than normal. Dr Keller indicated several dull yellow hoops that he assumed were earrings.

'They're gold,' she said. 'We also found this necklace and these bands.' She indicated the pieces all laid out in a row. 'They have one interesting detail in common; see here, these markings.'

He looked where she was pointing and she handed him a magnifying glass.

'Take a look on the inside. I haven't been able to identify them yet.'

He saw a series of symbols. At first glance he thought they were letters, but when he looked harder he realized they weren't from any alphabet he recognized. He studied them, wondering what they reminded him of.

'Romany,' he said at last, straightening.

'I'm sorry?'

'Some kind of Romany symbols. I've seen something like this before. I did a story a few years ago about a family of gypsies. A teenage boy was killed by some local youths. He wore a ring with markings like this.'

Dr Keller looked at him with interest, then peered herself through the magnifying glass. 'You might have something there. They could be of Romany origin.' She put the glass down. 'Any other reason why you might think that, Mr Turner?'

'Yes,' he said and indicated one of the gold bands. 'See if the police have something that matches that. It'll be in a property file from 1985. A gypsy girl went missing. Her name was Meg Coucesco.'

After leaving the hospital he phoned the *Courier* and asked Findlay if he could spare ten minutes of his time. When he arrived twenty minutes later Adam was surprised to find both Findlay and Janice waiting for him.

'How was the lovely Dr Keller this morning, Adam?' Findlay said, gesturing towards a chair.

Adam tried to hide his surprise. 'How did you know I'd seen her?'

'This is no' a big place Adam. I've someone waiting at the hospital who recognized you. I take it you were there to talk about the body they found in the lake? Though I doubt there's much left of it now, eh? Mebbe a pile of old bones.'

Adam saw no point in denying the obvious but he wasn't going to break his pledge to Dr Keller either. 'I can't talk about it, Jim. I gave my word.'

'Aye, fair enough. To tell the truth, Adam, I was surprised the good doctor agreed to see you. There's people from the national papers and the TV who'd cut off their arm to get inside that lab. Well, mebbe no' their own arm, but probably their mother's anyway.' Findlay chuckled at his own grim joke. 'Perhaps it's because of your charm and good looks, eh? What do you think Janice?'

Janice had so far said nothing, and when Findlay drew attention to her she seemed uncomfortable. She cast Adam a quick almost apologetic look.

'No, I don't think that's it,' Findlay said, rocking back on his chair. 'No offence, Adam, but our Dr Keller is no' easily swayed by such trivialities. She takes her work seriously, so she does. I think she must have had some other reason for agreeing to talk to you.' He leaned forward and tossed a newspaper across the desk. 'I wonder if this has anything to do with it?'

The headline was from seventeen years ago. The paper was dated 15 August 1985, and the story was about the disappearance of a gypsy girl whose likeness, drawn by a police artist, occupied a quarter of the page. Adam was aware that Findlay was watching his reaction intently.

'Listen, I know it's her body they found in the lake.' He jabbed a finger at the paper. 'The police are holding a press conference later today, but I cannae wait for that. We're putting out a special edition this afternoon and I need to know now what they're going to say in that conference. You have to be quick these days to get the jump on the competition.' Findlay glanced at Janice with heavy emphasis. 'So tell me, have they positively identified her?'

Adam shook his head. 'I gave my word, Jim.'

Anger flashed momentarily in Findlay's eyes, then he gestured to Janice. 'Give us a few minutes will you, Janice?'

She hesitated, obviously baffled by what was going on but nevertheless intrigued. However, she rose and obediently went to the door. Findlay watched her go. 'She's going to make a good reporter that one. She told me that it was you who tipped her off about what those fishermen found the other day.'

'We're staying at the same pub.'

'Aye, I know. I suppose you know the *Mail* had the story the next morning? I know that was Janice's doing. She's young and ambitious. I'm no' so old that I dinnae understand that. I was young once myself, Adam. But the kids today, they're ruthless, so they are.' He smiled ruefully. 'But mebbe they always were, eh? Mebbe I just didnae have the right attitude when I was her age. That's probably why I'm still here.'

Was there a wistful note in Findlay's tone, Adam wondered? When he'd known him years ago, Findlay had seemed older than his years. He'd been the paper's senior reporter, his solitary and individualistic habits tolerated because of his skills. But Adam had no idea what path Findlay had taken to arrive at the *Courier*. He supposed there had been certain choices along the way, maybe some he regretted.

Findlay pointed a stubby finger across the desk. 'You know something about this girl, Adam.' He wagged his finger before Adam could respond. 'Don't try and deny it. I knew it when she disappeared, and I know it now. I could've made you tell me back then. Don't think I couldn't have. But when they arrested that fella James Allen, I figured it didnae matter any more.'

Findlay leaned back in his chair. 'I knew a detective who worked on that case. He always believed that James Allen had killed her. Allen knew her, Adam. Did you know that? He had a lot of dealings with the gypsies. Selling stolen goods and the like. Anyway, after Allen was killed that was the end of it one way or the other. I thought so too. Though I often used to wonder what it was you'd been hiding. I should have made you tell me really. That's always been my trouble, I'm too soft. If I'd been more like young Janice there I wouldnae've let you off so easily. But the way I saw it, Allen was dead, and whatever you knew it was between yourself and your conscience.'

Findlay paused for effect. 'But now I hear you get in to see Dr Keller when naebody else could. That makes me wonder, Adam.'

Findlay was calling in an old obligation, Adam saw. He was telling him that once he'd gone easy on him, and now it was time to repay the debt. Perhaps he was right. Besides, when considered in light of the fact he had come here to ask for Findlay's help again, Adam didn't see that he could refuse.

'Okay, I can't tell you what I spoke about with Dr Keller,' he said eventually. 'But I can tell you this much. The police found something in Allen's van after he was arrested if you remember.'

'Aye, it was a bracelet.'

'That's right. It was you that told me about it. I think you'll find it was one of a set.'

Findlay regarded him shrewdly. 'And they've found others that match, is that it?'

Adam said nothing. Findlay stood up and came around his desk. He rested a hand briefly on Adam's shoulder. He seemed about to offer some philosophical observation on the nature of loyalty, but thought better of it. Eventually he went back around his desk and sat down.

'Now, Adam, you wanted to see me, what can I do for you?' he said.

Findlay, it turned out, knew a lot about Carisbrook Hall. Adam told him that Jane Hanson had been interested in somebody who'd been a patient there in the mid-eighties, but he didn't know the reason for her interest.

Findlay thought for a minute. 'Webster would've been in charge at Carisbrook around then.'

'Yes. I already spoke to him.'

'Is that so? And what was your impression of the good doctor?'

'Apart from the fact that he lied to me about having met Jane Hanson, I thought he was a bit of the old-fashioned type, I suppose. Authoritarian.'

'Aye, he was that. A cold-hearted bastard more like. I had to interview him a few times over the years. It would have been easier getting in to see the prime minister.'

'He didn't like journalists then?'

'He didnae like anybody that questioned the way he ran that place. Anyone that said a word against the way he did things was out. None of the good nurses ever lasted there very long. Only the bad ones stayed. Webster liked things to be regimented, everything to run smoothly. I don't think he was all that bothered about the methods his staff used so long as they got the results. I always felt sorry for the poor buggers who ended up there.'

'Are you saying the patients were abused?'

'Aye, I'm sure there was some of that. There were all kinds of rumours about the place. Most of the time things got swept under the carpet.'

'But surely there were complaints?'

'There were, but you have to remember that we're talking about an institution for the mentally ill, Adam. The powers that be, even these days, tend not to take complaints too seriously when the people who make them claim they were abducted by wee green men.'

'So, nothing was done?'

'Eventually they had to. It got to the point where they couldn't ignore it any more and that's when they started making moves to shut the place down. It was partly a way of getting rid of Webster quietly.'

'Can you remember anything specific happening there around the mid-eighties?'

'I did a few different stories on that place, but it was a long time ago now. The thing for you to do would be to check through the back issues of the paper.'

Findlay picked up the phone and spoke briefly. When he hung up he said, 'You remember the way to the records department? Speak to the guy down there, he's expecting you.'

'Thanks,' Adam said. As he got up he caught sight of Janice at her desk. 'What are you going to do about her?'

'I've given her a bloody good bollocking, but this time I'll let her keep her job,' Findlay said. 'But I'll be warning her if anything like this happens again she'll be out on her ear. Send her in as you leave would you?'

It was fair enough. More than fair really. As he left Adam made a detour past her desk. She glanced warily over his shoulder towards Findlay's office. 'What kind of mood is he in?'

'He wants to see you, but between you and me I think you're off the hook.'

She looked relieved and then her journalistic instincts took over from concerns about her self-preservation. 'What was that all about in there anyway?'

'Ask Findlay,' he answered, knowing as well as she did that Findlay wouldn't tell her anything. 'I have to go downstairs and look up some old back issues. I'll talk to you later.'

'Back issues? Would that have anything to do with the body they found?'

'No, this is about the protest.'

'What are you looking for?'

'I'm not sure yet.'

She regarded him suspiciously. 'You're no' holding out on me are you?'

'I'm not holding out. When I have something, I'll be in touch.' He paused. 'Just as a matter of interest, if this does turn into a story, what will you do with it?'

She glanced over towards Findlay's office and bit her lip. 'Good question,' she said, but gave no clue as to what she thought the answer might be.

CHAPTER TWENTY-EIGHT

The records room was in the basement of the building. Years ago part of Adam's holiday job had been to help file back issues, which were eventually transferred to microfilm. He took the stairs, and as he descended past the first floor each step was like going back another year in time. Unlike the upper floors the walls were painted dark green and hadn't seen a fresh coat since the last time he'd been there. In places the plaster was cracked and occasionally chunks were missing. A blown light tube added to the gloom of the stairwell. At the bottom a scarred wooden door led into the records room where a man in his thirties blinked behind his glasses when Adam appeared.

He introduced himself as Kenny. 'So, what can I do for you?'

'I'm looking for anything that was written during the mid-eighties about Carisbrook Hall. In particular 1985.'

'Right. You'll need to have a look at the microfilm records then.' He led the way to a table where a reader was all set up. He turned it on and showed Adam how to work it. 'I'll have to pull out the files for you. How far back do you want to start?'

'I'm not sure. Say the beginning of 'eighty-five.'

'Right.' He went to a bank of cupboards on the wall. 'You know, you're the second person to come in here looking for something about Carisbrook lately,' he said conversationally.

'The second?' Adam echoed, guessing what was coming next.

'Yes. A young woman was here back in the summer. August I think.'

'Let me guess, her name was Jane Hanson?'

'Yes, that's her,' he said, sounding surprised.

'Do you remember what she was looking at?'

'I'm not sure. Is it important?'

'It could be.'

'Let me think. She mentioned Carisbrook, I remember that. She was interested in somebody who worked there I think, but I can't remember the name.'

'Was it Webster?' Adam suggested.

Kenny frowned. 'No, that doesn't ring a bell. It was something simple. Smith or Black or something like that. No, Jones! That was it.' His excitement at being able to help quickly faded when he saw Adam's expression. 'Doesn't that help?'

'It might if I knew who it was.'

'He. I think he was a male nurse. I seem to remember her saying something like that. I'm pretty sure she found what she was looking for anyway, because she wrote down an address before she left. She asked me for directions.'

'I don't suppose you remember where it was?'

'Sorry. Wouldn't have a clue. I know it was local because I helped her look it up on the map.'

'But you don't know where she found this address?'

Kenny shook his head. 'If it was on the computer I could do a search. Enter the name and date and pull out any matches.'

'But it's not, I suppose.'

'Not back then. Sorry.'

It had been too much to hope for. Nevertheless, at least he had something to go on and he wouldn't be searching blindly. A story about Carisbrook that mentioned somebody called Jones, possibly a male nurse. The clerk brought over some files. They were in the form of large slides, and there didn't appear to be very many, which was heartening, at least until he started looking and he found that each slide contained a month's papers. Resignedly Adam sat down and put the first one in the machine.

It took him an hour and a half to find what he was looking for. The story had appeared at the end of June in 1985. It was a very small piece on the court pages and he almost missed it. The police had arrested a man called Chris Jones, aged thirty-eight, of Border Avenue, Carlisle, on suspicion of selling drugs in a city pub. Jones was found with amphetamines in his possession. He pleaded guilty and was given a six-month suspended sentence. According to the report he worked at Carisbrook Hall as a psychiatric nurse aide. That was it.

Adam went over to the desk where Kenny was reading a paperback science-fiction novel. 'Border Avenue, does that ring a bell?'

'Could be.' He produced a street plan and looked the street up. 'Yes. Here it is. Must be right because I circled it.' He spun the book around so Adam could see, and sure enough there was a red circle around Border Avenue, which wasn't far from the city centre. Adam wrote down directions.

'Do you know this area?' he asked.

'Not really.'

He didn't have a street number, but at least he knew that he was on the right track. He thanked Kenny for his help and went back upstairs. Before he left he went back to Findlay's office and poked his head around the door.

'Somebody called Chris Jones was caught selling drugs in a pub back in 'eighty-five. He worked at Carisbrook. Mean anything to you?'

Findlay snapped his fingers. 'Aye, now that you mention it. He was a shifty wee bastard that yen. The police thought he must have got the stuff he was flogging from Carisbrook, but Webster claimed there was nothing missing. Jones left a wee while afterwards.'

'Do you think Webster was lying?'

'I thought so at the time. Probably didnae want a scandal so he covered it up and quietly sacked Jones.'

'Right. Thanks.'

He looked for Janice on the way out but she was nowhere in sight. He almost bumped into her as he left. She was standing outside smoking, though it turned out she'd been waiting for him.

'I didnae want to talk about this in there, but I've some information for you,' she said.

'Time for a drink?'

'Aye, a quick one.'

They went to the pub on the corner where Adam ordered sandwiches and a couple of bottles of Stella. 'So what have you got for me?'

'It's about Councillor Fraser. Remember you asked me to see what I could find out about her? Anyway, I know a guy who works for an estate agent that specializes in farm property. He's been in the game for years so he knows most of the farms in the area. After you mentioned that the Frasers owned a farm I gave him a ring to see if he happened to know anything about it.'

'And he did?'

'Aye. Rural property isnae exactly a hot item around here these days, so news gets around fast when something is sold.'

'They sold the farm?'

'Not sold. But apparently they have leased about a third of their land.'

'Leased to whom?'

'That's the interesting part. A company called Wood Products, which is based just outside Newcastle. They want the land to plant firs. Apparently what they do is plant some fast-growing variety and the crop is sold as a futures commodity. The lease deal with the landowner is structured so that they get a share of this money up front. Basically what this means is that the Frasers get a lump sum, plus an annual lease of the land, all for doing nothing.'

'Nice work if you can get it,' Adam observed.

'Aye, but that's no' all. I did a bit of digging. A guy by the name of Leith Williams is listed as a major shareholder of Wood Products. He's an investor who lives in London, sits on the board of half a dozen different companies. And guess what one of them is?'

Adam had a feeling what Janice was going to say, but he didn't steal her thunder.

'Forest Havens,' she said, with a hint of the dramatic.

It could be coincidence, Adam thought, but he didn't believe in that kind of coincidence. So, perhaps Councillor Fraser had given in to temptation. But there was still no proof, and he still had no idea where an ex-nurse aide from Carisbrook fitted into any of it.

After Janice had gone back to work he walked to where he'd left Angela's car, thinking over what he knew. Jones had been prosecuted in late June, about a month after the last date on Marion Crane's medical records, though he didn't know what the connection was. Was it this man Jones that Jane Hanson had asked Webster about? If she had he doubted Webster would have told her anything, which meant she must have tried to track down Jones herself, hence looking through the newspaper files. Without a house number it would be a laborious process. Had she knocked on every door? He hoped it wasn't a long street.

Border Avenue, it turned out, was a crescent-shaped street of three-storey red brick Victorian terraces. Had it not been for the railway lines that bordered the back gardens on one side, it was the kind of street that might have been gradually taken over by affluent young couples with money and an addiction to DIY television shows. The proximity of the railway, and the nearby industrial yards, however, had ensured that the upwardly mobile had passed Border Avenue by. Consequently the houses were a mixed bag. Some had tiny neat front gardens and lace curtains at the windows, while others were neglected with peeling paint and weeds poking up around the edges of cracked concrete parking areas. An absence of trees added to the uniformly unappealing air of the street.

Adam parked at one end and considered his options. To knock on every door looking for somebody who might remember a man who'd lived there seventeen years ago seemed like a shot in the dark at best. Given that he was bound to come across houses where nobody was home it could take him days. He remembered passing a small block of shops around the corner in the next street so he went back on foot and ducked into a small newsagent's. An Asian woman stood behind the counter.

'I'm looking for somebody who used to live in Border Avenue,' Adam said. 'It was a long time ago but he could still be in the area. Maybe he has a paper delivered. His name was Jones. Chris Jones.'

The woman frowned. 'We have quite a lot of people called Jones on our list.'

'Do any of them live in Border Avenue?' She hesitated. 'Please, it's very important.'

She relented and went to the back of the shop and returned a moment later carrying a book. When she opened it she ran her finger down the pages, stopping briefly now and then. When she was done she closed the book. 'We deliver to one Jones in Border Avenue. Number twenty-three.'

'Thanks.'

Number twenty-three was in slightly better condition than the neighbours that flanked it on either side. The door looked new, though it appeared to be made of white plastic and had not been chosen to enhance the period features of the house. Outside on the paved front courtyard a couple of pots on either side of the door housed geranium plants. Adam rang the bell and waited. Across the street a woman walked past pushing a baby in a pram. She glanced at him curiously. Adam turned as the door behind him opened and a middle-aged woman appeared.

'Yes?'

'Mrs Jones?'

She hesitated a beat before answering cautiously. 'Yes.'

'My name's Adam Turner. I'm looking for somebody who used to live in this street during the mid-eighties. Chris Jones?'

'There's no one here by that name,' she said flatly.

He supposed it had been too much to hope for, though he felt his spirits flag as he contemplated the long rows of houses on either side of the street. 'Right, well thanks anyway.' He began to turn away and the woman started to close the door, but when he was almost to the pavement again she called out.

'What made you think he lived here anyway?'

'It was just the name.'

'Try fifty-seven,' she said, and before he could ask anything else abruptly closed the door.

Number fifty-seven was neat in a fussy kind of way. The front windows were draped with lace curtains and a plastic gnome stood alone in a square of manicured lawn in the garden. A card in the front window announced a room to let, and when Adam rang the bell musical chimes played the opening bars of a tune he vaguely recognized. The woman who answered was small and neat, her grey hair tied back in a bun. She wore a pink housecoat and had tiny ferret-like eyes. Adam introduced himself and explained why he was there. He added that somebody along the street had suggested he try here.

'That Mandy Jones I suppose.' The woman sniffed, and peered along the street as if she might see her standing at her door. The woman looked at him suspiciously. 'What do you want with Chris Jones anyway?'

'I'm looking for somebody and it's possible he might be able to help me. The woman along the road. Is she a relative of Chris Jones's?'

'His wife, or ex-wife anyway. He came here when she threw him out.'

'He lives here?'

'Used to, but it was years ago now. He only stayed three months. Left owing me a fortnight's rent, which that wife of his never paid me, though I only took him in as a favour to her. That's what you get for doing folk favours. A slap in the face that's what.' The woman folded her arms across her chest in an attitude of aggrieved hostility. 'What's he done anyway?'

'Nothing as far as I know.'

'Must have done something to make himself so popular after all this time. He was never as popular when he lived here.'

'Popular? You mean somebody else has been here looking for him? A young woman?'

'Might have been,' the woman said archly. 'It's not for me to go telling strangers all about my lodger's personal business.'

'I don't think it matters much after all this time does it?'

'It's the principle I have to think about. Where would I be if my lodgers couldn't depend on me for their confidences?'

'I thought you said Jones left owing you money.'

'Yes, well, that's as maybe.'

Adam glanced back along the road. He wondered if he should go back to number twenty-three and try talking to the ex-wife again.

'She doesn't know where he is, if that's what you're thinking,' the woman said, with a sly gleam in her eye.

'But you do?' he asked, grasping the implication.

'Maybe.'

Adam took out his wallet and produced a twenty-pound note.

'Jones left here owing me two weeks' rent. I charge fifty-five pounds a week for room and board.'

'You want me to give you a hundred and ten pounds?' he said incredulously.

'Suit yourself,' she said, and started to close the door.

'Alright, wait.'

She watched greedily while he went through his wallet. He wondered how much she had charged seventeen years ago, knowing it must be a fraction of what she was asking. And how much had the old crow managed to get from Jane Hanson? He took another twenty and a ten from his wallet. 'Fifty, and that's it. And only if you have an address for him.'

'Wait there.' She closed the door and when she opened it again a few minutes later she held a folded slip of paper. When Adam reached for it she snatched it away and held out her other hand. He gave her the money in exchange for the piece of paper and she started to close the door. He read what was written on it and quickly shoved his foot in the door.

'Wait. What is this?' The woman had written *Barstock Clinic, Durham* on the paper she'd given him.

'That's where he went after he left here.' She tried again to close the door, but Adam refused to move his foot.

'You expect me to pay you fifty pounds for this? That was seventeen years ago.'

'It's all I've got. He left it as a forwarding address and promised to send me the money he owed when he got his first wages. 'Course he never did. I should've known better. Pretending he didn't have any money when I knew better.'

'What do you mean?' The woman eyed him stonily. 'Listen, I already paid you more than this bit of paper is worth. If you want me to take my foot out the door you better start talking.'

'It's all I gave that girl that came around. She didn't complain.'

'Then I'd say you were doing pretty well if you sold this twice,' Adam pointed out. 'You said he had money?'

Reluctantly the woman gave in. 'Before he left I saw him in his room one day with a big roll of notes. He said it wasn't his, but I didn't believe him. I don't know where he got it from, but I expect it was from doing no good.' The woman glared. 'That's all I know.'

Adam removed his foot and she slammed the door. He went back to where he'd left Angela's car and read the note again. The

Barstock Clinic, Durham. Was that where Jones had gone to work after leaving Carlisle? It sounded like a private hospital of some sort. He wondered how Jones had managed to get a job in a place like that after being fired from Carisbrook for stealing drugs. And where had Jones come by the money that his landlady claimed to have seen him with?

It was almost dark by the time Adam got back to Castleton. He drove straight to Angela's house. There was no sign of David's Land Rover outside. Nor when he went inside was there any sign of Kate. Angela led the way through to the kitchen.

'I asked if she could stay for a few more days with the Cartertons,' she said when he asked where Kate was. 'I thought it would be a good idea.' She gestured towards the table, and fetched two glasses and a bottle of Scotch. 'So, what happened today?'

He didn't mention his visit to see Dr Keller, instead he told her about the old *Courier* story he'd found, about Chris Jones being charged with selling drugs, and how Jane Hanson had been there before him.

'Findlay told me at the time the police suspected Jones of stealing the drugs from Carisbrook, but Webster denied anything was missing. Then Jones was quietly gotten rid of.' He told her what he'd learned from Jones's ex-landlady. 'Jane had spoken to her too.'

Angela was thoughtful for a moment. 'I don't understand how Jones could have got a job at this clinic in Durham. Surely he wouldn't have got a reference?'

'I've been thinking about that too. Maybe it was part of the deal Webster did with Jones to keep him quiet. That could explain the money his landlady mentioned as well. According to Findlay there were all kinds of rumours about what was going on at Carisbrook, including patient abuse.'

'You mean Webster paid him off?'

'Possibly. Maybe Jones could've spilled the beans about more than just stolen drugs.'

'Which could be where Marion Crane comes in?'

'It makes sense, though what her connection is to the development is anybody's guess.'

Or to David and the deaths of three boys, was the unspoken implication, as they both knew.

'What now?' Angela asked.

'All I can do is follow the trail. Jane must have gone to this Barstock Clinic, so I will too. I'll leave in the morning. So, what about you? Did you have any luck tracing Marion Crane today?'

Angela reached for a pad on the table. There were lines of handwritten notes on several pages, many of them crossed out. 'After you left I thought about where to start looking and I had an idea. I thought she might be connected to somebody on the planning committee, so I started with them.'

'Good idea.'

'In theory. In practice I didn't find anything. I rang around digging up everything I could on wives, children, relatives, but no Marion anywhere as far as I can tell. I even checked the name of Henderson's first wife because I knew he'd been married before a long time ago, but no luck there either.'

'It was still a good idea,' Adam told her.

She smiled a brief acknowledgement. 'So then I resorted to the phone book. I rang every Crane listed. Nobody ever heard of anyone called Marion. Actually, I suppose we're lucky that it's a reasonably unusual name. If it'd been Jane or Mary or something there would probably have been too many leads to follow up. I've still got a few numbers left to try where nobody answered, but it isn't looking good.'

'I think you should keep at it. Something might turn up.' He hesitated a moment. 'That is if you still feel you want to.'

'Of course I do. Why wouldn't I?'

'No reason.'

'You mean I might have changed my mind. In case this all leads somewhere I won't like, is that it?' she said angrily.

It was exactly what he'd meant. He felt pinned beneath her accusing glare and then her expression softened. She shook her head wearily.

'I've been thinking. About why you think David is involved with all this. I thought it was just because of what happened. Because of us. But I get the feeling there's something else. Something you haven't told me.'

He wanted to tell her that she was right. He wanted to tell her about Meg, but what did any of it mean really? It was all just fragments and feelings. How could he explain that he knew David had something to do with what had happened to her? He had always known it.

'There's nothing else,' he said.

She held his eye. He didn't think she believed him. He drew her back to her notes and Marion Crane, and reluctantly she let it go.

'Maybe there's a way to narrow the field.' He told her what Janice had told him about Carol Fraser and her husband leasing part of their farm.

'Just because a director of the company that's leasing her land is also on the board of Forest Havens it doesn't mean she's corrupt,' Angela said.

'No. But it is a pretty big coincidence. I think she's worth another look anyway. Maybe if we dig a bit deeper Marion Crane will pop up in her past somewhere. Could be a relative or something.'

Angela nodded and made a note. 'I've also been working on this.' She pulled a sheet of paper from the back of her pad, which Adam saw was the phone account from the lodge. 'I've been calling some of these numbers, to see if they lead anywhere, but I haven't had much luck there either.' She started going through them. It turned out that some were to local supply businesses that dealt with the lodge, the international one was to a number in India, and the remainder were to innocuous places such as the local train station.

'What about the mobile number?'

'No luck. I get a recorded message saying the phone is either switched off or in an inaccessible area. There are still a couple of local numbers I haven't tried yet.'

Adam didn't think she was going to find anything more there. He already knew that the one significant number on the list was the one he'd circled, and that was Angela's own, which by her own admission Ben Pierce or one of the others had called the night they were killed. He put the list down.

'Let's concentrate on Marion Crane,' he said.

Angela found some cold chicken in the fridge and made a salad which they ate at the table in the kitchen. She wondered if she should ask him if he wanted to stay the night, but when she thought about how to phrase the suggestion there seemed an implication in the offer that she didn't mean. Or did she? The night before when she had gone to his room he had practically told her that she was the reason, at least in part, that he had come back. She couldn't believe even now that she'd had time to think about it that he had loved her so much all those years ago. To think that he had never forgotten her, that it was her image he'd sought through his relationships with other women. And yet she knew it must be true because he wouldn't lie, she would know if he had. He'd told her the truth. She could feel it then just as she could now. There was something intense about Adam. He felt things keenly, his emotions running like a live current near to the surface so that sometimes you could almost feel what he thought like a pulse in the air around him. He lived by his feelings, as opposed to David who was more logical, who kept what he felt in check, like many men she supposed. Perhaps if he had been more like Adam they wouldn't be in this situation because he would have talked to her instead of bottling everything up inside himself.

She came to, realizing abruptly that she had been so engrossed in her thoughts that neither of them had spoken for some time. The light was fading. Across the table Adam was watching her with that same look he had worn the night before. There was a kind of hunger in his eyes. She could feel his desire like something tangible and she couldn't deny that it affected her. Her pulse quickened. She could feel the flush of heat on her skin and a dull ache in her belly. It would be so easy to allow something to happen between them. How long had it been since she had felt so wanted, so needed? How long since she had felt the strength of a man's arms around her, of another body moulded against her own? There was the temptation to offer herself as a gift. To soothe his troubled mind. He was like a man with a fever and he was burning up with the heat of a long-held desire that was bordering on obsession. She wanted to hold him, soothe him and at the same time take some physical comfort herself. She could immerse herself in heat and passion and tenderness for a time, forget everything. In a way the possibility seemed natural, something that should have happened a long time ago, as if the past remained incomplete. He watched her so seriously, his eyes drinking her in, devouring her. Her breath caught in her throat. Part of her, a tiny voice of caution in the back of her head, struggled vainly to be heard. She knew that it would happen, that she would allow it to and he could see her silent acquiescence in her eyes.

He shifted as if to rise and as he did the sound of a car pulling into the front yard hit them like a blow. They froze and in that instant she knew it must be David. She got up to go to the door and as she did she switched on the light and the tension between them evaporated in an instant.

At the front door she watched as a van backed into the lane and drove away. She felt Adam behind her and hugged her arms about herself as a cold wind blew into the house.

'Just somebody turning around,' she said. Her voice sounded unnatural.

'I should be going anyway.'

She stood aside to let him pass. His car was in the garage. She told him somebody from town had come by and checked it that afternoon. 'He said you can drive it. Just don't overdo it. He did a temporary repair on the window.'

'Thanks. I'll call you tomorrow.'

'Goodnight.'

He raised a hand and she waited until he had driven away before she went back inside. The house was silent. There was a bolt on the top of the front door that was never used. If David came home during the night and the door was bolted he wouldn't be able to get in, short of breaking a window, which she supposed would be easy enough to do if he was that determined. Nevertheless she drew the bolt. It was symbolic of her need to be alone, of a distance she was putting between herself and David. Right now she didn't want to see him, she didn't want to confront him with the questions that filled her mind. It was, she acknowledged, a shift in her thinking because now she no longer truly knew what she believed.

She wondered about that call the night David had gone out. He must have gone to the lodge, she acknowledged. But he had never mentioned it. And that same night three lads had been killed.

She went along the passage to the stairs. The study door was half-open and as she passed by she reached inside to flip on the light. David was there. Not physically, but his presence was etched everywhere. In the prints on the wall, the books, the papers and bills scattered on the desk. Even in the empty glass that smelled of whisky. She was tired. She turned out the light and went upstairs.

It took her a long time to sleep. She lay in the darkness and allowed her mind to drift. She envisaged a sunny day, the willow by a bend in the river, and a girl laughing. It was herself, though younger, paddling barefoot while Adam with his serious, dark eyes watched her from the grass on the bank. She recalled the pulse and surge of her emotions, the strange thrill of power she'd felt at the effect she knew she had on him. The beginnings of the discovery of her womanhood. Briefly she yearned for the return of something that was long since gone. It was, she thought, life's greatest irony that the most precious state of all, that of innocence, has no value at all until it has been irrevocably lost.

CHAPTER TWENTY-NINE

Mad Mary. That's what people called her. She couldn't tell anybody about the Shapeshifter. Even if there were anybody to tell, nobody would believe her. Mad Mary. Don't listen to her, she's crazy. Even Nick told her it was in her head. But this time it wasn't. She knew it wasn't. She had seen it. It had a shifting face that turned from being a person into a hideous creature with a grinning, drooling mouth. Its eyes were red and puckered.

Christ! Stop thinking about it! Stop it! That's what it wanted because then she got scared and that's what it liked. Didn't she even know that much? Was she that stupid? She ought to fill her mind with other things, that's what. She ought to think of trees. Big leafy trees like the ones in the wood. She knew a place where there was a purple beech that stood more than a hundred feet high. Its branches skirted the ground and made a huge cavern-like space inside. Safe from the outside world. If she looked skywards the leaves were green on the underside, and the light filtered softly through them. She felt safe there. She hoped it wasn't one of the trees they cut down when they built the holiday camp.

I'm listening to you, Mary, you mad bitch. I'm listening to all your mad thoughts.

Snigger, snigger. Chortle, chortle. Stop thinking about fucking trees. Think about the Shapeshifter instead. Look, isn't it pretty? Picture it, Mary.

It wants to touch you.

It wants to taste you. It's going to take a big bite out of you and chew you up into small pieces.

SHUT UP YOU BASTARD!

That's not very nice, Mary. I don't like you to shout at me. It isn't polite. I'm going to punish you for that soon. Very soon.

Mary screwed her eyes shut tight until it hurt, until lights exploded in the dark. Sometimes that kept the voice out, for a little while at least. It laughed as it retreated. She knew it was only hiding, burrowing into nooks and crannies in her mind. It didn't seem to mind going away because it knew that it wouldn't be long now.

It's nearly time, Mary. Nearly.

The voice faded and died on a lingering echo. Once she'd thought the voice couldn't hurt her, but she'd been wrong, she knew that now. The Shapeshifter and the voice were really the same. The voice wasn't only in her head any more. Her madness had made it real. It had been born in her mind, but it had frightened her and it was her fear that made it real, made it grow, so the voice was both inside and outside of her now. Soon the Shapeshifter would come for her and she wouldn't be able to escape, it would do terrible things to her and laugh while she screamed and nobody would ever be able to help her.

Oh, yes yes yes. Terrible things. Scream. Scream all you like, Mad Mary. You slut. You deserve what you're going to get. You dirty little bitch. You've got this coming. Yes yes yes.

She opened her eyes. Mary had a little lamb, its fleece was white as snow. She paused, unable to recall how the rest of the rhyme went. So she said the first line in her mind again. Mary had a little lamb, its fleece was white as snow. She repeated it over and over again, and the repetition made the voice go quiet. It couldn't talk while she filled her mind with stuff like this. She looked at the table by the bed. There was a bottle of pills there. Her medication. If she took them, six a day, she would feel better. That's what the doctors said. The voice would go. Maybe it would, but she would shake and drool and feel like she was trapped in a cotton wool dream, her movements dulled, her senses coated in tar. It was like being half dead, and one day she knew if she took the medication she would never wake up. She would be trapped like a zombie for ever, and then the voice would come for her. She thought maybe it was a trick, it was what the voice really wanted. So she didn't take the pills.

Take them, Mary.

NO! Shut your mouth. She lay down on the bed. It was cold and dark, other than the soft, red light that flowed into the corners of the room from the lamp. A breeze through the window made her shiver, and made the light pulse like a beating heart, like blood.

Where was Nick? Why did he always leave her alone these days? But she was glad he wasn't there in a way. He had changed, she didn't like him that much any more.

She felt under the pillow. Her fingers closed on the cold metal of the gun barrel. It felt alien. Hard and cold, but it gave her some comfort to know it was there. She withdrew her hand and closed her eyes. She was tired now, and the voice had settled to a whispering background hiss. Sometimes bubbling when it laughed, mocking her, but she could stand that. She closed her eyes, and weariness overtook her. She was so tired. Being afraid made her tired. She slept.

Once she had been a happy, bright schoolgirl. She had grown up on a farm between Castleton and Carlisle. She'd gone to school at St Agnes. She'd ridden her horse, played the violin, had planned to go to university. When she was seventeen the voice had first started speaking to her, and afterwards her life had slowly fractured, splintered, eventually disintegrated. Her family hadn't understood and now she rarely heard from them. They had written her off. They couldn't see that she was changing into another person, not the Mary they knew, and that there was nothing she could do about it. Her parents hadn't understood why she drank until she was almost senseless, why she'd started taking drugs. Alcohol and drugs dulled the horror of what was happening as she slowly lost herself, but she couldn't explain. Every time she tried to talk, the voice in her head screamed at her so loud it hurt her. Only drinking or smoking dope, or eventually shooting up, soothed it. She left home. She lived in filthy places, and fucked people for money. Anybody. Old men. Men who stopped in cars. Youths who laughed and jeered at the things she did for five pounds. A lot of the time she was out of it, barely knew what was happening to her. She didn't care. She cut herself and wanted to die.

Nick told her that they had met in a pub in Carlisle when she was drunk. She didn't remember. He said he had beaten up somebody who was trying to drag her outside. Her parents were horrified when she moved in with him, though by then they had almost reached the limit of their horror. But it was Nick who had taken her back to hospital. She had stayed there for three months and they had told her she was suffering from paranoid schizophrenia, had got her on medication. When she came out she came to live at the cottages. After a year, when she told Nick she wasn't going to take the medication any more he hadn't argued. Sometimes she thought she loved him. Other times, in her half-lucid moments, she knew they merely existed together, two misfits, two loners. He had nightmares. He was sullen and moody and they didn't talk much. Sometimes he got angry with her and occasionally he punched her and then she hated him.

They never went anywhere together. But that wasn't his fault. She didn't like to go out. She was afraid to go anywhere, though she wanted to leave the cottages. She thought they were haunted. By the past. By ghosts. Nick said that soon they would leave. She knew that in a way he didn't want to because he'd grown up here, though she suspected his childhood had not been a happy one. He didn't talk about it and she didn't ask. She had her own problems.

She woke not knowing how long she had been asleep. At first she lay still on the bed, breathing normally with her eyes closed, trying to feel if there was anyone in the room with her. She couldn't hear anything, and she couldn't sense anything. The voice in her head was quiet. In fact it was silent, and suddenly Mary was filled with a deep rushing dread that threatened to engulf her. The silence overwhelmed her. She felt so alone. Like she was standing in a great limitless dark space and there was nobody near; no sound, no light, just nothingness and that was all there would ever be. While she had slept it had taken her and brought her to this place and left her here. She was absolutely, completely alone. The absence of sound, of even the voice of her madness that at least she was used to terrified her. Fear rose in her throat and threatened to gag her.

She opened her eyes, and the scream that had risen died on

her lips. There was light. Soft, red, comforting. She was in her room. She looked warily towards the door, but it was closed the way she had left it. Slowly she raised herself on one elbow and looked about the room. Nick wasn't there. Nobody was there. She started to breathe a little easier. The voice remained silent, and this fact disconcerted her. She was so used to it; even when it wasn't shouting in her brain, trying to drown out her own voice, it was there, whispering in the background, ever present like the constant movement of air through trees. But now it was gone and the empty space it left behind was unfamiliar. She glanced at the table to see if her pills were there, thinking that perhaps she had taken them and had forgotten. But the pills were where she'd left them, and when she held out her hand it wasn't shaking, and when she felt her face it wasn't wet with her own drool.

She rose from her bed and stood uncertainly on the bare floorboards. She wasn't sure what she should do. She trembled, and goosebumps rose on her arms. The window was open and the flimsy curtain fluttered in a freezing breeze. She went towards it and outside the moon suddenly appeared through a break in the cloud. A movement caught her eye. It was close to the wall of the last cottage, something dark and shapeless in the shadows. Fear leapt in her breast, and she stifled a gasp. Then it moved into the grey light of the moon and she saw that it was Nick. He paused briefly, looking one way and then the other as if he was searching for something. She wanted to call out his name but stopped herself before a sound escaped her lips. Instead she watched as he went towards the meadow and from the way he often stopped and looked around, from the way he moved with deliberate stealth, she knew he was searching for something. It was as if he was stalking.

Suddenly, a rustle in the undergrowth beneath her window made Mary look down. The moon vanished again and darkness returned, but not before she saw something down there. A shifting shape. She couldn't see it clearly now, but it was moving. She sensed rather than saw a change in the texture of the darkness every now and then as it slipped away from the cottages. She realized that it was getting closer to Nick. Fear paralysed her, freezing her to the spot. She couldn't move or make a sound. A shiver ran the length of her body as a blast of freezing air rippled over her skin. The clouds parted briefly, and the moon illuminated the meadow again. Nick was standing still, looking towards the woods. He held something in his hand. A shotgun she thought. Something emerged from the trees behind him and changed shape, becoming a man on two legs. The shape moved swiftly and silently and in the last second before it reached Nick, Mary opened her mouth and screamed.

Nick turned, startled, and started to raise his shotgun, but then a cloud passed over the moon and everything was plunged into darkness. She thought she heard a scuffle, a soft thump as her scream died in her throat. Then there was only silence before the moon reappeared to reveal the empty meadow.

CHAPTER THIRTY

While Adam ate breakfast in his room he watched the TV reports on local and national news. Following the story in the *Courier*'s special edition the previous evening linking the remains found in Cold Tarn to the disappearance of Meg Coucesco in August 1985, the police were admitting there was certain evidence to support this theory. The chief inspector holding the press conference remained tight-lipped about the precise nature of the evidence, even when a reporter referred to claims in the *Courier* that jewellery found with the remains matched items discovered in the vehicle of a man police questioned over the disappearance seventeen years earlier.

'Thanks, Findlay,' Adam muttered to himself. He imagined that questions had already been asked to try and find the source of the leak. He hoped that nobody linked it to Dr Keller.

On TV the chief inspector thanked the media for their attendance and attempted to leave the room. He remained wooden-faced while reporters crowded around him and hurled questions from all sides.

Given that the *Courier* story had included references to the tarpaulin and chains used to wrap and weigh the body down, it was a foregone conclusion that the victim had been murdered. A reporter shoved his microphone at the inspector and asked if the police were looking for anyone beyond James Allen, their original suspect in the Coucesco case, who was now dead.

'At this stage we're not considering making any further enquiries beyond establishing the identity of the remains with as much certainty as possible. Thank you very much.'

The scene switched back to the studio where the newsreader began recounting the events of 1985. An artist's image of Meg filled the screen and then was replaced with old footage of searchers combing the woods and the fells around Castleton. Again the image switched and showed James Allen as he was released from custody after police questioning. The final image was a still they had recovered from somewhere of the burnt-out wreck of Allen's van.

Adam switched off the set. He wondered if David was watching. Whatever had happened all those years ago, it was unlikely anyone would ever know the truth now. But fate, Adam had often thought, has a way of dealing with past wrongs. What goes around, so they say, comes around.

It was still early when he left the New Inn for the drive east across the fells past Alston and Stanhope. The road wasn't busy, and though the sky was leaden and ominous it remained dry. On the bleak high ground, where the hills were brown and windswept, the landscape broken only by stone walls, there was a sprinkling of snow from the night before. At one point near the old lead mines on Killhope Moor across the county border into Durham, Adam pulled over to get some air. It was freezing and he managed five minutes with his collar up and shoulders hunched against the bitter wind before he went back to the sanctuary of the Porsche. It took him a good ten minutes with the heater on full before he felt fully thawed out again. The weather report on the radio talked of a sudden end to the balmy autumn the country had experienced and predicted more winds from the icy north.

He arrived on the outskirts of Durham city just after eleven, and pulled over into a hotel car park. Inside he asked at reception if he could borrow a phone book, and found Barstock Clinic listed in the directory. When he called and spoke to an administrator he told her that he was a journalist and that he was trying to track down a man who he believed might once have worked at the clinic. The name meant nothing to her, which didn't surprise him. He doubted that Jones was the type to stay anywhere for long, whether he left of his own accord or was fired. The person he spoke to asked him to hold while she put him through to the director's office, and after a short wait he heard a woman's voice.

'This is Dr Hope speaking. How may I help you?'

He went through it all again. 'I was wondering if somebody there might know if Jones did work at the clinic in 'eighty-five.'

'Actually, I was here at that time.'

'Then you remember him?'

She took a few moments to answer, and when she did it wasn't directly. 'Why did you say you were interested in this man, Mr Turner?'

'It's a long story. I'd be happy to explain it in person if you can spare me a few minutes of your time. I'm calling from a hotel called the Rosedale just off the A690. I think it's quite close to the clinic.'

'Yes it is,' she answered, her reluctance evident. 'However, I really don't know that I can help you. Mr Jones only worked here for quite a short time, and I'm afraid I have no idea where he is now. It was a very long time ago.'

'I see. Perhaps I could speak to you anyway. Who knows, maybe something you remember might help me.'

'I'm afraid I'm really rather busy.'

'Well, maybe you can answer one question at least. Has anybody else contacted you about Jones recently? A young woman called Jane Hanson?'

'No, I'm afraid the name doesn't ring a bell.'

There was a note in Dr Hope's tone that struck Adam as off key. She'd hesitated before answering, as if she wanted to give the impression that she was thinking about it. But that was all wrong. It was the kind of thing people assumed was expected of them, like actors in a play. But surely she would have no trouble remembering if somebody else had come around asking about a man the clinic had employed seventeen years ago.

'Perhaps she spoke to somebody else,' Adam suggested.

'I really don't think so.'

'You seem very sure of that, Dr Hope.'

There was a short silence. 'Normally I would expect any enquiry of this nature to be directed through my office, as yours was. I'm not aware of any such enquiry, Mr Turner. Of course, I might be mistaken,' she added reasonably. 'Why don't I take your number and I'll check with our administrator. If I learn that anybody spoke to your Ms Hanson I'll certainly let you know.'

It was a good attempt to put him off, Adam was prepared to give her that. But it wasn't going to work. 'The thing is I really need to find Jones quickly. Perhaps if I came to see you now . . . if you could spare me just a few minutes?'

'As I said I'm really very busy.'

'Then perhaps I could talk to your administrator myself.'

In the face of his persistence she eventually relented, though her irritation was obvious. 'Very well,' she said crisply. 'Perhaps I could squeeze you in if you came now. Just for a few minutes.'

Adam smiled to himself. 'I appreciate it, Doctor. Thank you.'

'I'm glad to help,' she said, sounding not at all glad, and gave him directions on how to get there.

A discreet sign outside the gate announced the presence of the Barstock Clinic, which was surrounded by a high stone wall. Once inside the rest of the world receded. Gravelled walkways meandered along avenues of trees surrounded by rolling mani-cured lawns. Here and there seats had been placed where people could sit and immerse themselves in the tranquillity of the sur-roundings. As Adam drove along the entrance road he saw a dozen or more people doing just that, despite the cold. One or two watched with vague curiosity as he passed by, but most sat placidly ignoring him.

The clinic itself was housed in what must have once been a manor house. It was an imposing building made of local grey stone with gabled wings at each end. The entire façade was clad with ivy, adding to the sense of permanence the visitor immediately felt. A wide row of steps led to huge entrance doors, through which were a large hall housing a reception office and a grand staircase. The atmosphere was one of privilege, a sanctuary for the wealthy. It could have been an up-market health farm.

A young woman in a crisp pale blue uniform smiled politely as Adam approached and introduced himself.

'Of course. Dr Hope is expecting you.' She reached for a phone. 'Please have a seat and I'll tell her you're here.'

He thanked her, but rather than sit down he loitered in the hallway. One or two people passed by with the dazed expressions of the heavily medicated. He nodded to one who responded only with a vacant stare. Dr Hope, when she appeared, was tall and thin and dressed in a conservatively cut business suit. Her dark hair was cut short almost to the point of severity and the smile she greeted him with as they shook hands was controlled.

'Mr Turner. Please come this way. We'll talk in my office.'

As they entered a long oak-panelled corridor he asked questions about the building and the clinic in general, partly out of curiosity, partly in the hope that she would let down her guard a little. Her defensiveness bristled like quills beneath her outwardly smooth exterior. She told him that the manor itself dated from the fourteenth century, while the clinic had come into being during the First World War.

'Its initial purpose was to treat victims of what we would call post-traumatic stress disorder.'

'Shell shock?'

'Yes. Actually, perhaps treat isn't the right term. The aim then was to return the men to active duty as soon as possible. Shell shock wasn't officially recognized. Not at first.'

They came eventually to Dr Hope's office, where a small sign on the door announced her title of Clinic Director. The room inside was large and comfortably furnished. A desk with a computer on it stood at one end, and behind were lead-latticed windows deeply recessed into the thick stone walls. The furnishings were largely modern and comfortable, though a sprinkling of antiques sat unobtrusively among the rest. Dr Hope indicated that they should sit at a table where coffee things had been laid out. As they sat down a young woman emerged from an inner door and poured coffee for them.

'Thank you, Sarah,' Dr Hope said. She waited until the young woman had retreated again before she began. 'You said that you're a journalist, Mr Turner. May I ask which newspaper you work for?'

'I don't actually. I'm freelance.'

'I see. Well, since you phoned I've spoken to the administration staff, and also to the other staff members who worked at the clinic during the period that Mr Jones was employed here, and they each confirmed that they haven't spoken to the young lady you mentioned.' She smiled apologetically. 'I'm afraid you've had a wasted journey.'

'You spoke to everybody who was here in 'eighty-five?' He didn't try to conceal his scepticism. 'You didn't waste any time.'

'There are only a few of us, Mr Turner.'

'And you're certain that none of them spoke to Jane Hanson?'

The director carefully replaced her cup. 'That's correct. As a matter of interest, do you mind if I ask who this Ms Hanson is exactly? Is she a journalist like yourself?'

'No she isn't,' Adam said, noting the glimmer of relief in the director's eyes. 'Is that what's worrying you, Doctor? The fact that I'm a journalist?'

'I'm sorry?'

'I'm just wondering why you're so reluctant to speak to me.'

'I assure you that it's not a case of reluctance, rather of simply being unable to help. The man you're looking for was employed here for only a very short time.'

Adam looked around the room and out of the window at the well-kept serenity within the outer wall. 'The Barstock Clinic is a private psychiatric facility I understand?'

'Yes it is.'

'No doubt discretion is important to a place like this.'

Dr Hope regarded him levelly. 'The people who come here, and their families for that matter, have very high expectations. Aside from the assurance we give that the care and treatment we provide is exceptional, we have a reputation for the utmost discretion, it's true.'

'Are you worried that speaking to me will somehow compromise that reputation?'

Her response was a thin smile. 'In what way, Mr Turner?'

'I'm not sure. But I'm a little surprised that nobody's heard of Jane Hanson. I know that she was looking for Jones, and this was the last place he was known to be. I can't imagine that she didn't come here, but you say she didn't, which makes me wonder why.'

Ignoring his implication Dr Hope rose from her seat, signalling that their interview was at an end. 'I'm sorry that you've had a wasted journey. But I really can't help you.'

Adam remained seated, voicing his thoughts. 'Could it be that there's something you don't want me to know about? Maybe Jane discovered something about Jones you'd rather wasn't made public knowledge.'

'As I have said, Mr Turner, quite clearly I believe, Ms Hanson did not come here. I'm afraid your information is incorrect.'

'No, I don't think it is.'

The director regarded him coldly, then crossed to her desk and picked up the phone. 'I'm going to have to call security and have you removed.'

'Before you do, maybe I should mention that whatever Jane learned here may have directly or indirectly led to the deaths of three people.'

'I will allow you one more chance to leave of your own accord.'

'That doesn't bother you at all?'

'I refuse to be drawn into a hypothetical debate.'

'These people were students. Kids really, and there's nothing hypothetical about the fact that they're dead, Doctor.'

For a moment she appeared to waver, studying him as if she was trying to discern if what he was saying was true. Then she punched in some numbers and waited.

'If you speak to me now, I guarantee you won't read about it in the weekend papers,' he said.

There was a flicker of response and then it was evident that somebody had answered her call. Adam regarded her steadily. A second passed, and then another until finally resignation settled in the director's eyes. 'No, it's alright, John. I misdialled that's all.' She replaced the phone and returned to her chair, her expression thoughtful. 'What would you have done if I'd had you removed?' she asked.

'I don't know, but I might have called a friend of mine who works for one of the tabloids and told her that if she dug deep enough she might find a juicy story. Maybe something to do with a wealthy patient, possibly somebody well-known. The tabloids love a scandal, especially when it involves celebrities or aristocracy.'

She considered that. 'I think that now you're guessing.'

'True,' he agreed. 'But do you really want somebody from one of the scandal rags nosing around?'

She allowed herself a wry smile. 'No, I admit that possibility does not appeal to me. Alright, Mr Turner. You were right. I did speak to Ms Hanson.'

Once Dr Hope had agreed to talk, her icy exterior melted a little. She told Adam that Jane had phoned one day out of the blue wanting to know if Chris Jones had worked for the clinic during the mid-eighties. Just as Adam's call had been referred to Dr Hope, so had Jane Hanson's.

'But unlike me you agreed to see her?'

'Yes. I suppose I was taken aback to hear Jones's name again after such a long time. My immediate reaction was to discover why Ms Hanson was interested in him.'

'And to see if it would affect the clinic?'

'That was my concern, yes.'

'Because of something related to Jones?'

She nodded. 'As you guessed there was an incident during the time that Jones was employed at the clinic that I'm sure certain newspapers would love to hear about. Although it was all a long time ago now if what happened were ever to leak out the resulting publicity would have a disastrous effect. You may think by that I'm referring to the financial impact on the clinic, Mr Turner, but in fact though we are a private facility, what motivates myself, and I would say most of the people employed here, is the work we do. Mental health in this country is vastly underfunded. Not all of our patients come from wealthy backgrounds. Without this clinic many of the people we treat would never have the opportunity to rebuild lives that have been destroyed by their illness. It's only because of the income we derive from those patients who can afford to pay for the best of care that we're able subsidize the treatment of others less well off.'

'I'm only interested in what Jane wanted to know when she came here,' Adam assured her.

'She was looking for Jones. She asked how long he'd worked here and when I told her he left after less than six months she wondered if I knew where he might have gone.'

'And what did you tell her?'

'I gave her an address that we had on record, where Jones used to live.'

'I don't understand,' Adam said. 'Why would you give a total stranger the address of an old employee? Particularly one who you'd rather not be reminded of.'

'The answer is very simple: self-interest. You see, Ms Hanson struck me as a very determined young lady. It was quite clear to me that she would not desist in her efforts to locate Jones. If I didn't give her somewhere else to look she would have sought out other people to help her and in doing so she might have uncovered some matters that I would prefer remain where they belong. Which is firmly in the past.'

'And when I phoned?'

She smiled ruefully. 'Ms Hanson caught me unawares. This time I'm afraid when I heard that you were a journalist I tried to steer you away completely.'

'Did Jane tell you why she was looking for Jones?' he asked.

'She said that she was involved in a protest somewhere in Cumbria; something to do with preventing the building of a holiday park. She thought that Jones and another man had illegally influenced the outcome of a submission for planning permission. I believed her until you turned up. To be honest after you phoned earlier I began to wonder if perhaps she was a journalist too.'

'You don't need to worry on that score. Jane was telling you the truth. The other man she mentioned, did she tell you his name?'

'She might have, I don't remember.'

'Was it perhaps Johnson? David Johnson?'

Dr Hope frowned. 'I think she might have mentioned that name. Though I couldn't swear to it.'

'I don't suppose she told you why she suspected that Jones was involved in this scheme to influence the council?'

'Something she overheard by chance, I believe. But I don't know what it was.'

Adam recalled that when he'd spoken to Ellie at the camp she'd mentioned something Jane had overheard in a pub. Had that been Jones and David talking?

Dr Hope went to her desk where she retrieved a key from a drawer, which opened a filing cabinet. When she came back she was carrying an old faded manila folder. 'This is Jones's employment record, which I retrieved from the files downstairs when Ms Hanson visited me.' She opened it and copied down something on a slip of paper that she handed to Adam. 'This is the address that I gave her.'

Adam glanced at it. It was a number and street in Durham. 'Thanks.' He put it in his pocket.

'You mentioned something earlier. The deaths of three young people?'

'Yes.'

'What did you mean by that, and what does Jones have to do with it?'

'I wish I knew. There was a car accident at the beginning of September and three students were killed. It's possible the accident was connected to Jones in some way. I think it's linked to where he worked before he came here.'

'Carisbrook Hall?'

'Yes.'

'I see.' The director pursed her lips thoughtfully. 'Jones was originally employed on the basis of references he supplied from a man called Dr Colin Webster. Do you know who he was?'

'The director of Carisbrook. I've spoken to him. I also know about Jones being prosecuted for selling drugs in Carlisle.'

'A fact nobody here was aware of until much later. Since you know about that then perhaps I'm not telling you anything when I say that the reference supplied by Dr Webster was entirely misleading.'

Adam nodded. 'My guess is that he wanted rid of Jones to avoid a scandal. What exactly happened when Jones came to work here?'

Dr Hope seemed reluctant to answer. 'The only reason I ask is that it might have some bearing on the rest of this somehow. Though I don't know how.'

'This won't go any further?'

'You have my word.'

'Towards the end of 'eighty-five we had a patient here. She was a well-known television actress. In fact she still is. I won't mention her name. At the time she was quite young, in her early twenties. She had been in the papers a lot the year before she came here. She had a reputation for wild living, I suppose you could call it. Parties, drinking, drugs. Her picture had been splashed across the front of some of the more salacious tabloids on several occasions when she had been photographed in various compromising situations. I'm sure you understand the sort of thing I mean. Anyway, finally, after a suicide attempt that the press never heard about she was persuaded by her family to come here where she was diagnosed as suffering from manic depression. The drinking and drugs, the unpredictable behaviour were all aspects of her illness. Jones would have started working here about the same time as she was admitted.'

'As a nurse aide?'

'Yes. Although it soon became apparent that he knew very little about what goes on in a clinic like Barstock. At that time I wasn't the director of course. In fact, the actress I told you about was one of my patients, and Jones was assigned to work with me.' She paused. 'When I look back now, I realize that I should have had Jones fired immediately. It was quite clear to me that he had very little understanding or empathy for the needs of our patients. And apart from that I didn't trust him, or even like him for that matter. Part of the reason I didn't act was his glowing reference from Carisbrook, which puzzled me actually, but primarily it was because I felt guilty about my instinctive dislike for the man. A hazard of the profession I suppose. The tendency to analyse one's thoughts and reactions. Perhaps overly so.'

'I'm sorry, I don't follow. Why exactly did you feel guilty about the way you felt?'

'I was afraid that my feelings about Jones stemmed at least in part from his appearance.'

Adam looked blank.

'I assumed you knew. One side of his face was quite badly scarred. Of course, it wasn't his fault but it gave him quite a gruesome appearance. I was actually worried that some of the patients might find it disturbing. I was also concerned that my own professional judgement about Jones was coloured by what I can only describe as an instinctive revulsion. Of course now, with the benefit of time and hindsight I know that my feelings were normal. Jones was an unpleasant personality. His outward appearance had nothing to do with the way I felt about him. I was reacting to what I sensed about the man inside, but the psychiatrist in me resisted that interpretation. Until Jones proved my suspicions about him were correct.'

'How did he do that?'

'He had been here for several months, during which time I must admit his work did improve. At first he was practically incompetent, but I suppose once he got used to the way the clinic operated, which would have been quite different from Carisbrook, he began to settle in. Perhaps that was why I let my guard down. Unbeknownst to me, however, he began smuggling in alcohol, and some soft drugs too I suspect, which he was giving to the young actress I was treating. Though there were one or two occasions when I suspected that she had obtained alcohol from somewhere she denied it completely, and it was hard to see where she could have got it anyway. She had no means of paying anybody to bring it in for her. In the end when the whole thing came to a head, I discovered that Jones hadn't asked for payment of any kind. Instead he'd brought in a camera that he'd used to take semi-pornographic photographs of the actress when she was drunk. It turned out he'd used them to try and blackmail her family, threatening to sell them to the tabloid press if they didn't buy him off.'

'Nice guy. Presumably the family complied?'

'Actually, no. They came to the clinic, understandably furious, and Jones was forced to hand over all the pictures and then fired.'

'The police weren't informed?'

The director dropped her gaze for a second. 'I'm afraid not.'

'Because nobody wanted a scandal,' Adam guessed.

'Yes.'

All of which made it reasonable to assume that stealing drugs wasn't all Jones was doing at Carisbrook, Adam thought. What else had he been allowed to get away with in order to protect other people's reputations? 'Did he get a redundancy cheque and a reference from Barstock too when he left?' he asked scathingly.

'No, Mr Turner, he did not. I'm not defending what happened, but at the time it was considered the best thing. In the interests of everyone.'

'I'm sure. Did Jones threaten to expose what had happened?'

'I doubt it. As I said I wasn't the director then, so matters were quickly out of my hands.' She paused and then said, 'You may not believe this but I do know that there was a limit to what Jones was allowed to get away with. If he had forced the issue, scandal or not, the police would have been called in. Jones would have been under no illusion about that.'

'Okay. Maybe I was a bit harsh,' Adam conceded. 'Sorry.' He decided to try a long shot. 'Doctor, have you ever heard the name Marion Crane?'

It didn't register. 'I'm sorry, it doesn't mean anything.'

He explained briefly that he believed whoever she was, somehow she was connected with Jones and the development. Dr Hope could add nothing more about either Jones or Jane Hanson's visit, except that she had not told Jane about why Jones had been fired, and that Jane hadn't asked. When he thought about that Adam could only conclude that what had happened at Barstock wasn't directly relevant, though it did reinforce Adam's idea of the kind of person Jones was.

'There's something else you should perhaps consider,' the director said, as she led the way from her office. 'I don't know if you're aware of this or not, but Dr Webster would have treated at least some private patients at Carisbrook.'

Adam was surprised. 'I thought it was a public institution.'

'It was. But that wouldn't have precluded Webster from having an arrangement with the local authority whereby he was permitted to devote a proportion of his time and perhaps the facilities there to his own patients. And there's something else. You mentioned the name Marion Crane before. If she was ever a patient at Carisbrook, it's quite possible that wasn't her real name. The use of pseudonyms is quite common. The actress I mentioned, for example, was admitted under her own name, which wasn't, however, the name by which she was professionally known. A sort of reversal in that case.'

When Adam left Dr Hope escorted him to the front entrance, where they shook hands. Adam thanked her for her help and she apologized for her initial reluctance.

'If Jones has done anything wrong, I hope you find him and that he is punished for it,' she added. She handed him a slip of paper that she produced from her pocket. 'That's why I want you to have this. The truth is despite my justifications I've always regretted that Jones wasn't handed over to the authorities for what he did. Perhaps if he'd gone to prison we might not be having this conversation now.'

The consequences of guilt, Adam mused. He could certainly relate to that. He read what she'd written. It was an address in Tynemouth. 'What's this?'

'I wasn't sure I was going to give this to you. You see, Ms Hanson didn't find Jones at the address in Durham I gave you. He left there years ago of course. But during the time Jones worked at the clinic he became friendly with one of the gardeners, who was an ex-merchant seaman. Apparently something they had in common. Anyway, the gardener is still here. Ms Hanson came back and spoke to him, something I wasn't aware of until this morning, and he gave her this address. Apparently he's seen Jones once or twice over the years. He thinks Jones still lives here when he's not at sea.'

'At sea?'

'He went back to his old profession I gather.'

When he got in his car Adam looked at the address again. Here at last, he was somehow sure, was where Jane Hanson had ended her search for Jones. Here too, he guessed, was where she had gotten the copies of Marion Crane's medical records. A record of something that had happened seventeen years ago that Adam was now sure must somehow be linked to the planning committee. Perhaps Jones had heard about the development and realized the value of what he knew and then he had sought out somebody who would be willing to pay for that information. David. It fitted. A conversation Jane Hanson had overheard by chance in a pub, which had ultimately led her to Marion Crane's records.

But Jane had then returned to London. Perhaps finally being corrupted herself. It seemed likely. Add to that the fact that her relationship with Ben was nearing a natural end and it was likely she wouldn't have told him everything. Perhaps he had stayed on with the others hoping to discover the answers Jane already had. His motivation might even have been partly the hope that success might win him some favour with Jane again. A naïve and ironic hope if it was true, and ultimately tragic. Had Ben and the others found enough to expose blackmail and a rigged vote? Is that why they were killed?

Dr Hope had told him that it wasn't unusual for people to use pseudonyms. Marion Crane. Carol Fraser. Could they be the same person?

Adam was tempted to go straight to the address in Tynemouth. If he could find Jones there all his questions would be answered. Looking up the area on a road map he saw the quickest route would be to head for Newcastle on the Al and then cross the Tyne at Jarrow. But by the time he got there traffic would be building and it would be getting dark and he didn't know his way around. He would be better off going back to Castleton and heading for Tynemouth in the morning. He was still mulling over his options when his mobile phone rang. When he answered it was Angela.

'Adam, where are you?' she asked. She sounded distraught.

'I'm in Durham. What's wrong?'

'It's Nick. He's dead.' He heard her take a breath. 'David's been arrested.'

CHAPTER THIRTY-ONE

Karen settled herself into the passenger seat of Nigel's Jaguar. He closed the door and hurried around the front of the car, holding a newspaper above his head to protect himself from the rain. He got in and brushed the sleeves of his suit.

'Bloody weather,' he complained.

It wasn't raining heavily, just a light drizzle, but it had been falling steadily all afternoon. The streets glistened blackly in the light from the streetlamps. The air was full of a misty vapour.

Nigel adjusted the driving mirror to check his tie. 'Is that alright, darling? How do I look?'

'You look fine,' Karen assured him.

He caught her expression of suppressed amusement. 'You can laugh, Karen, but this dinner is important.'

There was a faint authoritarian reproof in his tone. It came through now and again, reminiscent of some Edwardian aristocrat in one of those BBC period dramas that she hated. It was an aspect of his personality that she didn't like. She supposed it was a legacy of his upbringing. Boarding school at Harrow, and home to the family pile in the holidays. Despite Nigel's frequent protestations about not being some old-fashioned stuffed shirt, sometimes she thought that was exactly what he was.

He glanced at his watch, exposing an inch or two of dazzling white cuff, which she personally hated with a striped shirt. She noted that he appeared to have been for a manicure.

'Let's hope the traffic isn't too bad,' he said.

She used to think he was good-looking. He was always impeccably turned out. She'd once surreptitiously inspected the closet at his London flat and counted twenty-nine individually tailored suits, which she had thought was a bit over the top considering they were all remarkably similar: dark, conservative, very bankerish. She still thought he was good-looking, but maybe he was a little too well groomed. She was beginning to think he was fastidious.

They hadn't moved and she realized he was regarding her with a slight frown. 'What?' she said.

'Nothing.'

She looked down at her dress, which was a Donna Karan. Black, elegant, and had cost a bloody fortune. Nigel, however, didn't altogether approve. She had spent hours getting ready for this dinner, which she hadn't even wanted to go to in the first place, and when she'd come into the living room feeling like a million dollars he'd eyed her critically.

'Haven't you got something a little more formal?' he'd commented.

'What do you mean by formal?'

Her tone should have warned him, but he was not always perceptive when it came to these things. 'Well, less showy perhaps. It's a lovely dress, darling, I'm just not sure it's entirely appropriate that's all. What do you think?'

What did she think? She hated it when he did that. Made some criticism of her and then asked her to agree with him, all wreathed in smiles. And she hated that he always called her darling too. My name is bloody Karen, she wanted to say. Darling made her sound like his wife.

His wife. Therein, she thought, lay the real problem. Since he'd proposed, she seemed to find herself looking for faults in him. Qualities she'd once liked, she now found irritating. Things she hadn't even noticed before got under her skin. Oh dear.

He wisely interpreted the look she gave him as a signal to drop it about her dress and pulled out into the evening traffic. At the end of the road he indicated left. 'Don't forget we have to go to Shepherd's Bush first,' she reminded him.

'Darling, we can't go now. We'll be late.'

'Nigel, you agreed.'

'Yes, I know, but look at the traffic. Can't you do it tomorrow? These clients are important, Karen.'

'I see. So my job isn't important, is that what you're saying?'

'Now, don't start that. You know jolly well that isn't what I mean.'

'Don't bloody well patronize me. I don't *jolly well* know anything,' Karen said acidly. 'I agreed I'd come to this dinner providing we went to Shepherd's Bush first, and now you're trying to wriggle out of it because what you have to do is of course far more important than anything I might have to do.' A little voice in her head said that she should stop now, having made her point. However, she ignored it. 'If I'm interpreting this incorrectly please explain it to me, Nigel. Otherwise you can stop your *jolly* car and I'll *jolly well* go by my *jolly* old self and you and your precious clients can have a *jolly* old time without me.'

He looked across at her, clearly taken aback. She glared at him angrily.

'Alright,' he said stiffly. 'There's no need to lose your temper. I'll take you to Shepherd's Bush first.'

'Thank you very bloody much.'

They drove in tense silence all the way. Streams of traffic were crawling along trying to get onto the Westway. Uxbridge Road was a nightmare, and to make things worse Nigel pointedly glanced at his watch every five minutes. He was doing it to irritate her, since there was a perfectly good clock in the dashboard display.

Eventually they turned into a maze of streets before East Acton. Nigel followed the directions she gave him, though with every turn she sensed his growing frustration.

'Is it much further?'

'No,' she snapped. 'Take the next left.'

'I suppose this has to do with the Hanson woman again.'

The corner of Garden Road was just ahead and Karen told Nigel to turn left. It was raining heavily now, and she peered at the houses looking for a parking space near number twenty-nine. This was the fourth time she'd been to the house and there was invariably an unbroken line of cars parked along both kerbs.

'In answer to your question, yes it is,' Karen said, and pointed ahead. 'Pull over there.'

'I don't know why you simply can't accept that she obviously doesn't want to talk to you,' Nigel grumbled, as he aimed the Jag into a space between a Volkswagen and a people mover. Karen ignored him. 'After all, she hasn't answered any of your messages has she?'

She flashed him an irritated look. 'It's important, Nigel, alright?'

'Yes, of course it is.'

She had her hand on the door, but his supercilious tone stopped her. 'What's that supposed to mean?'

'What?'

'For Christ's sake, don't give me that innocent bullshit. If you have something to say, just say it.'

'Alright, since you insist. You say this is important, but sometimes I wonder what exactly *is* important to you, Karen. I really do. I wonder about your priorities.'

'Go on,' she said, containing her anger with an effort. 'You might as well explain yourself now you've gone this far.'

'I think you know what I'm getting at,' he said, affecting a slightly bored manner. 'The past few days every time I try to get hold of you you're busy chasing this Hanson woman for Adam Turner. Last night you couldn't come to drinks with the Fletcher people, and now . . .' He paused and with an exaggerated movement looked at his watch. 'And now we're already fifteen minutes late for dinner.'

'You can phone.'

'That's hardly the point.'

She stared at him, incensed at the way he was behaving. The car smelt of leather and clubby aftershave. His manicured nails caught the light as he tapped them impatiently on the wheel. What was she doing here? The thought flashed in her mind, but before it gained a foothold she banished it. She told herself she was not going to be angry and she took a deep breath before she replied.

'Nigel, last night I spent two hours sitting in my car here hoping to catch Jane Hanson when she came home. In the cold, on my own. I didn't enjoy it, I didn't particularly want to do it, and I didn't do it just to spite you. I did it because the brother of a friend of mine is dead and I'm trying to help her find out what happened to him. As is Adam. And also because it's part of my job.'

'Are you sure those are really your reasons, Karen?'

'Yes,' she said slowly. 'And tonight I'm here because Jane's neighbour called and told me she was home. At last. Which is why I have to go.' She put her hand on the door again and started to open it. Outside it was pouring. She stopped. 'What did you mean, am I sure those are my reasons?'

He hesitated. 'I mean, are you sure that you're not here because of Adam? That he's not the reason?'

'Christ.' She stared at him and shook her head. 'Are you jealous, is that it, Nigel? Is that what this is all about?'

'Do I have reason to be? You told me once that you slept with him.'

'No. I told you that we once slept in the same bed. There's a difference.'

'Please, Karen. Don't insult my intelligence.'

'If I ever come across it I'll be sure to remember that.' Angrily she flung open the door and stepped out into the rain. She peered back into the car. 'You know what, Nigel. I don't understand you, I really don't. You asked me to marry you, and yet I don't know why. You obviously have very little respect for me.'

'For God's sake, I'm not going to argue in the street with you like this. Get back in.'

She ignored him. 'How can you respect me, if you don't respect what I do? You don't seem to appreciate that my job means every bit as much to me as yours does to you.' Suddenly she wondered how she could ever have even considered marrying him. 'I think you should go without me, Nigel. I really don't think it would be a good idea if I came with you tonight.'

He regarded her disbelievingly. 'Are you serious? You make me drive all the way out here and now you're telling me I should just go alone. You're expected, Karen. What am I supposed to tell them?'

'Tell them I have a headache or something.'

'A headache. How imaginative.'

'You know what? Tell them whatever the hell you like. And while we're at it, I really think we shouldn't see each other for a little while.'

He was incredulous, and then angry. 'Fine. If that's how you feel then perhaps you're right. Your job obviously comes before me on your list of priorities. Among other things.'

Ignoring the barb of his last comment she said, 'That is how I feel, Nigel. Go and find yourself a nice girl who rides horses. Someone whose idea of a career is to do a few afternoons in a gallery somewhere. I'm sure somebody like that would be much more your type.' She slammed the door shut, and walked away, not even looking around when she heard him start the car and drive off.

She was still fuming when she saw the taxi pull up outside number twenty-nine. A girl ran lightly down the steps carrying a small suitcase. Karen glimpsed short dark hair, and though she had never seen a picture of Jane Hanson somehow she knew it was her. She called out her name.

The girl paused briefly and looked in her direction, but the rain was falling in buckets and she barely faltered before she climbed into the taxi and closed the door.

'Wait,' Karen said and started to run, but the taxi was already moving. 'Come back, dammit!' she yelled. 'Why won't you speak to me?' But it was to no avail. She could only watch helplessly as the taxi drove off, a pale indistinct face looking at her curiously through the rear window. 'Shit,' she muttered under her breath. She cursed Nigel for holding her up those precious few minutes, and she cursed Jane Hanson for leaving her standing in the rain and not answering any of her messages.

Resignedly she started walking for the tube, bemoaning the fact that she hadn't brought an umbrella. When she arrived at the station, soaked and cold, she took out her mobile and called Adam. The phone rang, but instead of him answering she got his voice mail, which in a way was a relief.

'It's Karen. Sorry, but I just missed Jane Hanson.' She paused, wondering what she could add, feeling there ought to be something, but she didn't know what. Then it came to her. 'Oh, yes, and Nigel and I aren't getting married.' She hung up, wondering what he would make of that. Wondering how she felt herself. Why should she care what he made of it anyway? Bloody hell.

CHAPTER THIRTY-TWO

By the time Adam arrived at the tiny police station in Castleton it was dark. The yard beside it was clogged with vehicles and officers. A group of fifteen or so uniformed police were standing around near the back of a bus and some men wearing fluorescent jackets were clustered around several vans. There was an air of expectation about them all. They were smoking and talking in low voices, shuffling their feet restlessly. As Adam approached several glanced at him with brief curiosity before going back to their conversations.

When he tried to go into the police station a constable who'd been posted at the door barred his entry.

'Can I help you, sir?'

'I'm looking for Angela Johnson.'

Before he could reply a voice behind him said, 'Don't worry, I'll take care of this.'

Graham appeared and gestured for Adam to come inside, closing the door behind him. The reception area was empty.

'What's going on?' Adam asked, glancing towards the door to the inner office. 'Where's Angela?'

'She's through there,' Graham told him. He looked harassed and lines of weariness were etched around his eyes.

'What the hell happened? Angela said Nick had been killed. And what are all that lot doing out there?' Angela hadn't told him much on the phone, except to say that David had been brought here. Now, he had visions of somebody running amok through the town with a gun. And yet that didn't seem right. The mood among the officers outside wasn't right for something like that.

'They're not here because of Nick,' Graham said.

Then what were they doing there, Adam wondered, but for the time being he put the question aside. 'But Nick is dead?'

'Yes.'

'How?'

'Somebody bashed his head in.'

'Jesus,' Adam breathed. He'd imagined that somehow there had to be a mistake. Even though there had never been any love lost between them it still came as a shock to learn Nick was dead, though from the pained look evident in Graham's expression he was taking the news harder. 'So, it's murder?'

'Looks that way.'

Adam wasn't sure how to frame his next question. 'I heard David had been arrested,' he said tentatively. It didn't make sense.

'He's here but he hasn't been arrested.'

'Then why is he here? Is he a witness?'

'I can't tell you that.'

'For Christ's sake, either he's a witness or a suspect! Which is it?'

Uncertainty clouded Graham's expression. 'He's being questioned. That's all I know.'

'Then he is a suspect?'

'I can't say any more.'

'Come on, Graham. I'm here as a friend, not a journalist.'

Whose friend? He saw the unspoken question flash like an accusation in Graham's eyes. It was useless to argue. 'Where's Angela? Is she here too?'

'Wait here.'

Adam caught a glimpse of a crowded room as Graham opened the inner door. There were both uniformed and plain-clothes officers inside. When Angela appeared a few minutes later she looked as if the strain was getting to her though she smiled briefly when she saw him.

'Are you okay?'

'I'm fine. Tired that's all.'

'Where's David?'

She glanced at Graham, who hung back by the counter. 'Inside. But I think they're going to let him go soon.'

'What exactly is going on? Is he a suspect?'

Angela took his arm. 'Let's go outside.' She turned to Graham before she left and thanked him.

'He wouldn't tell me anything,' Adam said when they were in the street.

Perhaps picking up on the resentment in his tone she said, 'It was Graham who came to the house to tell me what happened. He's been good to me.'

'So, what happened?' He gestured around at all the vehicles and officers. 'And what's this all about?'

For the first time she appeared to notice all the activity. 'I overheard them talking inside. They're going to start evicting the protesters tonight.' As they began walking slowly along the street she explained that Nick had been found early that morning. 'I suppose this was planned beforehand, but I think it's all turned into a disaster. It was supposed to be kept quiet. The last thing the police wanted was a lot of journalists nosing around, but once they heard about Nick they started arriving, and then of course they realized the eviction was going to begin tonight. They all started leaving this afternoon. Heading for the camp I suppose. Your friend from the *Courier* was here earlier.'

'Janice?'

'Yes. She wanted to ask me some questions. She seemed surprised when I told her that I knew you.' Angela looked at him curiously. 'You didn't tell her?'

'I didn't get into specifics. She knows I grew up around here.'

'Anyway, she asked me to tell you that she'll speak to you later.'

'Thanks. What about Nick? Graham said he was murdered.'

She avoided looking at him, answering with her eyes on the ground. 'Yes.'

'So, why are they questioning David?'

'They brought him in late this afternoon.' She looked up, her face reflecting her inner conflicts and doubts. 'They haven't let me speak to him, but I gather that two nights ago David attacked Nick.'

'Attacked him?'

'Some sort of fight. It was in a pub in Halls Tenement. Apparently some locals had to hold David back.'

It was hard to imagine David and Nick fighting, but easier to see how the police would have reacted when they heard about it. 'What was the fight about?'

She shook her head. 'I don't know.'

'And that's why the police have been questioning him?'

'I think so.'

'There's nothing else?'

She looked at him quizzically. 'What do you mean?'

'Did anybody see what actually happened when Nick was killed?'

Comprehension flooded her eyes. 'You mean was there a witness who saw David?'

'I'm just asking the question, Angela.' But he already knew the answer. If there had been an eyewitness David would have been arrested.

'From what I gather Nick was found near the cottages. The girl he lives with, Mary, found him. I think she saw something, but it was dark and she wasn't sure what it was. She was upset.'

'Is she here too?'

'No. I think she was taken to the doctor. God, what must she be going through?'

She broke off as just then there was a sudden flurry of activity along the street as the assembled police started putting out their cigarettes and getting on the bus.

'Looks like they're leaving,' Adam commented.

A knot of people came out of the front of the building and as they dispersed Adam recognized Graham and David among them. They spoke briefly to one another and then Graham headed towards the bus. Doors slammed and engines started and first the bus and then the vans and police cars moved off. After they'd gone and the street was quiet again David stood alone, looking vaguely dazed, his expression ravaged. He seemed to have aged years in the past few days, the lines in his face chiselled deeper, his eyes sunken and hollowed.

'I have to speak to him,' Angela said. She touched Adam's arm as if to restrain him from following.

It was the first time she had seen David for several days. The changes Angela saw shocked her deeply. Had she passed him in a busy street she might barely have recognized him as the man she was married to, the father of their daughter. Thinking of Kate, something clenched her insides. What would she think if she saw her father like this? She blinked away tears and took a breath. This wasn't the time to fall apart, she admonished herself silently.

When she reached him she searched David's expression, trying to read what she saw there. It was as if he had sunk so low inside himself that he had all but vanished. Her heart went out to him in a spasm of pity, but then she realized he wasn't looking at her. A flicker of something heated gleamed in his bloodshot eyes. She glanced back herself though she knew what he was looking at. Adam stood a little way off in the gloom watching them.

'David, are you alright?'

His gaze flicked back to her but he didn't reply. She had no idea what he was feeling; he was like a stranger to her. One of his oldest friends was dead and part of her instinctively wanted to offer him some kind of comfort. Yet some other part of her shrank back. For a few seconds she couldn't trust herself to speak, but when she did her anger overflowed.

'Dammit, David, don't just stand there, you have to talk to me!'

A twitch at the corner of his eye was all the response he gave.

'Did you hear me? What happened today? What did you tell the police?'

'They wanted to know where I was last night.' His voice was a harsh croak. It didn't even sound like him.

'What did you tell them? Where have you been?'

'At the office. I don't know. I've been driving around.' He seemed dazed, uncertain. He ran a hand back through his hair, a gesture of deep weariness.

'Graham said that you and Nick had a fight.'

He stared at her and then lifted a hand with a vague motion and allowed it to drop again listlessly, which could have meant almost anything, though somehow it seemed to communicate that it didn't matter any more.

'What did you fight about?'

He didn't answer and she sensed that he was drifting away from her lost in his own thoughts. Frustration made her angry again. 'David!' He focused on her again. 'What happened between you and Nick?'

'Nothing.' He shook his head. 'It was nothing.'

'He's dead!' she said almost savagely, trying to provoke him from the confused lethargy he appeared to have sunk into. 'David, listen to me. Nick is dead. Somebody killed him!' She forced him to look at her by strength of will.

'You think it was me, is that it?'

'I didn't say that.'

'You didn't have to.'

His gaze shifted beyond her and once again she knew it was Adam he was looking at. 'I want to know what's going on, David. Everything. I want you to tell me what you know about those lads who were killed.'

He made a snorting sound, raising his face to the sky. When he looked at her his eyes glittered with a maniacal light. Suddenly he thrust his face towards her. 'What's the fucking point? What fucking difference does it make what I say? It's what *he* says that matters, isn't it?'

'Adam?'

'Yes! Adam! Who the fuck else did you think I meant?'

She took an involuntary step backwards, alarmed by his reaction. There was a crazy look in his eye. She wiped the spittle he had sprayed her with from her face.

'What has he told you, eh, Angela? The two of you been having cosy chats, have you? He must have liked that. Oh, I bet he liked it. I can see it now, stick the fucking knife in with one hand, use the other to pat you on the knee, tell you everything is going to be alright. I bet you liked that didn't you? I can see it now, the two of you. Is that what happened?' He stared at her, his eyes wide, his face inches from hers. 'I SAID, IS THAT WHAT FUCK-ING HAPPENED?'

'You bastard,' she said quietly. Her anger grew from a small knot of heat and burst into bloom like some startlingly red flower. It was all the more potent for being controlled rather than a maddened outburst. 'You've got the nerve to stand there and accuse me. You lousy bastard. After everything you've done.'

He backed off blinking, but she refused to let him escape.

'You drink yourself half to death, you stop sleeping in our bed, you don't talk to me, you don't even talk to your own daughter and all the time you refuse to tell me what is eating away at you, and then you've got the nerve to accuse me of disloyalty! Where the hell is your loyalty to me, David? To Kate? I want to know what happened! I want to know everything! Where did you go the night those lads were killed?'

Her question registered. He flinched as if she had struck him. Again he looked past her to where Adam was standing.

'Don't look at him! *I'm* asking you, not Adam. Me! I know somebody called from the lodge that night. Who was it? Where did you go?'

'I don't know what you're talking about.'

'Don't lie to me, dammit!'

'Fuck.' He turned his face skywards and when he looked at her again she saw there were tears in his eyes. 'It's all screwed up, Angela. Jesus, it's all a mess.'

For a mere fraction of a second she wavered, but he had taken too much out of her these last months. She should have done this before. She should have confronted him. Made him talk. A voice in the back of her mind told her maybe she hadn't wanted to know the truth. Not really. But not any more. 'What happened? Tell me.'

He shook his head. She didn't know if it was a denial, or more a gesture of despair. He held his hands to his head, his face contorted as if he was suffering from a physical pain and she realized that he had almost reached breaking point.

'You have to tell me, David. Everything,' she insisted.

Something gave way inside him as he looked at her, and then his gaze switched beyond her again and his expression changed abruptly, shutting her out as surely as if he had slammed a door in her face. She turned and saw Adam coming towards them.

'Wait!' she called out. But it was too late.

David turned away. She called out to him but he refused to

even look back. He walked along the street, rapidly vanishing in the darkness.

Adam stopped the car outside her house. Angela hadn't spoken on the way back and now she seemed surprised to see where they were.

'Will you be okay for a while?' he asked her.

'Why, where are you going?'

'I want to see what's happening at the camp.'

She looked towards the darkened house. 'Do you mind if I come with you? I don't think I want to be alone at the moment.'

'Of course.' He started the car, and reversed back out into the lane.

It was clear long before they reached the wood that word was out about the eviction. Despite the fact that it was dark and cold there were cars parked along the grass verges on both sides of the road and knots of people were making their way towards the camp. A bus and several police vans were parked at the head of the track where uniformed officers were doing their best to discourage people from going further, though most just went around them through the trees.

The scene at the main camp area was chaotic. Police and workmen wearing fluorescent jackets mingled with groups of defiant protesters. A perimeter had been taped off and was manned at intervals to make sure that no onlookers got too close. The ground vibrated from the generators that had been set up to power portable lights and power cables snaked across the ground. A sizeable media contingent was on hand, including crews with TV cameras doing on-site reports. When they reached the perimeter tape Angela turned to the man next to her.

'What's going on?'

'They've got some of them out, but there's more in the trees back there,' he said. He was watching it all with his hands thrust in his pockets, a look of quiet satisfaction in his eyes.

At that moment there was a shout as a group of men gathered around the base of a large oak scattered in alarm. Something heavy crashed through the branches to the ground and a brief cheer went up among the protesters who'd already been brought out. Some others were in a tree house high up in the uppermost branches and one of them had just climbed down and pushed away a ladder that was being used to try and reach them.

'They ought to cut the bloody tree down with them still in it if you ask me,' the man next to Angela said.

Nearby, a handful of protesters were shouting slogans, and Adam spotted Peter Fallow among them. Though he'd succeeded in getting the media to cover the eviction his expression was tainted with the knowledge of defeat. He shouted something to a group of police who were dragging a protester from the undergrowth.

'I'll be back in a minute,' Adam told Angela.

He made his way over, and slipped under the tape. 'I'm sorry it turned out this way,' he said when he reached Fallow's group.

Fallow tried to look defiant and replied loudly enough for some nearby journalists to hear him. 'It isn't over yet. It'll take them weeks to get us out of here.'

Obligingly somebody shoved a microphone towards him. The replies he gave to the questions he was asked were peppered with rhetoric and slogans and as Adam looked on he was struck by the image Fallow projected. People in their living rooms watching the news would be confronted with this odd-looking character with long greasy hair protruding from the bottom of his battered top hat, earrings winking in the TV lights. Though he spoke eloquently enough his philosophy was patently idealistic and his appearance made him both alien and faintly ridiculous. Some of his fellow protesters who stood in the background with their shaved heads and nose rings looked positively threatening.

Ellie stood on the fringe of the group and when Adam caught her eye she shrugged resignedly as if she had guessed what he was thinking.

'So, where to now?' he said, joining her.

'I think I'll go home for a bit. Then there's a place in Kent I heard about.'

'Maybe you should wait until after winter.'

She smiled. 'Maybe. Did you find what you were looking for by the way?'

'Not yet.'

'Perhaps it's not too late then.' Which he took to mean that she thought the development might be stopped yet.

'Perhaps,' he agreed, though without conviction.

'Though they think it is.' She nodded towards a group of men huddled in thick coats, who were watching proceedings from a discreet vantage point across the clearing.

'Who are they?'

'The developers,' Ellie said. 'Except for the one at the back. He's local.'

Belatedly he saw that David was with them, though he stood a little distance from the others, outside the light. 'You know him?'

'I've seen him before. Do you know about the guy they found this morning? The one who had his head bashed in?'

'You heard about that?'

'I was in town this afternoon. His picture was on the telly.'

'His name was Nick Allen,' Adam said.

'That's him.' She looked at him curiously. 'Did you know him?'

'I used to.'

'I heard it was his dad they think killed that girl they found in the lake.'

Adam didn't comment.

'Anyway,' Ellie went on, 'I saw them both.'

'They were friends,' Adam said, and then he realized what she'd said. 'Wait a minute, when did you see them?'

'The night him and his mates smashed up the camp.'

Adam stared at her and then across at David. 'You mean he was there?'

'I'm pretty sure he was. The other one definitely.'

'Why didn't you tell the police?'

'I'd never seen them again until today.' She shrugged. 'Doesn't matter now anyway, does it?' She gave him a sadly resigned smile.

When Adam made his way back to where he'd left Angela, Fallow was still obligingly answering questions for the media. When he found her she was talking to Graham, who said something quietly and moved away when he saw Adam approach.

'Everything okay?' he asked, joining her.

She nodded. A commotion signalled another group of protesters being dragged out. They let their bodies go limp, dragging their feet on the ground so that it took three or more men whose faces were becoming increasingly grim with frustration to manhandle them. To people watching it all on TV it would appear as if excessive force had been used, which of course was exactly the effect the protesters wanted. The journalists crowded forward and among them Adam saw Janice. When the protesters had been bundled out of the way she made her way over. In the lights her cheeks were rosy red and her eyes gleamed.

'Hi,' she said to Adam, and then looked at Angela. 'Hello again.'

'You look cold,' Adam said. 'How long have you been here?'

'Hours. I'm bloody freezing.'

'Has there been any trouble?'

'Not really. Just what you see. A few scuffles, you know, but nothing to get excited about. I wasnae expecting to see your husband here, Mrs Johnson,' she said to Angela, gesturing across the clearing to where David stood.

'I didn't know he was,' Angela said.

Janice regarded her thoughtfully. Adam knew she must be wondering about Nick's death. He caught her eye and shook his head a little, and taking his meaning she swallowed the questions she was clearly itching to ask, albeit reluctantly he thought. A chorus of jeers distracted them as a group of policemen and men in fluorescent jackets emerged from the trees. As they drew closer the two dirty, dishevelled-looking people of indeterminate sex being dragged by their heels flashed grins at the other protesters who shouted encouragement and commiserations. The reporters surged forward again in a pack, microphones and cameras at the ready.

'Tunnellers,' Janice remarked. 'That's the third lot they've brought out. Apparently there're dozens of them dug in there with enough food and water to last for weeks. I talked to a guy who was down there earlier. He said the tunnels havenae been properly shored up. The police are terrified somebody's going to get trapped.'

They watched the two people being shoved into the back of a van.

'Well, I'd better get back to it,' Janice said. She glanced regretfully at Angela, then flashed a look at Adam that told him he'd better make it up to her.

'It was nice to meet you again,' she said to Angela.

'And you.'

'I'll call you,' Adam promised. When she'd gone he looked for David across the clearing, but he had vanished.

Angela shivered. 'I'm cold.'

'Let's go,' he said. 'There's nothing else to see here.'

She was silent as they drove back towards town, huddled in the passenger seat with her collar up, her face all but hidden in the darkness. He left her to her thoughts, mulling over what Ellie had told him about seeing both David and Nick the night the camp was attacked. Had they been looking for somebody in particular that night? Had their purpose been to frighten Ben and the others away?

Angela broke the silence as they neared town. 'I'm worried about Mary, Adam.'

'Mary who?'

'The girl Nick lived with. Graham told me the doctor took her to the hospital in Carlisle, but she refused to stay.'

'They just let her go?'

'They couldn't stop her. Apparently she'd calmed down a lot, but she's sick. She could be in that cottage all alone. Graham said he was going to have a look later, but he could be stuck there all night.'

'You want to check that she's alright?'

'I think we should.'

He drove through the square and on towards Back Lane. At the bottom of the hill where the streetlights ended and the unpaved track vanished among the trees it was pitch black. They rumbled over the bridge that crossed the river and when they came on the cottages they were dark and silent.

'Looks like nobody's there,' Adam said.

Angela was already getting out. 'I think we should check.'

He grabbed a torch from under the seat and doused the headlights and it was only then that they saw a very faint reddish glow coming from behind an upstairs curtained window in the first cottage.

When Angela knocked on the front door the sound had a hollow empty ring to it, and though they waited there was no answering sound from within. As the crow flies they were only a mile or so from where the protesters were being evicted in the woods. A faint smear of reflected light was visible in the darkness, and distant sounds of shouting reached them on the still night air.

'What do you think?' Adam said. The temperature had dropped in the last half-hour. His breath appeared in clouds before him and he stamped his feet on the ground. The night was clear, the earlier cloud having been swept away late in the afternoon. Stars flickered in the sky and a three-quarter moon hung over the trees. A deer shrieked eerily from somewhere in the copse close by. There was still no sound from inside the cottage.

Angela tried the door, but it was locked. 'Let's try around the back.'

They picked their way through the rotting debris and weeds, the torch beam bobbing across thick overgrowth tangled from years of neglect. As they drew close to the back of the house they heard a sound and froze. It came again, a kind of grating noise. They started forward again and when they rounded the corner Adam shone the torch beam towards the door, which was partially open. When he pushed it gave way slowly, grating over the stone-tiled floor inside.

'Must have been the wind,' Angela said, though the night was still. 'Or maybe a cat or something.'

More likely a rat, Adam thought to himself. He shone the torch towards the weeds and brambles, but there was nothing to be seen.

They went inside and Adam felt around on the wall for a light switch, filling the room with weak yellow light from a single bare bulb in the ceiling.

'Hello?' Angela called out. 'Mary, are you there?' Her voice seemed to fall flat and vanish, sucked into the old plaster and brickwork. There was no reply. 'It's Angela Johnson. I've got somebody with me. We just wanted to see if you're okay.'

They made their way towards the door and through into the

hall. Angela called out again at the foot of the stairs before starting up. Near the top the stairs turned a corner where a dim red glow was reflected on the wall. When they reached the landing they could see it came from a partially open door across the passage. Angela pushed the door open and inside they saw a bed and a lamp covered with a red scarf on an old table. A figure lay on the bed with its back to them.

'Mary?' Angela said quietly.

The figure remained motionless, curled into a foetal position with her knees drawn tightly to her chest.

'Mary? Is that you? We called out but nobody answered.'

Adam waited at the door as Angela went towards the bed. The room was cold and bare, the wallpaper on the walls so old the pattern was faded and in places it had come away altogether. There were patches of damp on the ceiling. From outside the cottage looked abandoned, and it wasn't much better inside. A smell of mould and decay permeated the air. There was something dead about the place that seeped into his bones.

Angela drew close to the edge of the bed and slowly reached out.

Abruptly the figure sat up and shrank back against the wall. Her hair was matted and greasy, and her face was painfully thin, but Adam recognized her as the girl he'd seen the last time he'd been here. She looked wide-eyed towards the doorway where he stood, and opening her mouth she screamed.

CHAPTER THIRTY-THREE

'It's you she's frightened of, Adam,' Angela said as she sat on the bed, trying to calm Mary down. The girl seemed oblivious to her presence and remained shrunk back against the wall, wide-eyed and staring at Adam in an attitude of absolute terror. Her screams had withered to a kind of constant wailing moan that rose and fell in pitch.

Adam lingered in the doorway, unnerved by the effect he appeared to be having on the girl.

'You better go outside,' Angela told him.

He hesitated, torn between wanting to do something to help and the desire to escape the girl's mad, accusing stare.

'Please, Adam.'

He backed out of the room, and pulled the door closed behind him. For a couple of minutes he waited in the passage, listening to Angela trying to calm the girl. She spoke in a low, soothing voice and gradually the moaning ceased and instead became great heaving sobs interspersed with shuddering breaths, then that sound too slowly faded until eventually he could hear only quiet crying. He pushed the door open a fraction. Angela looked up and managed a wan smile. She held the girl in her arms, stroking her hair, murmuring softly. He mimed that he would see her downstairs, and she nodded.

Twenty minutes passed before Angela appeared in the kitchen. Adam had found some cups and instant coffee and had put a pot on the ancient stove to boil water.

'There's no milk,' he said, handing Angela a cup of steaming black liquid.

'Thanks. This is fine.'

Her gaze flicked around the room taking in the unwashed plates and pans stacked by the old enamel sink, the single scarred table and filthy walls.

'How is she?' he asked at length.

'Sleeping. Poor girl, we can't leave her here.'

'Do you want to call a doctor?'

'Not now. She's exhausted and frightened, she needs rest. We'll take her back to the house.' Angela reached into her pocket and brought out a bottle of pills. 'These were on the table beside the bed.'

He looked at the label and read a long complicated-sounding name. 'Her medication?'

'I suppose so. But the bottle was open and the pills were all heaped in a pile.'

'You think she was going to take them all?'

'I don't know. Perhaps.'

He was surprised that she had been allowed to come back here alone, though he supposed if she'd appeared rational earlier it wasn't a simple matter to commit her against her will. He wondered what had set her off. 'Why do you think she was so frightened of me?'

'Perhaps in the state she's in she thought you were Nick. She said his name a couple of times. I don't think she quite understands what's happened.'

He thought about the abject terror he'd seen in her eyes. 'You think he abused her?'

'It's possible I suppose.'

But maybe it wasn't Nick she was afraid of. 'Come and look at this,' he said.

He showed her something he'd noticed while she'd been upstairs. The key was in the back door on the inside, and it was actually locked. The jamb was splintered. 'This has been forced,' Adam said. The wood, however, was rotten. He demonstrated by tearing off a long splinter with his fingers. 'It could have been like this for weeks.'

Nevertheless he remembered what they'd heard when they'd arrived: the scrape of the door and something else, perhaps the sound of somebody slipping away into the tangled garden? Or perhaps it was nothing. Maybe the thought wouldn't even have occurred to him if he hadn't seen the way Mary stared at him as if he was some monster straight out of her dreams. Whatever the answer, he agreed with Angela that they couldn't leave her alone there.

Mary didn't wake when he lifted her from the bed and carried her down the stairs to the car. She was surprisingly light, no more than skin and bones. She didn't even stir when he put her in the back seat or when he lifted her out again to carry her upstairs in Angela's house and lay her down in one of the spare bedrooms.

Angela smoothed the girl's hair from her brow. Her skin was pale and her face thin. She would have been pretty once, but now she looked undernourished and ill. 'She's absolutely exhausted. I'll get her out of these clothes.' She had brought one of her own nightdresses in from her room.

Adam took his cue and left her to it. Downstairs he helped himself to a Scotch and left the bottle on the kitchen table while he went to the window and stared out into the night. The stars above the fells created a sense of deceptive tranquillity. It was hard to believe that Nick was dead, and difficult to escape the suspicion that his murder was linked to the development somehow. Did that make him the fourth victim? Jesus, it hardly seemed credible that something like this could happen in a rural backwater like Castleton.

So far he hadn't told Angela about what he'd discovered at the clinic, but he knew she would ask. He wasn't sure what he would tell her. He thought about the way David had looked earlier. He was coming apart. At one point it had seemed he was going to hit Angela. Was it David who'd killed Nick? Obviously the police thought so if they'd questioned him for so long, though they clearly couldn't prove it. Not yet anyway. Had it been another fight that had gotten out of hand? And why had David attacked Nick anyway?

He heard Angela come into the room, and turning he gestured with his glass. 'I needed a drink. I hope it's okay.'

'Of course. I think I need one myself.' She went to the table and poured herself a small measure.

'Is she okay?'

'For now. She's sleeping.'

'You look as if you could do with some of that yourself.'

She sat down wearily. 'I feel as if this day has gone on for ever. Which reminds me, you didn't tell me what happened at the clinic.'

He gave her the facts, without including any elaboration or his own interpretation. 'Jones worked at the clinic after he left Carlisle, though he wasn't there for long. He was sacked for attempting to pull off a little blackmail scam. I talked to the director, who confirmed that he arrived with references from Carisbrook.'

'I'm too tired to think. What does it mean?'

'Maybe there was more going on at Carisbrook than just a few drugs going missing.'

Angela frowned. 'Had Jane Hanson been to the Barstock Clinic?'

'Yes. I asked the director if she had heard of Marion Crane too. No luck though.'

'Speaking of which, I didn't have any luck finding her I'm afraid. I didn't really have much time.'

'It doesn't matter. I've got an address for Jones in Tynemouth. I'll go there tomorrow. I think that's where Jane got Marion Crane's records. Something else I learned today was that Dr Webster might well have treated private patients at Carisbrook. Apparently it's not uncommon for them to use a pseudonym, so Marion Crane may not be a real name.'

Angela looked at him questioningly. 'Adam, do you know what this is all about?'

'I think it's pretty clear that Marion Crane is the key. She was at Carisbrook when Jones worked there. I think he must have known something that linked her to the development and maybe when he heard about it he realized what he knew could be valuable. Jane overheard somebody talking in a pub. Maybe that was Jones.'

'Talking to who?'

'I'm only guessing. But it could have been the person Jones was trying to sell information to.'

She didn't ask who he thought that person might be.

'When I saw David tonight . . .' She faltered, groping for some way to express what she felt. '. . . it was like he was a different person. I've never seen him like this. I could never have imagined him this way. Perhaps I've been wrong. Maybe I just didn't want to face the possibility that . . .' She broke off. 'This is such a bloody mess. I don't know how much more I can take. Do you think he could have killed Nick?' She searched his expression for an answer.

'I don't know.'

'But you know something, don't you? There's something you've been holding back, isn't there?'

He came to the table and sat down opposite her. She was struggling to hold herself together. Who the hell wouldn't in her shoes? The last thing she needed was for him to make things any worse. 'I don't know anything for sure.'

She shook her head. 'No. You do. I've been thinking about it. Please, Adam. I want you to tell me. I don't have any right really I suppose, do I? I haven't believed much you've said so far.'

'You had no reason to.'

'No, you're right. I didn't. There was nothing to make me suddenly think my husband is a murderer. But you had a reason. And it's nothing to do with the past, is it? I suppose I thought you just wanted revenge or something like that. But it isn't that, is it? It's something else. Please, Adam, tell me. I need to know.'

And he knew he couldn't refuse. Maybe he should even have told her before. 'It is about what happened in the past, though not what you think,' he said. And then he told her everything. As best he could anyway. About Meg and David, and all the suspicions he'd once had but had kept to himself. But the more he talked the more it became apparent that it was all feeling and undercurrent as much as anything, and as she struggled to absorb it all, her brow deeply furrowed, he saw that she understood that. But she didn't dismiss any of it, she listened and she thought about it. She thought hard.

'It's incredible,' she said at length.

'You mean you don't believe it?'

'No. I mean, Christ I don't know what to think.' She stood up to pace the room. 'I need to get this straight. You're saying David knew that girl, and you never told anyone. But that doesn't mean anything even if he did know her. You don't even know if it's her that they found in the lake.'

'It's her, Angela. It's Meg. The police might not actually have said as much yet, but the jewellery pretty well clinches it. And I was thinking about this long before they found her. That was just one of life's strange coincidences. Or maybe it wasn't. Maybe it was fate.'

'Fate?'

'I don't want to sound like a crank, but I've felt guilty about Meg all my life. I have dreams about her. She has this look in her eye. Kind of a plea and an accusation at the same time. Look at the kind of work I ended up doing. I've spent the better part of my working life looking for missing people, children mostly. I've always felt I was doing it because of Meg, out of guilt, or that she was driving me, haunting me in a way. It was like she wanted me to make up for what happened. It was even as if she wanted me to come back here.' He saw the way Angela was looking at him. 'You're beginning to think I'm a lunatic.'

'No. No I'm not.' She shook her head. 'I just don't know what to think.'

'Do you know that it was me that told Shields where to fish?'

'Shields?'

'The man that found her. Did I do that deliberately, albeit subconsciously?'

'But you didn't know she was there.'

'Didn't I? I saw David once standing on the shore where she was found, not long after it was all over, after James Allen was killed. He was going to throw something in the lake but then he changed his mind.'

'What are you saying? What was it?'

'I don't know. But something struck me about the moment. I can't explain what it was. Maybe his expression, something about him. It wasn't a rational thing, more of a feeling.'

'Like how you felt when you thought he knew her.'

'He did know her, Angela. That much I'm certain of. It was David she was waiting for when I saw her in those trees across from the sawmill. You even saw her there yourself one day. We'd been walking along the river.'

'Yes, I remember that. But she was alone.'

'I saw her there the day she vanished and she was with David.'

'You weren't sure of that. You couldn't have been. You would have said something.'

'I was sure. I just didn't want to be. Why didn't he admit it himself? What was he hiding? And what did David and Nick put in Allen's van that day?'

'Alright, I see what you're saying,' Angela said. 'But if you were so certain that he knew something, why didn't you tell somebody? Or at least confront him? I don't understand that.'

'Because he was my friend, Angela. Because I was trying to prove something to him. That I trusted him. That he could trust me. I think Nick knew. I almost asked David outright the day I heard Meg was missing, but Nick was there and somehow I felt like I had to prove I was as good a friend as Nick was.'

He couldn't keep the bitterness from his tone. That was really it in a nutshell. He had kept quiet to demonstrate his loyalty. To show he was as good as Nick.

They stared at each other across the table. He wondered what she saw. Was it anger? Pain? Guilt? Maybe all of those things. Eventually she nodded her head, a small movement that signalled her understanding.

❧

Angela went upstairs to look in on Mary. She'd guessed that the scarf over the lamp in the cottage meant something to Mary and so she'd brought it with her when they'd left. Now the room was suffused with a red glow. She hoped that if Mary woke in the night having something familiar would be a comfort. For now she appeared to be sleeping soundly, her breathing regular and even.

In her own room after she had washed and changed into a nightdress, Angela lay down on her bed in the darkness, but though her body was weary and she tried to sleep her mind wouldn't shut down. She kept running over everything Adam had told her. She didn't know what to make of it all. She was confused. In the end she gave up trying to sleep and turned on the lamp. She sat up in bed and hugged her knees. She felt alone. Cut off from the normal world. She glanced at the phone beside the bed and considered calling Kate, but dismissed the idea immediately. It was past one a.m. and Kate would be safely asleep. Apart from anything else she ought to let her daughter have one last relatively untroubled night. Come the morning she would start to realize that nothing would ever be the same again in her own home. Angela wished there was some way to protect Kate from all of this, but she knew deep down it was a futile hope.

She got out of bed and paced to the window, unable to stay still. It dawned on her that she would have to tell Kate everything. Better that she heard it from her than from anyone else. But what was she going to tell her? She ought not to try and hide the truth because kids have a sixth sense for picking up when adults are hiding something from them. But what was the truth? She wished she knew. For both their sakes.

It came to her then, very clearly. Kate would never believe that her father was capable of killing anybody. Of murder. But Adam thought he was. He hadn't said it in as many words, but he thought David had killed Meg Coucesco. She found herself shaking her head in denial. It couldn't be. But her conviction felt false.

She saw with sudden clarity that the answers to everything lay in the past. She'd always thought she knew David, but perhaps she really didn't know him at all. He had never mentioned Meg Coucesco, and yet she felt he must have known her. That much at least was true. What if Adam was right? What if David really had killed her, impossible as that seemed? If he was capable of that, then he was capable of anything.

Suddenly she went to the door and down the stairs. The door to the study was partly open. Barely pausing she went inside and switched on the light. She gazed around the room, her eye lighting on a chair, a picture, the bookcase against the wall that was mostly full of books about fishing or hunting or sports. On the desk were some letter trays full of mail-outs and paperwork relating to the sawmill. She wasn't even sure what she was looking for, but she was looking for *something*.

She opened a filing cabinet drawer and it was bulging with household accounts. A desk drawer was full of accumulated office junk: a packet of spilled staples, some paperclips and Post-it notes, several pens and coloured markers. She rifled among them then closed the drawer and opened the one below it. This contained a mass of manuals and disks for the various programs loaded onto the computer that sat on the desk. The next one she tried contained fishing paraphernalia: line and hooks, lead weights, a small coil of wire and a pair of pliers and some feathers and coloured cotton.

Often in the winter David would sit in here making his own lures and flies. He had his favourites, guaranteed to tempt the wariest of fish. She took one out and turned it over in her hand. This was the one he swore by, a tiny delicate thing with bright yellow and purple cotton attached to a tiny reddish-coloured feather with bands of pale cream. It was a thing of beauty. A work of art really. And yet sometimes appearances can be fatally deceptive. The feathers with their fine markings masked the barbed hook underneath. The fly even had a name. It was called a Pretty Deadly. Perhaps like this, nothing about David was really what it seemed to be. As if to underscore this idea the hook pricked her skin as she turned it over in her fingers.

'Shit!'

A drop of bright red blood welled on the end of her thumb. She stared at it in fascination.

As she sucked the blood from her thumb she looked around the office, and then suddenly fuelled by an urgency she barely understood she began searching again. She gave up being careful to replace things as she found them. Instead she pulled drawers from the desk and tipped their contents onto the floor. Her attention fixed on the bookcase and she began pulling out the volumes one by one to check if anything was hidden behind, and each book ended up on the floor with everything else until the shelves were bare. She frowned, her restless eyes skipping over the room. She emptied the filing cabinet and went through the papers on the desk again, sweeping everything to the floor when she was done. Eventually there was nowhere left, and she stared around in frustration until her gaze came to rest on the old leather shotgun case in the corner.

She had never understood why he kept the gun in here. He never used it because the guns he used were locked in the garage outside. She picked it up and took it to the desk. The clasps popped easily, which surprised her, as did the lid when it opened smoothly. She'd expected it to be stiff and unyielding the way something would be if it hadn't been opened for a long time. When she saw the gun that lay inside she thought she knew what it was. She touched the wooden stock. Intuitively she guessed that this was the gun that David had shot Adam with. She didn't know how she knew, but she did. All these years David had kept it. She wondered why. Was it guilt?

She lifted it out and saw there was something lying underneath. It was a dulled golden band, a simple bracelet. She picked it up and turned it over in her hand, staring at it. There were markings inside. She felt numb. A sound behind her startled her and when she turned she saw that it was Adam.

'I heard a noise,' he said. He looked at the bracelet and the gun and whatever doubts she had been clinging to were swept away.

For a little while neither of them moved. His arms were around her but she couldn't remember how they had come together. Her mind was strangely empty. What she wanted now was a safe refuge, a place where she could be free of all of this, just for a little while so that she could gather herself together again.

She could feel his heartbeat, she thought, but in fact it was her own. She wondered why it was beating at such a heady rhythm, why she could feel the blood rushing through her veins. He was murmuring softly, words of comfort, and she remembered that she had been crying, unable to stop the tears that had welled up in her eyes. But she was no longer crying. His fingers were at the nape of her neck, stroking her skin, sliding through her hair.

She felt a change in him. What had been words and gestures of comfort subtly altered. She could feel his desire, and the fingers at her neck stilled as he fought to resist the temptation. In response she pressed her body against him. What am I doing? The voice was her own, inside her head, loud and almost startling in its clarity. She put her head against his shoulder and pressed her palms against his back. She didn't want to think. He held her tighter and she heard him breathe out, almost a sigh, almost a sound of anguish.

'Adam.'

She spoke his name quietly and he let her go and looked questioningly into her eyes. She saw a tangle of hope and desire, love and need, all colliding together like gaseous clouds of light and dark. There was a sense of utter inevitability about what was happening. Though their reasons might be different their need was equally felt. She leaned towards him and parting her mouth she placed her lips on his. She tasted whisky. His saliva. Him. His lips were fuller than David's, his mouth yielding, more pliant. She had never slept with another man. A clamouring voice in the back of her mind urged restraint. This was all wrong. How could she think like this when her world was falling apart? But maybe that was it. She needed this. She needed to be held. The hell with reason, with morals, with anything. She felt his need. She thought she'd sensed it the first day they'd met again. The sensation of kissing him took her back through the years to a sunny day by the river.

She couldn't think any more. He kissed her throat and she arched her neck. His hands slid across her body, caressing her hips, her breasts.

'Not here,' she murmured.

She led him by the hand through the darkened house, up the stairs. At her bedroom door she hesitated and then went on to the room he was using. Inside she turned towards him. When he guided her to the bed she lay down and watched his face as he undressed her, pausing when her breasts were naked, eyes greedily devouring her. Almost literally. As if he wanted to absorb every minute fragment of her, every cell. She was conscious of her power over him. It produced a heady feeling that mingled with her own physical need.

She saw his lips move and heard his voice as he told her that he loved her, that he had always loved her, that he had never stopped thinking about her all through the years, and she knew that it was true, that he had held a part of her inside himself, and she felt a sudden overwhelming sorrow for him, and it was accompanied by guilt because she had once loved David so powerfully it had rocked her to the core and she couldn't deny that. She drew him down

332

and they kissed again. His hands were on her breasts, on her belly, between her thighs. When she reached for the button to his jeans he shuddered at her touch, and trembled as he entered her.

'Adam.' She heard herself repeat his name again as he moved within her. She held him tighter, and closed her eyes tightly to shut out the tiny troubled voice that struggled to be heard. But she would not let it. She closed her mind and immersed herself in feeling. Nothing but feeling.

❧

She was sleeping. They lay together in the darkness. He thought it must be early in the morning. Her breathing was deep and regular. His eyes had grown used to the dark, softened by the light of the stars outside the window so that he could see her profile. Carefully, so as not to disturb her, he lifted himself and leaned on one elbow so that he could watch her. Her skin was smooth. He touched her hair, marvelling at the feel of it, or perhaps it wasn't so much that, but the fact that it was her hair, and she was lying here beside him. He replayed making love to her, trying to hold onto the feelings he'd experienced. Their bodies touching, moving, her breath on his cheek, her hand against his back, her whispering as they had moved together.

He remembered opening his eyes and seeing hers closed. Just for an instant he'd experienced a faint regret. All of his life he had wanted this to happen. He had never forgotten her and yet in the midst of the very act he'd dreamed of, of being close to her, he'd realized that, in fact, his dream was flawed. She might as well have been a million miles from him. He couldn't look into her mind and know what she was thinking, what she was feeling. He couldn't feel what she felt. Perhaps this is what is meant, Adam thought, by philosophers who muse on the fact that in the end we are all, each of us, alone, contained within ourselves. With sudden insight he understood that it was true that we enter the world alone as we leave it, and in between the only way to alleviate that sense is through a spiritual belief or by loving another. By being so close over a long enough time that two people become, as much as it is possible to be, inextricably immersed in one another. In reality

333

time had made them strangers. He'd imagined this moment as fulfilment, but in the realization of his dream there was the acrid taste of ashes.

The sheet that covered her had slipped when he moved, exposing her breasts. He followed the line from her throat to the swell of her flesh and the dark tips of her nipples. Then he gently covered her again. She stirred and reached for him, and he lay down beside her and closed his eyes.

In the room along the passage Mary shifted in her sleep. She was locked in a dream, tossing her head as sweat broke on her brow and she murmured something frightened and unintelligible.

She was back in her room in the cottage where the Shapeshifter had come for her. When she was a child she had accidentally put her favourite teddy bear in with the laundry and when her mother found it and gave it back the bear hadn't looked the same any more. The Shapeshifter reminded her of the bear.

In her dream it had emptied her pills onto the table.

Take these, Mary. They'll make you feel better.

The voice in her head was lying. But the voice had changed. She didn't know if it was from inside her head or if it was the Shapeshifter. She was afraid. She looked at the pills and doubt tugged at her mind. Perhaps they really would make her feel better. Perhaps there were no such thing as Shapeshifters, it was all in her mind. Sometimes she didn't know what was a dream and what was real any more. In her dream she looked at the face before her.

'Nick?' she murmured in her sleep.

He smiled and held out the pills.

Take them, Mary.

She dreamed she heard the sound of a car, and saw lights as they swept across the window. She closed her eyes, and when she opened them he was gone and the pills were on the table beside her and then somebody was holding her, stroking her forehead, talking quietly.

CHAPTER THIRTY-FOUR

Unable to sleep Adam finally rose at five and gathered his clothes in the darkness. He made his way to the door where he paused and looked back towards the bed where Angela was still sleeping. Part of him wanted to go back and wake her, to climb back beneath the covers and hold her. He imagined her drowsy awakening, her murmured voice as she turned towards him and pressed her body against his. Yet he didn't move. There was something unreal about the scene he'd imagined. It had the quality of a fragile dream that he preferred to leave intact, at least for now. Instead, he slipped quietly out of the door and along the passage. He checked on Mary, who also appeared still to be sleeping, then went down the stairs and through the darkened house to the kitchen.

Half an hour later he quietly closed the front door behind him and went outside. It was pitch black. During the early morning cloud had gathered, stealing the light of the stars. It was cold and there was a feeling of snow in the air. Adam started the car and drove slowly to the gate with the lights off. He looked back at the house, half hoping to see a light come on upstairs, and yet glad in a resigned sort of way when it didn't. He had left a note for Angela in the kitchen explaining that he'd made an early start for Tynemouth and that he would see her later. He had deliberated for a long time about whether or not he should add some line of endearment at the end, but he didn't know what to write. Everything he thought of either seemed corny or false. In the end he'd written simply: *Adam.*

He turned on the lights at the end of the lane and headed for the A69 that would take him all the way to Newcastle.

The address Geraldine Hope had given him turned out to be a nondescript street of Victorian brick semis in a rundown area of Tynemouth. The house that he was looking for turned out, in fact, to be two houses that had been knocked together to form a hotel. A sign outside advertised budget rooms and special long-term rates. It seemed that Jones hadn't progressed much during the years since he had left Carlisle. The Park Hotel was depressingly ugly from the outside. Two empty beer bottles that stood on the pavement by the gate seemed to eloquently say it all. It looked like the kind of place that might be a staging post on the slide downhill for life's perpetual failures. A brief stop before life on the streets.

The front door was open and led into a small tiled reception area. Behind a plain wooden counter a number of keys hung from hooks screwed into a yellowing pegboard. To the right a door with a sign identifying it as the guest lounge was closed, and straight ahead a staircase led to the upper floors. The whole place smelt strongly of fried food underlain with a general unpleasant mustiness.

The counter was deserted, though behind it a door led to what he assumed was an office. Adam hit an old-fashioned bell on the counter and in response a heavy-set middle-aged man wearing a greyish-white open-necked shirt eventually appeared from the office.

'Yes?' he said guardedly. His accent was indeterminate, but maybe central European.

'I'm looking for somebody who may live here. His name is Chris Jones.'

The man regarded him calculatedly as he used a toothpick to clean his teeth. 'What you want with him?'

'He's a friend of mine.'

The man's narrowed eyes betrayed his scepticism. Perhaps he'd decided that Adam didn't look like most of the people who crossed the threshold of the Park Hotel. 'You a friend of his you say? I never seen you before, and Mr Jones, he live here a long time.'

'Is he in?' Adam said.

'No. He's not.' The man watched Adam with slightly amused interest as if waiting to see what he would say next.

'When will he back, do you know?'

'I thought you said you were his friend. If you his friend how come you don't know when he will be back?'

'Listen, just tell me when you expect him, alright.'

The man shrugged. 'I don't expect him.'

'What do you mean? You're not expecting him back at all, or you don't know when?'

The man simply shrugged again. He made no move to go back to his office, however. Instead he seemed to be waiting for Adam to make the next move. Getting the drift Adam dug in his pocket for his wallet. He put a ten-pound note on the counter.

'So, when do you think would be a good time to catch him?'

Bright dark eyes glinted greedily and the note vanished. 'Maybe you try again in a couple a weeks.'

'A couple of weeks? You mean he's gone away?' The man didn't answer, so Adam took another ten out and put it down.

'For somebody who is your friend you don't know him so good, I think,' the man said, as the note vanished.

'You haven't answered my question.'

'Mr Jones, he works on the ships. A sailor you know? The last time I see him was in August.'

Adam remembered what Dr Hope had said about Jones keeping in touch with the gardener at the clinic who was an ex-merchant seaman. Something they had in common. 'When in August?'

The man looked pointedly at Adam's wallet so he took out everything he had left, which was about fifty-five pounds. 'You answer my questions, alright?'

'Okay.' He shoved the notes in his pocket. 'Beginning of the month some time. I don't remember exactly.'

Which had to be before Jane Hanson had turned up, Adam thought. His eye strayed to the open office door behind the counter. Against the wall was a photocopier.

'Did somebody else come here looking for Jones? It would have been some time later in August. A girl?'

'Sure.'

'You showed her Jones's room, didn't you? She used that photocopier there afterwards.'

'How you know that?' the man asked in surprise.

'Never mind. I want you to show me the room too.'

The man hesitated, then again the shrug. 'Okay.' He grabbed a key off the board. 'Follow me.'

The room was in keeping with the rest of the hotel. That is to say it was furnished cheaply and simply and the carpet was so old and worn it was hard to distinguish the pattern any more. A single window overlooked a car park at the back. Apart from a double bed the room contained a set of drawers and a large wardrobe, a small table and two chairs and a TV set. It turned out the man behind the counter, whose name was Nicos, was the proud owner of the Park Hotel. He leaned casually against the door as Adam looked around and seemed happy enough to answer his questions now that he knew there was no more money.

'He's not a very sociable man, Mr Jones. Not very happy, you know? Doesn't like to talk much. When he's here he spend most of his time in the pub along the road.'

'How often is he away?'

'Seven, eight months in a year. Depends.'

Adam opened the wardrobe door. It contained a few shirts and some jackets and a coat but not much else. Nicos was from Selonika. He kept up a nonstop commentary, partly about himself and partly careless observations about Jones. He described Jones as being taciturn and a heavy drinker.

'I never see him with a woman. Maybe his face put them off . . .' He shrugged, which was a gesture he used to complete many of his thoughts.

It turned out that Jones had worked on the ships ever since he'd arrived at the hotel five years earlier. The Park Hotel rented rooms to half a dozen or so sailors who were away for more of the year than they were at home, and when they were at home they just wanted a place to sleep.

'Where's he gone, do you know?' Adam asked.

'Who knows? I don't ask, he doesn't tell me.'

Adam fetched a chair so that he could reach to the top of the wardrobe. He lifted down the suitcase that was up there and put it on the bed. When he snapped open the catches he found it contained some more clothes, a pair of old shoes and half a bottle of whisky. There was also a large thick yellowing envelope.

'Did the girl who came here look in this case?'

'Yes.'

The envelope contained Marion Crane's original file that Jane had photocopied. A brief scan of the first page revealed things he hadn't been able to decipher from the distorted remnants he'd recovered from the wreck. Adam frowned as he flicked through the pages. There was still no clue to Marion Crane's real identity, or why Jones would have kept these records. When he came to the last page, however, something fluttered free, a single sheet that turned out to be a photocopy. When he picked it up he realized it was the third document he'd found, only the copy Jane had made had been too far gone to make any sense of beyond the fact that it was some kind of official-looking certificate. Now as he read it, everything started to make sense.

He compared the certificate against Marion Crane's file, checking the dates on one against the other. Something stirred in his memory and a vague unease settled over him. He turned to Nicos.

'The young woman who came here before me, can you remember exactly when that was? I mean the exact day?'

'Sure. It was the day my nephew he have his birthday.'

It was mid-afternoon by the time a car pulled up outside the house where Adam had been waiting for the past two hours. He watched the driver get out and open the garage door before putting his car away and going to the front door. Adam switched off his mobile phone and crossed the street as the man put his key in the lock. Hearing footsteps behind him the man turned and the slightly surprised smile he wore faded when he saw who it was.

'I suppose I've been expecting you,' Councillor Hunt said. 'You better come in.'

They went through to the kitchen where they had talked the last time Adam had been there. Hunt took off his coat and carelessly dropped it over the back of chair. He rubbed his hands together as he filled the kettle.

'Would you like a cup of tea? Mr Turner isn't it?'

'Adam, yes. And thanks, tea would be good.'

'I always come in here if I'm home early. It heats up faster than the rest of the house,' Hunt said, as he looked out of the window at the heavy sky. 'I think it'll snow later.' He got some mugs from a cupboard, pausing for a moment. 'Do you mind these or do you prefer a cup? I like a mug myself.'

'A mug's fine.'

The kettle boiled and Hunt poured hot water into a teapot in a routine Adam thought he probably went through every day. This time he suspected there was some comfort in the familiarity of the task, no doubt while he tried to order his thoughts. When he finally brought the tea to the table he seemed quite composed, like a man who had reconciled himself to what was about to come. As he sat down Adam noticed he glanced at the photographs of his wife and daughter on the fridge door. What had he said? A holiday in Spain? Now Adam looked with new eyes. He remembered Hunt's wife rushing out the door the first time he'd come, and her slightly over-frenetic manner. A symptom of a highly strung nature he now guessed.

'Councillor Hunt,' Adam said. 'When you voted in favour of the Forest Havens development, were you being subjected to some kind of pressure?'

A small smile touched the corners of Hunt's mouth. 'Do you mean was I being blackmailed?'

'Yes.'

'I suppose you already know the answer to that.'

'I think I do.' Adam took the documents he'd found in Jones's room out of his pocket and laid them on the table. 'These are the records for somebody called Marion Crane who was a patient at Carisbrook Hall in 1985. According to these she was admitted in April of that year suffering from acute depression after suffering a miscarriage in the thirtieth week of pregnancy.' He paused. 'Marion Crane was your wife?'

Hunt nodded. 'She used the name of a second cousin who lives in Devon.' He sighed wearily. 'My wife has never been what you would call a strong person. Mentally I mean. She was forty years old when she suffered that miscarriage. It was the fourth time, though all the others happened much earlier. We had given up hope of ever having a child, and then as sometimes happens, when we least expected it Anne fell pregnant.'

Hunt picked up his tea, and was silent while he drank a little. He looked tired, the evidence of a long-held secret scored in the heavy lines around his eyes.

'How did you know from this that Marion Crane was my wife?' he asked.

In reply Adam laid down a copy of an original birth certificate. The child named was Judith Hunt, born on 19 May 1985 to parents George and Anne Hunt.

'My guess is that Dr Webster arranged for this,' Adam said.

He had put it together during the drive back from Tynemouth earlier. His theory was that Anne Hunt, under the name of Marion Crane, had been admitted to Carisbrook under Webster's care as a private patient. Somehow or other Webster had found a way to switch somebody else's baby for the one Anne Hunt had lost, then he had signed the official birth documents and nobody was any the wiser. What Adam hadn't been able to figure out at first was how the Hunts had managed to explain the sudden presence of a baby daughter. Anne Hunt had suffered a miscarriage, at which a doctor must have been present, most likely at the local hospital. The answer he'd come up with was simple, and he put it to Hunt now.

'Your wife was admitted to Carisbrook before her miscarriage,' he guessed.

'Anne became depressed a month after she fell pregnant. Her condition became worse as time went on. You see, she was convinced that she would lose the child as she had all the others. With every week that passed her mental state deteriorated. Ironic really. It was the impending loss, as Anne viewed it, of what was rapidly becoming a fully developed child that was so hard for her to cope with. She was given more drugs, and it was probably those that did the damage in the end. A kind of perverse Catch 22. When she did eventually lose the baby she went completely to pieces.'

Hunt looked like somebody who was if not exactly making a plea for Adam to condone what happened next, then at least to understand it.

'If I had not agreed to what I did, I think my wife would never have come out of that hospital.'

Adam sidestepped offering any comment on the moral issue, concentrating instead on the remaining questions he had. 'Whose

341

idea was it to substitute a live baby for the one your wife miscarried?'

Hunt winced at the clinical description of what had been done. 'I tried to convince myself that it was only a matter of adoption really. Albeit without the normal documentation. That was the way Webster described it.'

'It was his idea?'

Lost in his recollection of the event, Hunt seemed momentarily confused. 'Webster? Yes. Yes I suppose it was. He said that it was really for the best. That, in fact, the baby would have been put up for adoption anyway. The mother didn't want her.'

'He told you that?'

'Yes.'

Adam didn't point out that an official adoption agency would never have granted care of a child to a couple when the wife was suffering from a severe mental illness, even if they hadn't already been in their forties. But despite that, with the benefit of hindsight and with the evidence of the apparently healthy young woman in the picture on the fridge, perhaps it would have been easier to be more understanding if Adam hadn't known there was more to it. This hadn't come about because Webster was such a compassionate soul, into whose hands circumstances had delivered the means to do good in the world.

Hunt looked at the picture on the fridge. 'She's a bright girl. She's due back from an exchange in Spain next week to do her last year at school before she goes to university. She wants to become a linguist and work for the United Nations.'

There was no mistaking his tone. It was full of the pride of a loving parent and Adam had no doubt that the Hunts had raised the girl as if she was their own. In the photograph they looked happy together. He wondered if Judith Hunt had ever wondered why she hadn't inherited either of her parents' features. Though perhaps she thought she had. No doubt she had heard all her life how she resembled one or other of them, most likely her mother.

'Anne doesn't know,' Hunt said.

It took Adam a moment to absorb his meaning. 'She doesn't know that Judith isn't her biological child?' he said incredulously.

'At least she doesn't allow herself that knowledge. Perhaps on some level she is aware of it, but she's never showed it. It's as if she completely blocked out the miscarriage. In Anne's mind Judith is her child. Quite literally.'

Christ, Adam thought. What would happen to this family when all of this came out?

'Why did Webster do it?' he asked.

'Because at the time I worked for the council department that was considering the future of Carisbrook,' Hunt replied.

Suddenly Adam understood. This question had plagued him during the drive from Tynemouth. Despite everything he'd discovered he hadn't been able to imagine this as a simple case of babies for sale. It hadn't seemed either Webster's or Hunt's style. But if Hunt had been able to influence the decision regarding Carisbrook, that made perfect sense. 'You bought him some time?'

'Yes. Closure was inevitable in the end of course, but I managed to delay it on several occasions.'

'How did you first learn that somebody knew about what had happened?' Adam asked.

'It was a telephone call.'

'From who?'

'A man. I don't know who it was.'

'But you must have met him?'

Hunt shook his head. 'I only spoke to him twice, whoever it was.'

'But didn't you ever see these documents?' Adam gestured to the papers on the table. 'Didn't you want proof?'

'Of what?' Hunt said. 'He knew everything that happened including the name my wife had used at Carisbrook. At first I thought he wanted money. When he told me that the price for his silence was that I should vote in favour of the development I agreed. Perhaps I considered very briefly going to the police, but if I claimed it was anything more than a fleeting notion I would be lying. I don't expect you to believe this, but I did it for my wife, and for Judith.'

Hunt appeared to contemplate the inevitability of his secret now coming out. The flesh of his face seemed to sag and turn a greyish pallor before Adam's eyes. It was difficult not to feel sorry for the man and for his family.

'Didn't you at least wonder who the blackmailer was?'

Hunt blinked and rubbed his temples. 'Of course. But the only person I could think of was Webster. But even if I did know who it was it would have made no difference to the threat and my compliance.'

Adam could see that made sense. 'Was there anything familiar about the person you spoke to?'

'He spoke with a local accent, that's all I can say.'

It had to have been either Jones or David, Adam reasoned. But Jones had no motive to try and blackmail Hunt beyond money, which he had never done before, probably because he hadn't wanted to risk his own criminal activities at the hospital coming to light if something went wrong. But if he had heard about the development and realized that Councillor Hunt was on the planning committee he might well have seen that the information was potentially valuable. All he had to do then was find somebody who would pay for it. Somebody like David.

Adam had guessed during the drive from Tynemouth that whatever Jane had overheard it must have been enough that she knew somebody on the committee was being blackmailed, but not who. Perhaps she'd overheard Carisbrook mentioned, or Jones's name. Probably both. And from there she'd gone searching for proof. He had followed her footsteps all the way. And eventually she'd found what she was looking for, and that was what bothered him.

'Councillor Hunt, I asked you if you knew Jane Hanson last time I was here. You said you met her.'

'Yes.'

'Did she mention anything about your wife? Or give any impression that she was aware you were being blackmailed?'

'No.'

'And did you ever see her again?'

Hunt shook his head. 'Why do you ask?'

But Adam didn't answer. He was thinking. Why hadn't Jane confronted Hunt with the evidence of the birth certificate? He'd been working on the premise that she had been bought off, but now he knew the day Jane had visited the Park Hotel was as Nicos had told him, the day of his nephew's birthday. September the fourth.

'What is it?' Hunt asked.

Adam shook his head. He'd had it all wrong.

344

Part Four

CHAPTER THIRTY-FIVE

Though it was only four in the afternoon, outside it was almost dark. Angela stood by the phone in the kitchen deliberating whether or not to call Adam on his mobile. Her hand hovered uncertainly over the receiver.

'Bloody hell,' she said quietly, turning away.

She had expected that he would be back from Tynemouth by now, or at the very least that he would have called to tell her what he'd found. Perhaps like her he was avoiding the moment. She'd resolved to phone him a dozen times that day, and each time her resolve had deserted her before she'd made the call. She'd imagined a conversation full of halting uncertainty and unspoken feelings.

She took the note he'd left her that morning out of her pocket and read it again. Not for what it said, but rather for what it didn't say. They needed to talk, though she wasn't sure that she was ready for that.

Outside the window the cloud above the fells was heavy and low. A feeling of pressure lay over the landscape, the forerunner of snow. As if on cue the first drifting snowflakes appeared. Jenny's mother would drop Kate home from school soon. At least her presence would return some normality to the house, though Angela knew she had a lot to explain to Kate. Things she didn't even know how to begin to tell her about. Prompted by the thought she picked up the phone and dialled the sawmill again as she had half a dozen times already that day. It was Mollie who answered.

'It's me again,' she said.

'Sorry, Angela, I haven't seen him. I've no idea where he can be.'

Mollie sounded almost as worried as she was herself. 'Alright. Thanks. If you do see him before you leave . . .'

'I'll phone you straight away.'

Angela thanked her again and hung up. Dammit, where the hell was David? She had woken that morning certain of perhaps only one thing, and that was that she needed to speak to him. In a curious way she felt stronger, more clear-headed. David was still her husband. He was the man she had been in love with all these years. Something like that you didn't just abandon.

From the front of the house she thought she heard the sound of a car, and thinking that it was Kate she went to the door. It wasn't Kate, however, but the local GP, Dr Armstrong. He got out of his car and looked up at the sky. The snow was falling steadily now, already covering the ground with a dusting of white.

'I was passing by on my way back to the surgery so I thought I'd look in. How is she?'

'Fine, still sleeping the last time I checked,' Angela said.

She had called the surgery first thing that morning, uncertain what to do about Mary, and Dr Armstrong had come over. By the time he arrived Mary was awake and Angela had persuaded her to eat some toast and drink some tea. She'd seemed calm, though quiet and still nervous. She'd allowed the doctor to examine her without protest and afterwards he'd taken Angela aside and said that he thought Mary was physically rundown. Rest and care was what she needed. He'd taken a look at her medication and noted that it had been prescribed almost twelve months earlier. He'd offered to call the clinic in Carlisle and arrange an assessment if Mary could be persuaded to agree, but Angela had thought about it and decided she would keep Mary there for at least another day. She thought the girl looked vulnerable and lost rather than psychotic and she wanted to help.

Angela led the way up the stairs where Mary was asleep. 'I got her to take the pills you left for her earlier.'

The doctor went quietly into the room and checked her. 'She seems alright for the moment,' he said when he came back out.

'The sedatives I left are quite mild but they'll help her to sleep. Has she eaten anything?'

'A sandwich at lunchtime.'

They went back downstairs to the kitchen, where Angela offered him a cup of coffee.

'What do you want to do?' he asked, when they were sitting at the table. 'I could take her to Carlisle now if we wake her and she agrees.'

Angela glanced out of the window at the falling snow. 'What will they do there?'

'Nothing much I shouldn't think. Try and get her to sleep tonight and then assess her mental condition in the morning. If they think it's warranted they would have her temporarily committed.'

'It seems unfair to move her now,' Angela decided. 'And she's been quiet enough today. Why don't I keep her here for tonight anyway.'

'I think that's a good idea if you're comfortable with the arrangement. If you have any trouble you can call me at home. With any luck she'll sleep through the night anyway. How well do you know her by the way?'

'Not at all really. I'd only met her a few times before now.'

'Yes, I can't say I've seen her around much either.'

'I don't think she went out much. From what I gather Nick used to do most of the shopping and so on.'

'They weren't married were they?'

'Not as far as I know.'

'He left her everything though, apparently,' Dr Armstrong said. 'I was talking to Bill Sanders earlier. He was Nick's solicitor you know. I happened to mention that Mary was here with you.'

'Does she know?' Angela asked, surprised.

'Bill said he went down there yesterday to speak to her but he wasn't sure if she understood anything he said. I understand she found him. Nick I mean.'

'Yes.'

'Hard to believe something like that could happen in a place like Castleton, isn't it? First all this business with the estate, now this. Did you know they started evicting the protesters last night?'

349

'Yes, I was there for a little while.'

'To be honest, I'll be glad when it's over. That kind of thing seems to bring out the worst in people.'

The doctor finished his coffee and rose to leave. At the door he put his coat on and turned up the collar, regarding the snow with a glum expression. 'Looks like it's setting in. Just my luck some farmer up on the fells will break a leg or something. Anyway, remember, don't hesitate to phone if you need to.'

'I won't,' Angela promised. 'Thanks.'

He waved and hurried across to his car. She watched him leave, the snow already thick enough that his car left tyre marks out on the yard. As she was about to go back inside a set of lights appeared at the end of the lane and moments later Alice Carterton turned into the gate. Kate jumped out of the back and ran over as Alice leaned across the seat and called out.

'I won't stop, I want to get home before this gets any worse.'

'Okay. Thanks for having her,' Angela said.

She and Kate hugged and then went inside and through to the warmth of the kitchen.

'Hungry?' Angela asked.

'Starving. What's for dinner?'

'Good question.' Angela went to the fridge. 'How was your stay?'

'Great. But it's nice to be home.'

Angela smiled. It was the first time she'd felt like smiling for days. 'It's good to have you home.'

'Where's Dad?' Kate asked.

'At work I expect,' Angela said with her back to her daughter, the lie coming easily. She changed the subject quickly. 'Kate, there's somebody upstairs who's staying with us.' She began to explain about Mary.

Making an early dinner occupied some time and kept Angela busy. Kate was unruffled to hear about Mary, though she was curious to meet her.

'She might come down for something to eat when she wakes up,' Angela said.

She made lasagne, since it was the only thing she could think of and she had the ingredients. The fact that it was easy but fiddly suited her state of mind. It kept her occupied without requiring too much concentration and prevented her from watching the clock and waiting for the phone to ring. Kate chatted about what she'd been doing for the past few days. She knew about Nick but only that he'd had some kind of accident. So far nobody had connected it with her father, though Angela knew that was only a matter of time. When eventually she went into the lounge to watch TV Angela tried the sawmill again, but by then Mollie and everyone else had left and if David was there he wasn't answering. She let it ring for several minutes, willing him to pick up if he was there, but finally she hung up defeated. She considered ringing Adam again, but in the end she didn't, convincing herself that she had waited this long for news that she may as well wait until he turned up, which she was sure he would eventually.

When dinner was ready she called Kate and they sat on opposite sides of the kitchen table. Kate took in the two place settings.

'Aren't we waiting for Dad?'

'I'm not sure when he's coming home. He's busy at the moment,' Angela said, and knew by Kate's expression that she didn't entirely believe her, but what else was she supposed to say?

'What about Mary?'

'I think we'll let her sleep,' Angela decided. 'I'll look in on her later.'

After they'd eaten Kate had homework to do, and Angela busied herself clearing away. By six-thirty it was completely dark outside and snowing heavily. A layer several inches thick already covered the ground. Distractedly she turned on the small TV in the kitchen to catch the weather report. There was footage of cars caught in a blizzard on the Pennines and the snow was predicted to continue through the night. The police were advising people to stay at home. She turned it off, and for the first time she felt a pang of worry that she hadn't heard from Adam. Finally she tried calling him but all she got was a voice telling her that the phone she had called was either switched off or outside the calling area. As she looked out of the window at the swirling snow a growing sense of unease took hold within her.

* * *

It was just after seven when she finally went to check on Mary. She heated some food and took a tray up with her thinking that if Mary was still sleeping she would wake her and try to get her to eat something. She pushed the door open and balancing the tray with one hand she felt on the wall for the light switch. When she flicked it on she was confronted with an empty room. She stared at the bed then hurriedly put the tray down and went to check the bathroom, but Mary wasn't there. She tried to think where else she could be, and then went back to the bedroom and felt the bed. It was warm, but only barely. She glanced out of the window and a horrible thought occurred to her. Please no, she pleaded silently and dashed from the room. Downstairs she checked the laundry room. She'd washed Mary's clothes earlier and she imagined Mary had somehow come down and found them, though she knew it was impossible because the laundry was reached by going through the kitchen. The clothes were still there, folded on top of the dryer. Frantically she started going through the house, checking every room and every cupboard.

'What is it?' Kate said in alarm when Angela burst into the lounge.

'I can't find Mary,' Angela said, her voice rising. She forced herself to calm down. 'Have you seen her?'

'No.'

'It's alright, she must be here somewhere.'

She ran back upstairs and checked Mary's room again, but it was still empty. From downstairs she heard Kate calling to her. Thank God, Kate had found her, she thought, and rushed back down. She met Kate in the hall.

'What is it? Have you found her?'

'No. But the door's open.'

'Oh, God.' Angela ran to the door. Outside a line of footprints led through the snow to the gate. She grabbed her coat and sat down to pull on a pair of boots. 'Stay here. I'll go and find her.'

Kate stared at her wide-eyed.

'It'll be okay,' Angela said. 'I'll follow her tracks and I'll bring her back.' She paused, wondering what else to take with her. In the hall stand drawer there was a torch, which she put in her pocket.

'Don't worry,' she said and kissed Kate quickly. 'And don't leave the house.'

Outside the snow felt wet against her face, the ground leaking cold upwards through the soles of her feet. She headed towards the gate with a mounting sense of fear.

A stranger stared back at David from the mirror lying against his office wall. His eyes were bloodshot and beneath them dark smudges like paint exaggerated their sunken effect. He turned away. The door was open, as was the outer door. Snow was already drifting inside from the top of the stairs.

He had spent the day on the fells and hadn't laid eyes on a single person since early that morning. He'd thought that it would clear his head. He supposed it had worked. He hadn't had anything to drink since the day before so he was sober and he saw things as they were now. It was all clear to him.

He went to the desk and sat down. When he was growing up his father had sat in the same chair at the same desk. This was where he always pictured him, or in the yard. He had never wanted anything else than to become like his father. The smell of cut wood and sawdust, the whine of the saws in the cutting shed, it was all imprinted on him from such an early age he'd never even thought of a life other than this. When he and Angela had married, and later when Kate was born, he'd sometimes thought he was the luckiest man in the world. If there was anything at all he would have changed in his life, it was in the past. Just one thing that had marred his otherwise perfect contentment. A guilty burr that had scratched at the back of his mind.

And now because of that, he had lost everything. The sawmill was finished, he knew that. Even if it weren't it wouldn't make any difference. When he'd stood in the dark outside the house the night before and watched Angela and Adam through the study window he'd felt his life drain away. Now all he felt was empty. He was a hollow shell. It was as if all the years that he'd loved Angela and she had loved him in return had been something he'd never really deserved. They were stolen years, and deep down he'd always been afraid that one day the past would surface and he would lose her. Now his fears had become reality. His entire life had collapsed. The business was gone, his marriage, even Nick was gone. Nothing would be the same again.

He stood up from the desk and went to the cupboard where he kept a shotgun. He took it out and loaded two shells into the barrels and put the rest of the box away. Two were all he needed. More than enough. He moved almost mechanically. Without feeling, without hesitation. He felt calm. This was the last thing he would do. Up on the fells he'd reached a decision.

When he left he neglected to close the door behind him. As he drove from the yard the snow continued to drift inside and blown by the breeze it began to settle on the desks and the carpet, and papers fluttered to the ground.

CHAPTER THIRTY-SIX

Karen started the engine and let it run. She was bloody freezing. It wasn't snowing in London yet the way it was in other parts of the country, but it would be soon, she thought. They were talking about climate change all the time these days. She couldn't remember it ever having snowed this early in London before, and the world was supposed to be getting warmer. The heater was on full, but it would take a few minutes for the engine to warm up. She glanced at the clock on the dashboard and saw that it was past six. Where the hell was Jane bloody Hanson? Why couldn't she just be a secretary somewhere who finished work at five on the dot and was home half an hour later? Or why couldn't all this have happened in July instead of October so at least she wouldn't have to sit here for hours on end while her bum went numb and her toes gradually lost their feeling?

She tried to decide how much longer she would wait. She'd been here since four. There had been no reply when she rang the doorbell. Two and a bit hours sitting there freezing to death. And the worst of it was she knew that this time she would stay all night if she had to. This time she wasn't going anywhere until she'd spoken to Jane face to face, and if she was going to refuse to talk for whatever bloody reason, then she could tell her as much to her face.

But first Karen planned on making Jane sodding Hanson listen to a few things. Like how her ex-boyfriend was dead in case she was interested, and how Adam needed her help to try and find out what had really happened to him, in case she was interested in that as well. Adam must have been right about her. She must have been bought off, though Karen doubted that meant being a party to murder. So how could she just ignore all the messages Karen had left for her? At the top of every note she'd written in big bold letters URGENT. She'd also written that it was about Ben Pierce. Whether or not Jane knew what had happened she couldn't have missed the tone, which no matter how you looked at it made her a cold-hearted bitch as far as Karen was concerned. And she had had enough.

The heater kicked in and gradually she began to de-ice, though she did feel guilty about sitting in her car while she allowed exhaust fumes to pollute the atmosphere. A better person would elect to suffer. What was a little discomfort in comparison to doing her bit for the health of the planet? The more she thought about it the guiltier she felt. Finally, driven to it by her conscience, she reached for the key to switch off the engine. As she did so a taxi pulled up ahead of her. Karen froze, her eyes glued to the rear door as it opened. Please let it be her, she thought. If it was Jane she would only buy organic vegetables from here on and she would donate to Greenpeace and make more of an effort to recycle her rubbish. Please let it be her.

It was. The same slim dark-haired girl that Karen had glimpsed before stepped out onto the road and slipped between two parked cars. As the taxi pulled away she skipped up the steps carrying a small suitcase and put her key in the front door. Karen got out of her car.

'Jane!' she yelled and the girl looked towards her with a startled expression. 'Wait.' Karen started to run. 'I need to talk to you.' She had a sudden fear that Jane would bolt inside and slam the door in her face, and as the door swung open her fear turned to anger. She ran faster and bounded up the steps. 'I said wait, dammit!'

'I was just opening the door,' was the startled reply.

'I need to talk to you,' Karen repeated, slightly breathlessly this time, though with enough force to remove any ideas the girl in front of her might have had about trying to put her off.

'Alright,' she said, with an air of resignation. 'You better come in.'

The flat was small, but tastefully furnished. It had recently been decorated in tones of cream and browns that lent the rooms a sophisticated feel. Once inside Jane Hanson seemed unsure of herself. She took off her coat revealing that she had a taste for expensive clothes. She wore a tailored suit that Karen was certain hadn't come off any chain store rack. They stood opposite one another in the living room. The younger woman gestured awkwardly towards a couch.

'Do you want to sit down? Or would you like something to drink?'

Karen started to refuse, but changed her mind. Now that she was here she decided she might as well thaw out. 'Do you have any brandy?' she asked. 'I think I've lost the feeling in my extremities.'

'I'll have a look. There might be some.'

She went behind the counter that separated the living room from the tiny kitchen and searched through a cupboard and when she found a brandy bottle she took down two glasses and poured them both a measure.

'Do you have anything with it?'

'This is fine,' Karen said. The first sip burned her throat but started a pleasant glow in the pit of her stomach. 'Thanks. I needed that.' She remembered that she hadn't introduced herself and fumbled in her pocket for a card. 'My name's Karen Stone by the way.'

'I know. I got the other three you put in the letter box.' She gestured again towards the couch. 'Do you mind if I sit down? My feet are killing me. I've been on the go all day.'

'It's your flat,' Karen said. She sat down herself.

Jane Hanson, she decided, wasn't what she'd expected. She seemed unsure of herself despite her clothes and her slim, dark-haired good looks and the fact that she came and went by taxi. Maybe she was a model or something. She was young enough, and attractive enough. But the fact that she asked permission to sit down in her own home and the slight air of nervousness Karen was picking up made her seem vulnerable. Karen noticed that she kept glancing at the clock on the wall.

'You did get my notes then,' Karen said, with only a hint of censure.

'Yes.'

357

The flat was tidy. Very tidy. And clean too. There was something impersonal about it. No loose change lying around, no half-folded laundry or knickers shoved under the cushions.

At least she had the good grace to lower her eyes, betraying a shadow of guilt. Karen decided that there was no point in trying to make her feel badly. What was important was that finally she had found her, and now she had to make sure that Jane co-operated.

'Look,' Karen began. 'I'm not here to question your actions. You must have had your reasons for not calling me, but I suspect that you're not aware of the situation. About Ben I mean. I didn't want to say anything directly in my note, but . . .' She paused, suddenly sure from the patient wide-eyed way that Jane was regarding her that she had no idea her ex-boyfriend was dead.

'The fact is,' Karen said gently, 'that I'm afraid Ben is dead.'

For a second or two there was no reaction, and then Jane looked down at the glass she held in her lap. At length she looked up again, her eyes troubled. 'Look, I'm sorry about all this,' she said. 'I think I'd better tell you that my name isn't Jane.'

Karen reacted with a puzzled look of incomprehension.

'Actually, I've never even met Jane Hanson.'

Half an hour later Karen was sitting outside again in her car. She didn't know whether to be angry with herself or the girl inside the flat she'd just left. Herself, she decided, was the appropriate answer.

'Shit!' she muttered.

It turned out that the girl's name was Joanna, and she worked for an advertising agency. Her boss, who ran the agency, also owned the flat at number twenty-nine, along with all the others in the house. Joanna had explained that the flat had been leased to Jane Hanson earlier in the year, but that she wasn't due to move in until September. When she didn't arrive even though she'd paid a month's rent, Joanna and her boss had decided to sort of use the place.

At first Karen hadn't understood. Use it for what? And then something in the girl's expression had made the penny drop.

Outside, another taxi pulled up and a tall man in his early forties got out. He had thinning hair and wore the kind of clothes that advertising people and men clinging desperately to their youth wore. Joanna's boss.

He was married, Karen had learned. They used to go to hotels, but when Jane hadn't turned up to take up her lease he had decided that for the time being he would use the flat as a place where he and Joanna could meet. He wasn't sure if Jane was ever going to turn up. When mail and then Karen's notes had begun arriving he'd told her just to play it cool. Jane's father had even phoned a couple of times when Joanna was there, but she had simply said that Jane was away, which he had seemed to accept. Even when somebody had called saying he was from the company where Jane was meant to be working Joanna's boss had told her not to worry. She had probably just met somebody during the summer and changed her plans.

In other words, Karen thought, he didn't give a damn so long as he had somewhere to carry on his affair. She almost felt like getting out of the car to confront him. In fact she felt like punching him on the nose. But before she could act on the thought he vanished through the front door.

Karen took out her mobile phone. She wasn't sure what any of this meant, but she knew she had to tell Adam. She dialled his number and waited. She heard a voice tell her that the phone she was calling was either switched off or outside the calling area.

Terrific.

CHAPTER THIRTY-SEVEN

Four young people sat on a stone wall in the sunlight. It was a simple enough photograph. The kind that might be found in any album of holiday snapshots. A memento of youth, of halcyon days. But look deeper, beyond the frozen smiles, and there were stories behind the image. The camera had captured a mere instant in time in the lives of four people but in that tiny fragment lay clues to what had passed before and to what had come afterwards. Glimmers of insight, there for anybody who cared to look with an open mind. But, Adam thought bitterly, he hadn't seen them.

He had been sitting in his room at the New Inn for some time. While he stared at the picture he fiddled with the pair of broken glasses he'd found at the site of the accident, turning them over and over between his fingers.

Three young men and a girl sat in a row. Ben's arm was around Jane Hanson's waist. The first time he'd seen the picture he'd noticed Jane's body language, the way her hands were clasped loosely in her lap and the way she leaned very slightly away from Ben. He remembered thinking they appeared unbalanced. Whoever had snapped the photograph had inadvertently captured the signs of a relationship breaking down. When he looked closely he thought he could see that Ben's smile was a little strained, while Jane appeared composed, almost self-contained. It was clear who was ditching whom.

But there was more than that. He focused on Jane alone. The more he studied her the more she came to life. She wore a faint smile, but hers was the expression of somebody suffering an interlude from the serious business of why she was there. If he had to say now what his impression of her was, he would say here was a strikingly attractive girl who exuded an air of seriousness. There was something about the set of her chin that suggested doggedness. Perhaps single-mindedness.

How could he have missed what now seemed so glaringly obvious? Everything that he'd learned about Jane supported what her image portrayed. She had been at odds with protesters like Peter Fallow. She thought their methods would ultimately fail, that in fact they actually alienated the community whose support they needed. So, when she'd heard about Janice Munroe's suspicions regarding the planning committee she'd seen an opportunity to stop the development. An opportunity that was altogether pragmatic and one that she had pursued relentlessly.

Ellie had told him that Jane had overheard somebody talking in a pub, and it was that conversation that had sent her looking for Jones. He himself had followed the same trail, dogging her steps all the way. First to Dr Grafton and then to Webster and the newspaper records and ultimately all the way to a rundown hotel in Tynemouth. That had taken a lot of determination. A singular sense of purpose, and it had been staring him in the face all along and he had ignored it.

He should have known that Jane wasn't corruptible. She hadn't gone to such lengths to stop a development she was philosophically opposed to, only to roll over at the end. Nor would she have simply returned to London. When she had left the camp it was Durham she had gone to, not London. At the Barstock Clinic she'd been given Jones's old address in Durham, but tracing him from there to Tynemouth must have taken some time. Time that Adam himself had been saved thanks to Dr Hope. But once Jane had arrived at the Park Hotel, where she'd discovered Marion Crane's patient records and a copy of Judith Hunt's birth certificate, she must have pretty well known what had happened. But she had never confronted Hunt with what she knew, and the following day Ben and the two people with him in the car had been killed.

Adam went to the window. Outside it was snowing heavily. He thought he knew now what had happened the night of the accident and he couldn't wait until morning before he discovered if he was right. By then the snow would be too thick on the ground and he would have to wait for the thaw, which could be days or even weeks away.

He grabbed his coat and headed for the door. He left the broken glasses lying on the photograph. He should have seen earlier what was now painfully obvious, but he'd been blinded by his own preconceptions. They were the same glasses, he had finally seen, that Jane wore in the picture.

It was dark and driving was difficult. The windscreen wipers flopped back and forth at full speed, but even so there was time for a thin covering of snow to settle briefly on the glass. As he climbed towards the fells it was several inches deep on the road. He drove in second gear, hunched over the wheel, peering at the narrow black and white world lit by the headlights. The landscape was uniformly white except for the bare trees and the stone walls which stretched across fields like pencil-drawn lines on pristine paper. The only evidence of life he saw was in the occasional glimpse of headlights in the rear-view mirror. Somebody else braving the roads.

It took him forty minutes to reach the place where the Vauxhall had left the road. When he got out the wind froze his hands and face and icy chips stung his eyes. He shone the beam of his torch down the slope through the trees where the snow hadn't penetrated much yet, forming only a thin layer. Recalling the last time he'd been there he pondered the wisdom of tempting fate. His knee was aching. While he hesitated snow settled on his shoulders and trickles of moisture found a way down his collar. It was the relentless snow that made up his mind. The reports on the radio were that it was expected to last all night with more predicted for the coming week. By morning there would be no chance of finding anything and he had wasted enough time already. He needed to know. He looked for the best route down and then making his choice he sat on the frozen ground and began slowly to slide.

He gathered speed quickly and felt as if he was plummeting into a chasm. The snow deadened all sound as he slithered and slipped past trees and rocks, everything flying past in a blur. The snow, however, not only made his descent quicker, it also smoothed the bumps where it had drifted and eventually he began to slow and finally came to rest a short distance to the right of the tree that bore the scar of the wreck's final impact. Here and there a branch sagged under its burden and dumped a load of snow on the ground. The same thing was beginning to happen all around. Minor cascades began in the upper branches and then there would be the occasional dull thump of another fall and again the whispering trickle of snow.

Adam got to his feet and gingerly tested his weight on his knee. It hurt, but not badly. Logic told him that if his suspicions were right, he would find what he was looking for further down the hill, so he began his search fifty feet beyond the place where the wreck had come to rest. Using the scarred tree as a reference he covered the ground in a methodical pattern, working sixty or so feet on either side, ranging back and forth in lines ten feet apart.

The slope was gentler than up by the road but working by torchlight didn't make his task any easier. Several times something caught his eye but when he got down on his knees to check there was nothing there. After almost an hour he was far enough down the hill that he couldn't see where he'd started. He rubbed his numbed hands together and thrust them inside his coat to get warm. As the circulation returned it felt like small blades jabbing the tips of his fingers. Countless snowdrifts punctuated the darkness. Any one of them, he thought, could hide what he was looking for.

He heard a movement close by, the sound of something skittering down the slope, but when he shone the torch he couldn't see anything. Once again he resumed his pattern, slowly moving back and forth in straight lines sweeping the beam before him in a narrow arc, looking for some disturbance, something out of place.

And then finally he found it.

Beneath a holly bush, where a patch of ground was partly concealed, the beam fell on disturbed earth. A rudimentary attempt had been made at concealment and there were signs of animal activity. For some time, maybe a minute or more, he couldn't move. Though this was what he'd expected to find, he supposed part of him had hoped that in the end he was somehow wrong. He was overcome by a sense of hopelessness. If he had missed this, and it had been there right before his eyes from the beginning, then what else had he missed?

He sat down heavily on the cold ground.

He wasn't sure how long it was before he became aware that he was no longer alone. Though he hadn't heard anyone approach he felt a presence nearby and when he turned around he saw a figure standing in the trees silently watching him, holding a shotgun loosely in one hand.

CHAPTER THIRTY-EIGHT

Angela stopped to catch her breath at the fence at the end of the lane. She was puzzled that Mary was heading away from the town. Beyond the fence a set of tracks led out across the snow-covered field until they were lost in the darkness. She was tempted to go back and phone for help but the snow was getting heavier and if she lost Mary now she knew the chances of finding her in open country on a night like this were remote. Mary would surely end up freezing to death.

'MARY,' she yelled, her voice sounding muffled. The beam of her torch penetrated no more than thirty or forty feet into the darkness and suddenly seemed laughably ineffective. She called out again but she knew it was hopeless. Mary's tracks were already softening as fresh snow began to cover them though it was still apparent that she was barefoot. She had come out shoeless and wearing nothing more than a cotton nightdress.

With a backward glance to the house where the lights of the windows beckoned invitingly, Angela climbed the fence and began to run across the field, stumbling as she lost her footing on the uneven ground and occasionally falling headlong. Her breath came in ragged gasps. Her clothes were wet but she barely noticed. Snow filled the air, turning a familiar landscape into something alien, disorienting her so that when she reached a stone wall she wasn't sure where she was. Mary's tracks led down the hill on the other side. Nearby an oak and two elms grew in a corner of the field and Angela suddenly thought that she must be heading towards the river where it skirted the bottom end. She guessed then that Mary was going back to the cottages.

She began to run faster.

*   *   *

Mary's tracks skirted the edge of Castleton Wood and then veered across the old meadow. Angela slowed to a walk. Her heart was pounding both from exertion and a rapidly growing sense of unease. A light flickered in the darkness from the direction of the cottages. It bobbed up and down and then abruptly vanished. Somebody with a torch. Was it Mary, Angela wondered? But she was sure Mary didn't have a torch. So who else would be out there on a night like this?

She switched off her own torch and started across the meadow. It was pitch black and she had to walk but by the time she drew close to the last cottage her eyesight had adjusted enough that she could make out Mary's tracks again. What worried her was the other set that had appeared. She stopped, her heart leaping in her chest, and then instinctively she moved close to the cover of the wall.

After a few seconds a dim glow appeared ahead of her coming from inside the end cottage. She hurried to the first window and looked inside. A faint light receded as somebody turned the corner at the top of the stairs. She ran around the back and when she reached the door it was half open, the kitchen inside utterly dark and silent. Angela hesitated. She was certain that Mary was in the house, but somebody else was in there too. She tightened her grip on the torch and stepped over the threshold.

The smell hit her at once. The same damp and cloying air of decay that she had noticed the night before, only now there was something doubly oppressive about it. She moved as quickly as she dared, feeling her way along the wall. When she reached the door to the passage she heard a creak from the floor above. She went quickly to the foot of the stairs. The light up there was very faint. She pictured the landing beyond the corner and at the end of it the door to the room where they had found Mary. Her heart was pounding hard now, pumping adrenalin through her system.

Don't think, Angela told herself. Just do it. She started up the stairs, feeling her way along the banisters, her eyes glued ahead. A step creaked slightly beneath her weight and she stopped dead, hardly daring to breathe.

Abruptly the light at the top of the stairs went out.

And then she heard something. A low moan. A terrified child-like sound that slowly grew in pitch and she knew she had to do something. She started to run and when she reached the corner she sensed rather than saw a shape in front of her and instinctively she raised her arm to protect herself. Something hit her and the force of the blow knocked her off balance.

In the brief instant before she fell backwards she screamed.

CHAPTER THIRTY-NINE

'What's the gun for?' Adam asked.

David came closer. He looked terrible but worse than the way he looked was the mad light in his eyes. He was holding the gun loosely with the barrel pointing towards the ground. Adam wondered how far he would get if he made a lunge for it. Not too far, he thought.

'You got what you came for then, Adam.'

'What I came for?'

David stopped a few feet away. 'You know where I was last night?' His tone was almost conversational, though it didn't match the way he looked.

Suddenly Adam had a premonition of what the answer might be and David almost smiled.

'I went to the house. My house. You know what I saw?'

Adam thought again about making a lunge for the gun, but as if David knew what he was thinking he changed his grip and held it with both hands across his body.

'I was looking through the study window,' David said, and now there wasn't a shred of humour in his eyes. 'How was it? Was it everything you'd dreamed of? Don't be bashful, Adam. I want to know. Did it feel good when you fucked her?'

'Listen, you've got all this wrong.' Adam started to get to his feet.

He barely saw the butt of the gun swing towards him. It smashed against his cheek and sent him sprawling to the ground, the mingling metallic taste of blood and snow filling his mouth. For a few seconds he was dazed. Pinpricks of light floated through his vision. He got to his knees, breathing hard, bent over on all fours. His head was spinning and he wanted to throw up. Fuck, he was going to die. He spat blood and a jagged fragment of tooth and when he probed the back of his mouth with his tongue he felt a splintered edge.

He kept his eye on David as he hauled himself to his feet, wary of being hit again. His knee hurt like a bastard. He must have fallen on it badly and it hurt even more when he put weight on it, but if he was going to have any chance at all of surviving the next few minutes he needed to be on his feet. The gun was pointing at him now.

'You shouldn't have come back, Adam.'

'Bit late for that isn't it,' he said thickly.

'None of this would have happened.'

'What are you going to do? Are you going to shoot me, is that it? Do the fucking job properly this time?'

David's glance flicked to his knee. Some shadow crossed his eyes.

'How're you going to explain that?' Adam said. He was talking fast, slightly manically, he thought. He knew he sounded scared, which was fine because he was. 'You'll go to prison, David. They'll lock you up and throw the bloody key away. What about Angela? What about Kate?'

There was a glimmer of response when he mentioned Kate.

'Think about it,' he went on, seizing the advantage. 'Think how she'll feel. Kids at school whispering behind her back. Making fun of her. Parents who won't want their children to hang out with her. Is that what you want? Think about what it'll be like for her when everybody knows her dad is a murderer.'

David snorted. 'What the fuck do you care? Ever since you got here you've been trying to prove I killed those lads.'

'I know. But I was wrong.'

That took David by surprise. The gun dropped an inch or two, and then it came up again.

'What's the problem, Adam? Wasn't it as good as you thought it would be, is that it?'

'Listen, this isn't about Angela.'

'Bullshit. You've wanted her since the day you came back. I

knew it the second I saw you. That's what this has all been about for you. You wanted her to think I killed those lads so you could get to her.'

Was that true? Yes. Partly. 'She didn't believe it though. Even now I don't think she believes it.'

'You're a fucking liar.'

But he wasn't lying. 'Alright, I'm not denying that I thought you killed them, or that I wanted Angela to think so too. I wanted her to see what kind of person she was really married to. But she didn't believe me. Maybe just for a while she had her doubts, but you know why? It wasn't because of me, anything I said. Not entirely anyway. It was you. You did it yourself. The way you've been, the drinking. You think she didn't know something was eating away at you? You should have told her, David. You should have talked to her. That's why we're here now. And last night? She didn't really want me. She never has. She just needed somebody to turn to and I was there.'

For the first time uncertainty appeared in David's eyes. And it was all true, Adam thought heavily. He'd known it last night. He'd felt it even as he and Angela had made love. He'd felt the distance between them, and he'd known then that he couldn't reach her. He couldn't make her feel about him the way she did about David. And David was at least partly right. This had been about her in a way. Only not the way David thought.

He looked at the gun that was still pointing at him, bitterness souring his throat. 'Go ahead. Pull the trigger. You could always say it was an accident. Say you thought I was a fucking deer.'

There was a reaction. An involuntary flinch. But Adam couldn't decipher it. Suddenly he wanted to know the answer to the question that had always been there in the back of his mind. Nothing else mattered. Whatever happened now he wanted to hear the truth.

'So, come on, David. You can tell me now, there's nobody here but us. Did you mean to do it? Did you know what you were doing?'

He was surprised at the bile in his voice, at the rush of venom. It erupted out of him.

'What's the problem? It's a fucking simple enough question! I don't think you planned it, did you? I never thought that. Well,

370

hardly ever anyway. I've always thought it was more likely a sort of spur-of-the-moment thing. You turned around and you saw something and you pointed the gun because you were bored and cold, and then what happened? Did you stop and think? Did you remember how you shouldn't ever aim at anything unless you're certain of what it is? That stuff must have gone through your head. Then what? It moved didn't it? But it wasn't a fucking deer! I fucking moved! It was me!'

Jesus. Adam gulped to catch his breath. His chest was heaving and his heart was thudding like a hammer against his chest. He looked away, turned his eyes to the sky. What a joke! His vision was blurred. There were tears in his eyes for fuck's sake!

When he looked back at David he had dropped the barrel of the gun so it pointed at the ground again. He supposed he should be relieved.

'You know what really got to me? When I was lying in that hospital and you and Angela came to visit, I knew. The second I saw the two of you together I knew what was going to happen. I mean, I wasn't even surprised. Did you think I hadn't noticed the way it was with you two before that? And you know what the joke is really? Before I woke up in that hospital. *I didn't fucking mind.* Not that much. Because it was practically over between Angela and me anyway. We were never going anywhere. I knew that.'

Adam laughed grimly. How come the hardest truths to reveal are always the ones we know about ourselves? The way he had known this all along.

'So, you see, you just had to talk to me, you fuck! You didn't need to blow my leg off! You didn't need to sneak around behind my back. None of it was necessary.'

And that was what had really hurt. The thing that had eaten into him like acid. It had blighted his soul. The absolute truth was that he really had known that he and Angela weren't going to make the distance. If David had come to him and said, 'Look, I can't help the way I feel and I think she feels the same way', then it really would have been okay. But David had betrayed him. Betrayed his fucking loyalty, their friendship. Which he had already proved for fuck's sake because he hadn't told anyone what he knew about Meg's disappearance. He had shown that he was as good as Nick.

But that hadn't mattered. When push came to shove, David had done something he never would have done to Nick. It was never really about Angela, it was never really even about Meg. It was about a single act of disloyalty, of fucking betrayal.

And he saw from David's expression that he knew it.

They stared at one another while the snow settled on their heads. It was cold and hushed.

'I didn't know it was you. I thought it was a deer,' David said at last.

Adam wanted to believe him. Even now he wanted to, but he saw a different truth in David's eyes. The truth was he didn't know himself. He probably never had.

But it didn't matter. He saw that now. It couldn't be undone now.

What mattered was the shallow grave behind him.

If there had been any doubts in Adam's mind they were dispelled when David saw what was under the holly bush. At first he was puzzled and then as he realized what he was looking at his expression turned to disbelief.

'Who is it?'

'Her name is Jane Hanson.' The name registered. 'You knew her?'

David tore his eyes from the grave. 'I met her a few times.'

'She asked you about the planning committee?'

'Yes.'

'You knew she and her friends were trying to prove that you had bribed some of the councillors for their votes?'

'Of course I knew.'

'Which is why you attacked the camp? My guess is you were trying to frighten them away.'

Guilt and shame jostled briefly with defiance in David's eyes. 'It got out of hand. Some of the men had been drinking.'

'And Jane wasn't there anyway?'

'No, it turned out she'd already left. At least that's what I thought.'

'You were right,' Adam said. 'But she went to Durham, not back to London.' It was clear David didn't understand the reference to Durham.

'Tell me what happened on the night of the accident,' Adam said. 'I know somebody phoned you from the lodge. You went up there didn't you?'

'Yes,' David admitted. 'How did you know?'

'Your number was on the phone account. I got it from the lodge.' David didn't know what he was talking about, which meant, Adam thought, it couldn't have been David who'd tried to kill him that night at the lodge. It must have been Nick. 'Who phoned you?'

'The lad. Ben. He said they had some information which would put an end to the development and they wanted to talk to me.'

Adam had puzzled over this part. If Jane and Ben had believed David was the person who was blackmailing Hunt, why not just go to the police once they had the evidence? Why talk to David at all? But he thought he knew the answer. They had wanted to persuade David that the game was up without involving the police, since it would have been Hunt's wife and their daughter who would have become the real victims had the whole story come out.

'But by the time I got there,' David went on, 'they had already left.'

'What time was this?'

'About nine. I went to the office before I drove up to the lodge. I needed time to think.'

'So, you didn't see them at all?'

David hesitated, and his eyes darkened with the haunted dreams he had tried to drink into submission.

'You found the car, didn't you?' Adam guessed. 'After the accident?'

'Yes.' There was a hint of relief in David's voice at finally admitting something he had kept secret since that night. 'On the way back from the lodge. They were all dead. There was nothing I could do. But I didn't know about this.' He gestured to the grave.

But there had to be more to it than that, Adam knew. 'You saw something else that night. And whatever it was you kept quiet about it, but you didn't feel good about doing that, did you? That's why you started drinking. It was something you couldn't even tell Angela about, wasn't it?'

He saw that he was right.

'It was Nick wasn't it?' he guessed. 'You saw Nick.' There was a kind of symmetry to it all, Adam thought. A grim sense of poetic justice.

David nodded heavily. 'I saw his car heading back towards town.'

'And after you discovered the accident you suspected he'd killed them?'

'No!' David said quickly.

'But you knew he stood to make a lot of money from the development by selling the cottages. You must have suspected something. Why else the guilt?'

David shook his head and a trace of anger returned to his voice. 'You never understood Nick. You always thought the worst of him, but he wasn't like that. Alright, I admit I thought *something* had happened. An accident. I don't know. The boy who was driving was drunk, remember.'

And maybe, Adam acknowledged, as he had done when Meg had vanished, it wasn't so hard to understand that David would believe, or would want to believe, that there was an innocent explanation. Or at least one less damning. Had David thought this was something else that had gotten out of hand, like the attack on the camp, only more so? Maybe David had tried to convince himself that Nick had just tried to scare them, or maybe he was trying to stop them. He hadn't meant to run them off the road. But that wasn't what had happened, as even David could now see. If it had been an accident, how come Jane Hanson had ended up buried a few feet away from where they stood?

'Ben wasn't drunk,' Adam said. Just as his sister had maintained, only he hadn't listened properly. Something else he'd put aside, chosen to ignore even though it should have bothered him more. 'And he wasn't driving. He didn't know how. Jane was driving.'

Adam explained what he thought had really happened that night. 'Jane found out that Councillor Hunt had been blackmailed to vote for the development.' Pieces clicked together in David's eyes. 'You must have wondered about that? My guess is that some time back in August Nick told you Hunt would come around, am I right?'

'Something like that.'

'But he didn't explain why, or how he knew?'

'No. I'd talked to Hunt, tried to persuade him but he wouldn't listen.'

'You didn't offer him anything to change his mind?'

'There was no point. He wouldn't have accepted.'

'But somehow Nick had managed to get him to change his vote,' Adam said. 'You must have wondered how he managed that.'

David didn't answer. Perhaps he hadn't wanted to know.

'Jane came back from Durham the night of the accident. She knew Hunt had been blackmailed and she told Ben everything when he called her on her mobile, and she probably told him to phone you and get you to go up to the lodge. One of the others probably picked her up at the station and my guess is that Jane saw somebody following them. Perhaps she recognized him. By the time you got to the lodge they'd left because they were scared. Somebody chased them and ran them off the road.'

This was always how Adam had envisaged what had happened. He saw now that David had thought much the same thing, believing it was Nick who'd chased them, while Adam had thought it was David. But then he hadn't known Jane was driving.

'Whoever chased them climbed down to the wreck,' Adam went on. 'The two boys who were thrown out were already dead but I think Ben was alive, albeit bleeding badly. Jane probably managed to get out and make a run for it. My guess is that when her body is examined the pathologist will find she was murdered. Somebody caught up with her and either bashed her head in or strangled her and then buried her here along with her belongings from the car. Nobody knew she was even in the area. She didn't register at the lodge with the others. As far as anybody was aware she had left a week earlier to go back to London. Whoever killed her knew that. He tipped whisky down Ben's throat and strapped him into the driver's seat and then left him. By the time you came along he was dead.'

He thought about the photograph of Jane and the boys he had

left in his room. It was another photograph that had made him see how the past and present were linked, and made him realize who the killer really was.

He recalled a spring day long ago when it had been unseasonably warm. A gypsy girl on horseback, her thin cotton dress stretched against her full breasts.

'You're wrong, Adam.'

He came to, realizing what David had said. 'Wrong about what?'

'You think Nick did this, but you're wrong. If Nick did it, then who killed him? I suppose you think that was me.'

'Nick?' he said. 'Who said anything about Nick?'

His phone rang, shattering the stunned silence. David's incomprehension turned first to surprise and then alarm as Adam answered and held it out to him.

'It's Kate. Angela's missing.'

CHAPTER FORTY

Mary heard the scream and the sound that followed it, of something heavy tumbling down the narrow stairs. And then silence. She lay paralysed by terror. Beyond the door she thought she heard the sound of breathing, a laboured sound that wheezed and rattled.

It's coming for you, Mary. This time you won't get away.

Shut up! Shut the fuck up! She screamed the words inside her head and clasped her hands over her ears. She couldn't tear her eyes from the door as it slowly opened and a figure appeared. Please. Please leave me alone. She dared not make a sound. She could taste blood on her lips from clamping her mouth so tightly closed to try to stop her teeth chattering. She was cold, shaking uncontrollably all over.

The figure came towards the bed and a whimper of fear escaped her. She looked up and saw the Shapeshifter. For a moment she thought it was Nick, but it was trying to fool her. It was changing its shape but something was wrong. It was like it had got stuck halfway between one shape and another.

Now it's going to get you, Mary. Now you're going to be sorry, you little bitch.

The voice in her head mocked her. It knew there was nothing she could do. She watched in fascinated terror as the Shapeshifter emptied some pills onto the table. They were white, not blue like the ones she was supposed to take. She tried to say something. Please don't hurt me. Please. But she knew she hadn't made a sound. She had only formed the words inside her head.

It won't do you any good, Mary.

The voice laughed at her. It liked her to be frightened.

The Shapeshifter bent down, and lifted her head. She couldn't take her eyes from its face. It was shiny and smooth on one side. Not real. Like plastic. She wanted to struggle but she couldn't. She was rigid with fear. It forced her mouth open and shoved a handful of pills inside, then clamped her mouth shut.

She couldn't breathe. The pills were bitter-tasting, medicinal.

Eat them up, Mary. There's nothing you can do. Just swallow them.

The voice in her head chortled merrily. It knew she was going to die now. It wanted her to die. She spluttered and choked on something that caught in her throat. Please, she wanted to say. I don't want to die. Please don't hurt me. But she couldn't speak. Tears clouded her eyes. The Shapeshifter held her mouth clamped closed. It was strong. Its eyes were pitiless. She was nothing to it.

She couldn't help it, she had to swallow or choke to death.

CHAPTER FORTY-ONE

When they reached the road again they left Adam's Porsche and took David's Land Rover instead. The snow was still falling heavily and progress was frustratingly slow. Adam drove so that David could call Kate again. He talked to her reassuringly. Though he still looked a mess the crazy light that had been in his eyes earlier had gone.

'Did you call the police? And you spoke to Graham?' David questioned. 'Don't worry, it'll be alright.' He broke off, listening to Kate, then said to Adam, 'They've just arrived at the house. They can't see any tracks but Kate thinks Angela followed Mary along the lane away from town.'

Ahead of them the bridge over the river appeared through the swirling snow and Adam slowed to take the turn. 'The cottages, tell them to go to the cottages,' he said, though he knew they would arrive first.

David relayed the message and then after a few more reassuring words to his daughter hung up the phone. He turned to Adam. 'You think Mary would have gone back there?'

'Yes.'

'There's something else,' David said. 'What is it?'

Adam glanced over at him. 'I'm worried. I think Mary's in danger. And if Angela went after her then she is too.'

'What kind of danger? What are you talking about?'

'Think about it. If Nick didn't kill Jane and those boys, then somebody else did.'

David was bewildered, and Adam didn't know how to begin to explain, except by starting at the beginning. 'This goes back a long time. Back to when you knew Meg Coucesco. You did know her, didn't you?'

'Meg? What the hell does she have to do with any of this?'

'Everything. She has everything to do with it.' They had reached the top of Back Lane. The snow was still falling heavily.

'The other day at the lake, you knew it was her they'd found, didn't you?' He looked across at David when he didn't answer. 'For Christ's sake!'

'Alright, yes, I thought it was her,' David admitted. 'Look, I knew her, I'm not denying it. We used to meet near the sawmill. That doesn't mean I killed her. I didn't even know she was dead.'

Adam didn't know how that could be true. 'You met her the day she vanished though. I saw you.' Though I never told anyone you bastard, he silently added.

'Meg wanted to run away,' David said heavily. 'She'd been talking about it ever since I met her. She asked me to help her, so I did. I put her on the bus that day on the road to Alston up on the fells, and I gave her some money. I never saw or heard from her again.'

'Why did she want to run away?'

'Her family treated her badly. She was unhappy I suppose.'

But there was more to it than that, Adam knew. 'You're saying that even after her disappearance was in the papers and on TV you never heard from her? Not even a phone call?'

'No.'

'If what you're saying is true, why did you and Nick put that bracelet in his dad's van?'

David couldn't hide his shock. 'You knew?'

'I followed you that day.' Adam held his gaze. And I didn't say anything then either, he thought, knowing he didn't need to say it out loud. 'You tipped off the police, didn't you?'

'Yes,' David admitted.

'Why?'

'Meg gave me the bracelet. Sort of a memento. We, Nick and I, thought if we made it look as if his dad knew something about what happened to her, he'd have to leave. Everybody knew he used to go to the camp, and Meg hated him.'

'So, you framed him for a murder he didn't commit.'

'There wasn't any murder. We knew the police would have to let him go without proper evidence and there wasn't any because Meg wasn't dead. But nobody else knew that. It was just a way of getting rid of him. If he'd stayed around the gypsies would have had their own revenge. He was a bastard, Adam, so don't waste any sympathy on him.'

'But if all this is true how did you know it was Meg they found in the lake? You said you didn't know she was dead. And why did you accuse Nick of killing her? That is what you fought about, isn't it?'

'How did you know?'

'A guess,' Adam said, though, in fact, he'd only just made the connection.

'A few weeks after it had all died down, after Nick's dad was killed I saw Nick with a bracelet. We were up at the tarn. It was like the one she had given me. She had four of them, all the same, that she wore on one wrist. When I asked him where he got it he said that she had come back. She wanted more money. It was the day after his dad was questioned by the police. He said he gave her some more money and persuaded her to leave because he was afraid that if she didn't his dad would find out about what we did.'

'And you believed him?' Adam said sceptically.

'Yes. Why wouldn't I?'

But Adam remembered the day he'd seen David contemplating throwing that same bracelet into the lake. Was it coincidence that it was the very place where she had been found, or had David even then suspected something that he hadn't been willing to face?

'So, when she was found that was when you attacked Nick in the pub? Because you thought after all these years he had lied?'

'Yes. But after I left the pub that night, I talked to him. He was waiting for me down the road. He told me what happened, he admitted that he'd killed her but he said it was an accident. When she came back he tried to persuade her to leave and she got hysterical. He didn't mean to hurt her. And afterwards he panicked and dumped her body in the lake.'

But Adam didn't believe that was true either. He thought the truth was Nick had killed her because he was afraid of what would happen if his father found out what he had done. But he didn't believe Meg had come back for money.

'George Hunt was being blackmailed because his wife had a breakdown when she miscarried her baby. She was treated at Carisbrook,' Adam said. 'The director there, a man called Webster, swapped the dead child for a baby girl a young woman had given birth to. It was 1985.'

David looked bewildered.

'It was Meg's child,' Adam said.

He should have seen the resemblance the day that he'd first gone to Hunt's house. Judith Hunt, aged seventeen, pictured on holiday in Spain with her parents. She looked like her mother. The same dark hair and eyes. It could have been Meg looking back at him from the photograph, but he hadn't seen it for the same reason he hadn't realized that Jane couldn't have gone back to London. He was blind to everything but his own agenda.

He remembered the day he'd first seen Meg. He'd been struck, as any adolescent boy would be, by the glimpse of her full breasts delineated against the fabric of her dress. He hadn't realized it but he knew now she must have been heavily pregnant then.

But there was no time to talk any more. The Land Rover crossed the snow-covered bridge over the river and came around the bend in view of the cottages. They were ominously quiet, though a light was on in one of the upstairs windows.

CHAPTER FORTY-TWO

Mary got up from the bed. She spat out the residue of the pills she had swallowed. She remembered hearing a moan from the stairs, and then the Shapeshifter had left her. The rest of the pills lay in a pile on the table. She knew it would be back and then she would be forced to swallow those too.

She rose unsteadily to her feet and switched on the lamp beside the bed. The bulb cast a dim yellow light, enough to see her reflection in the mirror. She was shocked at her own appearance. Her skin was pale and bluish so that she looked like a corpse. For an instant she had wondered if she was dead. Her feet when she looked at them now were the same colour and she could barely feel them any more.

Not dead yet, Mary. Not yet.

She heard a sound from outside the door and she flinched in terror before she realized it was coming from down the stairs.

Mary went closer to the door. She heard another sound, something muffled. A kind of dragging noise. She thought about the scream she'd heard earlier. Somebody had been hurt, she thought. And frightened. She wondered who it was, and she remembered the woman who had taken her away from here before. She remembered her voice. It had been soft and soothing. Listening to her had made the voice in her head go away. She remembered being in a warm room in a soft bed, being given something to eat. Somebody stroking her brow the way her mother had done when she was child, before she had become ill.

Mary knew that the woman who had helped her was the one who

had screamed. Tears sprang to her eyes and ran unchecked down her cheeks.

You can't do anything, Mary. Mad Mary. It'll be your turn next.

The voice in her head was happy. A crooning, happy voice. It wanted her to die. Her breath came in clouds in front of her and outside the window she could see that it was still snowing. A violent spasm of trembling racked her body. She was so cold. Freezing. Her blood was thickening in her veins, slowing down, her heartbeat thumping like a slow drum beat, getting fainter.

What are you doing, Mary? Don't go. Stay here. There's nothing you can do now.

Shut up! I'm not listening to you. She went down on her knees and felt for the gun. It was still there and she dragged it out. When she stood up she felt shaky and thought she would fall down. After a moment it passed and she started to move towards the door. She couldn't stop her teeth chattering now. They rattled like clacking dice in her head, and her hands and arms shook as she shivered.

When she opened the door it was dark in the passage outside. She paused, listening again, and from below she heard the dragging sound again. She went to the top of the stairs and down the first three steps to the corner, holding the gun in front of her. The dragging sound ceased and she heard laboured breathing, then it began again and she knew the Shapeshifter was somewhere near the kitchen door.

Go back, Mary. Go back, you little bitch!

The voice sounded desperate. It wasn't happy now. Somehow that made her feel better. She reached out for the banisters and felt her way down. She felt light-headed, and halfway had to stop. She was turning to ice, slowly freezing. She could hardly think any more. She thought about the woman's soothing voice, the touch of her hand on her skin. Perhaps she would take her back there to that warm room and make her safe again.

She moved along the passage towards the kitchen. She couldn't feel her feet or even her legs moving. Perhaps she was floating. A breeze was blowing in through the open back door, sending flurries of snowflakes into the house. The nightdress she was wearing fluttered around her body. Beyond the kitchen door the Shapeshifter was bent over, dragging the body of a woman backwards so that her heels made furrows in the snow. The Shapeshifter didn't see her. When she reached the open door she could hear his breathing. It came in ragged gasps. Like an animal labouring under a heavy load. Suddenly he stopped and straightened. It was dark and snow swirled about him so that Mary couldn't see him properly. He hadn't seen her yet. He reached for something that was stuck in the snow. Mary stopped, uncertain what she should do. Perhaps the figure wasn't a Shapeshifter after all. It seemed like a man. He was looking towards the corner of the cottage as if he was listening to something, and at the same time Mary realized that she had heard something too, like the sound of an engine, but she couldn't hear it any more.

Then the woman in the snow moaned.

The Shapeshifter looked down at her, and he lifted the thing in his hands, which Mary saw was a shovel, above his head. At the same time he saw Mary at the door and for a second he froze.

Adam ran around the corner and for an instant was confronted with a frozen tableau. Angela lay motionless on the ground while a figure stood over her poised to strike her with a shovel. He glimpsed Mary at the open door.

A roar of sound shattered the silence and a tongue of flame lit them all like a photographer's flash. The figure standing over Angela was lifted from his feet and flung backwards through the air.

And then everything was deathly quiet.

CHAPTER FORTY-THREE

Adam rose from his seat and shook hands with Findlay. Outside at her desk Janice waited anxiously for him to emerge. Findlay had banned her from hearing what Adam had to say until he had heard it first.

'What will you do?' Adam asked him. 'Will you give her the story?'

'Aye,' Findlay said. 'But I'll make her sweat a wee bit more first.'

'You know she'll want to know everything the second I walk out of here.'

Findlay put his hand on Adam's shoulder. 'Tell her. And when you've finished, tell her to come and see me.' He opened the door. 'You know, Adam, has it occurred to you that if you had told me all those years ago what you saw, none of this might ever have happened?'

Was that true, Adam wondered? Even if it was it made no difference, and Findlay knew that himself.

'But then I expect the world would be a very different place if we could all see into the future,' he said. 'If you're ever back this way again, come and see me.'

'I will, Jim. Goodbye.'

As he left Janice rose from her desk and when he went over she glanced over his shoulder towards her boss's office. 'You owe me,' she said.

'And I always pay my debts. Come on, I'll buy you a drink.'

They went to the pub on the corner, and when they were sitting at a table he told her everything. She didn't touch her drink, but put her recorder on the table and listened intently. Then she shook her head in amazement.

'So, Judith Hunt is Meg Coucesco's child?'

'Yes. We'll never know exactly what happened, but my guess is that the child Meg was carrying was unwanted by the gypsies. Perhaps she'd been raped, or perhaps the father was simply some boy she'd met outside their own community before they arrived in Castleton. Whatever the reason, James Allen had dealings with the gypsies and he also knew Jones, who was working at Carisbrook. Webster claims that it was Jones who came up with the idea of swapping the babies after Hunt's wife had a miscarriage. It doesn't really matter though; either way Meg's baby was sold, probably against her will. I imagine that was part of the reason she decided to run away.'

'And also why she came back,' Janice guessed soberly. 'She wanted her baby back.'

It was the conclusion Adam had drawn too. She had probably read about the search for her and about Allen's arrest. Perhaps she thought that in return for getting Allen out of trouble with the police, he would get her baby back. She wouldn't have known what Nick and David had done.

'Do you think Nick Allen meant to kill her?' Janice asked.

Adam considered his answer. He'd thought about what David had told him, that Nick had claimed it was an accident. But Nick must have been terrified of what would happen once his father found out what he'd done. 'Yes, I think he probably did,' he said at length.

Janice turned off her machine and they finished their drinks. As they went to the door she said, 'You know the development won't go ahead once all this comes out.'

'That's something isn't it? At least Jane got what she wanted in the end.'

Outside Janice put her hand on his arm. 'One other thing. When did you realize that James Allen wasn't dead?'

'After I saw Hunt and realized who his daughter really was. I knew Nick and the blackmailer had to be working together, but after Nick was killed I knew it couldn't have been Jones. With Nick dead Jones would have had nothing to gain from the sale of the cottages. He'd have had no claim on Nick's estate. That didn't leave too many options. And then I remembered something Dr Hope at the Barstock Clinic had told me. She said that when Jones had first arrived he was badly scarred, but I didn't pick up on it at the time. There was a gap of several months after he left Carlisle before he started at the clinic, something else I should have wondered about.'

'He was in hospital?'

Adam nodded. 'Dr Hope also said that Jones was practically incompetent when he arrived. Not surprising given that he had probably never been anywhere near a hospital for the mentally ill before that. I suppose Allen and Jones must have left Carlisle together. They both had their reasons to leave. After the accident Allen saw an opportunity to swap identities. I imagine he just walked away from the wreck and left Jones to burn. At least that way he'd never have to look over his shoulder for gypsies wanting revenge.'

'But why did Allen kill Nick? Nick was his own son.'

'There was never any love lost between them. David said that the night he'd confronted Nick about Meg he also told him he'd seen his car the night Ben and his friends were killed. Nick denied it was him but he must have known it was his father. I think at that point Nick knew his friendship with David was finished, which I expect he blamed his father for. They had an argument that got out of hand and Nick ended up dead. After that I think Allen planned to convince Mary to kill herself and then he was going to turn up and claim the estate.'

'How was he going to explain the fact that he'd been living as Jones all these years?'

'He didn't kill Jones, only took advantage of a situation. Considering what he had to gain I doubt that he was worried unduly.'

'Nice guy,' Janice said. 'So, you think he ran Ben and the others off the road and killed Jane?'

'Almost certainly.'

'Do you think it was him that tried to kill you too?'

'We'll never know,' Adam said, though privately he had his doubts. He thought that had probably been Nick. He turned up the collar of his coat. 'Anyway, you better get back to the office. Findlay said to tell you he wants to see you.'

Janice made a face. 'I expect he'll give me a lecture before he lets me have this story.'

Adam grinned. 'I expect you're right.' They shook hands. 'Look me up if you ever come to London.'

'You can count on it,' she said.

He had no doubt that he could.

❧

He was already packed, his bags waiting inside the door of his room. The girl at reception regarded him curiously as he paid his bill, no doubt wondering about the things she had heard. As he left she expressed the hope, American style, that he would have a nice day.

He lingered in the car park for fifteen minutes and then looking at his watch he thought that perhaps she had decided not to come. He didn't really blame her.

But in the end she arrived just as he was getting into his battered Porsche. They both got out of their cars. She was lovely, he thought, and even now an echo of regret lingered.

'How's the head?' he asked.

'I'll live.' Angela gestured to his car. 'You're ready then?'

'As I'll ever be.' Their awkwardness with one another was apparent to them both. 'What will you do now?'

She gave a small shrug. 'We're taking it a day at a time.' She hesitated uncertainly. 'What I mean is, I don't know if we can get past this, but we're going to try. I've accepted the offer to have my books published in America.'

'I'm glad for you. Both of you.'

She frowned slightly. 'Are you?'

'If it's what you want.'

'He's really not a bad person, Adam,' she said. 'But I suppose you can't ever forgive him for what he did, can you?'

'I don't know about forgiveness. I can't forget it though.'

'That's what he said. I wanted him to come and see you before you left, but he didn't think you would want that.'

And he was right, Adam thought, though he didn't say as much. Besides, he doubted David wanted to see him either.

There seemed little else to say. He sensed Angela's discomfort. More than anything he wanted to tell her that he was sorry. There was a distance between them that he thought was because she must have felt that he had used her in a way. He wanted to say it wasn't like that. He had believed that he loved her.

But some things are best left to lie because nothing either of them could say would entirely alter what had happened.

'Do you think you'll ever come back?' Angela asked.

'No. I don't think so.'

She nodded as if she hadn't expected any other answer, and perhaps also because it was one she approved of, then she leaned towards him and kissed his cheek. His cue to leave.

'Goodbye, Adam.'

'Goodbye, Angela.'

He watched her get in her car and drive away. Her life would change. The development was on hold and once the investigations over planning permission began it was likely Forest Havens would pull out of the deal. David might face criminal charges; at any event the sawmill, the entire town, would face tough times. Adam wondered if Angela and David would survive what was ahead, and he thought they would. When all was said and done they loved each other.

She stopped at the road, indicating right, and then turned and was gone. He didn't think that she had looked back. Something he ought to bear in mind himself, he mused.

CHAPTER FORTY-FOUR

On the way back to London he decided he should wait a few days before he went to see Karen. Though he'd already spoken to her by phone and given her the basic facts so that at least she could talk to Ben's sister, there was a lot he hadn't said. In the event, though, when he arrived in London that evening he changed his mind. He'd wasted enough of his life already and he drove straight to her flat.

She was surprised when she opened the door. 'Adam. You're back.'

'In the flesh. Can I come in?'

She stood aside and in the living room she gestured for him to sit down. 'Drink?'

'Thanks.' Suddenly he wasn't sure where to begin. Karen handed him a Scotch and sat down opposite him. He cleared his throat. 'There's a few things I didn't mention on the phone.'

'Oh?'

'The, uh, fact is . . .' He paused. This was harder than he had expected. How did he begin to explain it all?

'Just say it,' Karen said, watching his internal struggle.

He took a breath. 'You remember that night we, er, spent together? I made a mistake. I mean the morning after we . . . after I . . .'

'Got up and left?'

'Yes. I shouldn't have.' He paused. It wasn't really true that he shouldn't have left. With the benefit of hindsight maybe, but then at the time he didn't have that benefit. She watched him steadily and he saw that she wasn't planning on making this easy. Perhaps it was too late. Perhaps he had lost his chance.

'The thing is, I've spent a long time running away from the idea of getting too close to anybody,' he said.

'And?'

'And I don't want to do that any more.'

She considered this for what felt like a very long time. Finally she said, 'You know, I don't know anything about you.'

'There's a lot to tell.'

'I'm not going anywhere.'

He put his glass down and started to get up, but she raised a hand to stop him.

'That doesn't mean I'm about to fall at your feet in gratitude, Adam, in case you had any such notion.'

'No, of course.'

'I don't know what the hell went on up there in Cumbria, but I do want to know. All of it. Understood?'

'Understood.'

'Because I think there was somebody there you once knew. A woman.'

Women's intuition, he thought. 'There was.'

'Did you love her?'

'I once thought I did. The truth was that it was more a case that she represented something that I've never been able to forget.'

'Which is?'

Good question. It was complicated. He'd felt guilty about Meg all these years, he'd also thought he'd been in love with Angela, but neither thing was really at the root of the direction his life had taken. The mind plays tricks and sometimes hides the truth of traumatic events in dark chambers of the psyche, but the effects linger to ensure the past isn't entirely forgotten. Guilt over Meg translated into an obsession with missing children. His relationships with women who physically reminded him of Angela were doomed to failure. But in a sense these things were merely the visible effects of a memory that was too painful to confront. For a few crucial years he had been a lonely child in a strange place where he never felt he belonged. David had been the friend who had eased his loneliness, but it had been an unstable relationship, precariously balanced against David's sense of maintaining a status quo. He'd never really appreciated how hard that must have been for him. But when Meg had vanished Adam had demonstrated his loyalty to their friendship, a loyalty which had ultimately been betrayed. That betrayal had felt like somebody had ripped out his soul. Far worse than any shotgun blast that had mashed his knee, it had left him utterly alone. He'd been alone ever since.

He looked hopelessly at Karen. 'I want to tell you, but it's not just a case of relaying the facts. The truth is it's about explaining who I am.'

'It's about talking, Adam.'

'Yes.'

'Opening up.'

'Yes.'

'Do you want to?'

The big question. The test. He noted how unlike Louise she was, how unlike Angela too, and he knew if he could be with her then he would be lucky. Very lucky. 'Yes, I want to.'

She smiled and he saw that it was a signal that she would give him a chance, though he knew she would not tolerate him if he screwed up. He couldn't tell her everything at once; it would take time. He didn't really understand it all himself. Who did know themselves that well? The point was he didn't have to be alone any more. He remembered how he'd felt when he'd woken up with Angela. How he'd still been alone, his dream once realized proven to be an illusion. With Karen it wouldn't be like that. Over time they could become close. As close as two people can be. And it wasn't a physical thing, it was about knowing each other, and caring, and he did care. He cared about her a lot.

He went to sit beside her. 'I don't deserve you.'

'No,' she agreed, still smiling as she took his hand. 'You bloody well don't.'